THE
AFFAIR

SHERYL BROWNE

Bookouture

Published by Bookouture in 2018

An imprint of StoryFire Ltd.

Carmelite House
50 Victoria Embankment
London EC4Y 0DZ

www.bookouture.com

ISBN: 978-1-78681-462-3
eBook ISBN: 978-1-78681-461-6

For Paul-Jon, who is nestled safe in an angel's wings.

To Drew, my son, who is the inspiration behind
my next book. I love you.

PROLOGUE

I had never imagined what it would be like to hold a life in my hands. Once, I would have been shocked by the realisation that I was an inch away from killing someone. No more. Strangely, I feel nothing, as if I, too, am in a state of limbo, suspended in this moment, somewhere between life and inevitable death.

We're fifteen long floors up, the muted throb of the city, lit up at night, reaching me as if from another dimension. The ground below, hard and unforgiving, looms closer for an instant, as if silently urging me to let go.

Can I? I waver. Am I capable? I'd imagined, in my darkest hours, when dreams only ever came to haunt me, how lost love could drive a person to acts of despair or even madness. How cold-blooded murder might have its basis in love, or unrequited love. In being unloved, spurned or wronged. There is no other way.

I feel it, the undiluted fear emanating from the individual over whose future I have control. This person is petrified, literally: dissociated, yet aware, unable to speak, move or control their own body. Incapable. *Powerless*. Mine to do with what I will. We think that we're immortal, that nothing can touch us, but in reality, we're fragile creatures. Flesh and blood. On impact, the skull will smash like an eggshell.

Obliquely, I wonder what thoughts will occur as the body plunges, its downward trajectory stopped suddenly, violently. It's said a person's life flashes before their eyes when close to death, because the parts of the brain that store memories are among the last to shut down. Some who've had near-death experiences describe a loss of all sense of time – life events that last for a second or a century. They relive moments of sublime happiness and extreme pain, feeling also the pain they've caused others around them. I've heard it described as close to purgatory. Will this person live a century in purgatory? I hope so.

CHAPTER ONE

JUSTIN

Pulling wearily into the drive after a double shift on call at the hospital, Justin was relieved to see Alicia hadn't yet left for work. They rarely argued, preferring to talk things through. They'd come close to arguing last weekend, though, and hadn't yet resolved the issue. His issue, he'd realised. Justin hadn't much liked himself for acting like a suspicious prat and obviously upsetting her. He'd been sure he'd heard her crying in the bathroom, and that had gutted him. At the time, given he'd been inwardly fuming, he'd thought he'd been quite restrained. But thinking about it since, no matter how restrained he'd imagined himself to be, the unspoken accusation had been there, and that was bloody unfair. The last time she'd cried heartbroken tears, it had been for him, when his family had been so senselessly murdered. She'd been there unstintingly for him ever since.

She was there whenever he relived that awful night in his dreams, sweat pooling at the base of his neck and saturating the sheets beneath him. Unable to contact his parents or his sister, he'd gone to their house and let himself in with the key he still had. The first thing he'd noticed was the smashed mirror on the hall wall. Justin closed his eyes, feeling afresh the cold fear that had settled in the pit of his stomach when he'd realised the blood at the epicentre of the fractured glass belonged to his sister. She'd tried to run. Her assailant, not fit to be labelled an animal, had left her bleeding out from her knife wounds on the hall floor.

He hadn't been able to cry. He'd been numb, incapable of processing his emotions, unable to reach out to Alicia, until she'd forced him to, holding him like she would never let him go and crying with him. He had no idea what he would have done if she hadn't been there for him then. They'd not long been married. He'd been so wrapped up in his grief, he'd shut her out. She'd had every reason to walk away, yet she hadn't. He needed to apologise, end this awkwardness he'd caused between them. Grovel, if necessary. Luke was only six months old, for Christ's sake. Her sister's birthday party, which she'd needed some persuading to get dressed up to go to, had been Alicia's first night out after a complicated caesarean section that had nearly cost her and Luke their lives. What in God's name had possessed him to end up spoiling it for her?

'Whoops, sorry.' He found himself apologising prematurely as he opened the front door and narrowly missed hitting her with it.

'My fault.' Alicia shuffled around from where she was strapping Luke into his carrier. 'I'm a bit disorganised, as you might have gathered. We're running late, as per usual.' Pressing a kiss to Luke's soft, downy head, she smiled up at him, somewhat guardedly, Justin noted, which made him like himself even less, and then got to her feet.

'There are croissants in the oven. Still warm, just about. Don't forget to eat,' she said, heading for the kitchen, and then back-stepping to call up the stairs, 'Sophie! Clock's ticking.'

'I'm coming!' Sophie yelled from her bedroom. 'Do you want me to go to school naked or what?'

That would be minus her make-up, Justin gathered. Shaking his head amusedly, he crouched down to say hello to Luke, who jiggled happily and offered him a delighted, gummy smile.

'Pandemonium reigns.' Justin gave him a conspiratorial smile back. 'So, how're you doing, little man, hey? Keeping a low profile,

I hope.' Catching hold of one excitedly flailing hand, he marvelled again at the miracle of their surprise arrival. He was doing well – healthy and strong after a worrying premature birth. His mind drifted to the baby who'd undergone a complicated procedure in the early hours of the morning. Would she be strong enough to survive, he wondered? Admitted with an extradural haemorrhage caused by a head injury, and with no paediatric surgeon available, Justin had had no choice but to drain the blood off, thus reducing cranial pressure, himself. The next twenty-four hours would tell. She was a fighter though. All Justin could do now was pray she didn't succumb to any infection.

Reminding himself of all he had to be grateful for, Justin stroked Luke's peachy cheek in lieu of giving him a cuddle and got to his feet.

Massaging his aching neck, he turned tiredly to the stairs. His fifteen-year-old daughter was descending, clearly disgruntled about school days that started at such an ungodly hour they didn't allow time for her morning beauty regime.

'Good morning,' said Justin, as she stomped past to pick up her schoolbag.

'It's not. It's raining.' Sophie huffed moodily.

Justin smiled and waited, and sure enough, Sophie back-stepped to plant a kiss on his cheek. 'Morning, Dad,' she said, with a sheepish smile. 'Oh.' Looking him over, her forehead creased into a concerned frown. 'Fun night, I take it?' she enquired, obviously noticing his weariness.

'I've had better,' Justin admitted, and reached to give her shoulders a squeeze. 'You'd better get a move on or you'll be getting a black mark.'

'Again.' Sophie mumbled, hitched her bag over her shoulder and turned to the front door.

'Do you think you could help carry something, Sophie?' Alicia called after her, emerging from the kitchen, Luke's juice in one hand, handbag and baby bag in the other. 'I'm running out of hands.'

Sighing, Sophie turned back to relieve Alicia of the juice, rolling her eyes as she did.

Justin gave her a 'don't push it' look, and Sophie looked suitably apologetic. 'Bye. See you later,' he said to Alicia, hoping she'd make proper eye contact with him.

Alicia nodded. Her smile was tremulous, her eye contact brief. Justin inwardly cursed himself again. He really had acted like an idiot, cross-questioning her because some ex-work colleague had made it obvious he was interested in her. He wished they'd had time to talk properly since, but their conflicting schedules hadn't allowed it. His, mostly. As clinical lead in accident and emergency, his job was demanding – soul-destroying, sometimes – with insane targets to meet. The rewards of helping outweighed the endless bureaucracy and the heartbreak of losing patients, but it took its toll. Double shifts were a killer, meaning their time together suffered.

He should have made time. He'd been jealous, there were no two ways about it. He'd been furious when this guy, Paul Radley, had tried to get her to dance with him, grabbing her hand and dragging her away from her sister, sliding his arm around her waist – crossing the lines, in Justin's book. Alicia had pulled away, left him standing on the dance floor, and Radley had looked nonplussed, agitated. Justin had watched him watching Alicia walk away. He'd met him at the bar afterwards and there was something… the way the guy had looked at him – a challenge in his eyes, almost. It had caused Justin to wonder, just for a second, if something had gone on between Alicia and him, possibly because he'd been preoccupied with his own problems around the same time she'd worked with Radley in financial services.

He'd ring her at work, he decided. Order some flowers to be delivered beforehand. Hope she was available and ask if she fancied having lunch with a sad, jealous bastard. Meanwhile, if he had any hopes of being at his scintillating best, he needed to catch up on some sleep. After a demanding night, he was utterly exhausted. All he wanted to do was crawl into bed. Yawning, he climbed the stairs, tugging off his jacket as he went, and then stopped, as Sophie trudged back through the door.

Puzzled, Justin turned back. 'I thought you were late?'

'I am now.' Sophie sighed, with an obligatory roll of the eyes. 'Mum's outside calling the breakdown service. The car won't start.'

CHAPTER TWO

ALICIA

'Nope, it's not going anywhere,' Justin confirmed. 'You're out of petrol.' He nodded towards the dash and then glanced sympathetically up at Alicia.

'Oh no.' Alicia sighed inwardly. She'd been so het up when the engine had spluttered and died, she hadn't even noticed the petrol gauge. Her first job this morning was to arrange urgent accommodation for a young mother whose toddler had been assaulted by the child's father. She couldn't let that child down, or let her mother down, who wasn't much more than a child herself. With more families on their caseloads than they could cope with, there were no other social workers to cover for her. Alicia felt suddenly too close to crying the tears she'd been desperately trying to hold back since she'd realised the grave danger her own family was in, and how much Justin would hurt, her children would hurt, because of her.

Swallowing hard, she turned to the rear passenger door to start unbuckling Lucas, her precious baby boy. Justin would die to protect him, to protect Sophie. *She* would. Whatever hold Paul Radley imagined he had over her, she would kill to protect them. All of them, including her husband, who'd done nothing to deserve having the foundations of his life ripped from beneath him. Closing her eyes, she tried to still the image that Justin would see: another man's breath hot on her neck, his mouth close to her ear, whispering his love for her as he pressed himself into her, assuring her that her husband need never find out. It would destroy him. She *wouldn't* allow it. *Couldn't.*

'How long before the breakdown service gets here?' Justin asked, climbing out.

'An hour,' Alicia said quietly, lifting Lucas out, easing him close to her shoulder and breathing in that special smell that binds baby and mother together forever. 'Sorry, sweetheart. Mummy's been a very silly mummy, hasn't she?'

Silly and weak, and unforgivably deceitful. Her heart squeezing inside her, Alicia eased back to drink her little miracle man in, marvelling at the perfectness of him, his softly curled eyelashes, his perfect cupid lips.

'I'll drive you,' Justin offered. 'The only alternative is to fetch petrol from the garage and that will probably take just as long.'

'It's okay, Justin,' Alicia assured him, noting the dark circles under his eyes. He looked utterly exhausted. His job was demanding enough without her troubles to contend with. Her heart twisted as she thought about what he'd already had to deal with, the awful loss in his life. What he might still have to face, unless she could stop whatever was lurking, ready to twist and weave its insidious way through the fabric of their marriage.

'You've been working all night,' she reminded him, as if he would need reminding. 'You're possibly not even safe to drive. I could take your car.' She glanced towards it. 'As long as you don't need it before I get home?'

'I don't, but…' Justin looked uncertain. 'You haven't driven anything but an automatic for years, Ali. I'm not sure I'd get much sleep, worrying about you having an accident.'

'I'll be fine. I'll get the hang of it once I get going.' Alicia waved away his concerns.

'It's a forty-minute round trip. I won't die of sleep deprivation, I promise,' Justin assured her. 'I'll take you. I'm only going to be texting you otherwise.'

Guilt immediately lodged itself like a hard stone in Alicia's chest. He would text her. He always did, checking she'd arrived safely. *Just wanted to remind you I love you* – that was his latest subtle way of enquiring.

'Thanks.' Alicia glanced away. She couldn't meet his eyes, just then. How would he cope, if he knew? Losing his family all over again – how would he ever be able to deal with it? He couldn't find out. Whatever she had to do, she had to make sure he never found out.

'Are you getting in?' Justin asked her, his head cocked bemusedly to one side as he looked her over, clearly noting her mind was elsewhere.

'Yes, sorry, miles away.' Alicia turned to the door he'd opened in his own car, quickly strapped Lucas into the carrier that was already there and then hurried around to the front passenger side. 'Where's Sophie?' she asked, climbing in.

'Waiting in the hall rather than get rained on,' Justin supplied, smiling wryly as he climbed into the driver's side.

'Sorry about forgetting to fill it up,' Alicia said, for want of something to say, as she fumbled for her seatbelt. 'I meant to do it yesterday, but I completely forgot.'

'I'm not surprised.' Justin started the engine. 'You obviously have a lot on your mind.'

Alicia felt her heart thud. What did he mean?

'I did the same thing myself last week,' Justin went on, clearly attempting to make her feel less incompetent, rather than make any insinuation. 'It's not a problem. I can catch up on my sleep later.'

'I'll have to pin a note on the fridge or put an alert on my phone or something. My head's like a sieve these days. I swear pregnancy addled my brain.' Plugging in her seatbelt, Alicia babbled inconsequently, desperate to stay on safe ground.

'All done?' Justin asked her, checking she had belted up. He was always attentive in that way, making sure she was safe. That Sophie and Lucas were. Alicia had hoped to do the same for him, keep him safe, when he'd been floundering after losing his family in the cruellest possible way. A hope doomed to failure. Part of her had known that the truth would come out, causing her world to unravel. She'd ignored it. Hoped it would go away. And now Paul Radley had come back. The lie she'd told was in danger of being exposed. She couldn't ignore it. Not any longer.

'Good.' Justin went quiet, and then turned to glance towards the house, presumably checking for signs of Sophie.

For a long second, silence hung heavy between them, like a yawning chasm, and then he turned back to her. The icy chill running the length of her spine told Alicia he was about to broach the subject she'd prayed he wouldn't. She wasn't ready. He wasn't. He would never be. Her heart sank hopelessly. 'Alicia,' he started hesitantly, 'about the other night, I was—'

The passenger door being yanked open cut him short, allowing Alicia to breathe out the breath she hadn't realised she was holding in.

'God, what is it with this rain?' Sophie moaned, throwing herself into the back seat. 'It's totally ruining my hair.'

'Don't worry, Sophie, you're still irresistibly gorgeous, even with totally ruined hair.' Justin eyed her amusedly through the rear-view mirror as he pulled out of the drive. 'But not as irresistible as your mother, obviously.'

Alicia felt her heart drop as if down a lift shaft. 'I assume there was some kind of innuendo in there?' she asked him quietly.

'What?' Justin looked across to her, surprised. 'No,' he said quickly. 'There wasn't meant to be. Look, Alicia' – he glanced again in his mirror, careful of Sophie in the back – 'about the other night: I was out of order. Overreacting. A touch of the green-eyed monster, obviously. Can you blame me? You're a beautiful woman.'

Astonished by that, Alicia simply stared at him.

'So, have you two kissed and made up then?' Sophie asked, clearly aware of the awkwardness there'd been between them. 'Only Luke reckons all this not talking to each other crap is really juvenile, don't you, Luke?'

'I don't know.' Justin turned questioningly to Alicia as he slowed at the traffic lights. 'Have we?'

Alicia studied him, bewildered. How could he imagine she was beautiful? How could he ever have? Her heart felt too big in her chest, stuffed full of regret, of overwhelming love for this man, who actually had made her feel beautiful – even immediately post pregnancy, he'd told her she was gorgeous. Small lies, little white lies to make her feel better, whereas hers… Feeling as if it might be for the last time, she leaned towards him and pressed a soft kiss to his cheek. She wished there was a way to tell him, before his love turned to hatred, how deeply she loved him.

Justin reached to squeeze her hand, and then, a warm glint in his eyes, leaned towards her to steal a kiss of his own.

'*Urgh*, cover your eyes, Luke,' Sophie advised her baby brother. 'The parents are doing lovey-dovey stuff in public. *So* embarrassing.'

Alicia felt a laugh bubble up inside her. It felt good. For the briefest moment, everything felt normal. If only she could hold on to it. Never let it go.

'Sorry,' Justin mouthed, giving her an apologetic smile.

Gulping back her heartache, Alicia smiled back and cupped her hand to his face, needing to feel the solidity of him. Soon it would be gone. Soon her man – her strong, dependable man – would recoil at her touch.

'Er, excuse us, children present.' Sophie sighed disapprovingly, and then said, 'Dad, lights. You're stopping traffic.'

'Hell,' Justin mumbled, checking the lights and then pulling hurriedly out.

Alicia was still looking at him when her blood froze in her veins. 'Justin!' she screamed, clutching his arm hard.

Instinctively slamming his foot on the brake, Justin swung his gaze to the side window. 'Dear God…' The words died on his lips as the full impact of the collision hit the family.

CHAPTER THREE

JUSTIN

Justin saw nothing but deep, dark red. Heard nothing. Felt nothing but numbness throughout his entire body.

Then all his senses assailed him at once: searing pain in his ribcage, a cacophony of noise, too loud in his head. Horns blaring. People shouting. Petrol spilling. Sirens plaintively wailing.

Alicia. Screaming.

Sophie, her voice high-pitched, hysterical. 'Dad! Oh God. Oh God. *Dad!*'

Luke… No sound at all.

Justin's heart kicked hard. White-hot pain shooting through his shoulder, down his spine to his pelvis, he turned towards Alicia, registered the palpable shock on her face, the blood on her forehead, matted in her hair, tracing the contours of her face.

'Justin! The *children*!' she yelled. 'Please, God, don't do this. Not my children. *Please!* Not my *children!*'

Justin was already fumbling with his seatbelt, grappling with it, tearing at it. *Come on!* 'Fucking… *fucking* thing!'

'Dad!' Sophie's voice was the terrified sob of a child as he twisted to face her. 'Luke!'

Jesus Christ, no. Please, no… Twisting back to his door, Justin reached for the handle, cursing again loudly as he realised the locking mechanism was engaged. Reaching to release it, he tried again, only to find the door was stuck. Justin shoved his shoulder against it, his whole body against it, pushed with all his might, finally spilling from his car to land heavily on the pavement.

Blinking bloody sweat from his eyelashes, his breaths coming in short, sharp rasps, he planted his hands on the concrete, heaved himself up to all fours, reached for the buckled metal of the door to pull himself to his feet.

His legs almost failing him, aware of the bedlam of traffic around him, the shocked faces of onlookers frozen in time, Justin groped for the rear passenger door.

He was vaguely aware of other hands helping him to wrench it open. Justin couldn't see whose. His focus was on Sophie. She was choking back sobs now, close to hyperventilating. *Luke.* He couldn't get past her. Couldn't make her hear him.

'Sophie!' He seized her shoulders as she attempted to climb out, locked his eyes hard on hers as she screamed over and over, petrified, soul-crushing screams of pure fear. 'Keep still! You're okay! *Please…*' He moderated his tone 'Don't move, Sophie. You might have a neck injury.'

Luke. Someone was reaching into the other side. 'Don't!' Justin screamed it. He needed to get to him before they moved him.

Swiping at the droplets of crimson clouding his vision, Justin galvanised himself into action and made his way around the back of the car. It took a second, a slow thud like a death knell, before he registered the impossible angle of the carrier.

CHAPTER FOUR

ALICIA

Petrified, Alicia watched as a flurry of medical staff attended him, her tiny baby, lost on a hospital trolley made for an adult, monitors beeping and pinging around him. He looked so small, so fragile against the vast expanse of white sheet. His little face wasn't damaged. He still looked perfect. Her perfect little boy, his softly curled eyelashes brushing his cheeks as he slept. His perfect cupid lips. His little hands curled into fists. His tiny chest rising and falling. Breathing. *He's breathing.* Squeezing her eyes closed, Alicia felt the room shift, breathed in and out with him. *Please keep breathing, baby. Please keep breathing.*

She could hear someone talking about the positioning of his carrier in the car. *Back passenger seat, forward-facing.* The words reached her as if muffled by endless fathoms of swirling, icy water. *Responsive to pain.*

Oh please, God, no.

Folding her arms tightly across her midriff, Alicia felt the tear rip steadily through her heart, felt the tug in her womb where she'd carried him, kept him safe and warm until he was grown enough to come into the world. He was hurting! Her baby boy was hurting, and he *wasn't* grown. He was *tiny.* He was hurting, and she couldn't make it go away, couldn't keep him safe. She needed to. She was his *mother!*

'Please help him,' she begged, her voice catching on the sob in her throat. She didn't want Lucas to hear her crying. It would scare him.

Swiping a hand across her face, she gulped back another wretched sob. 'Please do something,' she pleaded. 'Don't let him be in pain. *Please…*'

A nurse came to her side, speaking gently, as if cajoling a child. 'We're doing everything we can, Mrs Cole. Why don't you come and wait in the visitor's room?'

Alicia felt the woman's arms close around her shoulders, trying to coax her away.

No! Did they think she would *leave* him? Did they think she would leave her baby? She needed to stay. She needed to talk to him. He would respond to her voice. He *would* respond. Oh God, she needed to hold him, feel his warm body next to hers, his tiny heart beating. 'Please help him. Somebody, please help—'

Justin. Her gaze shot to the resuscitation room doors as they crashed open.

'You need to step away, Dr Cole,' someone ordered, as he moved towards Lucas. 'It's too personal. You have a possible pneumothorax. You're in no fit state to—'

'He's my fucking *son!*' Justin shouted, struggling to get past two colleagues who were attempting to hold him back.

'Pulmonary contusions evident,' another doctor said, as he pressed a stethoscope to their baby's small chest. 'Get hold of paediatrics. Tell them—'

'He won't make it!' Justin screamed. 'He's about to go into respiratory arrest. You need to intubate. Now!'

The doctor looked towards Justin and then, his expression foreboding, back to the other medical staff gathered around him. 'Tell paeds to stand by,' he instructed a nurse, as Alicia's heart slowed to a dull thud inside her. And then to another, 'Get me an EZ-IO drill. And get the fast scanner here now.'

Alicia knew what he was about to do. She couldn't bear it. Didn't think she could stand to hear the sound of the drill whirring and cutting.

She felt Justin's arm around her. Instinctively, she turned to him, felt his other arm enclose her, pulling her towards him. Guilt rose inside her, her mind screaming what she already knew. It was her fault. All of it, *her* fault! This was her punishment for the wicked thing she'd done, the dreadful mistake she'd made. But it was *her* mistake. The punishment should be hers, not her baby's. Not Justin's. Not Sophie's. Her's alone.

'You shouldn't touch me!' She pulled away from him, feeling she might taint him. Everything she'd ever done had shaped his life, had brought him to this terrible place. He shouldn't be with her. She should never have made him be. 'You shouldn't be anywhere near me!'

Justin stepped towards her, tried to ease her back. 'Alicia, don't…' He stopped, drawing in a harsh breath. Hearing the wheeze rattle his chest, Alicia looked sharply up, saw the agony in his eyes, the perspiration mingling with the salty tears on his cheeks as he looked towards his broken baby. He was hurting. Hurting so badly. How could he ever forgive her? How would she ever forgive herself?

He would never come back from this. He would blame himself. He would never stop blaming himself if…

'Blood pressure's dropping.'

CHAPTER FIVE

ALICIA

Feeling closer to him there, Alicia had stayed in the same place for two solid days since coming home from the hospital: sitting in the chair in the nursery. It was an antique rocking chair. Justin had bought it – to make feeding times easier, he'd said. Lucas had been easy to feed, a contented baby. It was a perfect chair for cuddling and snuggling him, though.

Her heart squeezing painfully, Alicia caught a breath in her throat as she recalled how she'd woken from an exhausted sleep shortly after bringing Lucas home, panic immediately engulfing her when she realised it was past his feed time and he wasn't crying. Her heart rate had slowed to somewhere near normal when she'd found Justin's side of the bed empty; she'd crept tentatively along the landing to find her husband nestling his son in the crook of his arm, humming softly as he rocked him gently back to sleep.

He'd done it many times since, when he hadn't been working. Alicia accused him of quietly hoping she would sleep through, so he could spend precious alone time with his son, and Sophie made merciless fun of her dad getting in touch with his feminine side. Alicia had pointed out he'd taken his fair share of night-time feeds with her too, the only difference being they hadn't had a rocking chair. At this, Sophie had bemoaned her deprived childhood.

Alicia smiled at the memory, and then swallowed hard against the cold stone wedged like ice in her chest. Shivering involuntarily as Lucas's wind-chime mobile tinkled the softest of sounds, she eased his patchwork quilt higher towards her face, breathing in the smell of him. His smell was everywhere: on her clothes, in her hair. She couldn't bear to wash him away. He permeated every surface, every wall, every pore of the house.

Looking towards the mobile, sure she could hear his delighted chuckles and gurgles as it jangled, she realised Justin was standing on the landing, watching her, not moving. He didn't come in. He hadn't come into the room once since he'd been discharged. Because he couldn't cope with it. Because his pain was too raw. Alicia could see it. It was etched deep into his eyes.

He needed her. He needed his family, his baby. She couldn't bear it. Alicia looked away.

'Can I get you anything?' he asked hesitantly.

Alicia shook her head. She couldn't eat. Couldn't swallow. Couldn't breathe.

'Some tea or hot chocolate?' he tried.

'We'd only just started weaning him,' she said, for no reason other than she could see the confusion in Lucas's beautiful summer-blue eyes when she'd first fed a spoon into his mouth. 'He opened his mouth for the spoon on Sunday. Soft fruits. He liked soft fruits mixed with his milk.'

Justin breathed in. 'I know,' he said throatily.

Another minute stuffed full of silence passed by, then, 'You should try and eat something, Alicia. At least let me get you some tea?'

Alicia smiled sadly. Her mother had always gone for the kettle in a crisis. A tradition passed on from her gran. A 'cure-all cuppa', her gran had called it. It couldn't cure this, couldn't take away the ache in her chest where her heart should be. Her hand strayed to the soft round of her tummy. The emptiness where her baby had grown.

She wished her mother was here. That God, in whatever infinite wisdom it was, hadn't seen fit to take her away from her too. She would have judged her, no doubt she would have done that, but she would have kept loving her. It was selfish, but she needed that love. She desperately needed the love of someone who could know all there was to know and still keep loving her. To be held until her heart had stopped breaking and the unbearable pain went away.

But it wouldn't go away. Couldn't. Ever.

Justin, would he hold her? Could he bear to, now that he suspected? And he did. She could feel it. How could she let him? Only to tell him she'd betrayed him in the worst possible way a woman could betray a man? He was bleeding too, just as steadily as her, and she had no idea what to do.

She needed to try. Needed to help him get through this. Could she at least do that, before she broke him completely? Glancing away, she wiped a tear from her face. 'I'll come down soon,' she said, though she had no idea how she would. She couldn't bear to see Lucas's things in the kitchen – his little bowl and his feeding cup. Couldn't conceive the idea of throwing them out. Here she was, surrounded by his things, his tiny baby clothes, his toys, by him. There were no surprises, nothing that would leap out at her and force the air from her lungs.

Alicia listened to the landing clock ticking, loud against the silence, as Justin nodded defeatedly and walked away. How she wished she could wrench the hands of the clock back, eradicate time, her mistakes – and the cruellest second of all, in which God had taken their baby away.

Not God.

Her. Getting unsteadily to her feet, she walked towards the window. She'd been responsible for Lucas's death. If not for her lies, her weakness, none of this would have happened. She might have remembered to fill up her own car had she not been so distracted by Paul Radley. Justin wouldn't have been driving her. If only she'd been honest, neither of them would have been distracted that day from what mattered most in the world: their family. Justin wouldn't be facing pain after insurmountable pain. She should have told him the truth. It was too late now.

'Where are you, baby?' she whispered glancing up at the stars, twinkling brightly against a vast canvas of black. 'Where are you, my beautiful baby boy?' Closing her eyes, she pressed his little quilt close to her face and allowed her tears to finally spill over.

She wasn't aware Justin had come back until he reached for her. Alicia leaned into him as he eased her to face him. She couldn't help herself. She didn't deserve him, but she so needed him, wanted to morph into him, never let go of him. Knew, as the hand of the clock ticked past this moment, that he didn't want to let go of her either.

But he would. He was blaming himself. It wasn't his fault. None of it.

She'd wanted to save him and now she would destroy him.

Pressing her face hard into his shoulder, Alicia tried and failed to still the sobs that shook through her body. 'I'm sorry,' she choked wretchedly, blinded by snot and tears. 'So, so sorry.'

'Shhh,' he murmured, softly stroking her hair, as if she were a child in need of comfort. And she was. Oh God, how she was. 'You have nothing to be sorry for.'

Alicia heard a sob catch in his throat.

And her heart cracked wide open.

CHAPTER SIX

JUSTIN

She'd decorated the nursery herself, as she had most of the house – an old Victorian property, which had been badly in need of renovation when they'd moved in. Steeling himself to venture into the room on his own, once Alicia had finally gone downstairs, Justin recalled how he'd almost had a heart attack when he'd found her halfway up a stepladder in her fifth month of pregnancy. She'd laughed away his concerns when he tried to dissuade her.

'I know this is your protective gene kicking in, but I'm only two rungs up,' she'd pointed out. 'Being pregnant doesn't mean I'm suddenly made of porcelain, you know? I'm fine, Justin, I promise. Go on, shoo. Go to work.'

Still, though, with Sophie staying over at a friend's to work on the lyrics of their latest 'going to be phenomenal' pop song together, Justin had been reluctant to leave her.

'Justin, go. You're making me feel self-conscious,' she'd urged him, blushing as he'd continued to watch her. With artistic flair, she'd been using a template to paint the pale blue wall with white seagulls, her tongue protruding in that cute way it did when she was concentrating.

Justin had smiled, and then stepped instinctively forwards, as she'd stepped down to deposit her paint tray. With her wild, caramel-coloured hair piled on top of her head and wearing one of his shirts as an overall, she'd looked possibly more beautiful in his eyes then than she ever had. 'You look utterly gorgeous, Mrs Cole,' he'd assured her, leaning in to brush her lips with a soft kiss.

'And so do you, Dr Cole,' she'd said, sweeping her eyes over his business suit – compulsory attire when meeting with the hospital trust, and which Alicia apparently considered a 'bit of a turn-on'. There'd been a far too enticing look in her eyes as they'd come to meet his.

Unable to resist, Justin had eased her towards him, kissing her this time most enjoyably thoroughly. 'I may have to take this further later,' he'd said hoarsely, when they'd finally come up for air.

'I'll consider that a promise.' Alicia had replied, delicious innuendo dancing in her eyes as they'd lingered on his. 'Now, be gone, Dr Cole. You're late.'

Checking his watch, Justin had winced. 'Damn. I was obviously having too much of a good time. I'm gone. Be careful not to overdo it,' he'd said, helping himself to another quick kiss. 'Be good, baby Cole,' he'd added, bending to kiss her tummy, should baby Cole feel neglected, and then heading fast for the landing. 'And make sure not to overstretch,' he'd called back.

Now, gulping back the emotion climbing inside him, Justin's gaze strayed towards the cot. He'd found the baby butterfly wind chime hanging over it when he'd come home.

She'd painted the ottoman that day too. It had been her mother's, and Alicia hadn't wanted to part with it when she'd lost her, but they'd never quite found the right place for it. She'd rubbed it down and painted it white, topped it off with two cushions and a traditional teddy bear dressed in a blue striped nightshirt and nightcap. That had been the night Justin had learned their baby's name. Lucas Cole. She'd stencilled it on the front of the ottoman, leaving space for his date of birth underneath.

She'd added that the week after they brought him home – six months, almost to the day, before his short life was stolen away.

Justin swallowed as he looked towards it. He wasn't sure whether it was his heart, or the wound from the tube they'd inserted to drain the fluid from his lung, that ached so incessantly. Whatever it was, he felt he deserved it. He'd been behind the wheel, exhausted, distracted. He'd been responsible for what had happened to their son.

Dragging an arm across his eyes, Justin walked out of the room, easing the door closed behind him, and then stopped and pushed it ajar again. Alicia preferred it open. She didn't want to shut him away. She didn't have to say it.

Stopping on the landing, Justin glanced at the ceiling, blinking hard, wishing he could do something to ease Alicia's pain. *Can I get you anything?* He laughed scornfully at the thought of the banal question he kept asking her. *Yes*, she should tell him. *You can get me my baby back.*

God. Heaving in a breath which stopped somewhere short of his chest, Justin dropped his gaze, squeezing the bridge of his nose hard in a vain attempt to suppress the rage burning inside him. He couldn't bring Luke back. Couldn't undo the godforsaken day on which he'd been responsible for the death of her child. He would die himself, right here, right now, in exchange for his little boy's life back, if only God were merciful and would let him.

CHAPTER SEVEN

SOPHIE

Seeing her dad on the landing, obviously upset, Sophie had stepped back into her bedroom. He hadn't cried though. It was like he wouldn't allow himself to. Her mum, too. She'd been sitting in Luke's room mostly. Whenever she did come out, she moved around the house like a ghost, her arms wrapped around herself, as if keeping everything in. Keeping everyone out. She'd been shutting out her dad. Blaming him, obviously, because he'd been driving, which was just so fucking unfair.

Since he'd broken the news to Sophie at the hospital, his voice cracking and his face deathly white, her dad hadn't spoken to her much either, other than to ask if she was all right.

Her mum kept asking her the same question, as if she could ever be. As if any of them could. Or else she snapped at her if she moved anything of Luke's. And then she would apologise. Why didn't they just let it out? Stop tiptoeing around each other and scream at each other, if that's what it took?

She kept assuring them she was okay. How could she not, when they were hurting so much? But she wasn't okay – stuck here in her room, because wherever else she went, she felt in the way, as if she were somehow intruding. They'd be devastated if she said it out loud, but that truly was how she felt, like she daren't say or do anything that might touch a raw nerve.

Her teacher, who had rung her to see how she was, had suggested she write down her feelings. She needn't show it to anyone, she'd said. Some things, on reflection, are better left unsaid, but it might be therapeutic, she'd told her. It did help. Sophie glanced down at the notebook she'd been scrawling in, the contents of which would definitely devastate her parents, and then plucked it up and stuffed it well under her clothes in her chest of drawers.

She debated whether to ring her mate Chloe, but then decided against. Chloe had been texting her constantly. She made the right noises, but she didn't understand, not really, that she felt as cold and empty as the house did without Luke in it. That with his funeral somehow to get through, she didn't want to go out, to the cinema, clubbing to 'lose herself on the dance floor', or anywhere else. She didn't want to sing either. She listened to her music – Adele, mostly, whose soulful emotion fitted her mood. Sophie wished she might be as good as her one day. She didn't sing along though. She didn't have the heart. All she wanted to do was stay cocooned under her quilt, left alone, preferably. But she couldn't even do that for her mum or her dad coming up every two minutes, like they were on a rota or something, to ask the perpetual question.

Sighing heavily, Sophie wandered back to her bed, picked up her phone and plugged her earphones in. She was selecting her playlist when there was an inevitable tap on the door. Her dad, she guessed. He usually waited before entering – 'at his own peril', he once would have said. Would he ever joke again, Sophie wondered, or smile or laugh?

'Yup, I'm here,' she called. She wasn't sure why she'd said that. Because part of her suspected they were frightened she wouldn't be. That something terrible might have happened to her too.

Her dad did smile when he came in. A forced smile. He looked at her, worriedly, as Sophie had expected he would, as if she might fall apart or self-combust on the bed or something. 'I thought I'd get some food,' he said, trying to sound normal.

Sophie shrugged. She wasn't hungry. None of them were.

'I thought pizza, maybe?' Scratching his forehead with his thumb, her dad shrugged in turn, as if he knew that it would stick in her throat, whatever it was.

'If you like.' Sophie offered him a small smile back, when what she really wanted to do was go to him and hug him. She couldn't though. She'd tried that when he'd arrived home. She'd gone to him, wrapped her arms around him. She'd hurt his chest. She could tell when he'd winced. He'd said he was fine, just a bit sore from where they'd inserted the tube; that was all. *Bullshit.* He wasn't fine. It was utter bollocks, pretending he was coping, when he quite clearly wasn't.

'Pepperoni with extra cheese?' he suggested, his voice tight, trying so hard not to crack it was heartbreaking.

'Sounds good.' Knowing he needed her to, Sophie played along.

Her dad ran a hand over his neck, nodded and turned to the door. And then turned back. 'Sophie,' he said, walking across to her, 'if you want to talk about anything…' He faltered. 'About Luke… I'm here. You know that, right? I'm listening.'

Glancing down at her phone, Sophie swiped a hand under her nose. She didn't say anything. She wanted to. Wanted desperately to talk about Luke, about what had happened, but with her mum and dad clearly unable to, how could she?

'Sophie?' Her dad hesitated, and then sat down on her bed. 'It's okay to cry, you know,' he said softly, taking hold of her hand.

He had nice hands. Sophie swallowed. Clean fingernails. A surgeon's hands, those of a man who saved lives. But he hadn't been able to save his own son. Sophie had heard him at the hospital, cursing himself, cursing the 'fucking bastard' who'd hit them and run. Blaming himself.

Sophie looked up then, searching his eyes. Steel-blue eyes, Sophie would term them. She'd always been able to read them: a soft twinkle therein when he'd tease her, usually about her 'tarantula' eyelashes or her eyebrow stud – her face jewellery, as he called it; when he hugged her, which he'd always done often. Now they were stormy, almost gunmetal grey. Uncertain, tortured eyes. 'Is it?' she asked him.

Her dad looked away, which pretty much communicated that he didn't think it was okay, not for him anyway.

'Have they found him yet?' Sophie asked. 'The man who cut the lights?'

Her dad took a breath and shook his head. 'Not yet, no.' Sophie could feel his frustration.

'Will they?' She kept looking at him, willing him to look at her. To let down his guard and look at her properly.

'I'm not sure. I hope so,' he said, pressing a thumb hard to his forehead.

'Will they prosecute him? If they do find him, will they charge him?'

'I don't know, Sophie.' Again, he faltered, looking awkward, as if he wanted to protect her. But he couldn't. This was happening to her too. She wasn't a child. She read the newspapers, watched the news. Knew that, if they did find him and they did prosecute him, he might get no more than a slap on the wrist. 'It depends on whether they have enough—'

He was cut off as the telephone rang, yet again. Saved by the bell, Sophie thought wearily.

Her heart sank as her dad got to his feet, going to answer the bloody thing, talk to people who didn't have a clue what to say. *Talk to me!* She wanted to scream after him. *I'm listening!*

Her mum knocked and came straight in, catching Sophie unawares. She'd been going to watch Netflix stuff on her iPad, but nothing seemed appealing. She'd given up eventually and curled up under the duvet.

'I brought you some pizza,' her mum said, as Sophie poked her head out.

'Thanks.' Sophie nodded, squinting against the sudden light from the lamp.

'You will eat it, won't you?' her mum asked, worry flitting across her eyes as she placed the pizza on the bedside table.

Realising she looked worse than she had when she'd last seen her – drained and definitely in need of some sustenance herself – Sophie straightened herself up. 'I'm not really very hungry, but I'll try,' she promised.

Her mum didn't look convinced. 'You have to eat something, Sophie. You need to keep your strength—'

'And so do *you*!' Sophie snapped, and then felt immediately guilty. 'Look, I'll eat it, Mum. Okay? I don't need to be mollycoddled or treated like I'm incapable.'

Her mum looked bewildered at that. 'I wasn't aware I was treating you like anything.'

'Seriously?' Sophie widened her eyes. 'You're bringing me dinner in bed? I'd have to have been dying for you to do that normally.'

Shit! Shit, shit, shit! She hadn't meant to say that.

Seeing the stunned look on her mum's face, Sophie felt tears stinging the back of her eyes. 'Sorry,' she mumbled, dropping her gaze. 'I didn't mean…'

'I know.' Perching herself on the edge of the bed, Alicia reached out to place a hand on her arm. 'It's okay to grieve, Sophie,' she said softly. 'It's natural to be—'

'So *grieve* then!' Sophie yelled over her. She couldn't stand this any more. 'Talk to *each other*, why don't you – not me. Stop trying to act like you're not crucified inside!'

Alicia snatched her hand away, as if she'd been burned. 'You're angry,' she said, understandingly, deflecting the conversation away from herself. 'It's natural. You're bound to—'

'Yes, I'm angry!' Sophie shouted louder. 'Bloody angry!' Dragging her hair from her face, she glared at Alicia, whose face had now drained of the little colour she'd had. Sophie knew she was hurting her, but she couldn't stop. They needed to be told. They needed shaking out of this... stupor. To be there for each other. 'I'm angry at the injustice of it,' she went on furiously. 'The cruelty! Angry with *you*!'

'Me?' Alicia asked shakily.

'Both of you.' Sophie looked past her mum to her dad, who, clearly having overheard, had appeared on the landing. 'You're treating me like a *child*. Sparing me the details. I don't want to be spared! I want to *know* what's going on. I don't want you wrapping me up in cotton wool! Don't you understand?'

'Sophie...' Justin stepped in, his face taut, definitely angry. Good! She wanted him to be angry. She wanted him to do *something*. Shout, swear, throw things. Anything but walk around here like a dead-inside zombie.

'*What?*' Sophie turned on him. 'Luke was my *baby brother*. I might have said he did nothing but eat, puke and poo, but I loved him, Dad. I *loved* him. I miss him, and my heart is hurting so badly, and I can't talk to you, because we're all walking around on *goddamned* eggshells.'

Sophie glared at him, her expression defiant, her shoulders heaving.

Nodding slowly, Justin walked across to sit on the edge of the bed next to Alicia. He hesitated for a second and then reached out to take Alicia's hand.

Her mum curled her fingers around his, Sophie noticed, relief washing through her.

Pressing his thumb against his forehead, in that way he did, her dad took a breath and then reached for her hand too. 'There are several stages of grief, Sophie,' he said, glancing at Alicia. 'I think we've both been in the denial stage. We're getting there.' He tried to sound reassuring.

Sophie wasn't sure she was reassured entirely, but at least they were acknowledging it.

'I think you might be in the anger stage – with good reason,' her dad went on. 'I'm sorry if I… *we* appear to have been distant. Sometimes, I…' He hesitated. 'I find I struggle to say how I feel, because I think it might trigger emotions I'm not sure other people can handle. I suspect that might be true for your mum too, just now.'

Smiling sadly, he squeezed her hand. 'You're right, though: we do need to talk. We're not other people, are we? We're a family. We need each other.'

Sounding choked, he looked again at Alicia.

Sophie followed his gaze, to where her mum was sitting with her head bowed. Crying. She was crying. *Shit!* Sophie saw one tear plop from her chin, and then another.

'Oh God, Mum, I'm sorry.' She shuffled across to her. 'It's okay,' she said, sliding her arms around her. 'You can cry on my shoulder. I don't mind a bit of snot on my T-shirt, honest I don't.'

Sophie swallowed hard as her mum emitted a strangled laugh.

CHAPTER EIGHT

JUSTIN

Justin hadn't been sure why he'd decided to come to the hospital the day before his son's funeral, but once he'd arrived, he'd realised he needed space, to try and get his emotions under control. He'd worked hard at that over the years, since he'd discovered his murdered family and almost lost his sanity. Whenever his thoughts went there, images like sick movie stills playing through his mind, his moods swinging violently from the same paralysing panic he'd felt then, through despair, to angry disbelief that the bastard responsible – an opportunist thief needing to feed his drugs habit – had never been caught, he employed the coping mechanisms he'd learned: calming deep breaths; counting when he felt himself too close to the edge. Tiles on floors, fluorescent lights on ceilings, he counted until he was able to reach some kind of detachment. But the tidal wave of grief, shot through with sheer fury, that crashed over him every time he thought about Luke, about what kind of person could hit a car, clearly causing serious injury to a family, and then run – Justin stood no chance of detaching from that. From the fact that he was also culpable; driving whilst tired and distracted.

As hard as he tried not to dwell on why he'd been distracted, he couldn't help himself. Perhaps because of the irony of Radley resurfacing days before the incomprehensible cruelty that had taken Luke from them. Justin knew he needed to let it go. Alicia and he had taken a step forward since the accident, with Alicia, at least, no longer keeping all her grief inside – Justin knew how destructive that could be. She still seemed unable to talk properly to him though, hold eye contact with him, and he badly needed her to. He was assuming it was because he'd been driving, that there was part of her that couldn't help blaming him. Still, though, his mind would wonder about Radley. He simply wouldn't go away.

Taking a breath, Justin realised the parents of the six-month-old baby girl brought in with brain trauma would probably wonder what he was doing, staring down at her, and snapped his attention back to her.

He'd performed emergency surgery on this child the day before his own little boy had died. She was alive. A small miracle in the bleak madness his life had become. *Untouched, untroubled, untarnished.* He couldn't help recalling what he'd thought when he'd first gazed down in wonder at Sophie. At Lucas. He'd sworn to keep their world safe. To keep them safe. He'd failed. Failed in his most fundamental obligation as a father.

Swallowing hard as a new wave of grief sucked the air from his lungs, Justin tried to breathe through it, focussing on checking the little girl's vital statistics. And then, satisfied she was doing as well as she could be, he stroked her cheek softly with his finger and was rewarded with a delighted gurgle, which almost broke his heart all over again. 'She's going to be a knockout,' he said, composing himself and turning to offer the parents a reassuring smile.

'Thanks, Dr Cole.' The young father smiled awkwardly and then glanced away.

Justin guessed they'd heard the news about his son, which had travelled like wildfire around the hospital. He should go. He hadn't meant to make them feel uncomfortable, which inevitably they would be, but he'd needed to see for himself that she was thriving.

'I'll leave you in the capable hands of the nursing staff,' he said, smiling again as he turned for the door.

'Dr Cole,' the mother said, behind him.

Justin had only half turned back when she launched herself at him, throwing her arms around him, dropping her head to his shoulder and squeezing him hard. 'Thank you,' she said emotionally. 'For everything. For coming to check on her. You're a very special man.'

Justin didn't feel very special. No matter how hard he tried, no matter how much he counted, anger was all he felt. So much anger and guilt stuffed inside him it was fucking choking him. He managed to make it to one of the patients' toilets along the corridor before he gave vent to his tears.

CHAPTER NINE

ALICIA

Breathing out a sigh of relief, Alicia came from the kitchen to meet Justin as soon as she heard his key in the front door. 'Are you all right?' she asked him, almost before he'd stepped through it.

Justin glanced at her confusedly.

'I was worried,' Alicia said, trying not to sound accusatory. God knew, that was the last thing she should be. 'You've been gone a while. I rang the hospital. They said you'd left. And when you didn't come home, I wondered… I thought…' She trailed hopelessly off, the words she wanted to say to him dying in her throat.

He could talk to her – that was what she wanted to tell him. *Should* tell him. She was here for him. Every thought she had now was muddled. Everything she said to him would add an insult to the injury that would inevitably be caused when the truth came out. She could feel it, like a guillotine casting a long shadow over them, ready to drop, when Paul Radley chose to let it.

'Sorry,' Justin said, with an attempt at a smile. 'I should have thought. I was out walking, lost track of time. I meant to call.'

'But you're all right?' she asked again, knowing he couldn't possibly be.

Justin took a second, a long second, to hang his coat up, and then finally turned to look at her. 'Under the circumstances' – he paused, holding her gaze – 'yes, as well as I can be, I suppose.'

Alicia scanned his eyes. Usually so bright and intelligent, twin-kling amusedly whenever he smiled and always full of compassion, there was nothing there now other than deep-rooted pain.

'Dad?' Sophie called apprehensively to him from the landing, breaking the silence now hanging between them. 'Are you okay? You've been gone ages.'

Justin snapped his gaze away from Alicia to look up at her. 'Yes,' he said, quickly. 'Sorry, Pumpkin. There was a patient I needed to check on. I should have rung. I'm okay, honestly.'

Wiping a hand quickly across her cheek, looking small and vulnerable, and about as convinced as Alicia felt, Sophie looked him anxiously over, and then padded quickly down the stairs to throw herself into his arms.

Justin held her, hugging her back hard. 'We'll get through this, baby, I promise,' he said hoarsely, dropping a soft kiss to her hair and then looking back to Alicia.

Alicia saw a question in his eyes. Fear, too. The same fear that was eating away at her. *Will we get through this?* Alicia had no way to answer.

Justin turned his attention back to Sophie. 'Have you eaten?' he asked her, easing back to scan her face.

Looking pale and drawn, Sophie hesitated. She hadn't, but clearly she didn't want to tell Justin that. She wouldn't lie to him either, so she simply shrugged instead.

'How about some soup?' Justin suggested, talking to her encouragingly, as he might have done when she was a small girl tucked up in bed with some childhood illness.

Sophie nodded then. 'I'll have some if you will,' she said, turning to the kitchen.

'Deal,' Justin said. 'Alicia?'

Alicia felt all her emotions bubbling to the surface as he looked at her, with such uncertainty in his eyes, it tore another piece from her heart. She should eat. She should at least try – for his sake, for

Sophie's – but what she really wanted to do was curl up under her duvet until the unbearable tightness in her chest went away. The duvet on the bed where she slept with the man she'd loved with her very soul since she'd first met him. The bed in which they'd talked, about important and inconsequential things, laughed and made sweet love, he sensitive to her every need, touching her to her very core, creating the child God had called back to heaven too soon. Alicia held on to that thought: that that's where Lucas was, safe with her mum – his great-nanna – who would be making endless cure-all cups of tea. It was what sustained her when she woke in the darkest hours, feeling so lonely and empty, desperate to turn to the man she knew would offer the comfort she so badly needed. Yet, how could she? She *had* to tell him. Everything. What alternative was there?

'Soup?' he asked her.

Alicia swallowed. 'I'll join you in a minute.' She smiled, though her voice caught painfully in her throat. 'I'm just going to grab the blouse Sophie needs ironed for tomorrow.'

Halfway up the stairs, Alicia saw him glance down, massaging his temples hard. Staying where she was, she watched as he turned his gaze upwards, as if contemplating… How would he ever survive the day he buried his six-month-old son?

CHAPTER TEN

ALICIA

Alicia didn't have to shout upstairs to hurry Sophie on the next morning. Joining Justin in the hall, she looked towards her daughter as she descended the stairs. Her face was pale, her eyes awash with unshed tears. She looked frightened, lost and so very lonely.

Wanting to cry for her, wishing she could take her pain away, Alicia moved towards her as she reached the hall. Offering her a small smile, she held her gaze for a moment, trying to reassure her. She shouldn't have to go through this. No one should. It was too cruel. Crueller still for a fifteen-year-old girl who was struggling to be an adult because she felt her parents needed her to be.

Sophie was going to do the eulogy. It would be one of the most heartbreaking things she would ever do in her life, but Alicia hadn't tried to dissuade her. Justin had agreed it was something she needed to do, for her baby brother. He'd said he would step in if she couldn't get through it. Alicia wondered, though, how *he* would get through it.

He looked dreadful, more exhausted than she'd ever seen him. Even at his lowest ebb, she'd never seen him look so utterly bereft. Dark shadows under his eyes – in his eyes – he looked like a man who might never sleep again.

She didn't ask him if he was all right, reaching for his hand to squeeze it reassuringly instead. Justin squeezed hers back, briefly, and then pulled in a long breath and went to the front door to check whether the cars had arrived. Alicia didn't want them to arrive. Didn't want the moment to come when she would have to say a final goodbye to her child.

Gulping hard, she glanced down and then looked back to Sophie, whose eyes were now full of trepidation. Alicia reached for her hand. 'Okay?' she asked her, brushing a stray curl from her face. Cascading over her shoulders, Sophie's long, sable hair was darker than Justin's. Her eyes were a deep, rich chestnut brown, where Justin's were blue. Yet, in so many other ways, she was so like him. Her mannerisms, her deeply caring nature – these were the things they shared. Justin adored his feisty, funny daughter. He would kill to protect her, Alicia knew that to be true. She hoped Sophie knew that she would, too. That she knew in her heart that her mother loved her with all of herself, no matter what else happened.

Sophie nodded, and gave her a small, tremulous smile.

'You're a beautiful, special person and I love you very much. Never forget that, Sophie,' Alicia whispered, squeezing her into a firm hug.

Sophie hugged her hard back, and Alicia felt her heart hitch in her chest. It was enough, that hug, to sustain her. She would get through this. Somehow, her legs would carry her. She would keep standing. Sophie would need her to. And Justin, her husband, a good, honest man, who would never knowingly hurt anyone… Whatever the future held, he needed her now, and she would be there.

'Ready?' he said softly, behind her.

Bracing herself to face the worst day of her life, alongside the two people who mattered most in the world, Alicia nodded and turned to him, her gaze dropping from the immeasurable heartbreak in his eyes down to his tie. It was slightly askew, she noticed. She imagined his hands shaking as he'd tied it. Instinctively, Alicia reached to straighten it, another intimate gesture between them that sent an unbearable wave of sadness right through her. He used to smile when she fixed his tie – that languid, slow smile that would make her fingers all thumbs – and then invariably steal a kiss. He'd tugged it loose once, a glint in his eyes that told Alicia they were both going to be late for work.

Alicia dropped her gaze. She couldn't bear it, the hurt she could now see there.

Justin surprised her, reaching to gently lift her chin, so that she had no option but to look directly at him. 'We'll find a way through this, Ali,' he said, his voice hoarse. 'We have to.'

Pressing his forehead to hers, he tugged in a ragged breath.

Feeling his hand softly tracing the length of her back, Alicia moved towards him, threaded her arms around him and held him tight. He needed her to. And she needed it too.

They stayed like that for one long, precious moment, before someone tapped on the front door. She felt Justin stiffen, pulling himself upright as he eased away from her, turning to face the insufferable heartache to come.

CHAPTER ELEVEN

ALICIA

Alicia watched Justin carry Lucas in his arms, his gaze focussed on the catafalque. She wanted to scream at the injustice of it – right here, right now, in front of all the people gathered to mark the passage of their son's short life in respectful silence. She wanted to drop to her knees and sob. Or run as far away as she could from the nightmare that was never going to end.

But she couldn't.

She had to be there.

Her family needed her.

Her throat closing, her heart beyond breaking, she watched as Justin lowered the casket. 'Bye, little man.' She read the words on his lips as he placed a hand briefly upon it, wiped his eyes with his other hand and turned away. He didn't look at anyone as he took his seat. Alicia guessed why: he couldn't bear to see the sympathy in their eyes. He simply wouldn't be able to cope with it.

She reached for his hand, gripping it hard. She heard nothing of what the minister was saying beyond 'God has walked with Luke since before he was born.' Sophie took hold of her other hand and Alicia held on tight to her daughter.

It took a second to realise Sophie was easing away. Alicia couldn't breathe past the pain in her chest, couldn't focus through her tears, as her beautiful, brave daughter took her place at the pulpit.

She felt Justin's hand on her back, his arm sliding around her as she bowed her head, gulping hard against the sobs she couldn't seem to stop.

Haltingly, Sophie began. '"Do not stand at my grave and weep; I am not there, I do not sleep. I am a thousand winds that blow, I am the diamond glints on snow…"'

Alicia looked up, her heart breaking for her, as her baby paused, trying to compose herself.

'Luke did sleep.' Sophie glanced upwards, wiped a tear from her cheek and went on, as Justin got half to his feet. 'He slept a lot.' She laughed tremulously. 'I wondered what the point of him was at first. And then I realised. Seeing the pure innocence in his eyes, the little hand he trustingly offered me, his smile' – again, she stopped, her voice quavering – 'simply because he was delighted to see me. Luke taught me how to love, unconditionally and with all of me. He's nestled safe in an angel's wings now, but he will never leave me. He's here.' She pressed a hand to her heart. 'He will always be.'

Easing her daughter to her when she made her way back, Alicia kissed her temple, and then turned to Justin. His gaze was fixed downwards. She saw the tears spill onto the order of service resting on his knees, his other hand going to his forehead as he drew in a deep breath, trying to contain his emotion.

Outside, she would tell him how much she loved him. Would always love him. She had no idea what tomorrow would bring, but today, she was Justin's wife. He was her husband. His heart was tearing inside him, and he needed her to be there for him.

CHAPTER TWELVE

JUSTIN

Once outside the church, Justin's strength almost failed him. People were spilling out, glancing over to him, talking in hushed whispers about the beautiful service, the flowers, debating whose cars to follow to the reception. Alicia's sister had stopped her on the way out. Watching her sobbing now in Jessica's arms, Justin thought his presence might be an intrusion. Deciding to give them a minute, he waited, shaking hands and thanking people for coming.

Seeing someone approach her, seemingly without hesitation, Justin felt his already fractured heart splinter. It wasn't jealousy that consumed him as he watched Paul Radley, the man from Alicia's past, place a hand on her arm and lean intimately towards her. It was desolation. Standing there, amongst people he knew, people who cared deeply, Justin suddenly felt more alone than he ever had in his life. He had no idea what to do. How to be. He wasn't sure he even knew who he was any more, what his role was. He felt utterly and hopelessly lost.

Kneading his temples, desperately trying to hold back his tears, he turned away. He couldn't do this, stand here, feeling as if he was on the outside. The man had worked with Alicia aeons ago, for what, six months? A year? It had been a small financial services company. She hadn't really liked her job, she'd said, and had eventually left to retrain as a social worker. As far as he knew, she hadn't seen this man since. So what the hell was he doing *here*?

Realising his anger was way too close to the surface, Justin started walking. Whether he was getting things out of proportion or not, he couldn't handle this. Not now.

'Dad?' Sophie said behind him, as he reached the path heading towards the exit.

Justin turned back. The guy was still there, his hand still on Alicia's arm, his face close to hers. Too close. Justin looked away. He couldn't breathe.

'Justin?' He heard Jessica hurrying towards him. 'Justin, are you all right?'

Ineffectually attempting to compose himself, Justin nodded shortly.

Jessica stopped in front of him, placing a hand on his arm, as he glanced again towards Alicia. 'He's just an old acquaintance,' she said, looking kindly into his eyes.

Was he? Justin's gaze flicked again to Alicia and back. He was beginning to very much doubt that that's all he was, not least because her sister had just felt the need to convince him of it.

'I need to go,' he said, restraining himself from going over there and establishing the facts for himself. 'I have to… walk. Clear my head.'

Jessica looked surprised, and then nodded sympathetically. 'You need some alone time. I can't say I blame you. Go on, take all the time you need. I'll let Alicia know. I'm not sure she'll understand entirely' – she glanced anxiously back over her shoulder – 'but I'll make sure she knows you're okay.'

Justin laughed drily at that. Deep in conversation with her 'old acquaintance', he wasn't sure Alicia would even notice he'd gone. 'Will you take care of Sophie for me?' he asked Jessica.

'Of course I will,' Jessica assured him. 'Do you want me to tell Alicia you'll see her at the reception?'

Justin hesitated. He would be there: Radley, being way too intimate with *his* wife. And he was supposed to do what? Stand by and watch? 'Just tell her I'll see her later.'

'At home?' Jessica asked worriedly.

Justin nodded, and turned to Sophie, who was looking at him in bewilderment. 'Stay with your mum, Sophie, will you?' he asked her throatily. 'Please. Can you do that for me?'

Her expression now a kaleidoscope of confused emotions, Sophie nodded uncertainly, as Justin turned around again and walked away.

CHAPTER THIRTEEN

JESSICA

Jessica glanced after Justin and then back to Alicia, who was still talking to Paul Radley. Seeing him there was clearly more than a little disconcerting for Justin, given the attention Paul had paid Alicia at her party. She really couldn't blame Justin for leaving, after seeing the man attempt to monopolise her again, here of all places.

She should intervene, she supposed. Clearly, Alicia needed rescuing. Her daughter needed her right now. Jessica doubted she would do in lieu of her mother.

Seeing Sophie was extremely upset, Jessica placed an arm around her niece's shoulders and eased her towards her.

'Why is he going? Without Mum?' Sophie asked, tears cascading down her face. 'I don't get it?'

Jessica hugged her closer. 'I think he just needs some space, sweetheart,' she said. 'Don't worry, he'll probably be at home when you get there.'

'They're not coping.' Sophie cried harder. 'They're avoiding talking about him, about anything meaningful. I don't know what to do.'

'They're hurting, lovely,' Jessica said soothingly. 'Probably both feeling guilty and not sure how to reach out to each other. I know you want to help, but there's nothing you can do in reality.

Just give them some time, and remember they love you however preoccupied they might seem.'

Sophie nodded. 'I don't want to go to the reception either,' she sniffled. 'Not without Dad. People I've never even met will be trying to talk to me about Luke, and I know they'll mean well, but they didn't know him, did they? It's just…'

'Too much?' Jessica suggested.

Sophie's nod this time was one of relief.

'I tell you what, why don't you come and stay with me for a few days? We could have a good natter, try to put the world to rights, watch romantic films when that fails, and then have a good cry together.'

Sophie didn't look sure.

'It would be good therapy,' Jessica said. 'We could even go out for the odd pizza, or whatever you fancy. What do you say? I could use the company. I'm a bit fed up of knocking around my empty house on my own, to be honest, and it might give your mum and dad a bit of space.'

'I don't know,' Sophie said hesitantly. 'Do you think Mum would mind?'

Jessica glanced towards where Alicia was still talking to Paul Radley. 'I shouldn't think so. She'll understand you need some space, too. She's going to be tied up at the reception anyway from the looks.'

Sophie followed her gaze. 'Who's he?' she asked, perturbed.

'Just a friend,' Jessica supplied. 'An old work colleague. He's been working in Dubai for a few years. They've obviously got things to catch up on. Look, if you really can't face the reception, we'll have a word with your mum and slip off now. We could go and grab your stuff on the way. Your dad's probably headed off home, so you might be able to have a word with him before you leave. Sound like a plan?'

'But how will mum get to the reception?' Sophie asked, clearly concerned about her mum, which was commendable. Sophie was turning out to be a very caring young woman. Jessica would be proud to have a daughter like her. She couldn't help but feel a pang of jealousy as she recalled her own lost babies. The man who'd been in her life back then had seemed to think she shouldn't even grieve over them, since she'd never managed to get past the crucial three-month stage of her pregnancies.

She had grieved for them, silently. She'd even grieved for their indifferent father, pathetically, since a man who'd walked out on her while she'd been losing their child hadn't been worth wasting a single tear on.

Shaking off her sadness, because here wasn't the place if she wasn't to end up sobbing like a child herself, Jessica turned her attention back to Sophie, Alicia really should be paying her a bit more attention. She was bound to be emotional after standing up there and giving the eulogy so beautifully. But then, Alicia wouldn't know whether she was on her head or her heels right now. And Paul Radley reappearing certainly wouldn't be helping her emotional state.

'She'll travel in the funeral car,' she said, smiling reassuringly. 'And if she doesn't want to do that, I'm sure one of the guests won't mind taking her.'

Paul Radley, for one. Jessica debated the wisdom of allowing Alicia to be alone in his company for too long. But she clearly did need to talk to him. As Alicia had said, when he'd turned up at her party uninvited, she needed to establish why he'd reappeared after so long. She could hardly bury her head in the sand and ignore the fact that he was here.

She actually might be doing Alicia a favour, taking Sophie off her hands for a while. And with a bit of luck, they would catch Justin at home. Plainly, he'd been upset and angry, seeing Paul Radley here. Jessica really couldn't blame him. The least she could do was offer him a shoulder and try to reassure him.

CHAPTER FOURTEEN

ALICIA

'I really am so sorry, Alicia,' Paul said, his face earnest.

Alicia didn't answer. She was too stunned.

'I'm taking up far too much of your time. I know you don't want to hear about my reasons for not being able to get back to the UK until now, but if there's anything I can do.' He smiled kindly. 'Anything at all…'

Yes, there is, Alicia thought. *Please, please leave me alone.* 'No, there isn't,' she said quickly, her stomach tight with nerves as she looked past him again in search of Justin, who would be as confounded as she as to why Paul was here.

'I couldn't believe it when David told me your news.' Paul shook his head in commiseration.

David? Alicia tried to think past the chaos of jumbled thoughts in her head. One of Jessica's old flames. She recalled what Jessica had told her at the party, insisting that, though she'd been quite close to Paul Radley when they'd all worked together, socialising with him along with this David, she hadn't invited him to the party. He'd apparently arrived with David, who also worked in financial services. Presumably, they were friends. It made sense. But it didn't make her feel any better about him turning up out of the blue – again.

'I wanted to call by and pay my respects,' Paul went on, apparently oblivious to her growing desperation to end the conversation and get back to her family.

His respects? Alicia was doubly stunned at that. He didn't know the meaning of the word. If he had any respect at all, for anyone, he would *not*... Her thoughts ground to a halt as her gaze fell on Sophie, who was walking away from the church with Jessica. She couldn't see Justin. Panic clutched at her stomach. Where on earth was he?

'Paul, I have to go. My family needs me,' she repeated firmly, moving past him, now frantically scanning the immediate vicinity of the churchyard, the groups of people heading towards parked cars, preparing to go on to the reception. Where *was* he? She'd lost sight of him when Jessica had stopped her as they'd filed out of the church.

Hurrying towards Sophie and Jessica, she caught up with them. 'Sophie, sweetheart...' Her heart plummeted as Sophie turned towards her, tears now flowing unchecked down her face. 'It's all right, baby,' she said, her voice catching as she pulled her towards her. 'It's all right.'

'It's not though, Mum, is it? How *can* it be?' Sophie mumbled into her shoulder.

'She doesn't want to go to the reception.' Stroking Sophie's hair, Jessica filled Alicia in. 'I said she didn't have to, I hope that's okay? Justin's already left, by the way.'

Left? Oh God, no. Because of Paul Radley? 'When?' Alicia asked, panic tightening her chest.

'A few minutes ago. I think he needed to be on his own.' Jessica met her eyes, an attempt at reassurance in her own, and then glanced past her to Paul Radley, who was walking towards them. 'I've told Sophie she can come and stay with me for a few days, if that's okay with you. I said I'd take her back to fetch her things.'

Alicia shook her head, bewildered. 'I should take her,' she said. 'I should be with her. With Justin. Is he all right? I mean, did he seem...' She trailed hopelessly off. Of course he wasn't all right. How could he be? She looked at her sister in desperation.

Jessica wrapped an arm around her. 'He's fine. Well, as fine as he can be. He just needed some time alone,' she assured her. 'He'll probably go on to the reception.'

Alicia searched her face, unconvinced.

'Why don't you go straight there,' Jessica suggested. 'People will expect to see you. It was Justin's colleagues who paid for the buffet, after all. At least you can be there in lieu of him until he turns up. I'm sure he will, Ali.'

Alicia hesitated. She should, if only for a short while. Searching Sophie's face worriedly, she debated her options.

'I'll be fine, Mum,' Sophie said, wiping a black track of mascara sideways across her face. 'I'd like to go to Jess's for a few days, to be honest. You know, away from… things at the house.'

Alicia felt her heart wrench inside her. Away from reminders of Luke, she meant, which were far, far too painful for her. 'As long as you're sure,' she said slowly. She couldn't bear the thought of Sophie being on her own and hurting. How could she let her daughter out of sight of her right now?

Nodding, Sophie smiled weakly.

My beautiful daughter. She had to keep her safe. Had to.

Squeezing her hard, Alicia reluctantly let her go. Reaching to brush her hair from her face, she cupped her cheek with her hand and gently kissed her forehead. *It will be all right, baby. It will be.* Even as she thought it, Alicia felt the thread snagging, as if her life was already unravelling. 'I'll ring you,' she promised.

'I've called a taxi. Why don't you get off before everyone starts leaving.' Jessica suggested.

'I can give you a lift, if you like?' Paul offered, standing suddenly by Alicia's side.

Taken by surprise, Alicia jumped, and then glanced warily at him.

'No,' she said quickly, preferring him to have as little contact with her family as possible. 'Take the funeral car, Jess. I'll take the taxi.'

'Are you sure?' Jessica eyes flicked between her and Paul.

Alicia nodded. 'I'd be happier knowing Sophie's left safely with you,' she assured her, hoping her sister would get the message.

'Okay,' Jess said, looking a little reluctant. 'Watch what you're doing, Ali.' Giving her a firm hug, she slid an arm around Sophie's waist and led her on towards the car.

Her heart going into freefall, Alicia blinked her own tears back, determined to hold herself together, to harness the strength to try to hold her family together. She *had* to.

'The offer still stands,' Paul said, as Jessica and Sophie headed off. 'My car's just over there.' He nodded towards it. It will save you waiting around for a taxi.'

Hesitant to go anywhere with him, Alicia tried to read his expression. His dark eyes were intent, determined. His smile, though, was sympathetic – no innuendo, she noted, somewhat calmed.

Guardedly, she nodded. It would be a chance to talk to him alone, perhaps her only chance, and she needed to. She had no choice but to. She had to find out what he wanted and then get him out of her life, out of Justin's and Sophie's lives, whatever it took.

'Good,' he said, leading the way. 'It's the least I can do, after all.'

Alicia followed him, bemused by the fact that he didn't seem to realise the least he could do was to stay away from her, from her family.

'Do you want to give me the address?' he said, once they'd climbed into his car.

Alicia gave him the details, and then waited while he fiddled with the satnav.

'Bear with me.' He smiled in frustration. 'It's a rental car. I'm not quite sure where everything is yet.'

The address finally entered, Alicia looked out of the window as they drove slowly out of the cemetery. She wouldn't talk to him here, where she'd just laid her beautiful, innocent baby to rest. It would be a desecration of his memory to even begin to discuss something that would hurt his father so badly.

Bye, little Lucas. Mummy will be back soon, sweetheart. Alicia closed her eyes as they passed through the gates, feeling afresh the wound in her chest where a piece of her heart had gone with him.

Ten minutes. She swallowed, calculating the time she must spend with Paul Radley until they reached the hotel, then steeled herself and turned towards him. 'Why are you here, Paul?' she asked him. Though calm on the outside, her emotions were in turmoil.

Paul glanced at her and then back to the road. 'On holiday,' he said, repeating what he'd told her at the party. 'Looks like it's going to be a bit of an extended stay now though.'

Alicia's heart sank. 'Oh, how so?' she asked, bracing herself for what he might say.

'I've been offered a contract to stay and head up some investment seminars by Graham & Young Investments.' Paul turned again to look at her, his gaze lingering this time. 'Obviously, they value my expertise. Just a short-term contract,' he went on, smiling inscrutably and looking back to the road. 'I should be on my way back to Dubai fairly shortly.

'Okay?' he asked her kindly, a second later, as Alicia wiped away another tear, this time one of relief.

CHAPTER FIFTEEN

JUSTIN

Counting steadily, his gaze fixed downwards, Justin kept walking. He didn't much care where. He just needed space to think. He *had* to be getting this out of proportion. There was no way Alicia could have had an affair! He would have known. He *would* have known!

Had he read all the signs but refused to acknowledge it? He'd certainly wondered about her staying over at a girlfriend's more than once. The evasive eye contact when he'd asked her which friend. He'd dismissed it. Told himself he was being paranoid. His biggest fear, when he'd woken up to the fact that he'd been so wrapped up in his grief over his family that he'd barely paid her any attention, had been that he would lose her. So, what if she had? Justin felt his heart drift free from its moorings. What then? He had absolutely no idea what he would do. None.

Reaching his road, he was surprised to see Jessica's car parked outside the house. They must have left the funeral soon after he had. Probably *because* he had. He shouldn't have, but how could he have stayed? How could he have made polite conversation when he felt as if he were dying inside?

Groping for some sort of composure, Justin let himself through the front door, where he found Jessica and Sophie in the hall.

'Dad!' Relief flooding her face, Sophie flung herself towards him. 'Are you all right?'

Wrapping an arm around her, Justin squeezed her shoulders. 'I'm okay, Pumpkin,' he assured her, his throat tight. Glancing past her, he looked along the hall, and then, seeing no evidence of Alicia, looked questioningly back to Jessica.

'I think Alicia's gone to the reception to thank people,' Jessica supplied. 'Sophie was upset, so I offered to drive back with her.'

He shouldn't have left his daughter. Justin glanced down at her, his gut wrenching as he noted her swollen eyes and smudged make-up. He hadn't been thinking straight. Then again, maybe he had. Maybe he was now acknowledging something he'd refused to see before.

'Why don't you go and grab your stuff, Sophie?' Jessica smiled encouragingly in Sophie's direction. 'I'll have a quick word with your dad.'

Sophie looked uncertainly between them, and then nodded. She was halfway up the stairs when there was a knock at the front door.

Justin opened it to find Sophie's friend Chloe standing there. 'I just wondered if Sophie was okay,' she said, glancing towards the stairs. 'I can come back if you're busy.'

'It's okay, Chloe,' Sophie called, coming back down. 'Ten minutes,' she said to Jessica.

Justin smiled, feeling relieved, as she headed past him to go outside, probably wanting to talk in private. He was glad she had a friend who obviously cared. She would need one – perhaps more than she knew.

Jessica waited until the front door had closed. 'She's coming to stay with me for a while, if that's okay?' she said, smiling sympathetically at Justin. 'She was actually very upset after you'd gone. And Alicia was… Well, you know, busy talking to people. I thought it might be a good idea to get Sophie away from the house for a few days.'

'Right.' Justin nodded tightly, guessing Jessica had diplomatically stopped short of stating the obvious: that Alicia had been too busy talking to her 'old acquaintance' to notice how upset her daughter was. 'And is Sophie okay with that?' he asked, concerned that she might feel pushed out in some way.

'I think she could use some breathing space, to be honest,' Jess said, obviously well aware of the emotional toll all of this would have had on her. 'I thought we'd watch some girly films together, go out for a meal maybe. You know, do normal stuff. It might do her good.'

Justin guessed it probably would. Things had been far from normal here. Judging by their conversation the other night, pushed out was exactly how Sophie did feel.

'She needs you, Justin,' Jess reminded him – as if she needed to. 'Alicia's bound to be a bit preoccupied now, but Sophie's going to need someone to talk to.'

Preoccupied with what, exactly? 'So it would seem,' Justin said, heading past her to the lounge. He didn't want to have this conversation in the hall.

'I can't even begin to imagine what you must be going through,' Jess said, following him. 'I mean, I know Luke's death has devastated you both, but it must be so much harder on a man, when you're supposed to be the strong one, holding everybody else up. I could see how upset you were today. I just wanted you to know you have a shoulder, if you need one.'

'Thanks, Jess,' Justin said distractedly, and then, running a hand wearily over his neck, he headed for the drinks table.

Pouring a large whisky, which he felt badly in need of after the day's events, his gaze fell on one of their old Adele CDs that Sophie had left on the table. Would she get through this? Would he ever hear her sing again? They'd never derided her ambition to be a pop artist. She emulated Adele so beautifully; if Justin closed his eyes, he really believed it was her. She was good, though she probably needed to hone her individuality. He'd been partway through converting the basement into a studio – that was going to be his present to her for her sixteenth birthday. Now, he had no idea what the future would hold.

Taking a long drink of the whisky, which burned the back of his throat but did nothing to warm him, he placed the glass back on the table, stared at it for a second and then braced himself. 'Can I ask you something, Jess?' he said, looking cautiously towards her.

'Anything,' Jess assured him.

Justin doubted she'd be so ready to answer when she heard the question. 'Sophie…' He paused, not sure he actually wanted to hear the answer. 'Is she mine?'

'What?' Jessica paled.

'You're closest to Alicia, Jess,' Justin went on quietly. 'I have to know. Am I Sophie's father?'

Hearing himself speak the words, Justin felt like a complete bastard. How was he supposed *not* to ask though? He'd gone over and over it. Radley had worked with Alicia sixteen years ago, when she'd been with the financial services company. Justin remembered it well, the details brought sharply back into focus by the man's reappearance. It had been then that he'd lost his family. Then that, spiralling into a depression he couldn't seem to climb out of, he'd pushed Alicia away, rather than reach out to her. He'd finally woken up to the fact that he'd been so immersed in his grief he was paying no attention to her needs when she'd started staying out: spending nights with a girlfriend, she'd said. He'd hated himself for it, but he had wondered whether that was the truth. She'd had every reason to give up on him. With his emotions all over the place, he'd been impossible to live with. He'd tried to convince himself he was being paranoid, his suspicions based on nothing but the fear of losing her, too. They'd got through that rocky period. They'd been a strong family unit ever since. He'd thought they had. It had taken him a while, though, to stop looking for the signs.

Something else had also occurred to him as he'd walked, something which had turned his gut inside out. Justin had noticed it when Radley had been watching him, a challenge in his eyes, at that fateful party: the man's eyes were brown. Striking brown. Sophie's eyes were a rich chestnut brown, where his and Alicia's were blue. Genetically speaking, it was rare, though it was possible. He'd tried to rationalise it, but now… Was he being paranoid all over again? The fact that Radley seemed to pop up wherever Alicia was, was he imagining that? Imagining the fact that the man was all over her? Justin thought not. He hoped to God he was wrong.

His heart constricting painfully, he waited for Jessica to answer.

Jessica, though, didn't seem to want to answer, looking away instead, looking anywhere but at him. Looking guilty. 'You need to talk to Alicia,' she said, eventually.

And Justin knew. Without a doubt, he now knew what he so desperately *didn't* want to. Already bursting with grief and guilt, his heart damn near exploded.

CHAPTER SIXTEEN

SOPHIE

Sophie stopped in the hall, hardly able to breathe as she tried to digest what she'd just heard. Shaking her head in bewilderment, she swallowed hard and stepped closer to the partially open lounge door.

'Why the *hell* didn't she tell me?' she heard Justin say angrily from inside.

'I don't know,' Jess answered, sounding frantic. 'I don't know if there's anything *to* tell. I know she was unhappy at one point, but she never talked to—'

'Bullshit!' Justin cut furiously across her. 'What am I supposed to do with this, Jess, hey? I mean, *what*? Carry on as if it's an inconsequential little detail she forgot to mention? Be there for her and pretend it's not killing me that I've lost my son *and* my daughter? Jesus Christ. *How?* Does she even want to be with me?'

'Justin, *please*… You need to ask Alicia. Now's not the time to go into any of this.'

Justin laughed cynically at that. 'No, you're right,' he said bitterly. 'There never was a right time, I suppose. Not when she was carrying the child she forgot to mention wasn't mine. Not when she gave birth to her. Not when I held her for the first time, swore to devote my life to protecting her. How about before I walk her down the aisle? How about then, Jess? Will she tell me, do you think, as the bastard who had his eyes and hands all over her steps in to take my place?'

'Justin, what am I supposed to say?' Jessica beseeched him. 'She's my sister. I can't betray her trust.'

'How long did it go on?' Justin demanded, and then laughed again bitterly. 'Christ, I must be fucking blind. It's still going on, isn't it?'

Sophie stopped listening. Clamping her hands hard to her ears, tears streaming unchecked down her face, she whirled around to fly upstairs to her bedroom.

He wasn't her father. She felt as if her world had just been ripped from underneath her. Gulping back a sob, she clutched her tummy tight. She felt so nauseous she was sure she was going to throw up. How long had he suspected? How long had he been reluctant to talk to her, to look at her properly? And he had. She'd sensed it. When she'd needed him most, when she'd had nothing but ghosts for company, Luke haunting her dreams, he'd been distant. Not just distracted, but different.

And *she*... her so-called *mother*... Sophie had been so worried for her, hurt so much for her, but *she* obviously didn't care about anyone! *Liar!* Lies. All of it.

Who, then, was her father? Who had her mother had some furtive, dirty affair with, while married to the man she'd passed off as her dad? Was it someone Sophie knew? The milkman? The postman? The fucking odd-job man?

It was sick! Sick and disgusting and sad. Why would he put up with that? *Why?* Stuffing things randomly in her overnight bag, Sophie snatched it up, swiped a hand across her cheeks and headed for the door. She couldn't talk to him. She just couldn't. She couldn't bloody well breathe. Stopping halfway across the room, she paused and scrutinised herself in the mirror. She didn't even look like him.

She had no idea who she was.

Choking back another sob, she wondered at the cruelty of this happening on the same day they'd buried her baby brother. Half-brother. That realisation hitting her like a blow to the chest, Sophie determined she would never trust either of them again. *Ever.*

She had to get out. Going with Jessica was her best hope of avoiding him, her father who wasn't her father and was clearly furious at being deceived into thinking he was. He was probably planning how fast *he* could get away.

Away from her.

She needed to speak to her mother. She wanted explanations, as if there could possibly be any. But not here. Not now. They'd probably be so busy arguing, or more likely not talking to each other, they wouldn't even notice her.

CHAPTER SEVENTEEN

JUSTIN

Justin wasn't happy Sophie had left before he'd had a chance to ask her how she was feeling now that the funeral was over. As if he needed to ask. Devastated – that was how she would be feeling.

Choking back an angry knot in his chest, he considered this new twist in their lives, and how it was going to affect Sophie. Because if not now, at some time it would have to. Had Alicia not considered how many times she might be asked for her parents' medical history throughout her life when she'd decided to keep this huge secret to herself? *Jesus Christ.* It had been so many years. Everything – their whole relationship, as well as his relationship with Sophie – was based on a lie. To her, plainly, this had been too trivial to mention. How many other things might she have lied about? How many other details might she have neglected to tell him? Like the fact that the long-lost lover hadn't just *happened* to turn up after the funeral, for instance? Or that *fucking* party? Wasn't it more likely that she'd had contact with him over the years?

Following Jess and Sophie to the front door, Justin dragged a hand furiously over his neck, attempting to curtail his building anger. They would have exchanged emails, no doubt. Text messages, phone calls – the added thrill obviously being that it was all going on behind his back. Had they met up when Radley had visited the UK, which surely he would have done? She'd been away a couple of times over the years. On residential training courses pertaining to her ongoing social work training, she'd said. More probably she'd been in that bastard's bed, the topic of post-coital conversation being their future plans.

Christ, he felt sick.

Breathing in hard, he forced a smile for Sophie's sake. 'Bye, Pumpkin,' he said, wishing she'd unplug her earphones so he could say goodbye properly before she left. Seeing that she was distracted, obviously into her music, which she probably found therapeutic, he settled for giving her shoulders a squeeze and kissing her cheek instead.

Sophie offered him the briefest of smiles and followed Jess out.

Justin watched as, head bowed, she walked to Jess's car and climbed inside the passenger side. He'd thought she might wave as they drove off, but…

Oh God, no. Justin's heart flipped over. He'd thought she'd been outside. He'd seen her and Chloe through the window, walking away from the house. Might she have come back earlier than he'd realised, heard him and Jess talking? *Dammit!* He'd needed to speak to Jess, desperately needed to speak to her, but why hadn't he thought before broaching the subject with Sophie around?

Cursing himself, Justin pulled out his mobile and selected her number, hoping she would pick up, relief surging through him when she did. 'Sophie, I just wanted to apologise,' he said quickly.

'For?' Sophie asked guardedly.

'Leaving you earlier. I'm sorry, Sophie. It was a selfish thing to do. I just—'

'It's fine,' Sophie said over him. 'You're dealing with shit. I get it.'

'We all are,' Justin reminded her gently.

'And some,' Sophie replied quietly, after a pause.

'Are you sure you're okay?' Justin asked, trying to read the inflection in her voice. He could feel her slipping away from him already. 'Staying with Jess for a while, I mean?'

'Yeah, it's fine. Me not being in the way will give you two some space, won't it?' She sounded so indifferent. 'Crap, battery's dying. I'd better go.'

'Okay, but ring me when you get there, will you?' Justin asked, feeling extremely concerned by her reluctance to be drawn into conversation. Was he reading too much into it? She'd seemed all right when he'd come home, or as right as she could be under the circumstances. When she'd left, though…

'Sophie?' Realising she'd gone, Justin tossed his mobile onto the hall table and stared at it, uncertain what to do next.

He couldn't lose her. Above and beyond Alicia's deceit, which was crucifying him, his gut-wrenching fear was that he would lose Sophie. She would have to learn the truth eventually. Parental medical history was so important, for pregnancy as well as future health issues. He couldn't keep this information from her – as a doctor as much as anything else. Once she found out, he might become peripheral to her life. Imagining that *bastard* taking over his role, being there for her when she needed a father, was destroying him. He loved her, irrevocably. He'd loved her since he'd gone with Alicia to her first scan and glimpsed her tiny form on the monitor. She'd been his reason for focussing on the future, not dwelling on a past that was too painful to contemplate. Losing his family had almost destroyed him. He *couldn't* lose Sophie. Whatever her biology, she was *his* daughter.

He'd need to take a test. His heart wrenched again as that sickening thought occurred. Should he do that before confronting Alicia? He didn't understand. Why had she stayed with him if she was still involved with this… whoever the fuck he was? Why the *hell* hadn't she told him?

Kneading a temple, he reached for his phone, selected Alicia's number and then hesitated. She'd just buried her son. *He'd* just buried his son, he reminded himself, his grief almost choking him as he realised the death of the child he'd loved with every fibre of his being was in danger of becoming secondary to all of this. *Was* Lucas his child?

He stopped, feeling the foundations of his life crumbling beneath him as that thought occurred. He couldn't do this. He couldn't talk to her. Hear her voice. Feel another part of him die inside when she lied.

CHAPTER EIGHTEEN

JESSICA

'All right, lovely?' Warily, Jessica glanced sideways at Sophie. Jessica had heard her outside in the hall, and knew she'd overheard. She'd expected her to say something at the house. Or at least mention it when Justin had rung just now. Instead, she'd got off the phone fast and immediately texted someone. So much for her battery being dead.

God, she hoped Sophie would be all right. She'd have to try and talk to her. Jessica didn't agree with what Alicia had done, deceiving Justin all these years, to say little of putting her in an impossible situation. Obviously not as adept as her sister at subterfuge, she'd found herself completely unable to lie to Justin's face when he'd had asked her outright. She hadn't actually confirmed his suspicions – it wasn't quite as clear-cut as he'd imagined it was – but she was glad he knew now. Alicia loved him, Jessica was sure of that, but it wasn't fair to keep a man under false pretences. Frankly, she didn't think Alicia deserved him. It wasn't a little lie she'd told, after all. It was humungous. She should have told Justin the truth straight away, as Jessica had urged her to. Back then, after Paul Radley had disappeared off the scene, there had been no reason not to. Honesty was surely the best policy, given the risk that Justin would find out one day. If Alicia had just been honest, they might have been able to get past it. She would never, ever have wished Sophie to find out third-hand though.

'Sophie?' Jessica reached out, giving Sophie's arm a squeeze when she didn't answer.

Sophie tugged an earphone loose and looked at her questioningly.

'All right, sweetie?' Jessica asked.

Sophie shrugged. 'You know,' she said, and fixed her gaze on the side window. 'Can you do me a favour, Aunt Jess?' she said, after a second. 'If Mum rings, can you tell her I'm asleep or something?'

'Of course,' Jessica assured her, her heart skipping a beat. 'Are you okay?'

Another shrug from Sophie. 'I just don't want to talk to anyone. Not yet.'

Jessica felt a prickle of apprehension run through her. Sophie would definitely need some space now, and Justin would most definitely need a shoulder.

CHAPTER NINETEEN

JUSTIN

You need to come home. It's urgent.

Justin placed his phone precisely down, lining it up perfectly with the edge of the table, as if that could somehow put his world back in order. Then he paused. He was less puzzled by the tiny screw on top of the hall table than the fine dusting of plaster around it.

Instinctively, Justin glanced towards the alarm box to the side of him, and then reached to open it. It took a second to register what he was looking at; to realise, cold foreboding sweeping the length of his spine, that the two crucial wires were disconnected, meaning there'd been someone in the house. *Jesus.* Justin's mouth ran dry. When?

While they were at the funeral?

While they'd been here?

While Sophie had been upstairs…

'*Fuck!*' His gut clenching, his gaze automatically shooting to the far corners of the hall, Justin froze. Images of his sister, her blood bleeding into the hall carpet, his parents, walls and white sheets stained impossibly crimson, emblazoned themselves on his mind. He took a faltering step forwards.

And then, snatching his phone back up, he ran.

Propelling himself into action, he slammed into the front room. Scanning it as he jabbed 999 into his phone, he registered that nothing seemed to be missing, checked the other downstairs rooms and then raced to the back door.

Locked. He noted the key, hanging well out of sight on the hook in the utility.

No broken panes.

They'd come through the front door. Through the fucking *front door*!

His heart rate escalating, a pulse thrumming rapidly at the base of his neck, Justin grabbed hold of the banister and swung himself upstairs to push the nursery door open. Undisturbed. Everything as still as the grave.

Sophie's room? It was a mess: dresser drawers open, T-shirts spewing out like hungry tongues. More mess than usual? Taking in the clothes-strewn bed, Justin had no way of knowing.

Backing out, he headed for their own room. His pulse rate slowing, his adrenaline still pumping, he banged the door wide, stepped inside – and stopped dead.

His blood freezing in his veins, he stepped towards the dressing table and closed his eyes. When he opened them, it was still there, scrawled in red lipstick on the mirror, scorched indelibly on his brain.

SORRY FOR YOUR LOSS

Justin tried to breathe, but he couldn't pull air past the fury lodged like acid in his chest. 'Bastard,' he seethed, trying and failing to obliterate the image of the smashed mirror in the house of his parents from his mind. '*Bastard!*' Slamming his fist into the glass, ignoring the cut from the sharp shard that sliced through his flesh, he turned away, heading for the landing. His anger simmering steadily inside him, he went up to check the third floor.

Having scoured the whole house, including the bathrooms, and checked every window on the basis that the scum who'd broken

in might just get it into their fetid minds to come back, he went
back into Sophie's room and sank heavily onto the bed.

They'd refurbished this room together, he recalled obliquely, he
and Alicia. Sophie hadn't wanted prissy pink walls and florals, she'd
said. She'd wanted grungy, whatever that meant. Street art style, an
industrial theme, Alicia had knowledgeably informed him. He'd
come into his own on the DIY front, putting the metal bedframe
and wire storage lockers together. And then he'd put his foot in
the paint tray, which had had Alicia in hysterics, coaxing the scowl
from his face and making him laugh at his own ineptitude. She
had a knack for doing that. They'd fallen into bed exhausted that
night, taken time to make unhurried love together, despite their
exhaustion, falling asleep with bodies and limbs entwined. Had it
been less satisfying for her than for him? Had he been inadequate
in some way? Had he always been?

His mind went back sixteen years, to the day he'd asked her
about the girlfriend she'd supposedly been staying with. She'd
stayed three, maybe four times. She hadn't been well after the
first time she'd stayed over. A hangover, she'd said, and maybe
a bug of some sort. She'd also been subdued. He remembered
that well. That was when the doubts had first surfaced. She'd
originally said they were going out. Then she'd said they'd stayed
home, preferring girl-talk and a film. He'd asked her what
on earth they found to talk about. 'This and that,' she'd said
vaguely. He'd asked her what film they'd watched. She'd looked
panicked for a second, before she'd come up with a title. It was
a film he and she had already seen together. It was nothing,
he'd told himself. She'd clearly drunk enough to make her
recollection hazy. Yet, there was something: her body language
had been tense. He'd noticed the slight flush to her cheeks, as
she'd turned away from him. He'd found himself watching her
and, far from the evasive behaviour he'd expected, he'd found
her looking back at him, her eyes wide and uncertain, locked

right on his. He'd wondered whether it was because she was uncertain about him, his commitment to a marriage he'd been emotionally absent from.

He should have paid closer attention to his instincts. Maybe then, he wouldn't be sitting here now, watching his life fall apart. Everything, piece by piece, was disintegrating around him and he had no way to stop it. No one to turn to.

Staying where he was, trying to get a grip, he counted the words repeated on the graffiti-print wallpaper, starting with one strip, reading to the top, and then travelling down the next. His gaze snagged on a notebook lying on the floor, and Justin stopped counting and reached for it.

Idly, he flicked it open, his eyes immediately falling on a poem written in Sophie's neat handwriting, and his breath hitched painfully in his chest.

I say I'm fine, but I'm crying inside.
I daren't let you see, the tears that I hide.
I'm hurting.
It's like he didn't exist.
Why can't you talk about him?
Tell him how much he is missed.
They say time will heal pain.
But time can't bring you back again.
I'm hurting.
Truly, how I feel is heartbroken,
For your short life stolen.
The words left unspoken.
I miss you, Luke.
We all do.
Stay safe with the angels, sweetheart.
Until I find you.

Pressing a thumb and forefinger to his eyes, Justin gulped hard. She would be devastated by this. Already broken-hearted at the loss of her brother, Sophie would feel that everything that defined who she was, everything dear to her, had been stolen away from her. She might never recover emotionally. If she couldn't trust her own mother, her own father – if he wasn't honest with her, she might never trust anyone again. How would he tell her? How the *hell* was he going to talk to Alicia? What would he do if she said she was leaving? Would he beg her to stay?

No. Justin dragged an arm across his eyes and got to his feet. He wasn't going to do that. An affair he might have forgiven, given his own erratic behaviour. But the deceit, the lies she must have told since – he could never forgive that. How could he live with someone who couldn't possibly have loved him? Alongside the knowledge that Sophie might not be his daughter, that's what hurt most of all: realising that she probably never had.

Ignoring the rich droplets of blood on the carpet, which were his own, Justin made his way back to the hall. He was halfway down the stairs when he stopped, noting a darkly dressed figure approaching, visible through the opaque glass in the front door.

CHAPTER TWENTY

ALICIA

All sorts of scenarios having raced through Alicia's mind when she'd received Justin's text, her first terrifying thought that something might have happened to Sophie, she'd accepted Paul Radley's offer of a lift home. Once on the way, she'd debated the wisdom of arriving with him, but her first instinct had been to get here as soon as she could.

Arriving at the house, she fumbled her key into the lock and almost fell through the front door. Relief sweeping through her when she saw Justin standing on the stairs, she took a step towards him. 'Justin? What's—' *Oh God!* He'd been injured. Her heart lurching against her ribcage, Alicia flew towards him. And then she stopped uncertainly.

His face white, his expression inscrutable, Justin didn't move. He simply looked at her as if she were a stranger, and Alicia's heart, already heavy with guilt and unbearable sorrow, plummeted like a lead weight in her chest.

'Justin, you're hurt.' Her gaze dropped to the spatters of blood on his shirt, then back to his face.

'I'm fine.' Justin scanned her eyes, his own thunderously dark, and then looked past her, his expression hardening.

'Sorry,' Paul Radley said from behind Alicia. 'I wouldn't have come in, but I saw the door was open. You dropped your phone in the car, Alicia.'

Oh no. Alicia felt her stomach turn over. She'd asked him to let her out of the car away from the house. He must have known why she had. And now he was walking into the hall as bold as brass. Why would he *do* that?

'Paul gave me a lift to the reception.' She fumbled hopelessly for an explanation. 'He came to the funeral and when I got your—'

'Right. Well, now he's played the hero, *Paul* can just fuck off again, can't he?' Justin cut in angrily, his gaze fixed stonily on Paul's.

Cold fear pierced through Alicia like a knife. 'He offered me a lift, Justin,' she said, falteringly, willing God to strike her down dead if it saved her husband any more hurt. 'Jess brought Sophie back and I didn't have any transport, so—'

'Drives a taxi then, does he?' Justin interrupted bitterly.

'No, I…' Alicia shook her head, confused and, above all, frightened. He was *bleeding*. She needed to know why. She needed to know what had happened. 'Justin, *please*, the text. 'You said it was urgent. Please tell me what's happened. Where's Sophie?'

Justin's eyes flicked to hers. 'She's fine, I *think*,' he said, emphasis on the 'think'. 'She's with Jessica.'

Thank God. Alicia closed her eyes.

Looking between her and Paul, Justin finally came down the stairs. 'We've been broken into,' he said bluntly, causing Alicia's world to shift further off-kilter.

'Broken into?' She stared at him, shocked. 'But… how? *When?* Not last night. They would have noticed. As devastated as they had all been this morning, they would have noticed a break-in.

'Today,' Justin supplied, glancing away. 'The police are on their way.' He looked back to her. 'I suspect *Paul*, who has an uncanny knack for turning up uninvited, might be better off out of the way, if you don't mind my suggesting.'

His gaze travelled pointedly back to him.

Paul nodded understandingly. 'Of course. My timing couldn't have been worse, could it? This is unbelievable, when you already have so much to contend with. Please accept my sincere condolences. This must be a very difficult time for you both.'

'It is,' Justin assured him.

Someone had broken in while they were at the funeral? While they were burying their child! Alicia felt anger unfurl inside her. *The absolute bastards!* 'Have they touched anything?' she asked, her blood running cold as she imagined the things they might have touched, desecrated, stolen. Memories broken. Her children's things. Her baby's. Please… not her baby's. She swallowed back a jagged knot in her throat. 'Have they taken anything?'

His hostility seeming to wane, Justin turned his attention to her, focussing on her at last. 'I'm not sure. I've looked, but—'

'Have they been in the nursery?' Feeling sick now to her very soul, Alicia stepped shakily towards the stairs.

'Alicia, wait.' Catching her shoulders, Justin stopped her. 'You need to wait, Alicia. The police said not to go into any of the upstairs rooms. They said not to touch anything.'

Alicia wavered, every one of her emotions colliding. This was her punishment. She'd lost her dear precious child, but she would not let the lowlife who'd done this sully her baby's memories. She prayed his tiny space hadn't been invaded. It still smelled of him. Her baby!

Clamping a hand to her mouth, she pushed past him. She had to see. She had to know.

'Alicia!' Justin was right behind her as she stumbled up the stairs.

Finding the nursery untouched, Alicia gave way to the sobs climbing her throat, and thanked God for this one small mercy. Her next thought of her daughter, she squeezed past Justin to Sophie's room.

Seeing nothing obviously missing or touched, she allowed herself to breathe out, and turned to go to the main bedroom.

Close behind her, Justin caught her arm as she neared the door. 'You shouldn't go in there, Alicia,' he said quietly, his eyes now holding a warning.

There was something he didn't want her to see. Something he knew would upset her. She searched his face. There was no anger there now, just heartbreaking bewilderment and so much pain. Concern also, for her. Guilt consuming her, Alicia dropped her gaze. 'I need to, Justin,' she said. 'I have to know.'

Once inside the door, she stopped dead. Studying the mirror in disbelief, reading the cruel message left there, realising it was Justin's blood at the smashed centre of it, that her husband would be suffering because of it, because of her, Alicia felt her heart falter.

It wasn't whoever had broken into their house who'd sullied their memories.

It was her.

CHAPTER TWENTY-ONE

JUSTIN

It had taken every ounce of Justin's willpower to control himself when Alicia had come home with the man who might well be Sophie's father. Now he was restraining himself from asking her to stay, instead of going to her sister's and leaving things hanging between them. But then, knowing what he now did, Justin guessed it was him, rather than a houseful of tainted memories, she might prefer to be away from.

He supposed he should be grateful, given the lack of police resources, that the detective in charge of the hit-and-run case had turned up personally. They were giving the break-in some priority, but the scene of crime officers seemed to be taking their sweet time trying to establish whether they might have any forensic evidence to go on, meaning Alicia would most likely take up Radley's offer of a lift to her sister's. How ironic that when Justin had asked him to leave, wanting the bastard out of his house and away from his wife, the police had requested he wait around – to eliminate any fingerprints he might have left, they'd said.

He'd gleaned from Radley's expression that he'd been more than happy to oblige, eager to hang around Alicia. Was he getting some perverse kick out of it, humiliating the man whose wife he was having a seedy affair with? Justin glanced contemptuously to where he stood in the middle of *his* lounge, looking at him as if he were weighing him up. *Prat.* Justin sucked in a terse breath and turned his attention to Detective Inspector Taylor, willing him to hurry it up.

'What about the writing?' Alicia asked him, as DI Taylor scribbled in his notebook.

'We might have been able to get a handwriting analyst on it. Unfortunately, now the mirror's smashed and spattered with blood...' Shrugging hopelessly, Taylor looked regretfully towards Justin.

Justin glanced down. It had been a kneejerk reaction. Probably the only one who would understand why he'd reacted that way was Alicia, because she knew the circumstances under which he'd found his family.

'So, it's just the items you mentioned that you think are missing?' Taylor double-checked, referring to his notes. 'One half-carat diamond ring; one ladies' Radley watch; one ladies' nine-carat gold bar-and-chain bracelet; and one yellow gold locket, enhanced with a white gold floral motif?'

Alicia nodded. 'I'm not sure about Sophie's things. I'll have to speak to her,' she said, sounding and looking more exhausted than Justin had ever seen her. 'The locket,' she added, as Taylor closed his notebook, 'it has photographs of my children in it. The one of Lucas was the last one we'd taken of him.'

Hearing the heartbreak in her voice, watching the tears slide slowly down her cheeks, Justin choked back his own emotion. He had the photo of Luke on his phone, but it was the significance of it being stolen on the day of his funeral that was breaking her heart. He was halfway towards her when Mr Magnanimous himself beat him to it. 'I'll take you to Jessica's, when you're ready,' Radley said, smiling sympathetically.

Alicia looked up at him, and then got to her feet.

And Justin felt her slip away from him another inch.

'No,' she said, taking him by surprise. 'It's kind of you to offer, but I think I'd rather take a taxi.'

Radley also looked surprised, Justin noted, or possibly slightly irritated. 'Oh,' he said, his smile now on the tight side. 'Are you sure? It's no trouble.'

'Positive,' Alicia said, nodding adamantly. 'I have some things I need to do. You might as well get off.'

She wasn't looking at him, Justin noticed, but Radley was looking at her, definitely perturbed. The man was obviously a cocksure son of a bitch who wasn't used to being turned down.

'I'll show you out,' Justin said, pushing his hands in his pockets and nodding towards the front door. He would quite like to physically escort him out, but he guessed that wouldn't be a smart move with police in the house.

Closing the front door behind him, having declined to shake the hand the bastard had the gall to offer him, Justin took a second and then went back to the lounge.

Finishing her call, to a taxi company, it sounded like, Alicia wrapped her arms about herself in that way she'd adopted. She looked cold, haunted, alone with her grief.

She shouldn't be on her own, not now. He had to stay here until the forensics officers had finished their business, but… 'Why don't you call Jessica?' he suggested. 'She won't mind coming to fetch you.'

Alicia shook her head. 'I'd rather she didn't leave Sophie. And I don't want Sophie coming with her and seeing police here.'

Justin understood. Sophie would have to know, but they could break this news to her gently, he supposed. There would be no way to soften the blow regarding her parentage.

Swallowing back his anger, which would serve no purpose right now, he walked across to Alicia. Whatever was happening between them, she needed not to feel the kind of emptiness he knew she would be feeling. The kind of desolate loneliness that would drive her further into herself. He'd been there. He might not have surfaced, if not for her. If he wasn't misreading things here, which clearly spelled out that three was a crowd – and he didn't think he was – then maybe he should be the one to bow out.

Not gracefully though. He would fight for Sophie. Though he felt jaded to his very bones, he would never give up on his daughter. *Never.* As long as she needed him, he would be there. And if one day she didn't… Justin quashed a stab of anguish in his chest. He would cross that bridge when he got there.

Alicia didn't relax into him as he eased her into his arms. She didn't tense, though. Justin didn't read too much into that, but he was taken aback when she rested her head lightly on his shoulder, staying like that for a second, before looking up at him, her eyes awash with such raw emotion that it tore him apart. 'Will you ring me?' she asked him, her voice small and defeated. 'If you hear anything?'

Feeling a sharp lump slide down his throat, Justin nodded. 'I will, I promise,' he said hoarsely, and pressed his forehead lightly to hers.

CHAPTER TWENTY-TWO

SOPHIE

Sophie hesitated, her thumb hovering over her phone when she saw it was her dad calling. But she couldn't call him Dad any more, could she?

Was he ringing to break the news, say, *Hey, how're you doing? Oh, by the way, I'm not your father?* He could hardly just leave it, could he, now he'd finally found out something that was basically a life changer?

Her heart missed a beat at the thought that he would want to change his life – but he'd have to, wouldn't he? It's not like he'd want to stay with a woman who'd turned out to be a cheating, lying bitch.

She placed the phone on the bed and let it go to voicemail. Jessica's spare bed in her spare room, pretty and prissy and nothing like her own. Sophie missed it already. She missed him. Missed Luke so much it hurt. It felt like her intestines were all twisted up inside her. Turning away from the phone, she curled herself into a ball, clamping her hands to her tummy and wishing the cramps would go away, that everything would go away. Especially her mother. All of this was her fault. *All* of it.

Plucking at a loose edge of wallpaper, she ignored the phone when it rang again. He was a bit keen, wasn't he, to drop another bombshell in her life? She didn't have a life any more, though, did she? Not one worth living. Sophie's anger intensified, twisting itself into a tight knot, like a snake squirming around in her belly. She'd never hated her dad. She'd been pissed off with him sometimes, yes, but he'd never been a rubbish dad, distant like some of her friends' dads were, or overbearing: laying down the rules, expecting her to jump to his command. He'd always tried to talk to her, even when he completely didn't get it. He'd smiled when she'd needed him to, making her think that whatever trauma she was going through maybe wasn't such a big deal after all. She didn't hate him now, though she wanted to. She just wanted him to do what he'd always done – make things all right. He'd always looked out for her, taking the little dickhead who was bullying her at junior school aside and making him stop with no more than a succinct word. Wiping away her tears and bathing her knees when she grazed them, which she always seemed to be doing when she was small.

He'd taught her to ride her bike on her own in the hall, she recalled, rather than risk her skinning her knees again on the icy pavement outside. Sophie's mouth curved into a small smile as she remembered how he'd whooped like a big kid when she'd finally got the hang of it. His eyes had been so full of pride, she felt like she'd climbed a mountain. And then he'd gone slightly cross-eyed when one of the rugs that covered the flagstones had slipped from underneath him and he'd landed flat on his back.

She pictured herself dropping down to clamp her hand to his cheek. 'Are you hurt?' she'd whispered fearfully.

He'd lifted his head and given her a wink. 'Nothing damaged but my pride, Pumpkin,' he'd assured her. He had been hurt though. He'd dislocated his shoulder, they learned later, but hadn't said anything, in order to protect her impressionable five-year-old's feelings.

She wished she could be small again, his little girl, safe in the unshakeable belief that her dad would be there for her forever.

He'd never lied to her either. Was he going to now? Would he try to soften the blow with more lies, she wondered? Would he quietly distance himself from her, or just wash his hands of everything and walk away?

Unfurling herself as her phone rang for a third time, Sophie leaned her back against the wall, brought her knees up to her chest and reluctantly picked it up.

'Hi, Sophie, it's Dad,' Justin said when she answered, causing the icy dagger to inch further into her heart. 'Are you busy?'

'No. Just sleeping.' Sophie plucked nervously on her eyebrow stud. 'Sorry, I muted my phone.'

'Are you okay?' Justin asked, immediate concern in his voice.

'Yeah, just stomach cramps.' Sophie shrugged. 'You know.'

'Ask Jess for a hot water bottle,' Justin advised, sounding like he always did, as near normal as it was possible to be in the abnormal shit-fest their lives had become. 'Take a couple of paracetamol and curl up under the duvet for a while.'

'I will,' Sophie said, thinking that a truckload of paracetamol might be the only thing that would make this pain go away. 'So, why the call?' she asked him, bracing herself for bad news – which it would be, whatever he said. If he didn't tell her, he'd be lying, leaving her with the uncertainty of when the bomb would drop. And if he told her… Sophie tucked her knees closer to her chest. She didn't think she could bear it.

'I just wanted to let you know your mum's on her way over,' Justin said, causing her to immediately uncoil.

'Why?' she asked apprehensively. 'I mean, why's she coming here now? I've only just got here.'

Justin hesitated. 'There's been a problem… at home,' he said carefully.

Sophie almost laughed. That was one way of describing a total fucking catastrophe, she supposed. 'What kind of problem?' she asked warily, praying that if he couldn't tell her the whole truth, he wouldn't give her a load of bullshit. He'd be struggling with it as much as she was, after all. His pride would be badly bruised this time. His heart pulverised, all thanks the woman who had vowed to stay faithful to him. *Cow.*

'A break-in,' Justin supplied, after a pause. 'Nothing major taken,' he added quickly, obviously trying to reassure her. 'Some jewellery: your mum's gold locket, a few other things. No items of yours, as far as we can see. I think your mum will feel safer there with you and Jess though.'

'A break-in?' Sophie felt goosebumps prickle her skin. 'But… *when?*' she asked, disbelieving. How? How did this shit just keep happening?

'While we were out. At the funeral.'

It took a second for Sophie to digest. *While we were saying goodbye to Luke, someone had…* Tears springing to eyes, she glanced upwards.

'Okay, Pumpkin?' Justin asked softly, which only made it worse.

'Yes,' Sophie blurted quickly. She couldn't cry. All the hurt stuffed inside her would come tumbling out if she did. She couldn't talk to him either. How could she? From him, at least, she wanted honesty. She didn't want to be pacified. She wanted the *truth.* The unedited, ugly truth.

'You didn't notice anything missing or moved in your room, did you, Sophie?' Justin asked her.

Shaking her head, Sophie tried to focus. She hadn't. But then, she'd been in such a state of shock that she probably wouldn't have noticed if Santa Claus plus his reindeer had dropped down the chimney. 'No,' she said. 'What about you? Are you coming here too?' She hoped her broaching of the subject sounded innocuous.

'I, er…'

Sophie tried to suppress her growing sense of dread as Justin searched for an answer.

'No,' he said, eventually, over a long intake of breath. 'I'll, er, be staying in a hotel, just for a while. I… have a work trip, a conference,' he went on falteringly. Lying badly.

And Sophie's heart splintered. 'Right,' she choked, feeling the knot in her stomach tighten into a fist. 'I have to go. Dinner's ready. I'll see you… whenever.'

CHAPTER TWENTY-THREE

ALICIA

Alicia gazed out of the taxi window, seeing nothing of the normality going on around her, her mind instead full of disjointed snapshots of her life: Justin in the delivery room, nestling Sophie gently in his arms, swearing to his new baby girl that he would die to protect her.

His awe when he'd watched Sophie take her first steps. His fierce sense of pride as she'd accomplished each achievement in her life, big or small. The adoration that shone from his eyes whenever he quietly listened to her singing. The same adoration she'd seen in his eyes for Lucas, as he'd watched his baby boy grow.

The tortured, terrifying heartbreak when he'd realised he couldn't save him. Alicia would never forget that look in his eyes.

The thunderous look, bordering on hatred, she'd seen when Paul had followed her into the house. She would take that memory to her grave.

He knew – at least part of it. He would be beyond devastated, and she didn't dare hope he could ever forgive her, but if he ever found out about Sophie, the possibility she might not be his, it would kill him. At least Paul couldn't disclose that to him, though. He couldn't reveal what he didn't know. She'd never told him about her pregnancy. For Justin's sake, she'd sworn she never would.

Realising they'd arrived at Jessica's, Alicia paid the taxi off and climbed tiredly out. She needed to be with Sophie. To hold her close and never let her go. To try somehow to stop the hurt, the immeasurable pain her daughter would be going through. She had no idea how she could, apart from simply being there for her. She knew she hadn't been, through all of this. And now some heartless animal had invaded their home. Sophie would be terrified by that knowledge.

She'd barely taken a step when a car drew up as the taxi pulled off. *Paul Radley.* Alicia's blood turned to ice as she recognised his car. How in God's name did he know Jessica's address? Jessica had gone out with his friend for a while, not him.

'Alicia,' Paul called, winding his window down.

Alicia glanced towards the house, and then took a breath and walked towards him.

'I just wanted to check you were okay,' he said, smiling as she approached.

'So you followed me?' Alicia looked at him, astonished.

Paul furrowed his brow. 'Why would I do that? I know where your sister lives. I dropped David off here from the tennis club several times. I was just concerned, that's—'

'What do you want, Paul?' Alicia asked him tersely. Maybe he was genuinely worried – she'd always been rubbish at reading the signs where Paul Radley was concerned – but whatever his reasons were for hounding her, he must know that he was putting her marriage in jeopardy.

'Look, Alicia.' He sighed. 'I know I took off suddenly, and that you probably don't want to see me…'

Probably? Alicia laughed incredulously.

'Can we talk? Please?' he asked her. 'Five minutes. No more, I promise.'

Alicia glanced nervously back to the house. She didn't want him anywhere near her daughter.

'We can drive around, if you like? Or we can just sit in the car.'

Alicia hesitated, and then braced herself. 'Just five minutes. And we'll stay here,' she said, walking around to his passenger side. 'So?' she asked, climbing in.

Paul looked her thoughtfully over. 'I'm concerned, Ali, that's all,' he said kindly. 'I know asking you if you're all right is ludicrous. Clearly, you're not going to be, after all that's happened. I'd just like to help, if I can.'

Alicia glanced warily at him. Surely he must know that the only thing he could possibly do to help would be to leave her alone? 'There's nothing you can do, Paul, really,' she assured him. 'Thank you for the lift to the reception, and for bringing my phone back – it was kind of you – but I really think it's best if we don't have any further contact. I have my family to think of.'

Letting out another heavy sigh, Paul nodded. 'Your daughter,' he said.

'And Justin,' Alicia reminded him. 'Look, Paul, I really should go inside. I need to talk to Sophie.'

'Right,' Paul said, as she reached for her door. 'Give her my love.'

Her heart immediately skipping a beat, Alicia froze.

'Sophie,' Paul clarified, as she looked cautiously back at him. 'Give her my love, will you?'

'*What?*' Alicia stared hard at him.

Paul looked away, placing his hands on the steering wheel and fixing his gaze straight ahead. 'I've been wondering… about the timing of your pregnancy.' He paused pointedly. 'I talked to Jessica at her party. She mentioned she'd been thinking of having a joint party with Sophie for her upcoming sixteenth. Naturally, that gave me pause for thought.'

Alicia's heart stopped dead. *Jessica?* But, surely she would have realised she wouldn't want him to have her date of birth?

'Is she mine, Alicia?'

Alicia didn't answer. She wasn't capable of formulating an answer.

'I have a right to know, Alicia. If she is my daughter—'

He stopped, his grip on the steering wheel tightening. His eyes were dangerous, when they came back to hers. 'Well?' he demanded.

'I… I don't know,' Alicia stammered, completely destabilised. 'I…'

Paul sneered. 'I see. But you didn't think to mention the fact that you were pregnant?'

'No, I… You went away. I—'

'I rang you! I emailed you! You didn't return one of my calls. Not one! Why? I *loved* you. I couldn't stop thinking about you. *Why* didn't you—'

'*Loved?*' Alicia stared at him, stunned.

Paul tugged in a terse breath. 'I've missed her childhood, Alicia,' he growled, his jaw tightening. 'Those years of watching her grow up, they were mine.'

'That's rubbish!' Alicia countered, her anger unleashing. 'What happened between us was a mistake. It was wrong – you know it was. And what if I had told you? You left! Went off to your bright new career in Dubai. Why would I have imagined you would have been remotely interested in a child you might have fathered?'

'I didn't leave voluntarily,' Paul said, after a second. 'I had a spot of bother. With the Financial Conduct Authority.' He paused, embarrassed. 'An investment complaint. It was all cleared up eventually, but… The point is, I *was* interested. I asked you to join me. You didn't even bother to reply.'

'Join you?' Alicia studied him, now utterly bewildered. 'I was *married*. I loved my *husband*.'

'But you still came back. Made love with *me*,' Paul retorted. 'What we had was good, Alicia. Special. You can't deny that.'

Alicia laughed incredulously. To him, it had been. He'd kissed her tenderly before she'd left the hotel room that first time. He'd sent her flowers, she remembered, to the office. He really had thought it was special. A relationship. 'You're mad,' she said, and turned to shove her door open.

Paul idled for a second, after she climbed out. Alicia felt the hairs rise on her skin as she wondered whether he might try to follow her in. Then, at last, he eased away from the kerb.

'I'll be in touch,' he shouted through his window as he drove off, causing cold terror to rip through her.

Justin was going to find out, from *him*, and there was nothing she could do to stop it. She'd never said the actual words – told Justin that Sophie was his. Why would she? He'd trusted her, God help him. He'd never questioned her. He'd been the best father to Sophie that a man could be. She had to pre-empt Paul, talk to Justin before he did.

It would kill him. His heart would be utterly broken.

Swallowing back her deep sense of shame, the shame she'd carried, and which had intensified every time she'd lied, whether with words or by omission, she swiped a tear from her cheek and turned to the house, ringing the bell urgently, only to find Jess already swinging the door open.

'Ali…' Jess's face was white, her eyes filled with apprehension as they searched hers. 'Justin… He knows.'

Alicia felt her legs go weak beneath her. *Oh God, no.* 'How much?' she asked, her voice hoarse. 'How much does he know?'

Stepping back to let her in, Jessica glanced guiltily down. 'Sophie. He knows about Sophie,' she said, looking wretchedly back at her.

Alicia stared at her, uncomprehending. Surely Jess hadn't…? She'd *sworn* she wouldn't. She'd urged Alicia to tell Justin the truth years ago, but she'd promised she would never take it upon herself to do so.

'I didn't tell him,' Jess said quickly. 'I would never have done that, I swear to God I wouldn't. But when he asked me outright… I was vague, but couldn't lie to him, Ali. I'm just no good at it.

He guessed. I think he'd half guessed already. I'm so sorry.' She looked at her beseechingly. 'So, so sorry,'

Alicia nodded, the floor seeming to shift underneath her as she tried to digest, tried to imagine what unbearable heartbreak Justin would be going through right now. 'It's all right,' she said, closing her eyes. It was her fault. Not Jess's. Hers. She should never have expected her to lie for her. 'I need to ring him. Talk to him.'

'There's something else.' Jess caught her arm as she fumbled shakily into her bag for her phone.

Alicia looked sharply up. *What?* What else could there be?

'Sophie.' Jess's eyes were wide with fear. 'I think she might have overheard.'

Alicia felt the breath being sucked from her body, her world unravelling, her marriage crumbling. Her husband's life ruined. Her daughter's.

CHAPTER TWENTY-FOUR

SOPHIE

She was here. Having watched her mum climb out of the car and come through the front door, Sophie stepped back from the window. A car driven by another man, she'd noted. She obviously had him at her beck and call, just like she'd had Justin.

Sophie was disinclined to talk to her – what could she have to say, after all, that was worth listening to? On the other hand, what she did have to say would be important. For one, Sophie would quite like to know who her father was. She would also like to know why she'd decided it was okay to lie to her, as if she had some God-given right to fuck up her life because she'd given birth to her.

She intended to have an exit strategy in place, however. If her mum fed her more bullshit, as Justin just had, she wanted to be well away from them both. Justin could bugger off on fictitious business conferences as much as he liked, and her lovely mother could stew in her own mess.

Checking she had all she needed in her overnight bag, she glanced at her phone as it signalled an incoming call. Justin again. She'd guessed it would be. Obviously he'd heard the disillusionment in her voice when she'd ended their last call and was concerned. Or maybe he now realised that she knew what a complete screw-up her life was. Well, that was tough. If he were genuinely concerned, he wouldn't have lied – end of. Rejecting the call, she selected Chloe's number, and then waited worriedly as she took ages to answer. *Please pick up, Chloe,* she prayed silently, as she heard Jessica and her mum talking in the hall. She would be up in a minute, Sophie guessed.

Was she contemplating dropping the news casually into the conversation, Sophie wondered, saying, *Hey, what do you fancy for dinner? Takeaway?* And then, *Oh, and you're the product of a seedy affair I had, by the way, but I decided to pass you off as Justin's. Fancy some onion rings?*

Finally, Chloe picked up. 'Hey, what's happening ?' she said warily, aware from Sophie's texts earlier about her mum's dirty little secret that the shit was about to hit the fan.

'Everything,' Sophie said shakily. 'It's a complete nightmare. Mum's just arrived. I swear, if she tells me one more lie…' Sophie stopped and squeezed her eyes closed. 'I need to talk to you, Chloe,' she went on tearfully, despite her best efforts not to waste tears on people who obviously didn't give a damn about her. 'Can I come over?'

'Crap, I'm not in tonight, Sophe,' Chloe said worriedly. 'I'm babysitting.'

Shit! Panic twisted inside her as Sophie heard someone coming up the stairs. 'I have to go. Can you meet me somewhere?' she asked her. 'Please, Chloe. I really need to talk to you.'

Chloe hesitated. 'I'll get something sorted,' she said, after a second. 'Where and when?'

Sophie blew out a sigh of relief. 'Brum town centre. An hour? I'm taking the bus. I'll meet you in the Bull Ring, outside H&M, second floor.'

'Okay,' Chloe said uncertainly, as Sophie rang off.

Pushing her phone into her bag, she braced herself, turning to face the door as there was a light tap on it. If a single untruth came out of her mouth, if she tried to justify what she'd done in any way, Sophie would be out of the door, and *she* could rot in hell.

'Hi.' Coming cautiously in, her mum looked at her uncertainly. 'How are you?'

Sophie almost laughed at that. 'Ecstatic,' she said shortly. 'How would you be?'

Her mum's face paled.

'So, who is he?' Sophie asked bluntly, careless of the fact that her mum actually looked like shit. As far as she was concerned, she deserved to. 'The man you cheated on Justin with,' she clarified, as her mum grew an impossible shade whiter. 'You know, my father – as opposed to the man you passed off as my dad for the whole of my life!'

Her mum flinched, as if she'd just slapped her. Through narrowed eyes, Sophie watched the swallow slide down her throat, her arms going protectively around herself. It wasn't going to work. The fragile, defensive body language wasn't going to cut it. Not this time. '*Well?*' she demanded.

Alicia's eyes scuttled for the safety of the floor. 'I don't know,' she said weakly. 'Not for sure. I—'

'You don't *know?*' Sophie stared at her, incredulous. 'You mean it was a one-night stand?' Lie number fucking one. She'd heard Justin asking Jess how long it had gone on. Whether it was still going on. So, obviously he thought it was. How could she do that to him? *How?*

'No! I didn't mean…' Stumbling over her words, Alicia shook her head. 'I meant I wasn't sure whether—'

'*Who*, Mum?' Sophie kept eyeballing her.

'A colleague,' Alicia finally said.

'Ah, an office romance,' Sophie said facetiously. 'How boringly predictable.'

'No. It wasn't like that,' Alicia said, looking more flustered by the second. Trying to remember her lies, Sophie thought angrily. 'There was an after-work thing. A birthday party. I—'

'An office jolly.' Sophie widened her eyes girlishly. 'So, obviously it was perfectly reasonable to end it with a fun shag with the nearest bloke. *What*, was it *his* fucking birthday?'

'No! I didn't intend for it to happen, Sophie. I'd been drinking. I lost track of how much. Your dad… Justin wasn't well, and I—'

'Oh, nice one,' Sophie sneered. 'He's not well, so you feel sorry for yourself and decide to get a little attention elsewhere?'

'No. I didn't decide anything. I… He…' Alicia trailed off, tears spilling down her cheeks. 'Sophie, please… You've every right to be angry, but please sit down and let me try to explain properly. I know how it looks, and I did lie to Justin, but—'

'Who is he, Mum?' Swiping tears from under her own eyes, Sophie stayed standing. 'The man at the funeral, the man Justin was staring at, was that him? Is that why he left so suddenly?'

Alicia didn't answer. She didn't need to. The guilt in her eyes said it all.

'You're a real bitch, do you know that, Mum?' Sophie said quietly. 'He's just buried his baby! And now he has to deal with this shit! Of course, that's assuming Lucas *was* his baby.'

Alicia looked up sharply. 'Sophie, stop it,' she begged. 'Please stop.'

'I wish I could,' Sophie said, her heart pounding so hard she was sure it would burst right out of her chest. 'I wish I could stop my fucking life and get off!'

'It was never meant to happen!' Alicia sobbed. 'I didn't mean to hurt Justin. I didn't want *any* of this.'

Sophie studied her mum hard. 'So you regret it then?'

Alicia looked at her bewilderedly. 'Of course I do. I wish to God I could turn back the clock, but I can't!'

'Cheers, Mum,' Sophie said, her heart sinking without trace. 'You know what, you don't regret it half as much as I do. Have a nice life.' Swallowing hard, she turned away.

'Sophie, wait!' Alicia tried to stop her as she grabbed up her bag and turned to push past her. 'I didn't mean I regret having you. I've never for one second regretted—'

'I wish I was fucking dead!' Sophie spat.

Did her mum honestly think she wanted to listen to this crap? That she would want to hang around while they split up, tearing her apart in the process? Well, stuff that. She wasn't about to stay here *or* with her bitch mother – no way. And Justin was hardly going to want her living with him. He'd want out of the whole crappy situation. At least they had that much in common, she thought cynically, as she thundered down the stairs.

CHAPTER TWENTY-FIVE

JUSTIN

'Chloe, slow down.' Holding the telephone close to his ear, Justin tried to make sense of what Sophie's friend was saying. 'Where and when were you supposed to be meeting her?'

'In town, but I'm babysitting.' Chloe still wasn't making much sense, frustratingly. 'She rang me earlier, and then she rang me again, and she sounded so upset. I'm worried about her, Mr Cole. I can't take the baby with me and I—'

'*Whoa.* Chloe, please, slow down.' Justin felt a knot of panic climb his throat. 'Take the baby where? Why was she upset?'

Chloe didn't answer.

Justin pressed his fingers to his temple. 'Chloe, this is really important,' he said, working to keep the immense agitation he was feeling from his voice. 'I wouldn't ask you to share anything you thought was confidential otherwise.'

'Birmingham. The Bull Ring shopping centre. Outside H&M, on the second floor. Sophie said she was catching the bus in. She's probably already halfway there by now.'

'Okay.' Justin nodded. He needed to go. But first, he needed to know why she'd taken off. 'Can you tell me why she was upset, Chloe?' he urged her gently. 'Is it to do with Luke and the funeral?'

Again, Chloe was reluctant. 'She heard you, Mr Cole,' she confided, eventually. She heard what you were saying... about her not being yours. She was really upset. I should have told her to come here, but I didn't think, and now—'

'*Jesus Christ.*' Why hadn't he done something? He'd *known* she had. Cold dread pooled in the pit of Justin's stomach.

'I thought you should know. I wasn't sure what else to do,' Chloe was talking fast now, sounding scared. 'I'm sorry, Mr Cole. I—'

'It's okay, Chloe. It's fine. I'll find her,' Justin reassured her. 'Let me have your number and I'll text you.' He snatched up the newly delivered loan car keys and his mobile, noting several messages from Alicia as he did so. 'Meanwhile, will you let me know if she gets back to you?'

'Uh-huh, yes, I will, I promise.' Sounding relieved, Chloe reeled off her number. 'Do you want me to text her?' she asked tentatively. 'I thought maybe if I told her I was coming, but I was running late, that, you know, it might buy you a bit of time.'

'Good idea. You did the right thing, Chloe.' Justin quickly keyed in her number and sent her his. 'I'll be in touch.'

He was halfway out of the front door when Alicia rang. 'Justin, it's Sophie – she's gone!' she said frantically when he picked up. 'She heard… What you and Jessica were discussing. She… She's taken her overnight bag. She's not answering her phone. I've tried her a hundred times. I don't know what to do. I—'

'*Fuck!*' Justin's chest constricted. If she'd taken her overnight bag, she clearly intended to stay away from Jessica's. Would she come back here? Justin very much doubted it, now that he knew what she'd overheard. She had her key, but… *Dammit!* He needed to find her.

'I know. Chloe rang me.' Drawing in a tight breath, he braced himself. 'Is it true?' *Do not lie to me, Alicia.*

An agonising second ticked by, before she delivered the blow that would surely kill him. 'I… I don't know.'

'I see,' Justin said quietly. He felt close to exploding. 'So, what did you expect her to do, Alicia? Sit down and have a nice, calm conversation over a fucking cup of tea?'

'Oh God. Justin, I…' Alicia broke off with a sob. 'I'm sorry. I am so, *so* sorry. I never intended to hurt you or Sophie, I swear I didn't.'

'Right.' Yanking his car door open, Justin threw himself behind the wheel. 'That's not how it looks from here, Alicia.'

'I know. I'm sorry.' Alicia sobbed harder. 'I know you can't forgive me. I know you won't ever, but please, please help Sophie.'

'*Jesus!*' Justin slammed the car door. 'Did you honestly think I *wouldn't?*'

'No. I…' Alicia's voice caught wretchedly in her throat. 'I'm so sorry.'

'So you said.' Justin breathed in hard. 'Just tell me one thing, Alicia. Was he worth it? Was he worth *this?*'

Alicia didn't answer. Justin guessed from her choking sobs that she couldn't. 'I have to go. I have to find my daughter,' he spat. He simply didn't have it in him to be anything but angry. It was too late for apologies – way too late. The cold, hard fact was that her deceit had led to this. If he didn't find her tonight… anything could happen by morning. He might never find her. That thought slicing through him like a knife, Justin cut the call, started the engine and screeched the car out of the drive.

CHAPTER TWENTY-SIX

JESSICA

'Ali?' Jessica said tentatively, walking to where Alicia stood motionless in the hall.

'He hung up.' Alicia looked tearfully down at her phone. 'I've destroyed him. Destroyed my whole family.'

'Come on, Ali. Tears won't help anything. Let's go and sit down and think about what to do – calmly.' Sliding an arm around her sister, Jessica attempted to lead her towards the kitchen. She decided not to point out that Alicia wasn't the only one feeling terrible right now. Alicia might have brought this on herself, but Sophie had done nothing to deserve this. Justin definitely hadn't, and he'd no doubt be feeling awful. She would ring him, Jessica decided, as soon as she could. The poor man would be gutted, thinking he hadn't got a soul in the world to talk to.

'He'll call back,' she tried to reassure Alicia. And he probably would, because that's the kind of man he was: caring. 'He's bound to be shocked and upset. You need to give him some time, Ali. It's an awful lot to take in.'

'He hates me! He has every reason to. I *lied* to him, Jess, about the most important thing in his life! Even knowing he might find out, I kept on lying to him.'

'I know.' Jessica nodded sympathetically. 'I did warn you what might happen, but you were so adamant. You know, sometimes the biggest lie of all is the lie we tell to ourselves, sweetheart.' She sighed sadly, aware of her own propensity to do just that.

She'd lied to herself for years, telling herself Michael, the would-have-been father of her children, had they survived, wasn't a complete misogynist. He was – a controlling, self-centred woman-hater. He hadn't liked her friends, hadn't wanted her to meet his friends, the way she'd dressed, the things she'd said whenever they were in company. He clearly hadn't liked her very much in the end, as proven by the fact that he'd walked out on her when she'd realised she was miscarrying – again. She must have been mad, and obviously attracted to bastards. She hadn't known any man that wasn't a bastard in some form, apart from Justin.

She wished she'd spotted him before Alicia had called first dibs on him. She and Alicia had been working for the same company then, alongside Paul Radley. In fact, it was Jessica putting in a word for her that had got Alicia the job. In gratitude for which, Alicia had nabbed the only decent man for miles from right under her nose. Justin had been coming out of a seminar at the same venue in which they were holding their sales conference, and had walked right into her. They'd practically fallen into each other's arms, and that had been that. Jessica wouldn't have ended up with the misogynist if he'd walked into *her* first, and Justin wouldn't have ended up with his heart broken. But, of course, in falling into Alicia, Justin had fallen for her. It had been obvious that he was immediately smitten by her rosy blushes and self-effacing apologies. Alicia, with her complete inability to see her own attractions – to see that her shyness obviously *was* an attraction – had wondered what the handsome young doctor saw in her. Jessica couldn't help thinking that Justin might be asking himself the same question right now.

Alicia wiped a hand across her eyes. She really did look wretched. Jessica doubted she'd had a wink of sleep since Paul Radley had turned up, and this was without losing dear little Lucas. She couldn't help but feel for her.

'Convincing myself I was doing it for Justin you mean.' Alicia clearly got the gist, another crop of tears spilling from her eyes. 'He'd been wounded and broken and lost, and I made it my excuse to tear his heart out. He will never, ever forgive me. How can he? And Sophie... Dear God, Sophie.'

'You did it for the right reasons, sweetie.' Jessica assured her, stepping in front of her and taking hold of her hands. 'He'll call back.' She locked her eyes on hers. 'Whatever he feels about *you*, he loves Sophie, Alicia. He'll be there for her. You know he will.'

Alicia nodded, squeezing her eyes closed. 'I know. But that's what makes it so cruel, don't you see? He would have loved her anyway, if only I'd found the courage to tell him, been honest from the outset and given him a chance.'

'Possibly,' Jessica conceded, though he would have to be a saint to have stayed with her, in reality. It wouldn't be easy for any man to accept his wife might be carrying another man's baby, even someone as family-orientated as Justin, and that was obviously Alicia's real reason for not telling him. She should have been honest with herself and with him, given him a chance at another relationship, if that's what he'd wanted. 'We can't undo history, though, can we, sadly?'

Alicia glanced upwards. 'I wish to God I'd listened to you.' A shudder ran through her. I might as well have taken a knife to his heart.'

'You're being too hard on yourself. He will be hurting. Of course he will. But you know him well enough to know his thoughts will be on Sophie,' Jessica repeated firmly. 'Let him concentrate his efforts on finding her. It's better he's focussed on that.'

Shakily, Alicia nodded. 'You're right,' she said, making a visible effort to stem her tears. 'There's no point trying to offer him explanations – not now. He won't want to hear them.'

'Just give him some time,' Jessica said, giving her a hug and finally managing to lead her to the kitchen. 'Do you have any idea where she might be?'

'Thankfully.' Alicia nodded, running a hand under her nose. 'Chloe rang him at home. Sophie spoke to her, apparently. She probably felt she had no one else to turn to.'

Including her. Jessica felt sad and angry about that. She would never wish any harm on her niece. She'd been put in an impossible situation. Sworn to keep Alicia's secret for her, she'd lost the trust of people that mattered to her, too. One day, when she was less fragile, Jessica really needed to point that out to her sister.

'That's probably where she is then,' she said reassuringly, pointing Alicia towards the kitchen table and making sure she sat down. She looked very wobbly on her feet – unsurprising, given the shock she'd had. 'Don't worry too much, Ali. She might not want to come home right away, but Justin will make sure she's okay.'

'But what if she's not at Chloe's?' Alicia looked fearfully up at her. 'What then?'

'Then we start ringing around anyone else she might know. We'll find her, Alicia,' Jessica said adamantly.

'But what if we don't?'

Noting the look in Alicia's eyes now was one of palpable terror, Jessica felt icy trepidation sweep the length of her spine. She wouldn't wish that on her. On poor Justin. She needed to ring him, as soon as possible. Make sure he knew that she'd been absolutely sworn to secrecy. She couldn't bear the thought of him being angry with her, thinking she'd condoned Alicia's behaviour.

CHAPTER TWENTY-SEVEN

JUSTIN

A mixture of guilt and anger gnawing away at him, Justin keyed in a text to Alicia as he headed towards the shop Chloe had mentioned. As furious as he was, he couldn't leave her worrying herself sick. She would be beside herself with grief, feeling bereft twofold, as he was. Sorrow weighed like a cold stone inside him as he thought of his innocent baby boy, whose soul they'd laid to rest just a few hours ago. It seemed like a lifetime had passed since then. *I'll call you as soon as I know anything*, he typed, and then hesitated, not sure how to sign off, dearly wishing it was possible to turn back the clock to a time where their lives weren't irretrievably fractured and he would have ended his text with a single X, as always. Not any more. It was all gone, everything they'd ever had together, slipping through his hands as surely as water through his fingers.

Not Sophie.

He couldn't lose her. *Wouldn't.*

Leaving the message as it was, he hit send and quickly selected Sophie's mobile for the umpteenth time since he'd left home. His heart hitching, he slowed as the call began to ring, his gaze shooting towards a coffee shop ahead of him. Her ringtone: Adele. The tune that rang constantly around the house. It *had* to be hers. She was there, somewhere.

Shit! He ground to a halt as the phone stopped ringing. She was here. He could sense her. But where? Dragging a hand through his hair, his desperation mounting, he scoured the seated crowd – and his heart almost stopped pumping.

Looking every bit as vulnerable and lonely as he knew she must be feeling, Sophie was sitting on the far side of the coffee shop.

Dammit. He cursed silently as a group of kids scraped their chairs back, simultaneously rising from a table directly in front of him.

His gaze fixed on Sophie, Justin mumbled an apology and squeezed past them, and then faltered as she turned to him with a look of alarm. A feeling of sick trepidation clenched his stomach.

'Sophie,' he said, making sure to keep his tone calm.

Time seemed to freeze for one agonising second as she locked eyes with him, and then, as Justin took another tentative step towards her, Sophie shot to her feet, grappling her overnight bag from the back of her chair and almost stumbling over a table as she backed away. Backed away from *him*.

'Sophie, *wait*! Please,' he called desperately, as she turned away. 'Sophie!'

'No!' Sophie whirled back around, her expression now one of near hatred, which shook Justin to the core. 'Go away! Leave me alone!'

'Sophie…' Bewildered, Justin took another hesitant step. 'Please. Don't do this,' he begged. 'Come back. We'll talk, just you and me. We'll sit down and—'

'No!' Sophie dragged her hair from her face and glared furiously at him. 'I'm not going *anywhere* with you. Why the hell should I?'

'Because I'm telling you to!' Justin snapped, his frustration, coupled with gut-wrenching fear, spilling over. If she took off now, he'd have absolutely no idea where she was. And the way she was feeling… He couldn't allow that. 'Come back here now!'

'Fuck off! You've no right! I don't *want* to!' Sophie shouted tearfully. 'I don't want to be anywhere near you. Don't you get it? I just want you to go away and leave me *alone*!'

Justin felt the ground shift beneath him. He wanted to go to her, hold her, let her scream, kick him, punch him, if that would help. Anything. 'I'm your father, Sophie,' he tried, his voice catching. 'I'll always—'

'You're not!' Rage now emanated palpably from her. Justin could feel it, like an icicle through his heart. Rage, hate, hurt – all directed right at him. 'You're a liar! Both of you! *Liars!*'

Uncertain what to do; go forward or back off, Justin watched helplessly as two concerned women stepped towards her, one placing an arm around Sophie's shoulders, drawing her further back, further away from him.

'He's not my father. He's *not*.' Gulping back a sob, Sophie addressed the women, and then, seeing Justin step towards her, wrenched herself away from them.

His blood turning to ice in his veins as she turned to flee, Justin moved fast, almost colliding with the women as he raced after her, only to find two security guards blocking his path.

'I wouldn't if I were you, mate,' one of them said, the menacing look in his eyes telling Justin he wasn't about to let him get past.

'She's my daughter,' he said, holding the man's gaze, praying he would see the desperation in his eyes.

'Yeah, and he's mine,' the man quipped drolly, nodding towards his sidekick. 'Back off, mate,' he warned him. 'The police are on their way.'

The police? Given how efficient he'd found them so far in finding any link that might lead to who killed his son, Justin might have laughed, had he not felt like crying. 'She's upset,' he attempted to explain, tried hard to hold on to his temper. 'I need to go to her.'

Fuck this, he thought, as the two men stood their ground, like immovable mountains. Arms folded, feet splayed in a Neanderthal display of aggression, it was clear they weren't going to let him go anywhere. Determined to get past them any way he had to, Justin's attempt to push through was cut short by someone grabbing him from behind, seizing his arm and twisting it high up his back.

Christ. 'Sophie!' Ignoring the pain ripping through his bicep as his arm was pushed impossibly higher, Justin struggled to stay upright.

'Sophie!' He screamed it, his heart splintering as, brought heavily to his knees, he watched his daughter disappear into the crowd.

CHAPTER TWENTY-EIGHT

SOPHIE

Choking back her tears, Sophie kept going. What had she done? She'd wanted to hurt him. She'd wanted to hurt them both as much as she could, but not like this. She should have stopped those security guards. Instead, she'd made them think he was a bloody paedophile.

Oh God, she hadn't meant to do that. Pausing to catch her breath outside the shopping centre, Sophie squeezed her eyes closed, seeing again the hurt and confusion on Justin's face. They'd forced him to the floor. Held him down like the worst kind of criminal. And he'd done *nothing*. He might be ready to walk away from the nightmare his life had become, from the deceit and the lies her mother had fed him – she could hardly blame him for that – but he'd always loved her as a dad should love a daughter. He couldn't feel that way any more, that was clear to Sophie, but she couldn't stop loving him as a father so easily. Part of her, the biggest part of her, would always love him, yet there was another part of her that hated him for being naive enough to allow himself to be deceived. It didn't matter much now though, did it? She would never see him again. She didn't want to. Hearing him say out loud that he'd lost his daughter, listening to his lies, his invented reasons – work conferences, whatever – to extract himself from her life now Luke was no longer part of his, that would have been too much to bear.

Suppressing a sob, she wiped the back of her hand shakily under her nose and tried to think about what her next move should be. Where she could go. Chloe had obviously told Justin where she was. Realistically, she couldn't have gone there in any case. Chloe's mum would have been on the phone in a flash.

Holly! She'd moved away when her parents had decided to run a caravan park in Herefordshire somewhere. Sophie wasn't sure where, exactly. Holly had been a good mate, though. She might be able to crash there for a few nights, until she got her head around what to do. Holly might even be able to sneak her into one of the caravans, which would buy her some time. She'd be sixteen soon. She could get a job then. An office temp job or something in a shop, maybe. Anything. Stacking shelves in the supermarket would do until she'd secured some accommodation – a single room somewhere or even a bedsit. Then she might be able to apply for a student loan to cover her fees and living costs while she went to veterinary school, which is what she wanted to do.

It was a plan, at least. She didn't need them – treating her like a child one minute and then like she wasn't even a person the next, like she didn't have feelings. Knowing her mum, she'd probably flipped a coin: heads, an abortion; tails, she passes her off as Justin's and crosses her fingers. Pity she hadn't kept her bloody legs crossed, Sophie thought furiously. *What am I supposed to do with this*, Justin had said. What had he thought *she* was going to do?

Scrolling through her contacts, she found Holly's number and rang her. She couldn't go over there tonight, as Holly was out with her family celebrating her brother's birthday, but, after a quick catch up, she arranged to meet up with her in the morning, which left her with nothing to do but wait around. She could kill a few hours at the train station, she supposed, where she wouldn't look too conspicuous; check out the train times and then download something to read on her phone.

*

She was sitting in Starbucks at the station, wondering whether she could get away with hiding in the loos for the night, when her phone beeped an incoming text alert. From her bitch mum or her dad, she presumed, wavering for a second when she thought it might be him, and then steeling herself to ignore him if it was. She felt bad about what had happened at the shopping centre – none of this was his fault, after all – but he'd been pretty quick to announce he didn't have a daughter when he'd learned Alicia's secret, hadn't he? Warily, Sophie checked the number – one she didn't recognise.

Hi, Sophie, hope you don't mind me contacting you. I would like to have got in touch sooner, but Alicia begged me not to. I realise this all might be a bit overwhelming for you, but could we talk, possibly? I'd love to hear from you, if you'd like to. All best, Paul Radley, your father.

Stunned, Sophie stared at it, and then knitted her brow. How the bloody hell had he got her number? And why the contact now?

Thinking it might be some kind of scam, Sophie hesitated for a second, and then dismissed the idea. Given the content, it couldn't be anything other than genuine. Fiddling worriedly with her eyebrow stud, she debated and then texted back.

Were you the guy at the funeral?

Yes. I wanted to speak to you then, but it didn't seem appropriate. I'm so sorry for your loss. Px

Sophie chewed on her bottom lip, hesitated briefly again, and then – 'Sod it' – she phoned him. It couldn't do any harm, could it? Thanks to her bitch mum, the harm had already been done. And at least he'd acknowledged she'd had a loss.

'Sophie?' he asked, when he picked up.

'Uh-huh,' Sophie answered guardedly. He'd said Alicia had begged him not to contact her, which smacked of the truth, knowing now what a deceitful cow she was, but… 'How did you get my number?' she asked him.

'I've been talking to Alicia, hoping I could come to some arrangement about having some contact with you. Fifteen years is a long time to be denied access to your own child. I've missed you growing up.' He drew in a breath. 'She's okay with me having your number, apparently, so I guess she's relented for some reason.'

Yeah, and Sophie knew why. Because she wanted to pass the shit she'd caused on to someone else to clear up.

'It's great to hear from you, Sophie,' he said, sounding as if he might even mean it.

'Why?' Sophie asked cynically.

Paul laughed. It wasn't a derogatory laugh though, more an amused chuckle. 'I get why you'd be cautious,' he said. 'I've missed you,' he added simply. 'There's never been a day when I haven't thought about you.'

Sophie wasn't wholly convinced by that, but he sounded sincere.

'So why didn't you get in touch before then? I mean, you didn't have to just… *not*, did you?'

'No,' Paul conceded. 'Truthfully, I didn't want to mess up your mother's marriage. I cared too much about her to do that. I'd hoped we'd be together. Things weren't going too well between her and Justin… But that's history – probably stuff I shouldn't be repeating. I knew Justin was a decent guy, which actually didn't make me feel great about falling in love with his wife, and… well, I thought I was doing the right thing, for everyone. I didn't think it was the right thing by you, to be honest, and I didn't bargain on missing you so much it hurt, but it did – a lot. And then I lost my wife and kids in a boating accident – I think that was a wake-up call.'

'Oh, shit,' Sophie murmured, shocked. 'That's rough.'

'It was,' Paul said quietly. 'It took me a while to get over it – not that you ever do. I realised then that I needed to see you, make sure you were okay. Do you think we could be friends, maybe? Meet occasionally? It would be great to catch up. Not that fifteen years is going to be easy to catch up on.' He stopped, sighing heavily.

'Sixteen,' Sophie pointed out.

'Right. Ninth of October. Happy upcoming sixteenth, Sophie.'

Sophie raised her eyebrows at that. 'You've been marking days off on the calendar then?' she asked drolly.

'I think that might be deemed a touch obsessive.' Paul laughed. 'No, I just remember that date, that's all.' He paused. 'So, how are you, generally?'

Sophie went quiet. 'Generally,' she said, after a second, 'crap.'

'Oh, how so?' Paul asked, sounding concerned.

'Stuff.' Sophie shrugged vaguely. She wasn't actually sure she wanted to share her sad life story with him. 'Mum and me had a fight.'

'Oh,' he said, sounding as if he got it. 'A bad one?'

'Very.'

Paul paused, then said, 'You're not within earshot of her then, I take it?'

'Nope. I'm at New Street Station. Wanted to give her some space, you know, so I'm going to stay with a friend – just for a few days,' she lied. She wasn't sure she would ever want to see her again. 'Trouble is, my train's not until morning, so I'm killing some time.'

'You're there on your own?' Now Paul sounded surprised.

'Yeah. I'm a big girl now,' Sophie reminded him.

'Have you eaten?'

'No, not yet. I might grab some chips or something.'

'Look, it's only a suggestion,' Paul said, 'and you can say no – I'm not likely to be offended, since you don't even know me – but do you fancy meeting up? I could come and get you. We could grab a pizza or something. You could even crash here, if you like. Once you've established I'm not too weird, that is.'

Sophie wasn't sure about that.

'Or just share that bag of chips, if you don't fancy doing anything else. On me, obviously.'

'Last of the big spenders.' Sophie smiled. 'Okay,' she said. He sounded all right. Normal. And she couldn't sit around here all night. She'd already seen a few homeless people being moved on.

'Great,' Paul said. 'I'll be with you in half an hour. Maybe forty minutes. I just have to have a quick shower. I've been in the gym. Don't want to make a bad first impression, do I? Oh, where are you?'

'Starbucks, or else just outside. I'll keep an eye out for you.'

'I'm the tall, dark and handsome one,' Paul joked.

'And modest.' Sophie laughed. 'See you soon.'

She liked him, she thought, ending the call. He definitely didn't seem weird.

CHAPTER TWENTY-NINE

ALICIA

Hearing Justin come through the front door, Alicia stopped breathing.

He'd already told her what had happened over the phone. 'She ran from me,' he'd said hoarsely, and then stopped. 'I tried to…' He'd stopped again. Alicia had heard his voice crack, felt his unbearable, palpable pain, and her heart had torn apart inside her.

Sophie had worshipped him. She'd had the best relationship it was possible for a daughter to have with a father.

Alicia clenched her fists. Why had she *done* it? *Why* had she waited, knowing this would eventually come out? That when it did, it would tear her beautiful family apart. Jessica had been right. She'd lied to herself and everyone else. She was everything Sophie thought she was – a selfish, unfeeling bitch.

'So, she already had her overnight bag packed?' DI Taylor asked her.

Alicia hardly heard him, her gaze going past him as the lounge door opened – hoping to see what, she didn't know. If he met her gaze, which Alicia was petrified he wouldn't, there would be nothing but hurt and disappointment in his eyes. Open contempt, too – that would be there. How could it not?

Seeing the gash on Justin's cheek, his dishevelled appearance, Alicia felt another part of her curl up and die. 'Justin…?' She moved instinctively towards him, and then stopped as he fixed her with a stare that could freeze an ocean.

He didn't speak as she faltered, turning his gaze quizzically towards DI Taylor instead, obviously wondering why he would come again personally.

'What happened to you?' DI Taylor asked, turning to look at him.

Justin smiled ironically. 'Security guards weren't too keen to let me go,' he said, his expression wary as he glanced between Taylor and the woman police officer with him.

He looked utterly exhausted, jaded to his very bones. Alicia wished there was some way to take his pain away, but there was none. She couldn't go to him, hold him. Dear God, how much she wanted to do that. There was nothing she could do but take herself, the cause of his pain, away. Her guilt threatening to choke her, she glanced down as Justin's gaze came back to her. She could feel his eyes on her, studying her, obviously looking for some clue as to who this stranger he'd lived with, loved with all of himself, was. In the edge of her vision, she saw him walk across to her, stand a foot away. The space felt like an iceberg between them.

Tentatively, Alicia reached out to him, placing a hand on his arm, and Justin flinched, physically flinched at her touch, and Alicia knew. She'd lost him. There would be no going back. Even if their beautiful, precious daughter walked through the door right now, there would be no going back for any of them. She'd done that.

'So, what do you propose to do?' he asked DI Taylor. His tone was tight with pent-up emotion. Emotion that surely had to be vented, if he wasn't to go the same route he had once before, driven slowly and steadily out of his mind by grief.

'I'm afraid there's nothing much we can do at this juncture,' DI Taylor said, with an apologetic sigh.

'*What?*' Justin reeled where he stood. Alicia knew this was too much to take on top of his frustration with the police's lack of progress in regard to Lucas and the crash. 'My daughter is *missing* and you're telling me you're going to do *nothing*?' Raking a hand furiously through his hair, he stared at Taylor, stunned.

DI Taylor's expression was sympathetic. 'It's too soon to register her officially missing,' he explained. 'And then, the first thing we have to establish is the level of risk to the person who is missing. If she—'

'My daughter!' Justin's voice rose. 'The person missing is my daughter! Jesus!' He banged the heel of his hand against his forehead. 'She's fifteen! Doesn't that make her at risk? What the hell is *wrong* with you people? Why aren't you out looking for her?'

Taylor looked regretfully to Alicia, before turning uncomfortably back to Justin. 'We have your statement, Dr Cole,' he said quietly. 'We're doing all we can for now.'

'Which, as you've just pointed out, amounts to nothing,' Justin said furiously.

Again, Taylor glanced away, plainly unable to meet his gaze. 'She went of her own volition, according to Mrs Cole.'

Alicia nodded. There was no escaping the fact that Sophie had been driven out, her life shattered and her heart broken, by her own mother.

'Which means what, exactly?' Justin asked, his jaw tightening.

'If a person goes missing voluntarily, then it's generally an indicator of a problem in that person's life,' Taylor explained patiently. 'And you've obviously been having a few problems…'

'Obviously,' Justin said, his tone now bitter with contempt. 'Meaning, in your expert opinion, she's classed as a low-risk case?'

'For now, yes.' Taylor nodded ruefully. 'We have a list of her friends and acquaintances. I gather Mrs Cole has already contacted most of them, but we will contact them again and keep you posted if anything new comes up.'

'Right. Such as my daughter being found raped or murdered?' said Justin. Alicia's stomach tightened like a slipknot.

Taylor glanced quickly in her direction. 'We could use a recent photograph,' he said, offering her a commiserating smile.

Nodding, Alicia swallowed back the jagged glass in her chest. 'I have one in my bag,' she said, fighting tears as she turned to the sofa to retrieve the photo she carried in her purse. She couldn't cry. Though she wanted to curl up and weep like a child – for her children, for Justin, who once would have comforted her – now was not the time. Now, Justin would hate her as much as she'd known he'd once loved her – and it hurt. It hurt so very much.

Shoving his hands in his pockets, Justin watched as Taylor looked at the photo and then passed it to his colleague. 'So, have you made any progress in regard to whoever murdered my son? Just wondering whether you're even trying. You know, out of idle curiosity,' he said, his tone scathing.

'We don't take the death of a child anything other than seriously, Dr Cole,' Taylor assured him. 'We're following every lead, I can assure you. I'm afraid we don't have much to go on, other than the colour and type of the car.'

'A black Land Rover,' Alicia said.

DI Taylor nodded, and then sighed. 'Unfortunately, black Land Rover doesn't really give us much to go on without at least part of the registration. And, as we have no witnesses to the road traffic accident, we're—'

'No witnesses?' Justin almost choked.

'No independent eye witnesses who can provide a description of the driver of the car,' Taylor clarified. 'We've appealed for people to come forward with any information, but without a clear identification or fingerprints, we can't check the national database, which means we're at a bit of a loss, I'm afraid.'

'A loss?' Justin stared at him, incredulous. 'I don't believe this! You mean the bastard is going to get away with it?'

'What about CCTV footage?' Alicia asked, feeling as desperate as Justin looked.

'Not much use, I'm afraid.' Glancing apologetically at her, Taylor shook his head. 'We don't have a clear image of the driver's face and, unfortunately, the angle of the camera doesn't show us the number plate. I'm sorry, Mrs Cole. I can't give you any further information, as yet.'

He *was* going to get away with it. Nausea rose rancidly in Alicia's chest. She looked at DI Taylor in disbelief, while Justin simply laughed, a short, derisive laugh, and then walked away. He stopped at the door. His frustration was tangible, his anger emanating from him. Breathing out, eventually, he reached to knead his forehead, and then, 'Stuff it!' he growled, slamming the heel of his hand hard into the lounge door.

'Dr Cole,' DI Taylor took a step towards him, a warning edge to his voice. 'I realise how frustrated you must feel, but I'm not sure getting aggressive is going to help, is it?'

'He's upset.' Alicia went to Justin, placing a hand on his arm.

'Upset? *Jesus!*' Justin pulled his arm away, looking at Taylor in bemusement. 'You know what,' he said, after a second, his expression somewhere between cynical and bitterly disappointed, 'I think getting "aggressive" might just help, actually. Then again, maybe you're right. I mean, my son being murdered and my daughter going missing is hardly worth getting upset about, is it? I tell you what, why don't we go shopping instead, hey, Alicia?' he suggested flatly. 'Or maybe we could catch up with a few old "work colleagues" for a drink. What do you think?'

'Justin!' His words cutting her to the bone, Alicia called after him as he strode out, shaking his head at Jessica who was standing in the hall, looking alarmed.

I'm sorry! She wanted to scream, to break down right there, right then. But she didn't deserve his forgiveness. She'd ripped his life apart, thrown everything he'd ever given her – his love, his commitment – right back in his face.

Desperate, feeling utterly anchorless without him, powerless to help him, she stayed where she was as Justin slammed through the front door.

CHAPTER THIRTY

SOPHIE

'Nice pad,' Sophie said, glancing around the open-plan living area. It was a brand-new Central Plaza apartment, decorated in white and greys, with a hardwood floor, great globular chrome lights and a huge L-shaped leather sofa. It must have cost a bomb.

'It is pretty cool, isn't it?' Paul said, closing the front door and nodding her on in. 'It has a residents' gymnasium, twenty-four-hour concierge service and a fantastic view over the city centre. Not mine, unfortunately. I'm flat-sitting for a friend.'

'Ah. Nice friend,' Sophie commented, her eyes boggling at the size of the flat-screen TV, which had to be seventy-five inches at least.

'There are plenty of flats available though. Out of most people's price range, I guess. The building's still practically empty. I might buy one when I move back from Dubai.' Paul followed her awestruck gaze thoughtfully. 'With a bedroom decorated to your specifications, of course – assuming you'd like to stay over occasionally?'

'Yeah, maybe,' Sophie said, smiling in his direction.

Looking pleased, Paul smiled back. He really did seem all right. She'd been a bit worried when he'd suggested she crash at his – she'd never met him before, after all, and weird stuff happened – but she'd figured she was safe when he'd turned up with a bag of chips, looking like a nervous schoolkid. Handsome, but definitely nervous.

'What do you fancy?' he said, walking over to a table lined with so many bottles of booze that Sophie's eyes boggled all over again.

'Something seriously strong,' she said, 'but I'd better not. Mum and Dad would go ballistic.' Realising what she'd said, Sophie dropped her gaze. She was missing home already. Missing Luke so much, she didn't think her heart would ever stop hurting.

'How about a small wine?' Paul suggested. 'I promise I won't tell if you don't.'

Sophie nodded, but kept her gaze fixed down.

'Hey.' Paul walked across to her, placing a hand on her shoulder as her eyes filled up. 'It can't be that bad, can it?'

Sophie sniffed hard and dragged a hand under her nose. 'It's my fault,' she blurted. 'What happened with Justin. It's my fault.' She hadn't told Paul that Justin had found out he wasn't her dad – somehow she'd felt she would be betraying him – but she'd told him some of what had happened in the Bull Ring. 'I shouldn't have run. I should have at least gone back and told them it wasn't what they were thinking. Do you think they might have called the police?'

'I very much doubt it.' Paul smiled reassuringly. 'And, in any case, Justin's an articulate man. He would have soon put them right.'

Sophie shrugged. 'I suppose.'

Paul reached to ease her chin up. 'I have no idea why you would think any of this is your fault, you know,' he said gently, his smile now bemused. 'The problem is your mother, not you.'

Gulping hard, Sophie nodded. He didn't have the whole picture, but he was right. She'd done nothing wrong except be born. Lately, she'd been wishing that she hadn't been.

'Do you want me to drive you back home?' Paul asked her, his brow furrowed with concern. 'I don't like the idea of you going off to your friend's upset.'

Sophie scanned his eyes. Like hers, they were dark espresso-brown, sympathetic and kind. Justin's eyes had always been kind. She couldn't remember him once ever losing his rag. Why had her mum done it, strung him along for so many years? Sophie got that people had affairs, but she didn't get why her mum would have built such an elaborate web of lies. She must have known it was bound to come tumbling down like a house of cards.

And why had she done it in the first place – not just lie, but have an affair at all? It wasn't like they'd didn't get on or had monumental rows or anything. They'd had their mental moments, but mostly they'd been solid, or so Sophie had thought. Justin definitely loved her mum. Sophie only had to think of the way he'd looked at her, that quiet smile in his eyes, to know that. Whenever her mum had been upset about a child at work who'd been abused in some way, he would go to her and massage her shoulders, kiss the side of her neck and hold her. Her mum always turned to him, buried her head on his shoulder and told him how much she loved him.

She was a kind person. That's why she kept on doing the shit job she did, even though she said the traumatised kids, who had to live their reality while she was tucked safely up in her bed, haunted her dreams. What she'd done to Justin was plain cruel. It just wasn't her. It was no wonder he'd been so shocked. Sophie's mind went to him, and she tried not to hear the words he'd said about how he'd lost his son *and* his daughter. Whatever he was feeling, she knew he'd loved her too. She'd felt it. He could hardly love her now though, could he, the spawn of her mum's affair with another man?

Sighing, Sophie shook her head. 'No,' she said, though she wished more than anything that she could go back, to a home that felt like a home, like it used to. But that place didn't exist any more. Her baby brother was dead, her mother was a lying bitch, and Justin… After what she'd done to him at the shopping centre, Sophie doubted he'd ever want to set eyes on her again.

'They're going through shit,' she said, still not wanting to divulge too much. 'The house got broken into while we were at my little brother's funeral.' Trailing off, she shrugged and forced back her tears. There was no way to go home, as far as she could see. No home to go back to.

'I'll be okay.' She smiled tremulously up at him.

Paul didn't look convinced. 'You really are going through it, aren't you?' He shook his head in commiseration. 'Tell you what, how does a holiday sound? It might do you good to get away from everything for a while.'

Sophie gawked. 'A holiday? Where?'

'Wherever you'd like,' Paul said, going back to pour the drinks. 'Florida, maybe?'

'*Florida?*' Sophie's eyes grew wide. Accepting the glass of white wine, she drank thirstily. 'But… what about my passport?' She knitted her brow. This was happening way too fast. 'And clothes and stuff.'

'Well, now Alicia knows we're in touch…' Paul took her glass and walked back to the table to top it up. 'I'll ask her about it. I'm thinking, under the circumstances, she might think it's a good idea, a way of allowing you all some space.'

Sophie was happy to give them as much space as they needed – and then some. Still, she wasn't sure. A holiday to Florida? Was he made of money? Yeah, she was his daughter, but he hardly even knew her. It sounded a bit too good to be true. As far as he knew, she could be a total brat.

'And I'll buy you some new clothes,' Paul offered, causing Sophie to do a double take. 'You won't need much anyway, in that climate.'

Sophie searched his face, puzzled.

'I can see you're a bit cautious,' Paul said, handing her back her glass. 'I don't blame you. You're right to be. But I'd like to make up for some of the things I haven't been able to do for you. Why don't you ring her yourself, if you're worried? Put your mind at rest.'

Sophie took another drink. 'I suppose I could text her. I don't really want to talk to her.'

Placing her glass on the coffee table, she dropped her bag on the floor and delved into it for her phone. And then, her heart skipping a beat, she delved deeper. 'Shit,' she muttered, dragging the contents out of it.

'What's wrong?' Paul asked, watching as she searched.

'It's not here. My phone.' Sophie swept her hair from her face. 'Crap. I must have left it in the station.'

Paul sighed sympathetically. 'Looks like there's a new phone to add to that shopping list then.'

He obviously was made of money. Sophie didn't turn down the offer. She already felt lost without her phone.

'Do you want me to ring her?' Paul asked, just as Sophie was debating whether to ask to use his phone. 'It might save you some hassle if I speak to her.'

'Would you mind?' Sophie was actually grateful for the offer. Her mum would only text back, and then she'd be obliged to answer. She didn't really want to get into dialogue of any sort right now. Wasn't sure she would ever want to.

'No problem. It's probably a good idea to clear things with her before getting anything booked anyway. I have to go into town first thing tomorrow to see my bank manager. I was thinking of doing it then.' He smiled and crouched to help her collect up her stuff. 'Then, after everything's booked and I'm out of my meeting, how about we head off somewhere for the day? The weather's going to be mild, apparently. We might as well make the most of it.'

'Like where?' Sophie eyed him curiously.

'Your choice. Somewhere fun,' Paul suggested. 'It might help take your mind off your problems.'

Sophie thought about it. 'Blackpool,' she said. 'Maybe the theme park?'

'Okay. Sounds good.' Paul nodded, getting to his feet. 'But you might have to hold my hand.'

Sophie frowned at him.

'Scared of heights,' Paul explained, shrugging embarrassedly.

Sophie smiled, feeling more at ease with a man who would admit to his vulnerabilities. 'Don't worry, I'll look after you,' she said, checking her jeans and jacket pockets for her phone, just in case, though she knew it wasn't there. 'But don't you have work?'

'I'm on leave,' Paul said, offering her another reassuring smile. 'And I'm more than happy to devote my time to getting to know you. Shall we check out where you'll be sleeping?' he asked, reaching to pick up her bag.

CHAPTER THIRTY-ONE

ALICIA

Trembling from head to toe, Alicia stood under the freezing cold shower until her skin started to turn blue. It did nothing to numb the raw pain in her chest, the emptiness inside her where her babies had grown. A whole night she'd been gone. A whole *night*! Where was she?

Wiping away the tears, mingled with water, that were cascading down her face, she turned off the shower and climbed out, her body moving on autopilot; her mind on Sophie, imagining where she might be. In some dark, desolate place, as cold as she was? Her skin tinged blue? Wet and hungry, crying tears of anger and hurt, rather than fear and shame?

Please let her be safe. Clamping down hard on an image of her lying somewhere too lonely to contemplate, her body bruised and broken, Alicia clutched up a towel, pressed it hard to her face and suppressed a sob. She'd just heard someone pass on the landing. She hadn't been sure whether it was Jess or Justin, but she didn't want him to hear her. No doubt he'd think she deserved to cry on her own, but it would be another tug on his emotions, which were already in turmoil.

Staying where she was, she tried to think what to do, where to look. Sophie hadn't been in contact with any of her friends, other than Chloe. After that – nothing. It was as if she'd disappeared off the face of the earth.

Please don't let anything have happened to her.

Gulping hard, Alicia glanced upwards, praying that God might take pity on her for the sake of her daughter. Might Sophie call Justin, she wondered. If she couldn't – wouldn't – ring her, then surely, once she'd stopped to think, she would realise that Justin cared deeply. That whatever *she'd* done, he would never stop caring for her.

Contemplating sending her another text, her heart leapt into her mouth when her phone pinged on the shelf, echoing around the tiled walls of the bathroom. Not daring to hope, Alicia snatched it up and hastily read the message. And then reread it, her heart somersaulting in her chest.

I need to speak to you. I was going to call round, but I realise that might not be a good idea. I don't want to cause any upset, Alicia, I promise you. I just want to do what's best. Could we come to some arrangement perhaps?

Feeling her whole world shift, Alicia placed the phone back, staring at it as if it might bite her, and then scrambled, still damp, into her clothes. How had he got her number, she thought, as she pushed her feet into her flip-flops and squeaked open the bathroom door. She hadn't… he must have taken it from her phone, she realised, anger tightening inside her, which he'd so magnanimously returned to her, completely careless of the fact that he was walking into Justin's house uninvited. Squeezing her eyes closed, Alicia took a breath and hurried downstairs, moving silently so that Justin and Jessica, who were talking in the kitchen, didn't hear her.

She had to speak to Paul Radley. Whether or not she wanted to, she had no choice now. She couldn't have him coming anywhere near her. She had no idea how Justin might react if he did. Cold foreboding snaking the length of her spine, she eased the front door open, slipped out, walked away from the house, and then steeled herself and called him.

'Hi, Ali,' he answered on the fourth ring. 'I take it you got my text? I would have rung, but I guessed that might be a bit awkward.'

'Why are you doing this, Paul? What do you want?' Alicia snapped.

Paul avoided the question. 'Alicia, don't you think it might be an idea to discuss this face-to-face, rather than over the phone?' he said instead. 'Why don't we meet up and have a nice relaxed lunch, and then—'

'*Why*, Paul?' Alicia demanded.

Paul didn't answer immediately, then he said, 'Hold on a sec, I need to go somewhere more private.'

Alicia waited for what seemed like an eternity.

'Sorry,' he said, finally coming back on. 'I was in the foyer. There's still work going on in the building, workmen all over the place. I didn't want everyone overhearing our personal conversation.'

Alicia continued to wait silently. If he thought she was going to be drawn into actual conversation, he was wrong.

'I think we need to come to some arrangement, Alicia,' he said, obviously getting the message and getting to the point.

Her heart thudding, Alicia closed her eyes. 'What arrangement?' she asked him, attempting some level of calmness until she'd heard him out.

'A mutually agreeable one. I'm assuming you don't want Justin to know?'

Nausea churning her stomach, Alicia didn't answer.

'Look, Ali, I really don't want to cause any upset, especially to Sophie,' he went on – sounding concerned, Alicia noted with disbelief. 'I'm sure there's a satisfactory way forward that will suit us both.'

'Which would be?' Alicia asked, drawing in a tight breath and holding it.

'Like I say, I think it would be better if we discussed it face-to-face. How about I book a table at our favourite hotel? I could be there in, say, an hour? We could have something to eat and—'

'It won't work, Paul,' Alicia cut in evenly, determined not to give him the satisfaction of knowing how upset she was. 'He knows about what happened between us.'

Ending the call, she tried to still the palpitations in her chest. Unable to believe that he would do this, on top of all that they'd suffered, that Justin and Sophie had suffered, she stayed where she was for several minutes. The past had come back to haunt her. Almost in the blink of an eye, her life, and Justin's along with it, had unravelled. As if she'd made an arrangement with the Devil himself, she'd known deep down that one day it would. And it wouldn't stop here – Alicia could sense it. Paul Radley presumably didn't know that Justin was aware that Sophie might not be his. As far as he was concerned, he had one more ace up his sleeve. Would he try to use it? Would he cold-heartedly try to destroy her husband completely? She wouldn't let him. The twist in all of this was that Paul Radley knew she wouldn't.

CHAPTER THIRTY-TWO

ALICIA

Alicia watched Justin checking his texts, trying Sophie's mobile for the thousandth time that morning, pressing his fingers hard to his temples when he got no reply. Dragging in a long breath, he went back to staring out of the lounge window, undoubtedly seeing nothing but the same petrifying images she was.

Where was she? Why weren't the police doing anything? Why had they classed her as a low-risk case when, if she was out there on the streets, she was clearly at risk. It was *her* fault. All of it. She was the reason Sophie had left, the reason her husband couldn't look at her. Could hardly bring himself to speak to her. How could she ever have risked her child's future, her life, been naive enough to imagine that if she closed her eyes to it, it would all go away? She'd made bad decision after decision. She'd been so stupid and weak.

Justin would have no life without his children.

She glanced towards him from where she sat uselessly on the edge of the sofa. He hadn't slept, not a wink. Neither of them had even considered going to bed, watching the clock instead, endlessly pacing and hoping and praying. Jumping, physically, whenever a phone rang. When a floorboard had creaked overhead in the night, it was as a ghost had trodden lightly over their graves.

'Justin…' Tentatively, Alicia got to her feet and walked towards him. 'I'm sorry,' she murmured – a short, useless word that couldn't possibly convey the deep remorse that she felt.

Justin tensed, his broad shoulders stiffening. 'Don't, Alicia,' he said, after a second, his voice hoarse. 'Please don't. I can't deal with this right now. I just can't.'

'Please, talk to me,' she begged him. *Tell me to go if you want me to.* She couldn't bear the thought that she might be torturing him even further by being anywhere near him.

'About what?' Justin shrugged, his back still to her. 'What is there to say, Alicia? Luke's gone. Sophie's missing. Out there somewhere because of some *fucking*…' He stopped, breathing hard.

'Because of me. I *know*.' Alicia sobbed. 'I'd undo it if I could. I didn't mean for—'

'But you *can't*!' Justin turned towards her, his eyes smouldering with raw anger. 'You can't undo any of it! There's nothing to talk about, don't you *get* it? We have no past that I can contemplate even thinking about, let alone talking about. No future. There is *nothing* you can say that will make any of this—'

The ringing of his mobile cutting him short, Justin immediately answered it.

Alicia felt as if her heart might turn inside out as she watched him, praying it was news of Sophie.

Justin glanced at her. His disappointed expression told her it wasn't. 'Yes, thanks for calling back,' he said into his phone. 'I need to take some extended leave for personal reasons. Do you think you could organise someone to cover as clinical lead?… I'm not sure. Dr Paton, possibly?'

He waited, squeezing the bridge of his nose hard between his thumb and forefinger. 'Okay, thanks. Tell her to call me if she gets stuck on anything.' His frustration tangible as he ended the call, he glanced up at the ceiling.

'Justin, please believe that I never meant to hurt you,' Alicia tried cautiously, knowing how ludicrous it sounded even as she said it. Still, she had to try.

'Right.' Emitting a guttural laugh, Justin dropped his gaze. 'I need to go,' he said gruffly, turning suddenly to the hall.

'But where?' Panic gripping her afresh, Alicia followed him.

'To look for her,' Justin said, grabbing his jacket from the banister and heading for the front door. 'I can't just stand around here doing *nothing*, for Christ's sake.'

'Wait,' Alicia said, as he yanked open the front door. 'I'll come with you. Let me get my mobile and—'

'No,' Justin said adamantly. 'Not because...' He stopped, sighing heavily as he turned to her. 'It would probably be better if we split up,' he suggested, his eyes flicking briefly to hers. 'I'm going to be walking the streets, in the town centre, anywhere I can think of. You might do better to concentrate on local areas, places she might be known – café's, clubs she might have been to. And you could speak to her schoolfriends.'

Alicia glanced uncertainly away.

'It would look less suspect than a man hanging around the school. The police may have covered it, but...' Again, he stopped, making proper eye contact with her at last, albeit guardedly.

But they might not have. Alicia understood. And Sophie's schoolfriends might be more likely to talk to her mother than the police, particularly if they frequented the same clubs she and Justin both guessed Sophie snuck into. It made sense. She was sure he wouldn't want to be in her company, but he wasn't making a point. His thoughts were on Sophie's welfare. As she had known they would be.

Swallowing hard, Alicia nodded. 'Be careful,' she said, holding his gaze, wishing he could see inside her heart to understand how truly sorry she was.

CHAPTER THIRTY-THREE

SOPHIE

'It's Britain's highest rollercoaster,' Sophie said excitedly, her nerves tingling with anticipation as the car trundled to the top of the ride. 'Wow! Look at that!' Breathing in the crisp, salty air, she glanced out over the bird's-eye view of the seafront they had from almost sixty-five metres up. It had been raining when she and Chloe had come before, grey and gloomy, but today, with the sun bouncing like jewels off the water, the sight was spectacular. She was really glad she'd come now. She'd felt like crap when she'd finally woken up, woozy and headachy, having slept really heavily. She'd been sure she was coming down with the flu. Paul had said she'd feel better for a day out. He'd been right.

'You'll have to hold on tight.' Her adrenaline pumping, her chest now about to burst with anticipation, she turned to Paul as they reached the dizzying summit of the climb, from where they would hurtle back to earth, leaving their stomachs behind them. 'We're going to drop at, like, eighty miles an— Oh.'

Paul was holding on for grim death. She noted his white-knuckled grip, his eyes squeezed tight, his complexion, which was a sickly shade of green. *Shoot.* He really was scared of heights.

Sophie was about to try to reassure him when her breath was snatched from her mouth, her insides turning inside out as they plunged, rolled, twisted and spun.

'*Shit.*' She regurgitated her tonsils as they swooped to a stop, her heart thumping so manically she was sure it would leap right out of her chest. 'Are you all right?' She turned quickly to Paul, who was grappling to get out of his seat.

Scrambling out when the safety bars where released, Paul didn't answer, heading fast away from what had obviously been pure torture for him.

'Paul?' Sophie caught up with him where he'd stopped, clutching his thighs and taking deep breaths. 'Are you okay?'

'Yes,' Paul managed, and nodded.

'Are you sure? You look terrible. I didn't realise you were that scared. Do you want to go and find somewhere to sit—'

'I'm fine!' Paul snapped, causing Sophie to take a step back. He'd been really cool up until then, laughing and joking. He hadn't minded at all about getting soaked on the spooky water ride and he'd been fine on the Grand National. To Sophie, the ancient wooden rollercoaster, clunking and grinding, was way scarier than the ride on the Big One.

'Sorry,' he said quickly, straightening up and arranging his face into a smile. 'I felt a bit nauseous for a minute. I'm fine now,' he reassured her, placing an arm around her shoulders. 'Come on, let's go and do something tamer, where we can keep our feet on the ground.'

Sophie had quite fancied seeing the Tower, but maybe that wasn't such a great idea, given his phobia. 'Go-karting?' she suggested.

'And that's supposed to be tamer?' He arched an eyebrow.

'Oh, right.' Sophie guessed he probably wouldn't want to be whizzing around bends and stuff. 'The casino?' she ventured.

Paul didn't look impressed. 'I don't really approve of gambling, Sophie, sorry. How about the *Star Trek* exhibition?'

'Sounds good.' Sophie nodded. It wasn't exactly her first choice, but she supposed he was paying.

'Excellent.' Wrapping an arm around her shoulders, he gave her a smile and led her on. 'And then food,' he suggested. 'Hopefully, I'll have got my appetite back by then.'

Paul wasn't enthralled with the exhibition, Sophie gathered. It wasn't as exciting as she'd expected, but it was okay. She'd thought sitting in the captain's chair of the original Starship Enterprise was cool. Paul, though, didn't seem to rate it much.

'So what did you think?' Noting his pensive expression as they walked out, she tested the waters.

'Not worth the entrance fee, in my opinion,' Paul said. 'Considering how vast the *Star Trek* universe is supposed to be, the exhibition was extremely small, wasn't it? And I didn't see any evidence of the *Star Trek: Discovery* props as promised by the signage outside.'

He was obviously a Trekkie. Shrugging, she quickened her pace to keep up with him as he strode off.

'What do you fancy to eat?' he asked her, his smile back in place a second later.

Sophie plumped for chips. 'You have to have chips at the seaside.'

'Really?' Paul's smile dwindled. 'Well, it is your day out. Okay, chips it is.'

Five minutes later, his smile dwindled further as Sophie pointed out the pier-front burger and chips kiosk. 'I think I prefer to eat mine with a knife and fork,' he suggested, obviously not keen to eat his chips walking along the seafront, which Sophie had quite fancied. There was nothing quite like eating chips drenched in salt and vinegar straight from the paper, as far as she was concerned.

Noting his unenthusiastic expression, she shrugged easily. 'Okay,' she said. They'd probably come in a cone anyway, and that wasn't quite the same.

'How about here then?' she asked, pointing out a Burger King a few minutes later.

Again, Paul didn't look that taken with the idea. Sophie was beginning to wonder whether he even wanted chips.

'Kentucky?' she tried, another few shops on.

Paul looked no better impressed. 'What about over there?' He nodded across the road. 'It looks a bit more salubrious, don't you think?'

Sophie didn't quite get why eating chips had to be done salubriously, but the curiosity coffee shop he was indicating looked kind of cute, and now at the point where her belly was thinking her throat had been cut, she'd go for anywhere that served food.

Grabbing a window seat, Sophie perused the menu hungrily, though she'd already chosen her order from the board behind the counter. Veggie burger and chips – had to be. She was practically fantasising chips now. 'Done,' she said, handing the menu to Paul with a smile. 'What do you fancy?'

Paul frowned. 'A clean table,' he said, wiping two fingers along the surface of it, examining them and then sighing audibly. Taking the menu with a shake of his head, he scanned it leisurely, finally deciding on beef stroganoff.

Sophie wrinkled her nose. 'I don't know how people eat meat,' she said. 'I mean, I wouldn't judge anybody, but personally, I couldn't eat another living creature if my life depended on it.'

'It's dead, Sophie,' Paul pointed out, his smile a bit short this time. 'And I doubt many carnivorous animals would give you the same consideration if the situation were reversed.'

Oops. Sophie reprimanded herself. He probably thought she was criticising him. 'I know. It's just a personal choice and, like I say, live and let live. Or rather, eat and let eat.' She shrugged and gave him a bright smile.

Paul's smile was more relaxed then. 'I'll order,' he said. 'Why don't you go and wash your hands.'

Sophie followed his gaze as he nodded towards the loos, and then looked back at him, perplexed. She didn't need to go to the… Ah. She got the gist as he turned to summon one of the waiting staff. He meant *actually* wash her hands. A bit fastidious, wasn't he? She knitted her brow. But then, she supposed she had been hanging on to rides where a million other sweaty hands had been clinging on for dear life.

Fair enough. Hoping the food wouldn't be long, she humoured him.

Her hope faded when she came back to see a coachload of old-age pensioners coming in. Looked like the service was going to be slow. Sighing inwardly, Sophie took her seat and tried to ignore her rumbling tummy. 'So, what do you do in Dubai?' she asked him, distracting Paul from checking his watch.

'Investment advice,' he said. 'All a bit dull really, unless you're into financial planning.'

Sophie tried not to look too bored. 'Do you mind if I ask you when you lost your family?' she ventured.

Paul looked down at that. 'It's a bit painful, to be honest,' he said. 'Maybe another time. We don't want to spoil the day, do we? Tell me about yourself. What do you want to do when you leave school?'

'Veterinary surgeon,' Sophie answered straight off. 'I was hoping to do my undergraduate course at the Royal Veterinary College, but I'm thinking that might depend on whether I can get a student loan now.'

Paul eyed her interestedly. 'Oh, how so?'

'Stuff,' Sophie sighed. 'You know, at home.'

'Ah, I see. I wouldn't worry too much about that, Sophie. I can cover your study costs,' Paul said, smiling benevolently.

Sophie's eyes grew wide. 'Really?'

'I'd have to run it by your mother first, but yes, I don't see why not. I'm supposed to be looking out for you, aren't I?'

'Well, yes, but…' Her uni fees? *Wow*. How cool would it be to have those covered?

'Unless you want to have a word with your mother, that is?' Paul asked.

'No.' Uh-uh. She absolutely did not want to have a word with her mother. Not any words, any time soon. But what about Justin? How would he feel?

She was debating whether to broach the subject with Paul when she noticed he was checking his watch again and looking agitatedly around for signs of their food.

Justin would feel relieved, Sophie guessed, turning to gaze out of the window. He wouldn't want the responsibility now, would he? He'd hardly want to pay out thousands of pounds for someone who wasn't his daughter. It might have been different if he'd known she wasn't his from the outset. He would have had a choice then. Who knows, he might have decided he wanted to be her father. Her mum had taken that away from him, though, hadn't she? She should seriously consider Paul's offer, she decided. Show them that the choices about her life weren't theirs to make.

Paul was growing more agitated, she realised. He was rearranging the cutlery on the table, lining up knives and forks and condiments and then checking his watch again. Finally, breathing in a tight breath, he gestured a beleaguered looking waitress over. 'Is there any chance of actually getting served today?' he asked her irritably. 'We have a long journey home.'

The girl, not much older than Sophie, a student probably, looked flustered, and offered to go and hurry it up.

Five minutes later, smiling apologetically, she placed their meals in front of them.

Sophie had started ravenously on her chips when Paul plonked his knife and fork down, clinking his plate as he did. 'Waitress,' he called – loudly. 'This is lukewarm, undercooked and, frankly, inedible.'

Sophie shifted uncomfortably as the now embarrassed girl retrieved his plate and scuttled back towards the kitchen.

'Sorry about that,' Paul said, his smile back again as he wiped his mouth on his napkin, folded it up and looked in Sophie's direction. 'I hope it didn't spoil your meal.'

'No,' Sophie assured him. Hers had been fine. She was about to suggest he maybe should have had chips after all, but then thought better of it.

'Good,' he said, reaching for the hand in which she was still holding her fork and giving it a squeeze. 'I'd hate my daughter to be disappointed on her special day out.'

CHAPTER THIRTY-FOUR

JESSICA

Having had no news of Sophie all day, Jessica considered it the least she could do to help Alicia hand out leaflets that evening. It was freezing cold though. She wished she'd put her thicker coat on.

Shivering in a sudden deluge of rain, she glanced towards Alicia, and then, sensing trouble, sprang after her. Obviously despairing of people either declining to take the leaflet or else accepting it with barely a glance, Alicia had got it into her head to chase after a commuter from the rush hour train, which was possibly a bad idea.

'You could at least have looked at it!' Alicia yelled at the man, as Jess reached her, catching her by the arm. 'It's my daughter! She's *missing*!'

'Come on, sweetheart.' Jessica urged her away. People were beginning to stare. There was no point in shouting at random strangers. That wouldn't bring her daughter back. Jessica swallowed back a knot of guilt in her chest. It wasn't her fault she'd gone, of course – this was Alicia's own doing – but Jessica wished she'd warned Justin that Sophie had heard them talking. Sophie might not have wanted to discuss it, but it might have given him a chance to try and initiate a conversation with her. Justin would never get over the heartbreak if anything happened to her. Never.

Walking shakily back with her, Alicia stopped, crouching to fish the leaflet from the puddle it had landed in when the man had tossed it aside. Then she dropped her head to her knees and let out a wretched sob.

Jessica joined her, as people rushing homewards skirted around them. Taking the leaflet from her, her heart wrenched for her sister as she noticed the print had smudged, causing a black track to wend its way down Sophie's cheek. No wonder she was upset. Whatever she'd done, Jessica wouldn't wish this on her. 'We'll get some laminated posters made up,' she suggested, slipping an arm around her and helping her to her feet. 'I can get them done at work.'

'Thanks, Jess.' Alicia nodded tearfully. 'I have no idea what I would have done without you. Gone mad, probably.'

'Madder, you mean?' Jessica smiled, hoping to coax Alicia into doing the same. 'You're soaked.' Jessica squeezed her sister close and attempted to rub some warmth into her as they walked. 'Let's go and have a hot drink,' she suggested, nodding towards a McDonald's. 'And then, when we've warmed up a bit, we'll come back and hit the pub crowds. How does that sound?'

Tugging in a shuddery breath, Alicia nodded more determinedly.

'That's better,' Jessica said, squeezing her tighter. 'You have to hold it together, Ali, for Sophie's sake.'

'I know. I'm trying, but…' Another fat tear spilling down her cheek, Alicia brushed it away. 'I'm sorry, Jess. I just feel so bloody *raw* inside. So empty.'

'You're bound to.' Jess sighed understandingly, leading the way into McDonald's and steering her disorientated sister towards a seat.

'Not here.' Alicia stopped short. 'Do you mind if we grab a seat at the window?' She nodded towards the high stools and headed towards them. 'I can watch people passing by then.'

In hopes that Sophie walked past, Jessica realised, glad that Alicia did still seem to be functioning and thinking, albeit sluggishly. She didn't want her having a breakdown. Justin would be bound to be sympathetic – it was in his nature – but it wouldn't do him any good.

'I'll go and grab us a drink. Won't be a second,' she said, leaving her leaflets and coat with Alicia, but taking her phone with her. Having Alicia privy to all her calls out of work hours, she'd found, was a touch awkward.

Coming back with toasted bagels and two hot chocolates, she noticed Alicia was staring vacantly into the distance. Not much people-watching going on here then.

'I'm so relieved Justin's keeping me updated on where he is,' Alicia said, as Jessica deposited the tray and hitched herself up next to her.

'He said he would, didn't he? He's always been dependable, Ali.'

Alicia looked immediately guilty. 'He must absolutely hate me.'

'He doesn't hate you.' Jessica reached to squeeze her hand. 'He's not going to recover from this easily, but I don't think he hates you.'

Alicia didn't look very reassured by that, but she could hardly tell her he'd forgive her and that they'd walk off into the sunset together. That was highly unlikely. The man's whole world had collapsed around him.

'Eat something,' she said, pushing the bagel towards her. 'It'll make you feel better.'

Alicia shook her head. 'Sorry, Jess, I really don't have any appetite.'

'You have to eat, Ali.' Jess looked her over-worriedly. 'You'll be no use to anyone if you make yourself ill.'

Alicia gave her a small smile. 'I will. Later.'

Jessica wasn't convinced. 'Have you tried to talk to him?' she asked, wondering what explanations Alicia might have offered Justin – not that she imagined Justin would be receptive to anything she had to say, if his reaction to her attempts to apologise to him yesterday were anything to judge by.

Alicia placed the hot chocolate back down. She'd barely taken a sip. 'There's nothing I can say that will detract from the fact that I deceived him, Jess – horribly. I lied to him. He's not likely to want to listen, is he?'

'No,' Jessica started, with a sigh, 'but—' She stopped as Alicia's phone rang, causing Alicia to jump.

Scrambling to retrieve it from her bag, her face hopeful, she checked the number. 'It's Paul,' she said, debating for a second and then answering it.

Jessica had guessed as much from her expression. She was only surprised Alicia was taking the call. She picked at her bagel and tried to listen without making it too obvious.

'What do you want, Paul?' Alicia asked him. 'Why do you keep ringing me?'

She listened for a second. 'But I don't want to see you,' she said adamantly. 'Or talk to you. If you have anything to say, then I suggest you say it through a solicitor.' And with that, she ended the call.

A solicitor? Oh dear, it looked as if Paul was intent on laying some claim to Sophie then. God, how dreadful. Jessica certainly hoped she was going to tell Justin about that.

CHAPTER THIRTY-FIVE

SOPHIE

'Sorry about that,' Paul said, coming back into the lounge area, having gone to his study to make an urgent phone call. 'Business, I'm afraid. An irate client. Clearly, he thinks I'm available even when I'm on leave. Some people never cease to amaze me.'

Shaking his head, he walked across to the drinks table, dropping his phone on the coffee table as he went, Sophie noted.

'Wine?' he asked her, waving a glass in her direction.

'No, thanks.' Sophie smiled. 'I think I've still got a hangover from last night.'

'I doubt that. You only had two small glasses. It's probably motion sickness from the rollercoasters. Maybe later, yes?'

'Yeah, maybe.' Sophie thought not. She'd thought she must have been coming down with something last night, but the wine, which she hardly ever drank, had made her feel so woozy, it had been all she could do to undress and crawl into bed. And then she'd had some really weird dreams. 'Do you mind if I watch some TV?' She nodded towards the telly.

'Help yourself,' Paul said, glugging back a red wine and topping up his glass. 'There's Netflix on there, if you fancy selecting us a film for later. I'm just going to take a quick shower and then how about I cook us a proper meal? You haven't tasted anything until you've tasted my creamy mushroom linguini.'

'I'm impressed,' Sophie said, flashing him another smile as she located the remote and seated herself on the sofa. 'I don't know my cannelloni from my spaghetti.'

Paul looked pleased at that. 'It's perfect with parmesan,' he said, pulling off his trainers, and placing them by the front door. 'And garlic bread, of course.'

'Can't have pasta without garlic bread,' Sophie concurred, watching him over her shoulder.

'A girl after my own heart,' Paul said, stepping away from the trainers then cocking his head to one side and surveying them. He stepped back again to arrange them just so.

'Won't be long,' he said, walking between her and the TV.

He straightened the magazines on the table and the cushions as he went, Sophie noticed, knitting her brow; one cushion, in particular, required much realigning, and he then stood back and studied it as if it were a piece of art or something. He was obviously a perfectionist. She'd have to remind herself not to leave her crap all over the place, but that was no big price to pay for crashing here for a while. It was a hell of a better option than a caravan in Herefordshire, assuming Holly had been able to swing it. She doubted she would have been able to stay there for long, in any case, and her job options would have been far fewer than in Brum. Here would do nicely, until she could find a place of her own, and if her mum didn't like it, that was tough after treating her with nil respect. It would certainly show her that she was perfectly capable of managing without her *or* Justin, and the shit they'd dumped on her because they thought they had a right to.

'Help yourself to anything you need,' Paul said. 'There's Coke in the fridge if you don't fancy anything stronger yet.'

'Will do. Thanks,' Sophie called, noting him refilling up his glass as he headed for the bedroom area. He drank a lot. Again, not a big deal. It's not like it was whisky he was knocking back, and he was okay – good fun, bar the perfectionist thing. Sophie could live with that. She'd survived a lot worse lately.

She hadn't asked him about the new phone. She'd thought that might be pushing her luck after all the money he'd spent on her and his offering to pay her uni fees. She was still slightly gobsmacked about that. But then, he was her father and he wouldn't have offered unless he'd wanted to.

She eyed his phone on the coffee table, wondering whether she should maybe send her mum a text, just to let her know she was okay. On the other hand, she'd never given a stuff about her feelings, had she? Her deliberations were cut short as Paul reappeared, heading swiftly across to the table to sweep the phone up.

'Forgot to mention something to the client who thinks I've got nothing better to do,' he said, glancing despairingly up at the ceiling. 'Work – I swear I'm thinking about it 24/7. Selected that film yet?'

'Not yet, no,' Sophie said, flicking through the list. 'How about *10 Cloverfield Lane* or *American Psycho*?'

Paul looked doubtful. 'Aren't they 18s?'

Sophie swung her gaze towards him. Was he serious?

'Don't look so alarmed, Sophie.' He laughed, obviously noting the look. 'I'd hardly allow you wine and then censor your TV viewing. In any case, *Cloverfield Lane*'s a twelve, I think.'

Sophie blew out a sigh of relief. 'You're bit of a Netflix geek then?'

'I watch a lot of TV, yes,' he said, smiling sadly. 'I tend to have a lot of time on my hands, without the woman I love.'

Oh, shit. Raw nerve. 'Sorry,' she said. 'I imagine that's really hard.'

'It is.' Drawing in a long breath, he glanced down.

'So, which one?' Sophie asked, guessing he didn't want to go there.

Paul thought about it, a not very enthusiastic look on his face. 'I don't really like psycho stuff, to be honest,' he said, reaching to relieve her of the control and flicking through the genres. 'How about we compromise and watch *Once Upon a Time in Venice*?

John Goodman stars in that, too, and Bruce Willis. It's supposed to be pretty good.'

Sophie had quite fancied *10 Cloverfield Lane*, but she could compromise. That's what being an adult was supposed to be all about, after all. 'Sounds good.' She nodded, feeling pleased when his smile brightened.

'Five minutes,' he said, heading jauntily off to the bathroom. 'And then I'll get that pasta on.'

'Food is served, Madame,' Paul called from the dining area an hour later.

'Cool,' Sophie said, flicking off the TV and going to where Paul was placing the plates down. Blimey, he really did things in style, she thought, noting the fancily folded napkins and what she supposed were crystal glasses on the long chrome and glass table.

'I feel like the Queen,' she said, as he took the tea towel from his arm, dusted her seat with it, and then pulled the chair out for her.

'Nothing but the best for my daughter,' he said, tucking her in and going around to pluck up her napkin, flick it with a flourish and place it on her lap.

'I thought an unoaked Chardonnay to complement the meal,' he said, topping up her already half-filled glass. 'I find the earthy flavours from mushrooms can leave mild wines tasting like water,' he added knowledgeably, placing the bottle down and taking his seat at the other end of the table.

Sophie looked warily from her glass to him. 'I'm not sure I should,' she said uncertainly.

'You can't have creamy mushroom linguini without a good white wine,' Paul said, nodding at her glass as he took a mouthful of his food. 'Sip it. I promise you'll appreciate it. Don't worry, I'll keep an eye on your intake.'

Just the one wouldn't hurt, Sophie supposed. And now he'd poured it… Picking up the glass, she took a sip and squeezed her eyes closed as the fruity, acidy flavour hit the back of her throat. *Wow*, that was seriously strong.

'Well?' he asked, clearly interested in her view.

'Excellent,' Sophie said, not entirely sure whether it was. 'It's kind of…' She had a think, not wishing to sound like an ignoramus. 'Sharp and crisp, and fruity.'

'You obviously have a nose,' Paul said, leaving Sophie perplexed. 'You'll probably notice there's no buttery vanilla taste. Some people call it the naked wine.'

Now Sophie was definitely perplexed, but he clearly knew his stuff. Obviously, he had lived the high life, which was fair enough, since he'd earned it. Plus, he'd had a shitload of tragedy on the personal front, problems even worse than hers, and he was getting on with his life. And *that*, Sophie decided, picking up her glass and taking a larger swig, was exactly what she intended to do. 'Cheers,' she said, nodding him a toast.

Paul did likewise. 'Eat up,' he said, indicating her meal with his fork. 'Don't want all the chef's hard work going to waste, do we?'

Grabbing her fork, Sophie dug in, swirling the linguini around and taking a huge mouthful. 'Do you think I should ring Mum?' she asked conversationally between chews. 'Just to let her know I'm all right?'

'Probably a good idea,' Paul said, taking another sip of his wine. 'Maybe not tonight though. Don't want to ruin our film night, do we?'

'No.' Sophie slowed her chewing, knitting her brow as a realisation began to dawn.

'I've spoken to her anyway. She's fine with you being here, as long as you want to be.'

Sophie stopped chewing, grabbed up her wine, took a huge gulp and swallowed hard. It had meat in it. She'd just swallowed part of a pig. *Shit.* What did she do? She felt sweat prickle her forehead. She couldn't not eat it, not after all his careful preparation.

Reaching for her glass, she took another drink, feeling definitely nauseous as she did.

'All right, Sophie?' Paul eyed her curiously over his glass.

'Yes,' Sophie said quickly, looking down at her plate, and then, seeing the small chunks of ham there, feeling dangerously close to actually being sick. 'I, um… 'Scuse me,' she said, scraping her chair back. 'I feel a bit…'

Getting to her feet, Sophie turned for the bathroom, and found herself groping for the walls as the room shifted worryingly off-kilter.

'Sophie?' Paul was behind her, sounding alarmed.

'Sorry,' she mumbled, her head reeling, her stomach churning. 'I'm not feeling very well. I…' Trailing off, she stumbled forwards, and the walls tilted. Attempting to stay upright, the room now revolving steadily, like a merry-go-round on slow spin, Sophie tried another step, but her limbs felt heavy, sluggish.

'Sophie!' Paul caught her as her legs gave way like butter beneath her.

'I thought you were coming down with something.' Her eyes shut tight, Sophie heard him as he swept her up into his arms and carried her towards the bedroom. 'You probably have a vitamin deficiency. You really should be eating meat, you know.'

CHAPTER THIRTY-SIX

JUSTIN

A whole week he'd been searching. Seven dark, grey days and cold nights. Tonight, it was raining. Icy, slashing rain, which seemed to be seeping into his bones.

Debating whether to ring Alicia again, Justin decided against. He had no news, and with each passing day, that was definitely bad news. Alicia had promised to ring him the minute she heard anything from Taylor, which might be never. The police had had no sightings of Sophie, though that didn't surprise Justin. She was obviously going to stay a low-priority case. Bitterness, like corrosive acid, rose painfully in his chest.

Alicia was out there too, handing out leaflets, visiting the various places they'd discussed, talking to kids at the school. Endlessly searching faces in the street. Justin had no doubt she would be doing that. He wished he could talk to her properly, communicate on anything but the most basic level. The fact was, though, he simply couldn't talk about anything that touched on who they were before. Who he'd thought they were. Couldn't bear to allow his mind to think about the future they didn't have. He needed to stay focussed on finding Sophie. It was the only way he knew how to get through each day.

Concentrating his efforts, Justin walked on through the city streets, counting paving stones as he went, which at least occupied his mind if it did nothing to help calm him. Sleep might help, but that only ever came now to haunt him. Reaching the area he'd been heading for, where young and old slept rough in the city centre, Justin pulled out his photo of Sophie, showing it to a few people, getting no information. Then stopped, his chest constricting as he noticed a young girl around Sophie's age.

She was a drug user. Justin noted the paraphernalia around her but didn't judge her. One week observing the people here had altered his thinking. These kids were hooked. And once they were, it seemed there was rarely any going back. No going forward either, becoming the people they could be. They were stuck – slaves to their addiction. It was a lesson well learned in regard to the drug users who came into accident and emergency.

Seemingly oblivious to him as he walked towards her, the girl concentrated on her endeavours. Her head shot up as he stopped directly in front of her, her expression one of alarm.

'Sorry,' Justin said quickly. 'I didn't mean to scare you.'

'Are you after my stuff?' she asked, a panicky look in her eyes.

'No,' he assured her. 'I'm looking for my daughter. I wondered whether—'

'Haven't seen her,' she said immediately.

Justin sighed and massaged his forehead. 'I haven't shown you her photo yet.'

She shrugged and continued with her task, drawing her brew up into a syringe and flicking the needle. A long-term user then, Justin surmised, a knot of anger tightening his stomach. No matter how much he counted, he couldn't seem to reach a point where his emotions weren't pivoting between fury, fatigue, fear and despair.

'Do you mind if I sit?' he asked her.

She looked up again, seeming to measure him. 'Not if you don't,' she said chirpily.

She was pretty. Unusual coloured eyes, somewhere between hazel and green – pupils constricted, meaning she was possibly a heroin user. Lowering himself down beside her, Justin felt his heart constrict. Seeing the eyebrow stud, in the same place as Sophie's, he looked away, trying hard not to see his daughter sitting in the same place as this young girl. If she was still alive. He clamped down hard on that thought.

'Is she missing?' she asked him. 'Your daughter?'

Justin nodded wearily and dragged a hand over his neck.

'So why did she split?'

'We had some problems. Her mother and me. We argued. Things were said. Things that Sophie overheard. Things she shouldn't have.' Justin paused, his gut aching, tears too damn close, he realised, gulping back a lump in his throat. 'Do you ever wish you could turn the clock back?' he asked her.

'Every day,' she assured him, with a wry smile.

'I should go,' Justin said, attempting to compose himself.

'Do you have that photo?' she asked, as he got to his feet.

Relieved she was prepared to at least look at it, Justin pulled it from his inside pocket and handed it to her.

She scanned it, then looked back at him. 'I think I might have seen her,' she said, her brow furrowed thoughtfully. 'About a week ago, hanging around New Street Station. I remember thinking she shouldn't be. She didn't get on a train though.'

'Oh?' Justin said, his heart rate spiking.

'She left with some bloke, eventually.'

Fuck. Justin swallowed hard. 'Can you remember what he looked like?' he asked, hoping against hope that she might.

'Not really. An older bloke, quite tall, dark. They left eating chips together, so I figured she must know him.'

'Do you remember what clothes he was wearing?' Justin tried to keep the desperation from his voice.

She shook her head. 'Jeans and trainers. I can't remember what jacket. They were clean though. He'd didn't look like a deadbeat.'

Tall, dark; wearing jeans and trainers. Justin sighed inwardly. She could be describing half the male population.

CHAPTER THIRTY-SEVEN

SOPHIE

Sophie awoke with absolutely no recollection of where she was. Panic slicing through her, she pulled herself to sitting position, squinted hard against the thin, wintry sunlight filtering through the blinds and then glanced hurriedly around. *Paul's.* Closing her eyes, she breathed a sigh of relief. She was at Paul's apartment, in his guest room, though how she'd got here from the lounge, she hadn't the slightest clue. No, not the lounge, the dining table. Sifting through her dysfunctional memory, she eased her legs over the edge of the bed and felt immediately woozy. A dull throb, like a band slowly tightening, pounded at the base of her skull. She massaged her neck, trying to recall anything beyond taking her seat at the table, but the images were grey and wispy.

Shit! He must have put her to bed. She certainly didn't remember getting into it herself. Glancing quickly down at her attire, she emitted a huge sigh of relief, and then jumped to her feet as there was a tap on the door, only to end up plopping heavily back down again. 'Yes,' she called croakily. God, her throat felt like sandpaper. What the hell was the matter with her?

'Are you decent?' Paul called, pushing the door open a fraction.

'Uh-huh,' Sophie said, guessing she was decent enough for his eyes, being dressed, though had no clue what she must look like. Had she been sick? She'd definitely caught a whiff.

'Morning – or rather, afternoon.' Paul smiled as he came in, bearing a tray. 'Are we feeling a bit better?'

'Ugh, no, I feel awful,' Sophie said miserably, blinking against the light that flooded in from the lounge. 'What happened?'

'At a guess, the flu bug going around happened. It's a nasty one, apparently.'

He could say that again. 'Did I pass out?' she asked, guessing she must have.

'You don't remember the doctor coming?' Paul placed the tray on the dressing table and turned to her, surprised.

'Doctor?' Sophie's eyes boggled. 'No.' She shook her head, bewildered. She was obviously sicker than she thought she was.

'You were running a fever,' Paul said. 'She gave you a shot.'

A shot?

'Just something to bring your temperature down,' Paul said, as her eyes drifted to the small pinprick on her arm. 'She said to call her again, if you got worse, but I'm guessing you must be slightly improved, since you're back with us. You had me really worried there, I can tell you. I must have checked on you at least ten times in the night.'

Oh. 'Thanks,' Sophie said weakly, feeling grateful and guilty. 'Sorry for all the trouble I seem to be causing.'

'It's no trouble,' Paul assured her. 'I think you might need to take her advice though.'

'Which is?' Sophie asked, wondering whether she could make it to the bathroom. She seriously needed to shower.

'She's in agreement with me about you possibly being lacking in essential vitamins and minerals. If you really can't face eating meat, and I'm guessing you can't, you need to supplement your diet. I've bought you some vitamin pills. I've left a couple on the tray.' He nodded towards it. 'There's scrambled eggs there, if you're up to it. And then I'm thinking you might want to get changed.'

'Thanks,' Sophie said again, feeling still puzzled. He must have remembered she didn't eat meat if he'd discussed it with the doctor, so why had he put meat in the meal? She shrugged it off. He must have forgotten, and then been reminded when she'd thrown up.

'Like I say, no trouble. You can't help being ill, can you? I've rung your mum, by the way. She sends her best.'

Her best? She passes out and her mother sends her best? *Cheers, Mum.* At least she was finding out how wanted she really was now. The cow was probably out there having a ball. Shagging the latest boyfriend and test-riding a few more from Tinder.

Sophie shrugged. As far as she was concerned, she and Justin were well shot of Alicia. Her eyes suddenly filling up, Sophie hurriedly wiped her nose.

'I'll come in and strip the bed while you're in the bathroom,' Paul said, heading for the door.

'Strip it?' That was a bit OTT, wasn't it? She wasn't that niffy.

'Mascara.' Paul turned, nodding past her to the pillow, upon which, Sophie realised, were several tell-tale black patches. 'You might want to not bother with it while you're ill.'

'Oops. Sorry,' she said, wiping a hand under her nose again.

'Oh, and Sophie?'

She looked sheepishly back at him.

'Use a tissue to blow your nose, yes? There's a box on the bedside table.'

'Oh, right.' Sophie plucked one and fiddled with it. She didn't actually want to blow her nose.

'Your bag's over by the window,' he reminded her. 'I'll leave you to it. Shout when you're ready and I'll give you a hand to the bathroom.'

'Okay, thanks,' Sophie said, as he went out. 'Oh, where are my boots?' she called, assuming he'd taken them off last night.

'You were sick on them.' Paul poked his head back around the door and gave her a sympathetic smile. 'Looks like we'll have to get you a new pair, when you're up to it.'

Crap. Sophie's heart sank. She found a use for the tissue after all, dabbing at the tears that sprang from her eyes, despite herself. She shouldn't feel bereaved over a bloody pair of boots, but those were her new Red or Dead boots. More importantly, Justin had gone with her to buy them the week before their world had been blown apart. It shouldn't matter. But it did.

Testing the floor with her feet, Sophie heaved herself up, feeling in need of Luke's little pink elephant toy, the only link to her past and something she had made sure to bring with her.

Wobbling as she went, she dropped to her knees and delved into her bag, and then delved deeper. It wasn't there! She did the whole pulling-stuff-out thing all over again. She'd had it here. She was sure she had. Hadn't she? And now it wasn't here.

She'd lost it. The one thing she'd wanted to keep above everything else.

'I'm so sorry, Luke,' she whispered, tears spilling down her cheeks. 'So sorry.' She was sure she could hear his happy little gurgles above the distant rumble of traffic, that she would see her beautiful baby brother again soon. She missed him so much. Sometimes, she would close her eyes, sure that when she opened them, he would be here. Sophie's heart twisted inside her as she remembered Luke's flailing little arms, his squeals of delight as she laughed and cooed at him and pressed his pink elephant to his cute button nose, the way his true baby-blue eyes would grow wide with excitement when they alighted on her coming into his nursery.

She'd been sure she could do this, survive on her own. She had no choice but to.

But now, her chest felt so tight she could hardly breathe.

CHAPTER THIRTY-EIGHT

ALICIA

'Paul again?' Jessica asked, obviously noting Alicia's wary expression as she checked her incoming call.

Alicia nodded, her heart, already heavy with guilt and confusion, plummeting like a lead weight in her chest.

'Persistent, isn't he?' Jessica gave her an unimpressed look. 'Are you going to answer it?' she asked, turning to fill up the kettle.

She had no choice but to, Alicia realised. However much she told him she didn't want to speak to him, have anything to do with him unless through legal channels, he just wouldn't stop. *Why?* What could he possibly hope to gain? He didn't want to suddenly take an interest in Sophie. He hadn't even enquired after her, for God's sake. And if, by the remotest, most unbelievable chance, he did want to figure things out with Sophie, then surely he must realise that this way wasn't going to achieve anything.

Hesitating for a second, Alicia steeled herself and took the call.

'Why are you doing this, Paul? Why are you harassing me?' she said, before he could speak.

'Harassing?' Paul laughed, incredulous. 'I'm not harassing you, Alicia. I'm simply trying to have a civil conversation with you about my daughter. Surely you have to concede you owe me that much?'

His daughter? Hearing him speak the words, laying claim to her as if she *was* his, not even caring enough to ask how Sophie might feel, how she might be, *where* she might be, Alicia swallowed back her contempt. *She's not here!* She wanted to scream at it him. *She's not here – because of you!* She would never let him near her. Never.

'Look, Alicia, I just want to see you.' He sighed heavily. 'I don't want to cause you more heartache. That's the last thing I would ever want to do. I just want to talk, that's all, one-to-one, not over the phone. We can sort this out, surely? I'm not an unreasonable man.'

Didn't want to cause her more heartache? Alicia could hardly breathe.

'You said your husband knows about us,' Paul went on.

Alicia didn't answer. How could she, without playing into his hands?

'Does he know there's a possibility Sophie might not be his?'

Alicia gripped her phone hard, praying this conversation wasn't heading where she thought it might be.

'Look, all I want to do is to see you and to talk, Alicia. That's not too much to ask, is it? We had something good once. We shouldn't be pulling each other apart. We can work together on this, can't we?'

'I don't want to see you, Paul,' Alicia repeated forcefully. 'There are no circumstances under which I want to meet you, don't you see? I love my husband.'

Paul went quiet.

Alicia waited. He was still there. She could hear him breathing.

'I think you might want to see me, Alicia,' he said, eventually, 'given the results of the paternity test.'

Oh God, no. Alicia closed her eyes, feeling sick and claustrophobic, the noise of the kettle boiling and the clink of the cups behind her grating on her nerves, as the room closed in on her.

'I don't want to cause any upset, Alicia, I promise you. I just want to do what's best,' Paul continued, sounding quite calm. Kind, almost. Reasonable.

Feeling as if she might be going slowly insane, Alicia scrambled feverishly through her muddled recollections. He couldn't have. How could he have, unless… Had he been in touch with Sophie?

'How?' she asked him, her mouth dry, her throat parched. 'How did you get a test done? You'd need to have something of hers.' *A toothbrush? A strand of her hair?* She tried to think, hoping that he was lying. Yet, there was a part of her that was desperately hopeful that he might have seen her in the past week.

'Her hairbrush,' Paul supplied, killing all hope Alicia might have had dead. 'When I was at the house.'

After they'd been burgled? When they'd just laid Lucas to rest?

'You left me no choice, Alicia. I have a right to know. I think your husband has a right to know, too, don't you?' Paul said, as if anything could excuse the vileness of his actions. 'I'll leave it with you. I really do think we need to meet though, don't you? For Sophie's sake.'

Realising he'd ended the call, Alicia felt her blood run cold. What did he mean? A hard kernel of apprehension knotted inside her.

'Not a good outcome then?' Jessica enquired, glancing at her worriedly as she carried the tea to the table.

'No. Struggling to draw air past the lump in her throat, Alicia shook her head wretchedly. 'He claims to have had a paternity test,' she murmured, her mind still reeling, her heart plummeting to the depths of her soul. 'He's calling her his daughter,'

'Oh my God!' Jessica stared at her, aghast. 'You have to tell Justin, Alicia. He needs to know.'

CHAPTER THIRTY-NINE

ALICIA

Coming into work had been a bad idea. If not for the little girl on her caseload who'd rung in claiming her father had deliberately burned her, she wouldn't have. How could the mother have blamed the child, she wondered, bewilderedly. How could she have demanded that the child be removed from the family home, rather than the father, even after the hospital had concluded the injuries were non-accidental? Looking away from the manager who was heading the team meeting, Alicia swiped away a tear.

She couldn't do this any more, she realised. How could she hope to remain detached, to try to hold families together – which had been her naive reason for wanting to do this in the first place – when she'd been responsible for tearing her own family apart? When her own daughter was missing? She'd often felt upset after the type of visit she'd had today, but this time she'd been devastated. She'd rushed straight from her car to the toilets, where she'd locked herself in a cubicle and sobbed her heart out.

She wasn't any help to anyone like this, least of all the children. They needed someone who was level-headed, and strong enough to fight back for them.

Lost in her thoughts, her heart leapt in her chest when her phone buzzed. Justin, she realised, her pulse racing – though in a very different way to how it always had whenever he'd texted her before. Grabbing up her bag, she mouthed an apology to the manager and hurried towards the office exit, collecting her coat as she went.

Clutching her coat around her against the cutting wind, her thoughts immediately going to Sophie and how cold she might be, Alicia made her way to where Justin had said he'd parked and scoured the road, left and right. It was only when he flashed his lights that she remembered he wasn't driving his own car any more, which had been written off the day their baby boy had died.

A crushing wave of grief washing over her, Alicia closed her eyes, working hard to compose herself before heading towards him. She felt as if she were hanging on by her fingernails, but she couldn't let go in front of him. She knew that would only compromise him into offering her comfort he couldn't possibly want to.

Sliding into the passenger seat, her heart missed a beat as she looked Justin over. He looked dreadful: unshaven, exhausted, his eyes those of a haunted man.

'How are you?' he asked her awkwardly.

She had no way to answer. 'Getting through the days,' she said, turning forwards as Justin fixed his gaze on the windscreen. He still couldn't look her in the eye. Alicia didn't blame him. She couldn't look herself in the eye.

'Have you spoken to him?' he asked after a second, resting his hands on the steering wheel.

Alicia swallowed. 'Yes,' she said, and took a deep breath, bracing herself to tell him what she desperately didn't want to. Lies hadn't kept him safe. She had no idea how she'd ever hoped they would.

Justin simply nodded. 'Do you think he might have been touch with her?'

'I don't know,' Alicia answered honestly. 'I think not, from the things he said. He hadn't spoken to Sophie before she left. I'm not even sure he knows she's missing.'

Justin ran his thumbs pensively along the steering wheel. 'You're not having in-depth conversations then?' There was a sarcastic edge to his voice.

Alicia's heart dipped an inch lower, if that were possible. 'No,' she said simply. To try to explain would mean to explain everything, and Justin had given her no indication he wanted to hear it. 'I texted him this morning.' On the back of what he'd said, she had no choice but to contact him. *For Sophie's sake*, he'd said. She'd gone over it and over it. She thought he'd been talking about Sophie's future, but there'd been something in his tone that she couldn't quite figure out… 'To ask him whether he'd been in contact with her,' she went on. 'He didn't answer.'

Justin glanced at her, his expression a mixture of wariness and surprise.

'His voicemail said he was at a one-day conference. I confirmed it with his office. He seems to be behaving perfectly normally.'

Again, Justin nodded. 'You know where he works then?' There was that sarcastic edge again to his tone, though now clouded with weary resignation.

'Jessica knew, through her friend, David,' she supplied, wanting to soften the blow she was about to deliver; knowing she couldn't possibly. She'd never before reached a place where she'd thought life wasn't worth living. Now, whenever she dozed, in the hours between the thin light of dawn and daylight – the only hours that sleep allowed her some escape – she would open her eyes to the harsh truth of an existence without the people she loved, and she simply didn't want to be in this reality any more. If not for Sophie, for the further pain she would cause Justin, she doubted she would be.

'There's something I have to tell you,' she said, feeling physically sick at the thought of delivering another knife wound to his chest. 'Something he told me.'

Justin didn't respond, stilling his hands on the wheel and seeming to brace himself instead.

'He said he'd had a paternity test.' There was no way to soften the news that would surely crush him. She waited, praying, futilely. How would he not be destroyed?

Justin didn't react immediately. And then, shaking his head, he emitted a short, scornful laugh. 'And he's had the results?' he asked, his tone flat.

'I believe so, yes.' Her throat tight, Alicia looked away. If he looked at her now, if she saw what was in his eyes, she would crumble. 'He threatened to tell you,' she whispered, using her sleeve to wipe her eyes, rather than delve into her bag for a tissue. 'Or at least he hinted he would, so yes, I suppose he must.'

'Threatened?' She felt Justin turn to her. 'To what end?' He sounded incredulous, confused.

Alicia hesitated. 'I'm not sure,' she said, not knowing how to share her suspicions with her husband.

'Because he wants future contact with her?' Justin's voice rose. 'The daughter he's had no contact with whatsoever, and who is now *missing*?'

Feeling sick to her very soul, Alicia pressed a hand to her forehead. She had to talk to him, properly. She couldn't undo the lie she'd told, but she had to talk to him, try to explain. 'I don't think that's his reason, no,' she said guardedly.

Justin didn't say anything – nothing at all – staring straight ahead instead.

Alicia looked towards him. His face was taut and white, a tell-tale twitch tugging at his cheek. 'Justin,' she started, 'I know you won't want to hear it, but—'

'I need to go,' he said tersely, and started the engine. 'You might want to tell him to have a rethink.'

CHAPTER FORTY

SOPHIE

Waking with a jolt, Sophie sat bolt upright, looking frantically around. Seeing Paul coming through the door, she breathed a sigh of relief and then sank groggily back down.

'How are you feeling?' he asked, walking across to put a glass of Coke on the bedside table.

'Shitty,' Sophie answered honestly, blinking up at him. She felt like she had the worst bug ever.

'Language,' Paul said, smiling tolerantly as he looked down at her. He wasn't very impressed though, Sophie guessed, from the slight narrowing of his eyes.

'Sorry,' she said, attempting to lever herself up. She'd have to watch her mouth, she realised. The fact was, though, she did feel like shit. It must be the worst superbug ever. 'Do you think I should maybe go to the doctor's?' she asked him, as he reached to help her.

'I've rung them,' he said. 'They can't prescribe antibiotics for flu bugs, unfortunately. You need to drink plenty of fluids though. Don't worry, it'll be out of your system soon, I promise. I've had it myself.'

Sophie nodded. She supposed he was right. And the fluids made sense. Her throat still felt like the bottom of a birdcage. She reached thirstily for her Coke.

Paul beat her to it. 'Don't want to have to strip that bed again, do we?' He smiled and guided the glass to her mouth. 'You should think about going without make-up,' he said, watching as she took a huge glug. 'Natural is so much nicer, don't you think?'

Sophie managed a small, indulgent smile. *Yeah, right*, she thought.

'You should lose the eyebrow stud, too,' he said, nodding towards it as he placed the glass back on the table.

'Why?' She gawked up at him. She liked her stud. It had taken her ages to pluck up the courage to get it done, and it had hurt like hell, but she was quite proud of it.

'Just a suggestion,' Paul said. 'If you're hoping to get onto your veterinary course, they're likely to frown upon it, for hygiene reasons.'

Oh. That gave Sophie pause for thought.

'Plus, it does look a bit juvenile, to be honest,' Paul added.

'Does it?' Sophie frowned. 'I thought it looked pretty cool.'

Paul closed one eye and shook his head doubtfully. 'Childish,' he said. 'I'd take it out if I were you, but that's just my opinion.'

Not entirely convinced, Sophie reached for it, wincing as she pulled it out. He might be right, she supposed. She could always put it back in later.

'Better,' he said, nodding approvingly. 'Much. Trust me. Now, will you be all right for a couple of hours, do you think? I have a seminar I have to head up at the local office. I shouldn't be too long, though.'

'I thought you were on leave,' Sophie said, though she'd already guessed he was off somewhere, since he was wearing a grey business suit, crisp white shirt and red tie. He definitely looked dapper. Not as handsome as Justin though. She quashed an overwhelming sense of homesickness and wondered again where Luke's little pink elephant had gone. Paul had said he hadn't seen it but would ask his cleaner. Sophie hadn't seen a cleaner, but then she'd been pretty zonked out for a while.

'Seems I'm in big demand.' Paul rolled his eyes. 'My overseas investment knowledge is invaluable, apparently. There's more

Coke in the fridge, but drink plenty of water, too. That fizzy stuff's no good for you. Way too much sugar. Don't want to get fat, do you? I'll make sure to get Diet Coke next time. Help yourself to anything else you fancy, obviously.'

'Cheers,' Sophie said. She actually was feeling marginally better – possibly well enough to have a potter around. She'd rather watch TV than lie around in here, and she could really use another shower.

'Shouldn't be too long,' Paul said, heading for the door. 'I'll bring some Florida brochures back with me. That should be worth getting better for. Oh, and don't forget to take your vitamins. I've left a couple next to your Coke.'

CHAPTER FORTY-ONE

JUSTIN

'Christ, you look rough,' Taylor observed, looking Justin over as he came into the station reception area.

'You need to talk to someone,' Justin said, dragging his hands up over his face, exhausted and disorientated from endless hours spent searching for Sophie. He'd crawled the streets, checked shop doorways and car parks, trawled shopping precincts, and all the while, he hadn't been able to shake the thought rattling around in his head: *tall and dark*. That fitted Radley's description. He told himself he was being paranoid, counting how many tall, dark men he saw as he walked, but after his conversation with Alicia, he wanted Radley checked out. The man's interest, which he hadn't even tried to hide, was obviously more in Alicia than Sophie, but Justin needed to be sure he'd had no contact with her. He wanted the fucker out of his life, which might never happen, unless Justin did something about it. Sophie was his daughter. In his heart, he didn't need any proof of that. On paper, though... he had to do something about that. Go to the hospital and get the test organised. Today. Whatever the outcome, he would fight to make sure he stayed part of her life. He'd file for custody if he had to. First, though, he had to find her. He *would* find her.

Justin took a breath, knowing that what he was about to say might give Taylor more reason to class Sophie a low-risk runaway. It was possible that Radley had had no contact with her, but if he had any information regarding her whereabouts whatsoever, then Justin had to take that chance. 'Paul Radley, the man who was at our house on the day of the break-in, he and Alicia, they…' He faltered, the words sticking in his throat. 'They had an affair.'

Taylor's eyes widened.

'Years ago,' Justin went on, awkwardly, 'around the time Sophie was conceived.'

'Ah.' Taylor's brow furrowed in consternation. 'You'd better come through.' He gestured for the PC behind the desk to release the security door. 'So, am I to assume there's some doubt around her parentage?' he asked, leading Justin through to his office and nodding him towards a visitor's chair before seating himself at his desk.

Justin declined the invitation to take a seat. He was so wound up, he was finding it difficult to stand still, let alone sit. 'Possibly,' he said carefully. There was no way he wanted Taylor privy to the information about the test, which might sway his thinking in regard to whatever rights Radley had. 'Alicia and I haven't really… Look, I don't know for sure, okay? For Christ's sake, do you need the details? Can you not just send someone to his—'

'Slow down, Justin,' Taylor interrupted. 'Take a breath and explain slowly. I can't do anything until I have the facts.'

Justin sighed agitatedly. 'You have them. There's a possibility Sophie might not be mine. This guy turns up out of the blue and—'

'He's had no previous contact with Sophie then?'

'As far as I know, no. Jesus, what does it *matter*?' Justin snapped. 'My concern is that he might be in contact with her now.'

Taylor looked puzzled. 'Have you spoken to Alicia about this?'

Justin's frustration, which was already way off the scale, multiplied tenfold. 'Not in great detail, no. It's a little difficult, as you might imagine.'

Picking up his pen, Taylor began tapping it repeatedly on his desk, which was immensely annoying. 'Do you think he might have taken her?'

Kneading his forehead, Justin sighed heavily. 'I don't know,' he said exasperatedly. 'His interest seems to be more in my wife.'

Taylor stopped tapping. 'And was Sophie aware of this, shall we say, dilemma?'

'Yes,' Justin said, guilt rising him. 'She overheard me talking to Alicia's sister.'

Taylor nodded slowly. 'So, if Sophie is in contact with this… Paul Radley… it would be of her own volition?'

Justin clenched his teeth hard. 'Yes, of her own volition,' he said. 'The point is, he might well know something about her whereabouts.'

Again, Taylor nodded. 'And the address?' he asked, poised to put his pen to its proper use.

'*Christ almighty!* I don't know! If I did, I wouldn't be here, would I?'

'I see.' Taylor downed his pen and laced his hands in front of him. 'So, let me get this straight. According to what you've told me, it would appear that, if Sophie has had any contact with Mr Radley, it would be willingly. Do you agree?'

'Willingly?' Justin eyed him incredulously. 'He's had nothing to do with her! Played no part in her life whatsoever. He doesn't give a damn about her. If he has been in contact with her, it's part of his plan to get to Alicia. I simply need to know whether he's heard from her, so I can get my daughter back. What part of this don't you *get?*'

Obviously unimpressed by the outburst of temper, Taylor glanced down at his desk and shuffled around some paperwork. 'How old is Sophie, Justin?' he asked.

Immediately realising the significance of that question, Justin felt his heart go into freefall. Neither he nor Alicia had mentioned it when they'd spoken, but he hadn't doubted that his wife would have been thinking exactly what he was: that the milestone that marked Sophie's sixteenth birthday tomorrow would carry their daughter further away from them, that she might always remain low priority to everyone but them. Unless something happened to her, of course, and the worst-case scenario that had been haunting Justin day and night came to pass. Then they would mobilise all available bodies, or whatever it was police did when there was a *real* crime to solve. Someone raped and strangled, bludgeoned or knifed to death. Then they would cordon off areas, go house to house, investigate – while he buried another child.

Justin felt a cold shiver run through him. He didn't answer Taylor's question.

'A man eliciting contact with his sixteen-year-old daughter isn't a criminal offence, Justin,' Taylor said regretfully.

Justin swallowed back a tight lump in his throat. 'And if he's not her father?'

'We don't know, though, do we?' Taylor pointed out, confirming what Justin had already concluded: that they were going to do absolutely nothing. 'If he's had contact with her and he's not, obviously we will want to speak to him,' he went on, his expression now apologetic, as if impelling Justin to understand his hands were tied. 'But there's nothing we can do without proof of parentage, other than make a general enquiry. Not unless Sophie herself actually comes forward with a complaint. I'm sorry.'

'Right. Well.' Justin shook his head, disbelieving. 'Thanks for your help, Detective Inspector.'

'Justin…' Taylor called after him, as Justin strode furiously towards the door. 'Dr Cole! Don't do anything rash.'

CHAPTER FORTY-TWO

JUSTIN

Nice premises. Justin surveyed the Portland stone exterior of the 1930s art deco building from which Graham & Young Investment Advisers operated. The lease would undoubtedly be extortionate. Is that what Alicia had been impressed with, he wondered, his wealth? His emotions were swinging between disbelief that she would ever have got involved with Radley and gut-twisting fury. From where Justin was standing, the man had no redeeming features whatsoever.

They'd had an affair right under his nose. And this *wanker* had swanned back into her life and was resorting to threats, using *his* daughter as some kind of hold over her, presumably so he could pick up where he left off. That was a huge error of judgement on Radley's part, and Justin had decided to point out just how huge. He was obviously the type of person who got off on getting what he wanted, whatever the cost. Not used to being turned down. Justin recalled the challenge in Radley's eyes the first time he'd had the misfortune to meet him at the party, his obvious irritation when Alicia had turned down his offer of a lift to Jessica's after the break-in, the day she'd buried her child. And this was supposed to be someone who *cared* about her? About Sophie?

Bastard! There was no way he was going to have contact with Sophie. Not while Justin still had breath in his body would he allow someone like that anywhere near her.

Curtailing his temper, Justin sucked in a breath and pushed his way through the revolving doors at the front of the building. Checking the list in the foyer, he ascertained the location of the company, nodded a greeting at the security guard and bypassed the lift, preferring to take the stairs up to the third floor. Counting the steady rhythm of his footfall against the stone steps did little to calm him.

Reasonably composed, he walked into the reception area and waited for the girl behind the desk to finish her call. 'Paul Radley?' he enquired pleasantly, when she acknowledged him.

'He's in a meeting,' the girl said, with a bright smile. 'Do you have an appointment, Mr…?'

'Cole. Dr Cole. I need to speak to him urgently,' Justin said. 'Is his meeting here, on the premises?'

'In the conference room.' The girl pointed behind her, her forehead creased in obvious concern that a doctor was calling. 'If you take a seat, I'll ring through and get someone to let him know you're here.'

'No need. I'll go straight through. He needs urgent medical attention,' Justin said, his tone serious, his gaze on the conference room doors at the end of the corridor. *Or he soon fucking well will.*

'Excuse me…' The girl twirled in her chair as he walked purposely around her. 'Excuse me! Dr Cole? You can't go in there.'

Clamping his jaw tight, Justin walked on, shoving the double conference room doors open and walking straight across to where Radley had obviously been heading up the meeting. Plainly, he was some company bigshot, and Justin was about to bring the bastard right down to size.

His gaze shooting towards him, clearly registering who he was, Radley stopped mid-sentence, a startled look on his face in place of the smug expression Justin had seen what seemed like a lifetime ago. 'What do you want?' he said, taking a step back. 'You can't just walk in—'

'To break your neck,' Justin cut across him. 'But I'll settle for an arm or a leg. Maybe two.'

Radley was scared, he noted, stopping in front of him. He searched his eyes – rich chestnut-brown, deceitful, dark eyes. Nothing like his daughter's.

'Look, I have no idea what this is about, but I'm sure we can sit down and discuss it civilly.' Loosening his tie, Radley glanced around him, presumably wondering whether he could get past. *Not a chance, sunshine.*

'You threatened my wife.'

'*Threatened?*' Radley laughed nervously. 'Don't be preposterous. I rang her to ask if we could meet to discuss things going forward, that was all. I have no idea where you would get the idea that I—'

'Do your colleagues realise what a slimy piece of shit you are, Radley?' Justin cut him short. The 'things going forward' business-speak really hadn't helped the man's case. He was talking about his *wife*, his *daughter*, his fucking life!

'This is ridiculous,' Radley snapped irritably. 'Rachel, call security,' he instructed one of the employees Justin could sense hovering uncertainly behind him.

Justin's mouth curved into a scornful smile. 'Good idea, Rachel,' he said, his gaze never leaving Radley's. 'Why don't you call the police while you're at it? Mr Radley and I can have a nice cosy conversation with them down at the station about why he's stalking my wife.'

'Mr Radley?' the girl asked uncertainly.

Popping the top button of his shirt, Radley shook his head. 'It's fine, Rachel,' he said, coughing nervously.

'Tell them to leave,' Justin said, working to hold on to his temper now he'd established the man was a spineless prick. He was as tall as him, and looked pretty fit, but he was shaking in his designer shoes.

Radley paled. 'What?'

'I'm not asking you twice, you bastard,' Justin bellowed. 'Tell them to leave!'

Perspiration wetting his forehead, Radley swallowed, and then glanced at the audience behind them. 'Can we have the room, please?' He smiled shakily. 'Dr Cole and I have some things to discuss.'

Justin waited while people filed out.

'Satisfied?' Radley asked, as the doors closed.

'Not quite.' Justin looked him contemptuously over. 'Do those windows open?' He nodded behind him towards the long picture windows that gave a scenic view over the city.

'What?' Radley glanced confusedly in that direction. 'No!' he said, his expression now petrified.

'That's a pity,' Justin said, stepping towards him. 'Means I'm just going to have to put you through one, doesn't it?'

Radley swallowed. 'Look, I realise you're upset,' he said, holding his hands defensively up in front of him, 'I don't blame you. You should know, though, that I don't go around having random affairs with married women. Alicia was lonely, upset. She approached me, truth be known.'

Justin narrowed his eyes.

'She contacted me when I got back from Dubai,' Radley babbled on, spouting crap, his eyes all the while flicking nervously towards the window. 'I tried to put her off, I swear I did. Obviously, now I can see how distressing this all is for you, I'll avoid any future contact. As for Sophie, I'm happy to back off. I'm not an unreasonable—'

His fury unleashing inside him, Justin seized Radley by the throat, shoving him back towards the window before he could blink.

'Don't!' Radley screamed as he rammed him hard against it. 'I'm terrified of heights. 'Please. God... *Don't.*'

Justin stared hard at him, his emotions swinging wildly as he realised, with a jolt, that he didn't actually care if the man went through it.

Twisting his collar tighter, Justin eyeballed him meaningfully. 'Do not even breathe my daughter's name,' he warned him. 'And do not *ever* attempt to contact my wife again. If you do, I *will* kill you. Am I making myself clear?'

His eyes wide with fear, Radley nodded quickly.

'I didn't fucking hear you!' Justin lifted the man off his feet.

'Yes,' Radley rasped; his Adam's apple bobbing in his throat.

Justin breathed in hard. 'Good,' he said, more quietly, and then, counting silently backwards, he gained a tenuous grip on his emotions and relaxed his hold.

Crumpling with relief, Radley almost slithered down the window. 'Rachel!' he shouted croakily, as Justin turned away. 'The police!'

Bad move. Justin turned back. 'You'll want something more substantial than threats to report,' he suggested, bringing his fist back, getting little satisfaction as he heard bone and sinew crack. 'You're scum, Radley,' he spat, turning to walk away as the man dropped to his knees.

CHAPTER FORTY-THREE

ALICIA

Recognising his ringtone, Alicia grabbed her phone.

'Hi,' Justin said, as soon as she picked up. 'I just wanted to check you were okay.'

'Yes,' Alicia assured him, amazed he cared enough to even ask after the news she'd given him. 'Why?

'No reason. I just thought I'd check.' There was a pause on the line, then, 'Radley,' he said, almost spitting the word out. 'If he gets in touch, will you let me know? Regarding Sophie, I mean.'

'Obviously I will,' Alicia said, wondering why he'd think she wouldn't. Then she thought of the paternity test, her heart aching for him as she imagined what his line of thinking might be: that she might decide her future was with Sophie's father.

'And you'll let me know if he bothers you? Assuming you don't want him to contact you unnecessarily, that is,' Justin went on, sounding awkward now, uncertain.

'Justin…' Alicia paused. It would be so easy to just say it, to blurt it out. But then what? The endless questions, the disbelief. Him thinking she was incapable of doing anything but lying. Things were so clouded and confused in her mind now, she couldn't even be sure she wasn't lying to herself. She couldn't bear that Justin might think she had ever wanted to be with anyone but him. That she would entertain the thought of talking to Paul Radley now, unless through a solicitor. God forbid he should ever go down that route, but he well might now that he'd had the paternity test, meaning she would receive some cold, official letter in the post. 'I don't want any contact with him. Not ever,' she said.

She wished she could be with Justin now. Hold him. She wished there was something she could do to prove how very much she'd always loved and cared for him, even when she'd done the most careless thing in the world.

'Okay,' he said, drawing in a tight breath. 'I needed to check, for my own peace of mind.'

His peace of mind? Alicia looked upwards, blinking hard… Would he ever have that again?

'I'd better go,' he said, after another awkward pause. 'I have some places to check out.'

'Wait,' she said urgently, wanting to at least check how he was. 'Are you all right?' she asked him, stupidly. She knew how he was: a jaded, broken man. He missed Sophie and Lucas as much as she did: every minute of every waking day, in her dreams and her waking nightmares, she thought of them. Yet they couldn't reach out to each other, comfort each other. The void between them, where their children should be, was too vast.

'Tired,' he admitted. 'I've moved rooms. Renting nearer the area I'm going to check out later tonight.'

'Is it clean?' she asked him, grieving for what they'd lost, for the ability to talk naturally that they'd once had. There was nothing between them now but stilted conversation.

'Reasonable,' he said, then, 'What about you? You're going to be staying with Jess for a while, I take it?'

'Yes, for now,' she said, not sure what else she could say. She couldn't contemplate the thought of going back to a house where the ghosts of her family would haunt her. She hadn't even broached the subject of the house with Justin, whether he would want her going back there, whether he would ever want to go back.

'Jess is here now.' She glanced towards her sister as she poked her head curiously around the kitchen door.

'Justin?' Jessica mouthed.

Alicia nodded.

Jessica nodded in turn, and then waggled her phone in Alicia's direction, indicating she was going to make a call.

'We're just back from distributing leaflets at district train stations,' Alicia went on. 'We have lots of shops and supermarkets putting up posters, too,' she said, as if her efforts amounted to anything compared to what he was doing.

'Good. That's good.' Justin sounded relieved. 'Tell Jess thanks.'

'I will,' Alicia said, and then wondered what else to say. There was no subject that was safe. There was no future they could discuss, as Justin had pointed out. No present. No past. Every memory they'd made together had been tarnished.

'Right, I'll get off,' he said, when it was clear they'd exhausted all topics. 'Talk tomorrow.'

'Okay.' Alicia's heart fractured a little further. 'Be careful, Justin.'

'I will. You too,' Justin said, and ended the call.

Alicia listened to the empty silence. There had been no coldness in his voice – he'd sounded like Justin – but it was as if he'd been talking to a sister or a friend, not his wife, not his lover. But then, she wasn't either of those any more.

Going to the fridge to pour herself a large wine, Alicia swallowed hard on the thought that one day he would stop calling. That would be the day she would stop breathing.

CHAPTER FORTY-FOUR

JUSTIN

Justin ended his call to Alicia. He'd been relieved to hear that Radley hadn't been in touch. Fury driving him, he hadn't been thinking clearly, hadn't considered what the consequences for Alicia might be when he'd stormed into that office. He hadn't been capable of anything beyond his fervent wish to do him permanent damage. He almost had.

Realising the man was a coward and likely to react in the way cowards did and pick on someone physically weaker than him, Justin had been worried he might retaliate and choose Alicia. He hadn't wanted to admit to her he'd been aggressive. In the normal run of things, he considered himself level-headed, and hated violence or confrontation of any sort. It rarely solved anything. Knowing Radley had threatened Alicia, though, that he thought he had a hold over her and was continuing to contact her when it was clear she didn't want him to, that had been beyond discussion of any sort. The man was pond scum, which begged the question again: what the bloody *hell* had she ever seen in him? He doubted he'd ever know the answer to that.

Pocketing his phone, he checked the time on the dashboard. Two weeks, he thought, his gaze flicking back to the windscreen. Fourteen days. He focussed, calculated the hours, the minutes, the seconds Sophie had been gone. The time he and Alicia had been apart. He tried to pinpoint the exact moment things had started to fall apart and he hadn't noticed. Or had noticed – he dragged a hand hard over the back of his neck – but had chosen to ignore it.

Why hadn't he quizzed her? Why had he ignored it and allowed her lie to perpetuate? His breathing suddenly shallow, indicating an imminent panic attack, Justin concentrated on the coping techniques he'd learned when he'd lost his family the first time around: breathing in to the count of four, holding for seven, breathing out for eight, repeating four times: re-oxygenating his body, attempting to get his anxiety back under control.

He'd conquered this once, found a way to get a grip on his emotions when the anger at their senseless murder; the guilt that he hadn't been able to help them, threatened to assuage him.

He didn't stand a chance this time. No matter how hard he tried, he couldn't get the images out of his mind: of Radley and Alicia together; of where Sophie might be, in some dirty, flea-bitten dive. On the streets. His fault. Whatever Alicia had done, he was the one who'd driven Sophie to run. He recalled the words he'd spat in anger when he'd found out. He'd played those words over and over ever since. And no matter how many times he did, what he'd said sounded exactly the way it would have to Sophie – that he no longer considered her to be his daughter. He would never forgive himself.

He should have done something when he'd suspected she might have overheard. He should have gone straight to see her. He wasn't able to even begin to process the knowledge that the child he'd brought home from the hospital, loved with every fibre of his being since before she'd been born, might not be his; that his wife had had an affair with another man, had sex with another man.

He missed her. Missed what he thought they'd had.

Missed his children, so much his heart physically ached.

He might never have a chance to tell Sophie how much he loved her; that's what hurt most of all. Whatever a paternity test might prove, she was his daughter. No one could take that away from him.

Apart from Sophie.

Justin swallowed hard on that thought. He would give his life to go back and undo the damage he'd caused the day he'd climbed into his car exhausted, distracted. But he couldn't. All he could do now was pray. Pray and keep scouring the streets in the hope of unearthing some small piece of information that might lead him to her. He would keep searching. Had to. His past had been obliterated. He had no life now, no purpose, other than to keep searching. Without Sophie, without some knowledge she was safe, there was no future.

CHAPTER FORTY-FIVE

JUSTIN

Heading towards the canal towpath, planning to cover a section of the main line out of Birmingham, Justin stopped at the doorway of a derelict shop to talk to a guy who was tucked into his sleeping bag.

'Spare some change, mate?' the guy asked as Justin approached him. His look wasn't hopeful – more resigned. Any vitality he might have once had in his eyes had been dulled; by booze, Justin guessed, noting the several empty beer cans to his side.

Justin offered him a smile. 'I'm looking for someone,' he said. The guy recoiled, shuffling further into the doorway, assuming he was something to do with the police. 'My daughter,' he elaborated, drawing Sophie's photo from his inside pocket.

The guy looked warily up at him and then down to the photo. Looking at it for a second, he shook his head. Justin sighed. Even if alcohol hadn't addled his brain, the chances were the guy wouldn't remember anyway.

Sighing, he nodded his thanks and reached into his pocket again, this time for money, though it went against the grain. Maybe the guy would buy food; maybe he'd spend it on booze. The dog would get fed, though. Justin was certain of that. Checking his watch, he bent down to pat the animal, then headed for the towpath, hoping that this time he might get lucky.

The wind was bitter, channelled by abandoned factory buildings, converted warehouses and high embankments. It stung his face and sliced through his clothes. Pulling his collar high, chilled to the bone, he thought about Sophie, and the clothes she'd been wearing, which would do nothing to warm her. He walked on, speaking to homeless people as he went. Receiving nothing but negative answers to his questions, some incoherent mumblings, he searched all the likely places: benches located within walking distance of one-stop shops and garages, bridges that provided sparse protection from the elements, counting them off as he went.

He'd gone a fair distance when his phone buzzed. Pulling it from his pocket, Justin checked the caller display, and then furrowed his brow and took the call. 'Jessica?'

'Justin, I have to be quick. Alicia doesn't know I'm calling you.' Jess's voice was a hurried whisper, which immediately rang alarm bells.

'And?' Apprehensively, Justin urged her on.

'I wouldn't normally go behind her back, but I think she won't want to tell you, so—'

'Jess, can you just cut to the chase,' Justin interrupted, his gut clenching.

'He's had a test. Paul Radley, he's had a paternity test, apparently, and I think you should know. I did suggest to Alicia that she should—'

'I do know,' Justin cut across her.

'You do?' Jessica sounded surprised.

'We talked. She told me.'

'Oh.' Jessica went quiet. 'Well, that's good,' she went on, after a second. 'That's she's finally decided to talk to you, I mean. It's a pity she didn't years ago. She's my sister and I love her to bits, and she's beside herself with remorse now, but I told her she needed to tell you everything from the beginning.'

Justin ran his hand over his neck. He was too tired for repeat conversations. 'I know, Jess. You said.'

'She hasn't told you everything, has she?' Jess asked, sounding tentative.

'No,' Justin said tightly. However well-intentioned Jess was, ringing him several times to see if he 'needed a shoulder', he really didn't want to discuss this, not now.

'I have no idea why she saw him as many times as she did,' Jess carried on regardless. 'You can understand how she might have been—'

'Jess! I don't want to hear it,' Justin snapped, images of his wife in bed with the bastard assailing him all over again, images that counting all the stars in the universe wouldn't make go away. 'I really do *not* want to know.'

'Oh God, I'm sorry,' Jess said quickly. 'I wasn't thinking. I just wanted you to know that I don't condone what Alicia did. I couldn't tell you, I was sworn to secrecy, and I had to be there for her. I still do, but I wanted you to know I'm there for you too.'

Nodding tiredly, Justin drew in a breath. 'I know. I just can't deal with it right now.'

Ending the call, Justin felt the knife that had been plunged into his heart twist an inch deeper. A sharp, violent twist, made more painful by the knowledge that Alicia must have known this would all come out while he'd been burying his son. That cocksure bastard had been right there at the funeral. She must have suspected he would find out what had gone on between them, and still she'd kept the truth from him. Attempting some level of control, Justin tried to breathe through it. It didn't work. He didn't stand a chance of ousting the images now in his mind: Luke smiling at him on that fateful day of the accident, his little arms flailing delightedly. He'd sworn to keep his son safe. He hadn't. Justin breathed in, kept counting.

Sophie's words whispered on the wind as he walked. *He's nestled safe in an angel's wings now, but he will never leave me. He's here. He will always be.*

Where was she?

CHAPTER FORTY-SIX

SOPHIE

Still feeling lethargic and majorly bored, Sophie flicked through the channels, but nothing grabbed her. She wished she had her phone. She could at least download something to read then.

Heaving herself up from the sofa, she went to the kitchen. Nothing much took her fancy when she peered into the fridge, but she pulled out the Coke. She was halfway through filling a large tumbler when she stopped, debating. Should she? Had Paul been subtly hinting that she was getting fat? No, he was just pointing out that it wasn't very healthy to stuff herself full of sugar. He was probably right. She usually drank sugar-free. Maybe she could go and get some when she felt better. And when she had some shoes. Glancing down at her bare feet, she wiggled her toes, noticing her chipped nail polish as she did. There were a few things she needed, in actual fact – nail polish remover being one of them. She didn't want to ask Paul to fork out though. Then again, as he kept reminding her, he was her father, and he'd been pretty cool about buying her stuff so far.

She hadn't seen any evidence of a phone yet, but then, he had been busy looking after her. She'd remind him later – casually, though. She didn't want him thinking she was going to milk the situation. That would be a shitty thing to do when he'd already been treated so crappily by her mum.

Opting for water instead, she grabbed an apple and mooched around the apartment. She hadn't liked to poke into too many spaces and cupboards while he was here – not that she'd been capable of nosing around – but she needed to know where stuff was and how it worked. The music system, for one. There was a fabulous wireless multi-speaker system. She really wished she had her phone. There was a turntable too, she noticed, going over to it. Not many CDs or vinyl records to choose from though – classical stuff, mostly. She guessed he probably used his phone with Spotify or something. And it wasn't his apartment anyway, she reminded herself.

The motorised shutters at the windows were something else. You really had to be making serious money to afford one of these places, Sophie surmised. Bored with opening and shutting them after a while, she ambled towards Paul's bedroom. Nothing much to see in there. Sophie hadn't thought there would be. Having noted his obsession with having everything in its right place, she guessed he'd have all his stuff put away in drawers and cupboards. She inched open the top dresser drawer. Yup, all neatly folded.

Feeling guilty being in his personal space, Sophie closed the drawer and then had a quick peek in the wardrobe, where his suits and shirts were all pressed and hanging with military precision, like soldiers on parade. His bed was made up with the meticulousness of a hospital. Fastidious, definitely. Still, if his obsession with tidiness was his most annoying habit, Sophie could live with it. She'd just have to remember to clear up after herself. It was no biggie.

Heading back out, she wandered towards the door furthest from the lounge area – his study – where she hesitated. But then, curiosity getting the better of her, she squeaked the door handle down and went on in. She wasn't really spying on him, she was just curious to know more about him, as anyone would be, having just learned that a complete stranger was their father.

Nodding righteously to herself, Sophie walked across to his desk, and then stopped as her eyes fell on the framed photograph there. It was of her mum, Sophie realised, astonished. She was less surprised by its presence than by the fact that it was a recent-ish photograph, taken by her at a hotel they'd stayed at in London early last year. Sophie remembered it distinctly. The London Eye had been lit up in the background. And wasn't Justin supposed to be in the photo, too?

How had Paul got it?

Plonking herself moodily down in his office chair, Sophie yanked open the top desk drawer and pulled out an envelope folder she found there. Her mum had sent him the photo, she supposed. Paul had been married in Dubai, and he was still grieving, Sophie had assumed. It might have been that her mum and him had started corresponding after he'd lost his family, which is why Justin might have suspected something. Her mum might have sent the photo and…

And Sophie had absolutely no clue why she was bothering to think it through. There was no point asking her mum about it – she hadn't been honest with anybody. Not that Sophie intended to speak to her anyway. She'd ask Paul about it. At least he seemed to think she had feelings worth considering.

Peering into the folder, Sophie knitted her brow, and then… *Shit!* Hearing the front door open, she almost died on the spot.

'Sophie?' Paul called.

Shit, shit, shit! Hurriedly cramming the folder back in the drawer, she shot to her feet, scrambling to think of an explanation as to why she was in here that would sound remotely feasible.

'Sophie?'

'Coming!' she shouted. She had no way of not being caught snooping. There was nowhere to go but out of the door, where she'd be on full view before she had a chance to nip back to her bedroom.

She snatched up a pen just before Paul came through the door. 'Looking for something?' he asked her, his gaze travelling warily from her to the desk.

'Yes. I, um…' *Crikey.* Sophie's eyes grew wide. Had he been in some sort of fight? 'Are you okay?' she asked.

Paul's fingers went gingerly to the definite blue-black bruise forming under his eye. 'Fine. I had a fall, at the gym. Did you find it? Whatever you were looking for?'

'Paper,' Sophie ad-libbed, holding up the pen.

Paul frowned, clearly not buying it.

'I thought I'd write to her, my mum,' Sophie elaborated, her face, she hoped, the picture of innocence, though her heart was beating a rat-a-tat-tat in her chest. 'I didn't want to text her or ring her,' she went on. 'I thought a letter might be better. You know, more personal. What do you think?'

Paul studied her for a second, then, nodding slowly, he walked towards her, and then past her, his gaze lingering on the desk drawers as he did.

Pulling a filing cabinet drawer open, he retrieved what she'd supposedly been looking for. 'Paper,' he said, handing her a sheaf of printer paper.

'Brilliant. Thanks.' Sophie took it and beamed him a smile.

'No problem,' Pushing one hand into his pocket, his other going to the bruise on his face, Paul considered her thoughtfully for a second. 'Don't come in here again without asking, Sophie – please. I have client information in here. Data protection rules require me to keep that information confidential.'

'Oh.' Sophie looked suitably apologetic. 'Sorry, I didn't think.'

Again, Paul nodded and offered her a smile.

Not an overly effusive one, Sophie noted. There was something in his body language that made her feel uneasy, along with the wary look in his eyes as his gaze went once again to the desk drawers, the contents of which Sophie was now exceedingly curious about.

Come to think of it, she pondered, as she took her leave, why wasn't there a photograph of his family on that desk? His wife and his children. Why would he have picture of Alicia instead?

CHAPTER FORTY-SEVEN

JUSTIN

'Can I leave now?' Justin looked up from his bruised fist as Taylor came back into the interview room. He had been left there while they waited for the officer in charge to report back on whether 'Mr Radley' was going to file charges. He'd obviously hit him harder than he'd realised. Should have hit the fucker harder.

At least he wasn't being held in a cell, Justin supposed, though that was where he might well end up, Taylor had warned him, if he didn't get his emotions under control. Justin wanted to challenge him to do the same, to remain perfectly calm while some bastard was using his missing daughter as leverage over his wife.

'Tell me something.' Folding his arms across his chest, Taylor studied him curiously. 'Did it make you feel better? Punching the man, did it solve anything?'

Justin noted the edge to his tone. 'Not much, no,' he admitted. He hadn't felt very proud of the fact that he'd given in to his base instincts. As to whether it had solved anything, that remained to be seen. If Alicia didn't want Radley contacting her, then the man needed to understand that. He also needed to know that if he even spoke Sophie's name, then Justin was very close to making sure he wouldn't ever again.

'Just so you know,' Taylor said, 'I get why you did it. I'd probably have done the same myself, to be honest.'

Justin glanced at him.

'I have kids.' Taylor shrugged, now looking sympathetic, at least. 'I also have a wife. Ex, that is. I'll leave it to your imagination as to why.'

Surveying him thoughtfully, Justin nodded, supposing that he would have some inkling of how he felt. It didn't really help.

'Look, Justin…' Taylor dragged out a chair and sat down opposite him. 'I understand your frustration. I can't imagine what it must be like to lose a child so young under such tragic circumstances, to then to have your teenage daughter go missing. I promise you, we're doing all that we can.'

Rubbing his eyes in exhaustion, Justin declined to answer. As far as he could see, that still amounted to nothing.

'He's not filing charges,' Taylor went on. 'I'm not majorly surprised, under the circumstances.' He smiled wryly, and then drew in a breath. 'In regard to your certainty that he may have had some contact with Sophie, we asked him the question, obviously.'

Justin looked sharply back at him. 'And?'

Taylor's expression held a warning. 'He has.'

What? Justin's first reaction was bewilderment. His second – gut-clenching fury that the bastard hadn't said. His third was overwhelming relief. She was alive. He'd *known* it. He could feel her. 'When?' he asked throatily.

'Two days ago,' Taylor said.

Justin sucked in a breath, buried his head in his hands and suppressed an overwhelming urge to cry.

'He phoned her,' Taylor continued, as Justin struggled to formulate any words. 'He didn't know she was missing, so he says. He was, and I quote, "simply initiating contact with his daughter".'

'My daughter,' Justin managed to sputter.

Taylor didn't comment on that. 'She said she was staying with a friend.'

Justin nodded, trying very hard to do the simplest thing in the world and breathe. 'She didn't say where?' he asked, and then coughed, attempting to clear the hard knot in his throat.

Shaking his head regretfully, Taylor sat back in his chair. 'Apparently not.' He paused while Justin attempted to compose himself. 'I know this is painful, Justin,' he said, after a second, 'but possibly less painful than the alternative you were imagining, yes?'

Swiping a hand across his eyes, Justin nodded, vigorously this time.

'We're keeping our ears to the ground, Justin. We're still pursuing any leads we can in regard to the hit-and-run that took your boy away. What you need to do now, if you care to take some advice from someone who knows, is be there for each other. You and Alicia. Right now, you need each other.'

Justin didn't respond. He doubted he could get the words past the fractured pieces of his heart, which still seemed to be lodged in his windpipe.

'You can leave as soon as you're ready,' Taylor said kindly. 'Just promise me you'll seek counselling if you need it,' he added, as Justin got to his feet. 'I would offer you some numbers, but I imagine you have access to people of your own. Think about it, Justin. You and your wife both.'

Answering with another short nod, Justin swallowed and turned towards the door. What kind of counselling would best help Alicia, he wondered, bereavement or marriage counselling? His chest constricted.

What wasn't she telling him? How did Radley get Sophie's number? From Alicia? Was it possible he'd accessed it from Alicia's phone? Did she know he'd been in touch with Sophie?

CHAPTER FORTY-EIGHT

ALICIA

'He's leaving! Going back to Dubai,' Alicia said, turning in disbelief to Jessica, having worriedly read her incoming text from Paul Radley.

Her wine glass halfway to her mouth, Jessica eyed her with surprise. 'Really?'

'Apparently.' Joining her at the kitchen table, Alicia hesitated, then said, 'He suggested we should meet before he goes.' She inhaled a tight breath.

Jessica furrowed her brow. 'Why?'

'He has some things he wants me to give to Sophie, so he says. I have no idea what things.'

'And are you going to meet him? Jessica searched her face, her expression curious. She was probably wondering why she'd even read the text.

Alicia had almost deleted it, but as she'd actually been expecting threats in regard to Sophie, she'd thought better of it, thinking she needed to prepare herself as to what those threats might be. Some attempt at custody, or at the very least access rights, she'd thought. Now, she wasn't sure what to think. She felt utterly bewildered. And very wary. Would he really just go?

'I think I've said all I have to say to him.' She sighed wearily. 'I can't help wondering what the catch is. Why he would just decide to leave, after going to such great lengths to tear my marriage apart?'

'You don't know that he's done that yet, Ali.' Looking at her sympathetically, Jess downed her glass and reached for her hand. 'If you are thinking of meeting him, though, you should really let Justin know. If he finds out—' She stopped as Alicia's phone rang.

It was Justin's ringtone, as if he knew he was under discussion. Realising it was much later than he would normally call, Alicia immediately jumped up to snatch it up from the work surface. 'Justin?' she said, glancing nervously back at Jess. 'Has something happened?'

'Sorry,' Justin said quickly, 'I should have thought. Calling you at a different time was bound to worry you.'

'It's fine,' Alicia said, her eyes filling up. Only a truly special man would worry about her at all under the circumstances. 'Are you all right?'

Topping up her glass, Jessica picked up her own phone and made a face at her, indicating she was off to make one of the many calls she preferred to do in private. Vaguely, Alicia wondered whether there might be a new man in her life. A man she was possibly avoiding bringing home, thanks to her sister moving in with baggage by the trunkful.

'As all right as I can be,' Justin answered. 'I just wanted to check you were.'

Now Alicia was definitely taken aback. 'Yes,' she said. 'Ish. Why?'

'No specific reason. It's just…' Justin faltered. 'The things I see when I'm out walking – homeless people, young people,' he went on tiredly. 'It gets to me sometimes, to be honest.'

Immediately empathising, Alicia's stomach wrenched as she imagined how affected he must be, the things that must inevitably go through his mind. Witnessing such things in her job, they went through hers too, causing her to tear herself from the warm bed in which she lay sleeplessly every night. And then, for fear of waking Jess, she would end up standing silently, gazing uselessly out of the window, where the images would only be starker. Justin was in the thick of it. She doubted he would even bother to lie down at night half the time. 'Do you want to talk?' she asked him, tentatively, wondering whether there was anything specific troubling him.

Justin sighed. 'No, not really. I think I just needed to hear a familiar voice,' he said. And then went quiet.

Unable to bring himself to talk more, Alicia guessed, to someone he'd once trusted implicitly with his inner feelings and who'd so badly deceived him.

'So, are you back at work?' he asked her, changing the subject.

'No.' Alicia sighed, despairing of her apparent inadequacy on all fronts. 'I tried, but I couldn't handle it. The children…' She left it there, guessing he would understand what she meant. 'I'm keeping busy though. I've set up a Twitter account and a "Find Sophie" Facebook page. I thought it might be a good way for people to communicate anything that might help, any likely sightings. I also thought that if her friends wanted to message us privately for any reason…' She trailed off, realising Justin would gather what she meant there, too.

'Good idea,' he said. And went quiet again.

Alicia waited, sensing there was something else he needed to say.

'Can I ask you something?' he asked, after what seemed like an eternity.

Alicia felt a prickle of apprehension run through her. 'Yes, obviously.'

'Radley,' he said, causing Alicia's insides to turn over. 'You said he'd had no contact with Sophie, right?'

'Yes,' Alicia said quickly. 'I mean, no. He hasn't, as far as I'm aware. Why?'

Justin breathed in long and hard. 'It seems he has.'

What? A million emotions assaulting her, Alicia felt her legs turn to rubber beneath her. 'He's spoken to her?' she whispered.

She had to see him. She headed for the hall. Went back for her keys. *Why* hadn't he mentioned—

'He rang her. Just once, according to Taylor,' said Justin. 'She's staying with a friend. She didn't say where.'

'When?' Alicia asked, feeling desperate. She needed to do... *something*.

'Two days ago, apparently,' Justin said. 'Alicia... did you give him her number?' He paused, giving her a few seconds as she tried to assimilate the information. 'Did you give him Sophie's number?'

'No! I wouldn't. Why would I have?'

Justin's silence spoke volumes.

'Justin, I didn't. I swear to God, I didn't,' Alicia repeated, tears streaming down her cheeks, the phone clutched tight to her ear. 'I don't want him to have access to her. He must have got it from my phone, or from someone else. Please believe me,' she begged.

'I have to go,' Justin said, over another tight intake of breath. 'We should talk,' he added.

'About?' Alicia asked fearfully.

'Things,' Justin replied vaguely. 'At some point, I mean. Take care, Alicia.'

He signed off, leaving Alicia emotionally floundering. The 'things' he wanted to talk about were presumably to do with their marriage. At 'some point' soon, she would have to face the reality that they would have no future together.

Hesitating for a second, Alicia steeled herself and then rang Paul Radley's number, only to get his voicemail. After trying again minutes later, she grabbed the wine from the fridge. It would do nothing to anaesthetise her beyond the first alcohol-induced hour of total oblivion, after which she would end up going over and over things, until her recollection was more clouded than ever. Yet she needed it – needed somehow to try to numb the pain.

Did Justin believe she hadn't passed Sophie's number on to Paul? Why would he? He would never be able to trust anything she said ever again.

Draining half a glass in one, she topped it up again.

Why hadn't Paul Radley rung her?

CHAPTER FORTY-NINE

JUSTIN

After fruitless hours ringing around Sophie's friends again, hoping to find out the identity of the mysterious friend with whom Sophie might be staying, Justin headed to the hospital. He wouldn't stay. There was no way to concentrate. He couldn't possibly trust himself with people's lives until he knew his daughter was safe. Whether he would still have a job then, Justin felt didn't much matter without his family.

Picking up the results he'd come for, he went to the hospital restaurant, where he bought a coffee but didn't drink it. A colleague spoke to him. He hardly heard her. Dragging his hands over his face, he sat motionless, staring out over the car park, watching people coming and going, attempting to digest this latest news, until his coffee went cold. Then, sucking in a long breath, he left, going straight from the hospital to room he was renting.

Weary with exhaustion, yet knowing sleep would elude him, he barely noticed the sparse furnishing as he dropped his keys onto the single chest of drawers. He'd stopped craving material things the day Sophie had disappeared and his marriage had disintegrated. Before that, when Luke had been cruelly snatched away from them, he'd begun to wonder how much one really needed in life. The fancy cars, flat-screen TVs, the latest in technology – they were just things, accumulated throughout a life. Stuff you couldn't take with you when you ceased to exist. It was all meaningless without someone to share it with.

Justin didn't miss those things. He didn't need them. There was no point in living luxuriously any more. He wondered whether there would be any point in living at all if he didn't find Sophie. Whatever the hell was going on with Radley, he knew Alicia felt the same: she was existing, rather than living, waiting and praying for news, for any shred of information that might lead them to her.

Refusing to entertain the thought that he might never find her; that she might choose never to contact him again, he pulled off his coat and dropped onto the bed. He should ring Alicia. He'd wanted to believe her – badly needed to – but how could he? How could he begin to believe anything she had to say when their whole life together had been a lie?

But would she really be carrying on with the charade if it was Radley she wanted to be with? Justin had considered that too, but had reached no conclusion. Part of him hated her for what she'd done, but part of him still loved her. It was pathetic, but there it was. He wanted to reach out to her. A couple of times he almost had, when he'd seen the tortured look in her eyes and felt her palpable pain, but he'd stopped himself. He couldn't take any more hurt. There just wasn't room inside him for any more.

He had to stay in touch, though. If he couldn't say what he wanted to, ask the endless questions going around in his head, they needed to communicate about Sophie.

Retrieving his phone from his pocket and selecting Alicia's number, his gaze strayed to the one thing he didn't want to be without – a framed photograph of her with Luke and Sophie, which he kept on the bedside table. He felt like it had been taken eons ago, in another lifetime, when they were a family, happy and healthy, a smile dancing in Alicia's dazzling cornflower blue eyes. Despite the pain she'd caused him, he hoped she would smile again one day. That she would have a life beyond the purgatory they were living in now.

'Hi, Justin, it's me,' Jessica said, picking the call up. 'How are you doing?'

'Not great.'

'I know.' Jessica sighed sympathetically. 'I honestly don't know how you're getting through each day.'

'Willpower,' Justin joked half-heartedly.

'*Yes*, it's a good job you're a strong man, that's all I can say,' Jessica said dourly. 'Some men would have walked away from it. Most men, in fact.'

'I haven't always been, Jess,' Justin said, reminding her of the time he hadn't been strong. Then, Alicia had had to be the strong one, while he'd learned how to feel normal again.

'You'd lost your family,' Jessica said softly. 'To have discovered them the way you did… To have had to bury them, try to carry on, never knowing who had been responsible, why someone would commit such an atrocious act of violence…'

She stopped. Justin was relieved when she did, every desecration of his family inevitably searing itself again on his mind.

'It's wonder you didn't break down completely. The fact that you got through that makes you strong,' Jessica went on forcefully. 'You shouldn't be bottling your feelings up now, though, Justin, not when you're going through the same heartbreak all over again. I know you'd probably feel a bit awkward about it, but if you do ever want to unburden, I'm here. Just because I'm Alicia's sister, it doesn't mean I can't be a friend to you, too.'

Justin ran a hand over his neck. Knowing exactly what had gone on, Jessica was possibly the only person he could talk to, but he wasn't about to do that. It wouldn't be fair on Alicia – or Jessica, come to that. There was also the fact that he didn't think he could talk about any of this without breaking down, and he was desperately trying not to do that.

'I know. Thanks, Jess,' he said, wanting her to know he appreciated the offer.

'And if you don't fancy unburdening, we could just get drunk instead,' Jessica suggested.

Justin smiled wryly. He didn't think that was such a good idea either. He doubted his problems would look much better at the bottom of a whisky glass.

'Has he been in touch?' he asked, bringing the conversation around to why he'd called. He should ask Alicia, and he would, but he'd taken to asking Jessica for information first, which didn't make him feel great.

Jessica hesitated. 'He texted her,' she said, sounding reluctant. 'Apparently, he's going back to Dubai. He's asked to meet with her. And now I've said enough. I'd hate Alicia to think I was going behind her back. You'd do better to ask her about the detail.'

'I'll do that,' Justin assured her, already bracing himself. The fact was, he was scared. Terrified she would lie to him again. He had no idea what he would do, how he would react.

Whatever the future held for Alicia and him, he was hugely relieved Radley was scuttling off back to Dubai. He'd been shocked by the realisation he'd been an inch away from inflicting possibly fatal injuries on a man. Despite his assurances to DI Taylor, he wasn't certain he would be able to control himself if he found himself in Radley's company again.

'Is she around?' he asked, assuming from the tone of Jessica's voice that Alicia must be out of earshot. And then he immediately felt pig-sick as he wondered where she was – and with whom.

'She's busy. That detective guy has just arrived.'

'Taylor?' Justin was surprised.

'He said he was passing, so he decided to call in to check on Alicia,' Jessica said. 'I'll get her to call you back as soon as she can.'

'Cheers, Jess,' Justin said, feeling wary. He wasn't sure why Taylor had decided to pay Alicia a visit. It certainly wouldn't be because 'he was passing', but it wouldn't be to announce they'd suddenly decided Sophie was a high-profile case, that was for sure.

CHAPTER FIFTY

ALICIA

Hearing his ringtone, Alicia knew Justin had just called. She was desperate to call him back after the way their last call had ended, but first she needed to hear what the detective inspector had to say. 'You're sure you won't have some tea or coffee?' she asked him, having already established that he wasn't here with news of Sophie and then gone through the awkward civilities.

'No, thanks, Alicia. I can't stay long.' Giving her a brief smile, DI Taylor checked his watch.

'Something stronger possibly?' she asked him, making a supreme effort to be cordial, despite the fact that all she wanted to do was scream at him to do his job and bring Sophie home. She'd rung around all her friends, only to be told Justin had already called, and to receive the same news he presumably had. She'd supposedly been with this mysterious friend – whom no one had any idea about – two, getting on for three days ago, which meant she could be anywhere now. The nagging thought had also occurred to Alicia that this 'friend' might not even be a girlfriend. A boyfriend would be worrying, but what if it were neither? What if it were some predatory adult?

'I'd love something stronger,' DI Taylor smiled, regretfully this time. 'I'm still on duty though, unfortunately.'

'Right, well.' Alicia smiled back. 'What can I do for you, Detective?'

'Do you mind if we sit?' Taylor asked, and walked across to seat himself on the sofa anyway.

Alicia took the armchair, uneasiness creeping through her as she noted the troubled look on his face. He hadn't called by with news of Sophie. And Justin had just phoned, so what on earth was this all about?

'Paul Radley,' Taylor said, and paused. Alicia's stomach turned over. 'I believe he's an old acquaintance of yours?'

Oh no. Alicia dropped her gaze, feeling an immediate sense of deep humiliation.

'Mine's not to judge, Alicia.' Taylor smiled kindly. 'I'm merely trying to ascertain all the facts in regard to your daughter.'

Alicia drew in a breath and nodded. 'Yes, of course. Yes, he is,' she confirmed falteringly.

Taylor nodded thoughtfully. 'Justin came to see me,' he said. 'He was rather irate at the time – exhausted, clearly, having been searching for Sophie.'

Alicia nodded, immense sadness settling inside her. She had no idea how Justin was pushing himself on. He wouldn't be sleeping. She could tell he was barely eating. He'd lost weight. She suspected the only thing keeping him going was his determination to find Sophie.

'He seemed very concerned about Mr Radley having any contact with your daughter. I take it he told you Mr Radley did in fact speak to her on the telephone?'

Alicia nodded. 'Yes,' she said tightly. 'He did.'

Taylor studied her for a second. 'And what about future contact, Alicia? If Sophie turns up, which I'm quite sure she will, would you want Mr Radley to be in contact with her?'

'No, absolutely not,' Alicia stated categorically. 'He's… a womaniser,' she added. 'Not the sort of person who would be a good influence on an impressionable young girl.'

'I see.' Taylor nodded. 'Would that be why Justin would want to warn him off, do you think?'

'Warn him off?' Alicia's gaze shot worriedly to his.

'We had a call-out,' Taylor explained, 'from one of the staff at Mr Radley's place of work. Apparently, Justin paid him a visit.'

He let it hang, watching her carefully, then said, 'He attacked him, Alicia. Quite aggressively, by all accounts.'

'*What?*' Alicia stared at him, stunned. *Justin?* He'd never been violent in his life. He simply didn't have it in him to be violent. 'Was he injured? Paul?' she asked, fear that Justin might be arrested causing her chest to constrict.

'He did have an injury, according to my officer's report. Sustained earlier at the gym, according to Mr Radley. It seems he wouldn't confirm the initial report we received. Said there'd been some misunderstanding.'

Now Paul's sudden decision to fly back to Dubai made sense.

'The strange thing is, the attack took place before your husband learned of this contact.' DI Taylor paused. 'A reaction to the difficulties he found himself him, no doubt. Understandable.' He sighed expansively. 'Nevertheless, Justin is still at fault. Please try to persuade him to stay away from Mr Radley, Alicia. He could very easily have been charged with assault, which would have done no one any good, would it?'

Still uncomprehending, Alicia shook her head and nodded all at once. 'He's leaving. Paul... Mr Radley. He says he's going back to Dubai.'

'Ah, right.' Taylor's smile brightened. 'In which case, hopefully that will be one less obstacle on the road to recovery, hey?' he said, getting to his feet. 'I'll see myself out.'

Walking him to the door anyway, Alicia maintained her composure. But when she'd closed the door behind him, she leaned against it and pressed a hand to her forehead. He'd attacked a man. But Justin wasn't aggressive. He'd never condoned violence of any sort. It was because of the paternity test, she realised. He was as determined to be a good father to Sophie as he was to find her. And Justin *was* her father – the person who'd nurtured her, loved her, laughed with her, cried for her. He would never give up on her, never bow out of her life. If there was anything positive to gain from this, it was that Paul Radley at least knew that now.

But what about Justin? What state of mind must he be in?

She picked up her mobile, unsure what she was going to say to him or how much she should reveal of her conversation with DI Taylor.

Justin picked up straight away. 'Hi,' he said. 'Thanks for returning my call.'

Hearing the formality in his tone, the politeness, Alicia felt another crushing wave of sadness.

'Obviously, I would,' she started, and then stopped. He was keeping her at a distance. He'd hung a no-admittance sign on his emotions, one he wouldn't easily let her past, not now. 'Sorry I couldn't get back sooner,' she said, trying to keep the devastation from her own voice. 'DI Taylor was here.'

'I gathered. Did he have anything to say worth listening to?'

'Not in regard to Sophie, no,' Alicia answered cautiously.

Justin sighed wearily. Clearly, he'd expected as much. 'So, why the visit?'

Not sure what his reaction would be, Alicia hesitated. 'He wondered whether I knew that Paul Radley had been in touch with Sophie. He was a bit concerned, I think.'

'About?' Justin asked curiously.

'You. He said… He told me you attacked Paul Radley. He was—'

'He said what?' Justin sounded immediately agitated.

'He was worried about you, Justin. About the consequences. If you'd been charged with assault…'

'It would have been worth it,' Justin assured her.

'It would have affected your job, Justin,' Alicia pointed out, feeling scared that he didn't seem to care. 'Your future.'

Justin didn't answer immediately. 'I don't have much of a future, though, do I, Alicia, without my family?' he said quietly.

Alicia felt fear pierce through her like an icicle. There had been no contempt in his voice, no accusation. Nothing. He'd sounded empty. Flat. As if he truly didn't care.

'I'm sorry if it upset you,' he went on, drawing in a long breath, 'but he had it coming.'

'Sorry?' Alicia shook her head. 'Justin, I'm only upset for *you*. I don't care about—'

'We need to talk,' Justin said quickly over her, as though he had steeled himself to say it.

Alicia nodded, closing her eyes. He needed answers, none of which he would want to hear. 'When?' she asked, gulping back the heavy weight of remorse.

'Tomorrow,' he said. 'At the house.'

Surrounded by the ghosts of what had been, and the future that could never be. It would hurt meeting him there, seeing him there, being reminded of everything she'd thrown away. She didn't think that was Justin's intention, but it was fitting.

CHAPTER FIFTY-ONE

JUSTIN

Covered in a slick film of sweat from his efforts working in the basement, Justin wiped his arm across his forehead and checked his watch. It was early morning, he realised. Time he called it quits. He wasn't sure why he'd decided to come here, to carry on working on the studio. And then he realised it was because he saw Sophie and Luke wherever he went in the house; he would hear them. It was to be in touch with his children.

Tidying up his tools, double-checking he had all the equipment he would need, he turned his attention to the additional LED lighting he'd been installing. The soundproofing had already been done when he'd suspected the existing lighting wasn't sufficient. Wanting the studio to be finished for Sophie's sixteenth, he'd been planning to strip the insulation away and replace the spotlights. Her sixteenth had come and gone. The lighting had never been done. He'd come here on her birthday, but he hadn't been able to bring himself to disturb anything; not that day.

He would finish it. He was determined to. It was his way of keeping hope alive, he supposed. Hope that when she came back, it would be ready. When he'd finished it though, what then? What if Sophie didn't come back? He wasn't ready to contemplate that. Wearily, he climbed the steps back to the hall, where the melodic sound of a child's innocent laughter greeted him. He'd heard it when he'd come once before. It had worried him then. Today, it didn't bother him. He found it quite soothing.

She'd learned to ride her bike, stabiliser-free, here in the hall, he recalled. It had been snowing that day. His gaze travelled the length of the long flagstone floor, where he could see her pedalling furiously, laughing delightedly when she'd realised he'd let go of the saddle and she was doing it all on her own. She'd abandoned her bike and run back to him, when the rug had slipped from under him and he'd ended up flat on his back, cracking his head on the tiles. 'Is it hurting, Daddy?' she'd asked him, her beautiful chestnut eyes wide with alarm.

'It's hurting, baby,' he said now to the wispy spirit of her. *So much, I don't think I can bear it.* Closing his eyes, he swallowed and headed for the stairs, planning to take a shower before leaving. Where he was staying, hot water was a luxury in the bathroom he shared with the other tenants. He didn't need luxury. He needed to function, to wash himself awake, wash the grime from his soul after endless days traipsing the bowels of the city, seeing things he'd always been aware of but could never have truly imagined.

The hallucinations, if that's what they were, were worse upstairs, where the smells of his family were overwhelming: Alicia's lingering perfume; the faded scent of the joss sticks Sophie burned. The sounds. Wherever he went, he couldn't escape them: Sophie's soulful singing; the butterfly wind chime Alicia had hung in the nursery to encourage Luke's hand movements; Luke's gurgles of pleasure as he batted it or managed to catch hold of it. That was the sound that haunted him most. Even in the basement, he heard it. In his single room, he heard it. It would haunt him for the rest of his life.

Hearing the chimes as he bypassed the nursery room door, Justin didn't try to block it out, accepting it instead as part of the insanity his life had become. It was possible, he supposed, that he might be going out of his mind. He couldn't seem to keep a rein on his thoughts – definitely not on his emotions. Everything seemed to mingle into one lately: days, nights, dreams, reality. He'd be thinking, only to realise he'd been verbalising his thoughts. Talking, only to realise he'd stopped and drifted off into some distant memory. When he counted, he sometimes found himself counting out loud, which earned him wary looks from people passing by.

Would it bother him, he wondered as he showered, if the only sounds he heard were those of his kids? If he simply stopped functioning in other areas of his life? He wasn't sure it would. He didn't want to let go of them. Couldn't.

Towelling his hair ten minutes later, he was halfway down the stairs when he realised there was someone at the front door. Justin quashed his irritation as he pulled the door open to find Taylor standing there. Was he doing follow-up calls now, checking up on victims of crime? As if they gave a damn any more who'd broken into their house. That was history. The here and now, the painful reality, was that their daughter was still missing. They still had no idea where she was. And this paragon of the law, what was he doing? Nothing.

Sighing, Justin draped his towel around his neck and eyed the man questioningly.

'We have the forensics team here.' Taylor offered him his short smile – and a completely nonsensical explanation for his visit.

'Forensics?' Justin squinted at him, confused.

Taylor knitted his brow. 'I left you a message, on your voicemail. I spoke with your sister-in-law, too. She said she would pass the information on to Alicia. I assumed she might have told you.'

'No.' Justin shook his head. It seemed Alicia wasn't in the habit of telling him very much at all. 'No, she didn't. So, what is it you're looking for?'

'Anything we might have missed,' Taylor supplied. 'There's been another break-in in the area. It's not exactly a crime wave, but we found some footmarks at the other property. I thought it was worth taking another look here. We'll be concentrating mainly on the gardens, but if it's inconvenient…? It's just, as we already have the men here…'

'No, no major inconvenience.' Justin sighed, thinking he would need to call Alicia, assuming she didn't call first to postpone their meeting now the police were here. It occurred to him she might have thought this was a useful way to avoid facing him. It wouldn't be easy for her: explaining why she'd cheated on him, and then compounded that deceit with a decision that might ultimately crucify him. 'Help yourself.' He shrugged indifferently. 'Have a field day.'

Taylor looked mildly amused at that. 'Am I to take it you're moving back in?' He nodded past him, to where Justin's tools made it obvious he'd been working.

Justin shook his head. 'Under the circumstances, no,' he said, holding the man's gaze. 'We might well sell up. I just came to check the house over and attend to a few things.'

'Oh.' Taylor nodded awkwardly. 'That's a shame. It's a nice property.'

'A family property,' Justin said pointedly. 'Can I do something else for you, Detective? It's just that I'd quite like to get on with searching for my daughter.'

Taylor glanced down and back. 'We are looking, Justin,' he said, with a heavy sigh. 'Every one of my officers has her photograph.'

'You're not looking hard enough,' Justin said, attempting – and failing – to quell a rush of anger as he turned away. 'Fuck it!' he cursed, managing to trip over the drill he'd left in the hall.

'Emotions not entirely under control then?' Taylor observed drily behind him.

'You know what?' Disentangling himself from his drill, Justin turned around, making no attempt this time to hide his anger. 'No, they're not. Would yours be? I mean, look at it from my point of view: my daughter's missing and the people who are supposed to be out finding her are digging up my fucking front garden!'

Taylor drew in a breath and stepped inside, nudging the front door closed behind him. Obviously, he didn't want to be embarrassed in front of the officers whose resources he was wasting on a completely futile task. 'You need to get some sleep, Justin,' he said, his expression dour. 'You're exhausted.'

Justin laughed. 'Shrewd observation,' he said. 'I can see why you're a detective.'

'And make sure you stay away from Paul Radley,' Taylor added, his eyes holding a warning. 'He's leaving for Dubai shortly, isn't he? Just let him go quietly and try to get on with your life.'

Dragging a hand over his neck, Justin smiled contemptuously. 'I'd love to,' he said. 'Unfortunately, thanks to that bastard, I don't have one.'

'I get that.' Taylor nodded empathetically. 'I've been there, remember, though not under such tragic circumstances. But you have to let it go, Justin. Let him go back, and then try to pick up the pieces of your life.'

Justin said nothing. There were no pieces. Clearly, Taylor didn't get it.

'Violence rarely solves anything, Justin,' Taylor went on, echoing what Justin had once thought – in another lifetime. 'You could well have been up on a charge of grievous bodily harm with intent. How would that have helped anything?'

'Oh, the intent was definitely there.' Justin couldn't help himself.

Shooting him a despairing look, Taylor ignored that. 'Between you and me, I have no doubt he had it coming, but you don't deserve the repercussions, and nor does your wife. I might be completely out of line here, and you can tell me to mind my own business, but she cares about you, Justin. Don't let her go without a fight.'

Justin eyed him with ironic amusement.

'Of the non-physical variety,' Taylor added wryly.

CHAPTER FIFTY-TWO

ALICIA

Seeing Justin's car parked outside the house as she pulled into their road, Alicia felt an overpowering sense of heart-crushing homesickness engulf her, and then a flash of panic as she noted the police car beyond it. Parking behind Justin's car, she scrambled out, her insides twisting as she realised two white-suited officers were poking around in the soil of the garden. What on earth were they looking for? Her panic escalating, she hurried towards them and was surprised to see DI Taylor coming around the side of the house.

'Morning,' he said, smiling as he came towards her. 'Oh. I take it you didn't get my message either then? I left one with your sister.'

'No.' Alicia looked at him with a mixture of alarm and apprehension.

'We were investigating another property in the area,' Taylor filled her in, 'and we thought we might take the opportunity to check we hadn't missed anything forensically here. I did run it by your husband, obviously, when we arrived. I hope it's not going to cause you any inconvenience?'

The knot of tension in Alicia's stomach slackened. She'd been imagining all sorts of things in those few seconds climbing from the car. 'No,' she said, 'not if Justin doesn't mind. So, have you found anything?' She nodded curiously towards one of his men, on his hands and knees brushing at the mud.

'Nothing much, no.' DI Taylor followed her gaze. 'Although I did spot your rather nice rose tree. Climbing Lady Hillingdon, isn't it, if I'm not mistaken?'

He was a gardener then? Alicia looked at him interestedly. She hadn't really considered the man beyond the policeman. 'That's right,' she said, an immediate sense of sadness overwhelming her as she glanced towards where the huge creamy butterscotch flowers would bloom come spring.

'I wouldn't mind a cutting sometime,' DI Taylor said. 'I have the perfect space for it outside my patio window.'

'Of course.' Alicia's eyes filled up, despite her best efforts. Would she ever see it bloom again? See her daughter coming through the front door again?

They'd painted the outside of the house together, she and Justin. They'd chosen a cheery yellow for the door with a white trim to complement the red brickwork. They'd wanted something bold and sunny to brighten up the grey days. She could almost see Sophie coming through the door now. Dressed in her jeans, puffer jacket and a furry bobble hat, earphones strung around her neck and her phone in her hands, she was turning to chatter nineteen to the dozen to Justin, who was coming through the front door behind her. Listening attentively, he was wearing his patient expression, as ever, an amused smile playing around his mouth as he glanced towards where Alicia waited in her car.

They'd been going Christmas shopping, she remembered. They'd made it a rule, even in the midst of the Christmas madness, to spend family time together. They'd go out for their own pleasure only, browsing the shops, pointing out things they hoped Santa would bring them. They'd do lunch, stroll, take in the sparkling decorations and twinkly bright lights, refusing, just for one special day, to put themselves under any pressure.

They would never have that again.

Pulling in a shaky breath, Alicia attempted to suppress the tears that would come if she held on to the memory for too long.

'I'll let you get on,' Taylor said, his smile sympathetic. 'He's inside.' He reached to squeeze her arm, which, ridiculously, made her feel even more like crying. 'You two should talk.'

Alicia smiled faintly and then braced herself and headed towards the house. The locks had been changed since the break-in. Justin had organised it. She hadn't asked him for a key. In truth, she hadn't wanted to ask, terrified that he might suggest she didn't need one.

Answering it a minute after she'd rung the bell, Justin offered her a small smile. Alicia took some comfort from that, from the fact that he didn't appear to openly loathe her.

'Can I come in?' she asked him, smiling hesitantly back.

'Yes. Of course. Sorry. I, er…' Looking distracted, as he per-petually seemed to be, and utterly exhausted, Justin stepped back.

He'd been in the basement. Alicia noticed the door was slightly ajar, the tool bag outside it. He'd obviously been working on the studio – Sophie's sixteenth birthday surprise. Alicia's heart wrenched as she looked back at him. 'How's it going?' she asked, for something to say.

'So-so,' Justin shrugged. 'It's something to do.'

He didn't want to talk about it. Of course he wouldn't. He wouldn't want to talk about anything to do with the house. The material things and joint projects they'd shared in it. The memories. Alicia cursed her insensitivity.

Dropping her gaze, she turned and walked to the lounge. She didn't sit. She wasn't sure what to do. She felt bereft, a devastating sense of sadness encompassing her again as she stood in the middle of the room that was truly the heart of the home they'd built together, that they'd lived and laughed in together. Her breath caught painfully in her chest as her eyes fell on the TV remote, abandoned where Sophie always left it: on the arm of the sofa at the end she'd always claimed as her own.

Alicia squeezed her eyes tight shut and tried to breathe. If she caught sight of anything of Lucas's, her legs would fail her, along with her courage. She *couldn't*.

'Can I get you a coffee?' Justin said, his tone awkward as he followed her in.

Alicia shook her head. *Don't be polite. Please don't be polite*, she begged silently. She couldn't bear that he didn't know how else to be. 'No,' she said quickly, her throat tight. 'Thanks. I'm… not thirsty.'

Justin nodded, glancing down and back again. His eyes, finally meeting hers, were full of dark shadows, such insurmountable pain.

'I didn't realise DI Taylor was here,' she said, again for want of something to say. The awful empty silence hung like a guillotine between them.

'Jessica didn't tell you he was coming then?' Justin eyed her curiously.

Alicia shook her head. 'No. It must have slipped her mind.'

His eyes narrowing briefly, Justin nodded, and walked past her to the window, where he stood with his back to her.

'Justin…' Alicia noted the stiff set of his shoulders, as if he too was bracing himself – for more hurt than had already been heaped on him, more weight that he couldn't possibly carry. 'I'm sorry,' she blurted, the same two stupid, ineffectual words she'd uttered before. Words that could never communicate how desperately sorry she was.

Justin drew in a tight, ragged breath.

The tick of the carriage clock on the mantel grew louder in the heavy silence between them, punctuated by the scraping of the officers at work outside. Alicia was uncertain what to do, whether to go to him. Should she stay? What could she say? It was too late. There'd been no way for her to explain it years ago, and there was no way to explain it now. Whatever she said, she couldn't undo the damage, the pain she'd caused him. She was supposed to be the nurturer, the carer for her family. She'd broken everything. And she couldn't fix it.

'Justin?' She tried tearfully again, needing a response from him – accusations, questions, a release of the fury that was surely stuffed inside him. Anything.

'Would you like me to go?' she asked him, after another hour-long minute ticked by.

Alicia waited, working to stifle the tears he wouldn't want to witness and with which he couldn't possibly sympathise.

But still Justin didn't answer.

He didn't want to hear it. That was his answer. As the tiny sliver of hope to which she'd dared cling began to fade, Alicia turned quietly to the door. He could never forgive her. She'd finally lost him. He would never know that she would never be whole again without him.

'Why, Alicia?' Justin said simply, as she reached the hall.

Alicia's heart lurched.

Stopping, she turned and walked slowly back. 'I don't know,' she said, her voice barely a whisper.

'I see.' Justin shook his head.

'I didn't mean it to happen.' Alicia took another step in. 'I don't know why I—'

'How many times, Alicia?' he asked. 'How many times did you not mean it to happen?'

And there it was. Alicia closed her eyes. The reason he could never, ever believe she hadn't meant to hurt him as cruelly as she had. It was impossible. 'I'd been drinking. More than I normally would. I…' She trailed hopelessly off, the ominous tick of the clock growing louder still as she struggled for any way to explain herself that didn't scream her guilt.

'I think it might be an idea if you did go, Alicia,' he said, his tone hoarse.

And Alicia felt her heart fold up inside her. Swallowing, she half turned to the door, and then wavered. 'I thought she would save you,' she murmured. 'Sophie. I thought she would give you something to live for.'

'She did,' Justin said throatily.

But Sophie wasn't here any more.

And now he had nothing.

CHAPTER FIFTY-THREE

JUSTIN

Justin didn't even hear the door close as Alicia left. He was deep in thought, his mind going back to the time he now guessed it had all happened: the nights she'd supposedly stayed at a girlfriend's. To the first time she'd stayed, when she hadn't been very well. A hangover, she said. She hadn't looked well.

Painful though it was to be in there, Justin went up to their bedroom, feeling compelled to check their photo albums. He wasn't sure what for. A need for visual clarification of the milestones in their marriage, maybe?

They'd been to one of her friend's weddings a few days after; Alicia had been a bridesmaid. Justin remembered that bleak time in their relationship painfully well, because that was when he'd made up his mind he needed help. Seeing Alicia so closed in on herself, realising how badly he'd shut her out, he'd made a monumental effort to be more social, to be there for her. She'd been pale and drawn at the wedding and the reception, only half listening to the conversation around her, to him. He'd been scared they might be about to split up, and he'd redoubled his efforts. Depression, like a suffocating grey blanket, was still pressing down on him, but he'd woken up to the fact that, while trying to deal with his grief, he'd been pushing her away for a long time. If he didn't do something about it, he was going to lose her. The day of the wedding, he'd desperately wanted to show her how much he'd loved her, and had prayed it wasn't too late. She'd still had the bug in her system, though, so intimacy hadn't been an option. He'd hoped that was the truth. That she'd still wanted him.

It had been the night after that when they'd finally talked, when he'd opened up to her about how he felt. Guilty. As guilty as hell. He hadn't been able to get it out of his mind, the image of his sister bleeding out from her knife wounds on the hall floor. She'd tried to run. She'd been breathing, barely. But she'd been alive. Might have lived, had his medical knowledge not deserted him. By the time the paramedics had arrived, it had been too late. He'd watched the lifeblood ebb from her body, powerless to stop it. There'd been no way to move on, to even begin to process his grief. He been stuck, unable to forgive himself, unable to shed the tears he'd desperately needed to.

He'd broken his bloody heart when he'd ashamedly confessed all that to Alicia, which had been therapeutic in itself, releasing the stop valve on his emotions. They'd moved forwards after that, been stronger as a couple. There for each other. Or so he'd thought.

Pulling open the drawer they kept the albums in, he pulled a few out, flicking through them. Realising the top few were more recent ones, where Alicia had painstakingly recorded memories of Luke, he placed them carefully aside, the pain of his loss far too raw. Delving further, he found another recent one: photos of Alicia, pregnant with Luke, radiant, smiling, never in her worst nightmares imagining she would be burying her son before his first birthday.

Swallowing emotionally, Justin placed that along with the others on the bed. He searched in the drawer for older albums, rifling through various bits of paper and certificates, and realised they were missing. Simply not there. Surely to God they hadn't been stolen? Hadn't Alicia kept her scan photos in here, too, for both Sophie and Luke? Where the hell were they?

He pulled his phone from his pocket and headed up to the third floor, where he knew their disorganised collection of older photos were still boxed in the spare room. The ones he'd been particularly interested in looking at would most likely be in there. In the meantime, he would very much like to know where the others were. He couldn't imagine why anyone would want to steal family photographs, unless they were a member of that family – namely Alicia. He knew this meant that she didn't intend to come back.

His thumb hovering over her number, he hesitated. Did he really want to speak to her now, after the conversation they'd just had? No, not yet. That was still too raw as well. Going into the spare room, he located the box he was looking for and began sifting through it as he selected Jessica's number.

'Hey, Jess, sorry to bother you,' he said, pulling photos out and examining them as he spoke. 'I'm guessing you're at work.'

'Trust me, I'd rather talk to you,' Jessica said brightly.

'Not that scintillating then?'

'The work? No. Talking to you, however…' Jessica joked.

Justin wasn't sure he'd ever been scintillating. 'Can I ask you something, Jess?'

'Ask away.'

'Do you know if Alicia brought some photographs with her to your house? Family albums?'

Jessica thought about it. 'I'm not sure. Are they not there then?'

'No. Definitely missing. Most of them, in fact, apart from very recent ones and some older photos going way back. But I can't imagine anyone would want them.'

'Apart from Alicia.' Jessica echoed his own thoughts. 'Oh dear, she probably has then.' She paused. 'Look, I wouldn't worry about it, Justin. That's not necessarily a bad sign, is it? That's she's taken them, I mean. She probably just wants some reminders of her children around her.'

Or more likely she was taking things she definitely wanted to keep before they reached the stage of dividing their property. It was clear from what Jessica had said that she was thinking along the same lines.

'I take it you didn't get much chance to talk then?' Jessica asked. 'With that DI Taylor being there, I mean. His timing wasn't great, was it?'

'No.' Justin frowned. 'No, it wasn't. You did let Alicia know they were due to arrive this morning? Taylor said he'd left a message with you.'

'Yes.' Jessica said assuredly. 'I knew she was meeting you, so I made sure to. Why?'

So why the hell would Alicia lie about it, Justin wondered. She hadn't used it as an excuse to postpone. She'd met him there, as they'd arranged. She hadn't actually said very much – but then he wasn't very receptive to hearing anything she might have to say. It made no sense to him whatsoever. 'No reason,' he said, then, finding the photos he was looking for, added, 'I'd better go. Thanks, Jess.'

'No problem. I'm worried about you, Justin. I'm here if you ever need to talk.'

'Er, yes, thanks.' Justin's frown deepened as he ended the call.

CHAPTER FIFTY-FOUR

ALICIA

A deluge of freezing rain soaking through her clothes, seemingly to her bones. Alicia pulled her coat tight. Shivering as the wind whipped overhanging branches and fat raindrops plopped moodily around her, she wrapped her arms about herself and continued through the part of the cemetery where once proud Victorian headstones had submitted to the elements. Walking on, past weathered stones and wingless cherubs, she avoided reading the inscriptions. She didn't need any reminders of how short life was.

Reaching her destination, a secluded spot surrounded by beech trees and overlooked by the church, she stopped. *I don't think a cup of tea's going to fix this, Mum,* she said silently, gulping back the lump like granite that was wedged in her chest. Swiping a tear from her cheek, she took a step closer, then looked to the pregnant grey sky and sank to her knees. 'Sorry, baby,' she said out loud to little Lucas. 'Mummy's not crying, sweetheart. It's just rain. Just the rain.'

Her jeans already saturated and heavy, she didn't care about the wet mud seeping through to her skin. She just wanted to stay here a little while with those she needed to hold her, those she needed to hold so badly.

She didn't hear her phone at first, buried deep in her pocket. A message alert. She felt sure it was Justin, but she didn't scramble for it. There didn't seem to be much point any more. There was nothing she could say to him. Nothing she could stand to hear him say. Not just now. They couldn't fix each other's hurt. They had been able to once. They'd talked all night, made love the next morning and she'd held him then, held him so tight that she'd been scared she might hurt him physically. He'd bared his soul to her. Told her how scared he was, how inadequate he felt after losing his family. She'd sworn she would do whatever she could so that he would never hurt like that again. She would extract herself from the situation with Paul Radley by any means possible. But then Paul Radley had extracted himself from her life – suddenly. Miraculously, she'd thought then. She'd truly thought it was a sign that not telling Justin the child she was carrying might not be his was the right thing to do. Her man was hurting, and she could help him. She could provide him a family.

Oh God. Burying her face in her hands, Alicia allowed the tears to come. How wrong had she been? Had she been mistaken about everything? Every time she thought about it, every time she'd listened to Paul talking about her deceit, her denying him the right to see his child, a new doubt crept in.

Going over it yet again, half of her screaming at her that she *was* right, the other half telling her she could have been so wrong, she stayed where she was for a while. Rain and tears dripping down her face, she told Luke she had a cold, that was all. That's why she seemed a little bit teary-eyed. A little white lie, this time to protect her child.

She checked her phone eventually. Justin had sent a text. *Did you take the photograph albums?* That was all it said. No sign-off. Nothing. She'd hoped he might have been trying to contact her to say he'd changed his mind and wanted to talk after all, to listen to what she had to say. Though what she could actually tell him she was growing steadily more unsure of. There was no hope now. She knew that. In looking for the albums, he'd obviously been seeking to salvage what memories she hadn't poisoned. Or perhaps he was trying to clarify in his mind that they were all fake memories, woven around the lie she'd told, the life they'd built based on that lie. It had all come crashing down. The foundations had been crumbling since day one, and now it was submitting to the elements, just like the forgotten Victorian headstones. She couldn't stop it. She was too weak. She always had been.

No. She texted back. And then she muted her phone. Not because she thought he might ring or text again. But because she thought he might not.

CHAPTER FIFTY-FIVE

JUSTIN

As Justin walked towards the pub, he passed a couple who were obviously worse for wear. Seeing the girl hunched under her boyfriend's arm, which was possessively draped about her, he couldn't help but notice the bruising on her arms. Justin felt his gut clench. He'd seen it too many times, in his work in accident and emergency, treating women with smashed faces, broken bones and bruises that had obviously been caused by a fist.

Pulling his attention away from where it very probably wasn't wanted, he attempted to focus on his own problems, on what he would do next in regard to Sophie, and his marriage.

He needed to talk to Alicia again – obviously he would need to do that. Unfortunately, she wasn't answering his calls or his texts. She was okay; she'd a hot bath and gone to bed early with a glass of wine and a book, Jessica had said. But after their conversation earlier, had she really? He couldn't see it. Just couldn't.

Following the couple into the pub, he noted the inside was much like others he'd been in in the area: decor circa nineties; depressing smoke; yellow and brown. Stepping into the lounge, which was much the same as the bar area, dark and dingy, he didn't draw much attention. Wearing jeans and a T-shirt, he made sure to fit in with the general clientele, rather than be mistaken for the law, which he had been once or twice. At such times, he'd found, people weren't very forthcoming.

Locating the man's whereabouts at a table at the back wall, Justin saw he now had his arm hooked around the girl's neck, yanking her towards him. Judging by the girl's body language, she wasn't a willing participant in the not-so-loving embrace.

'Dean… Get off!' she said, scowling and clearly upset as she attempted to pull away from him.

The guy only tightened his grip, his expression one of obvious contempt as he snarled something in her ear.

'I did not!' the girl refuted. 'Dean, for God's sake, pack it in!' she shouted, struggling to break free of him and then scrambling hastily away.

The 'boyfriend' was up in an instant, grabbing the girl's wrist and dragging her back. 'Sit the fuck down!' he bellowed, shoving her hard onto the bench seat. 'Where're you going, hey? To that tosser you've been having it off with, is that it?'

'No!' she screamed. 'You're mental, Dean. I haven't been near anyone else, I keep telling you. Those drugs are doing your head in.'

'You're going nowhere.' The guy leaned in to clutch a fistful of her top and pull her up again. 'You fucking *slut*.'

It was the slap, a stinging blow across her face, that had Justin's temper snapping, launching him across the room in a second flat.

'Let her go,' he seethed, as the man clamped a hand around the girl's throat, shoving her hard against the wall.

'Fuck off,' the guy spat in his direction, and squeezed harder.

Justin looked from him to the girl's face. She was gagging – literally gasping for breath. What the hell was the matter with everybody, standing around letting *this* happen?

'I said, let her go!' Justin took a step forward.

'You want some an' all, do ya?' The man glared at him, his bloodshot eyes bulging with fury. 'Back off!'

Seeing him turning his attention back to the girl, Justin reacted instinctively. 'I said let her go,' he warned him. 'You'll *kill* her.' Intending to drag him off her, he moved meaningfully towards him, and the man turned on him like a rabid dog. Spitting obscenities, he seized Justin's shirt, pulling him forward and landing first one, and then two, heavy blows to his jaw.

Stumbling backwards into a table, Justin held his footing – just – as the man advanced towards him, his face puce and contorted with rage. 'You really shouldn't have done that,' he said. His own temper spiking, he righted himself, wiped the back of his hand across his mouth and stood to face him.

The man stopped, his chest heaving, his eyes full of violent malevolence, though Justin saw a flash of uncertainty.

A coward, Justin thought, standing his ground. They all were – cowardly scum, picking on people who didn't have a chance of fighting back.

'Tosser.' The man's mouth curled into a snarl as he stepped towards Justin, and then shoved violently past him.

Cursing liberally as he went, the man strode on and banged out of the exit, and Justin breathed a huge sigh of relief. The guy was bigger than he was. Heavier. Justin wasn't sure he would have been able to hold his own. 'Are you okay?' he asked, turning back to the girl.

She nodded shakily. 'Yeah, thanks,' she said. 'He goes a bit mental sometimes. He'll cool off eventually.'

Justin sighed inwardly. It sounded like she'd probably accept his apologies, which would no doubt be profuse – until the next time. 'Do you want me to call anybody?' he offered. 'Give you a lift somewhere?'

'No.' She shook her head and indicated her phone. 'I've called my brother. He's on his way.'

Justin nodded. 'I'll be at the bar,' he said, intending to stick around until the brother showed up. 'You might want to do yourself a favour and find someone who doesn't talk with his fists,' he suggested. 'You only get one life. Why waste it on someone like that?'

'I don't intend to,' she assured him. 'I'm going to college. Gonna get away from him.'

'Sounds like a plan.' Justin smiled, despite the sharp ache in his jaw.

Going back to the bar, keeping one eye on the girl until the brother arrived, Justin rang Jessica. He needed answers. If he wasn't going to get those answers from Alicia, then he needed to meet up with Jessica, in private – something, it was occurring to him, she seemed pretty damn desperate to do. She might not have all the answers, but she was Alicia's bloody sister. She would have some of them. Or she ought to. If she'd been 'sworn to secrecy', as she'd repeated more than once, Justin wanted to know exactly what about. The affair? The pregnancy? If she'd known about the affair, and he was working on the assumption that she had, then he needed the details. He hadn't wanted to hear them before, but he did now, every single sordid one of them.

Arranging to meet Jessica the next evening, Justin ended his call, and watched as a man came into the pub and walked directly across to the girl. Seeing her jump up to meet him, he waited for her to pass by. Relieved when she gave him a thumbs up as she did, he knocked the dregs of his pint back and headed out after them.

He'd gone no more than a few yards when his progress was cut short, by first one, then two, and finally three thuggish men. Justin didn't have time to consider his options before he was dead-legged from behind.

'Oh dear, poor sod's legless, ain't you, mate?' someone said tauntingly, close to his ear.

Justin felt his collar being clutched and tugged tight to his throat. An arm slid around his upper torso. They were obviously going to kick the shit out of him, he guessed, his gut turning over. He would stand no chance of fighting back against three of them. All he could do was pray they stopped before they killed him.

Justin guessed wrong.

Jesus Christ, no. Seeing the sharp glint of the blade in his peripheral vision, he felt sweat prickle his skin, saturating the shirt on his back, as he realised what was about to happen.

'Don't,' Justin begged, swallowing against the arm now constricting his airway. '*Please*, don't...' His words died on his lips as he felt the knife going in, sliding slickly under his ribs, then a sharp, violent twist, before the blade was pulled out.

Please, God, no. Justin sank from his knees to all fours as the men backed away. This wasn't happening. *Please don't let this be happening. Sophie.* As searing pain ripped through his side, Justin blinked the perspiration from his eyes and struggled to get to his feet, only to find the use of his limbs had deserted him.

He stared at the pavement and sucked in a breath. It stopped painfully short of his chest. Nausea churned his stomach. His heart thudded, loud and sluggish in his head.

No! He started counting.

Tried to control his involuntary shuddering as the crimson stain on the hall floor seeped towards him. Shaking his head, he blinked against the bright light that shone through the cracked mirror. Then blinked again, hard, as blood seeped from the cracks, rich red globules, tears for his children. *Warm blood. His blood.*

His mind screaming, he attempted to shut out the sounds – melodic laughter, chimes tinkling. But they weren't chimes. They were church bells. And his baby was singing.

Justin jolted, gulping back the salty taste in his throat as the dark closed in around him.

CHAPTER FIFTY-SIX

JESSICA

Finally, Jessica thought, tearing the note of the address Justin had given her from the pad and slipping it safely into her handbag. He was a typical man, bottling up his emotions, trying to be macho when his poor heart was steadily breaking. But he'd reached the point where he needed to share, and she would be there for him.

She wouldn't tell Alicia, obviously. She had brought it all on herself, but she was utterly devastated, poor soul. She'd come home soaked through to the skin and covered in mud. Jessica's supposed-to-be-amusing quip about her having been rolling around with a rugby team hadn't raised even the smallest of smiles. Quite the opposite, in fact. She handed her their usual cure-all cup of tea, and Alicia had promptly burst into tears.

Pouring herself a glass of wine, Jessica supposed she ought to go up and check on her. She'd been worried she'd drowned herself in the bath at one point. Now, since she hadn't heard a peek from her – not so much as the squeak of a floorboard since Alicia had gone to her bedroom – she was worrying she might have taken more than the one sleeping tablet she'd suggested might help her rest.

Five minutes later, a tray in her hands, Jessica nudged the spare bedroom door handle down. 'Only me,' she said quietly, in case Alicia was sleeping, and then went on in.

Oh, not sleeping then. She saw her sister silhouetted against the window. What on earth was she doing standing there in only her skimpy pyjamas? She'd catch her death of cold after coming home soaking wet. She really was a worry.

'Ali?' she said, placing the tray on the dressing table. 'Are you all right, sweetie?'

Alicia didn't answer. She simply continued to stare up at the stars, as if looking for the answer to the universe.

Uh-oh. She was swaying on her feet, Jessica noted, her gaze shooting to the bedside table and an almost empty bottle of wine. Oh dear, it looked like Alicia was attempting to anaesthetise the pain again – as if alcohol ever could, particularly if you didn't partake on a regular basis. And Alicia didn't. Or at least she hadn't for a very long time. Obviously, she'd snuck the bottle up in her bag. She really ought to let Justin know about this, Jessica thought. Alicia obviously wasn't coping at all.

Sighing, Jessica went across and placed an arm around her. 'What are you doing, sweetheart?' she asked kindly. 'You know drinking doesn't help anything. It only ever brings things into sharp focus.'

'It doesn't,' Alicia said, reluctant to let go of the glass Jessica was attempting to prise from her hand. 'It just makes everything more fuddled.'

'Muddled,' Jessica corrected her, steering her gently away from the window.

'Blurry.' Jessica nodded, allowing herself to be led to the bed. 'It's like there's two voices in my head. One's saying, "Stop doubting yourself." And the other one's saying—'

'You've drunk too much, Alicia. You really shouldn't—'

'*Exactly.*' Alicia plopped down. And swayed. 'I'm a lush. A drunken slush. Someone who gets para… paral… as drunk as a fish and then throws herself at the nearest man.'

Oh God. Jessica sighed again, heavily. Now she was slurring her words. 'A skunk, Ali.'

'Sorry?' Alicia closed one eye and looked at her askew.

'It's as drunk as a skunk or drinks like a… never mind.' Jessica smiled tolerantly. 'Come on, tuck up under the duvet and have a nice sleep, why don't you? I've brought you some toast.' She tried to tempt her in hopes of getting something down her to soak up the alcohol. 'You'll feel better for a bite to eat and a nice cup of tea.'

'No. Uh-uh.' Alicia shook her head and got unsteadily to her feet. 'I'm going on Facebook.'

Jessica watched, perplexed, as Alicia groped for her phone and jabbed randomly at it. 'Do you think I am?' She looked back to Jessica after a second, her eyes slightly unfocussed and full of uncertainty. 'A drunken trollop, I mean. I bet Justin thinks I am. Do you think I am, Jess?'

Definitely worried now, Jessica felt her heart sink. She didn't want her going gaga on her. Justin was bound to ask how she was and she could hardly lie to him about that. He might well talk to Alicia. She couldn't tell him she was fine if she wasn't. 'No, Ali, I don't think you're a trollop. And neither do you. It's just the drink, lovely. It's making you emotional.'

'Justin will think I am though, won't he?' A tear spilling down her cheek, Alicia went back to her phone. 'So, *c'est la vie*.' She shrugged and tried to focus on the screen. 'I might as well live up to my reputation, mightn't I?'

'Right.' Jessica heaved in a breath. 'Alicia, what are you doing exactly?' she asked, as Alicia continued to squint at her phone.

'Picking up a man,' Alicia supplied, with a determined nod, which was completely at odds with the tears now streaming down her face.

'From Facebook?' Shaking her head, Jessica eyed the ceiling. 'I think you need a bit more practice, sweetie,' she said, reaching to ease the phone from her hand as Alicia plopped back down on the bed – and almost missed it.

Damn. Jessica swallowed as a thought occurred. 'You haven't taken the sleeping tablet I gave you, have you?' she asked worriedly.

Wiping her hand under her nose, Alicia shook her head. 'No,' she said, her voice full of anguish. 'They make me feel ill in the mornings.'

Thank God for that. Jessica blew out a sigh of relief. Having to ring Justin in his medical capacity to tell him his wife was popping pills and washing them down with wine wasn't something she would have relished doing. Then again, should she tell him, for Alicia's sake?

'You need to lie down, Alicia,' she said firmly, as her sister leaned precariously to one side, 'before you fall down.'

Encouraging her to lie back, Jessica played mother – not that it was a role she wanted right now. 'There we go,' she said, making sure her feet were in and then fluffing up her pillows and tugging up the duvet.

Flicking on the bedside lamp, she fetched the tray and offered her the toast.

'I can't, Jess.' Alicia shook her head, looking a little green around the gills. 'I'm sorry.'

Jessica huffed inwardly. She had her hair to wash and her nails to do. She didn't want to be playing nursemaid half the night. 'All right,' she relented. 'But you have to promise to eat something in the morning. You need to stay strong for your family.'

The last came out a little more stridently than she'd intended, and Jessica felt a bit guilty as she watched another tear slide down her sister's cheek.

'Come on, Ali,' she said, holding on to her patience and smoothing her hair away from her face. 'Things will look better in the morning.'

'Do you think?' Alicia emitted a strangulated laugh at that.

Jessica actually didn't think they would. And Alicia would definitely be feeling ill after drinking that lot on top of no food. She did hope she wasn't going to have a complete breakdown. Her eyes were bloodshot, red-rimmed and, frankly, looked like two peepholes in the snow against her pallid complexion. She'd lost an awful lot of weight – Jessica felt the tiniest bit peeved about that, having been struggling to lose even a pound over the last two weeks. She'd barely uttered a word since she got back, and when she did speak it was distractedly, with a glazed, faraway look in her eye.

Jessica sat with her a while. When, at last, Alicia's eyelids finally grew heavy, Jessica was hugely relieved. She had things to do.

CHAPTER FIFTY-SEVEN

SOPHIE

'What did you say this was again?' Sophie asked, referring to the classical music he was fond of playing while she helped him clear up after their meal. It had been pasta again – which it seemed he was also fond of – but without the meat. Garlicky mushroom penne he'd said it was, and it hadn't been bad.

'Beethoven's Moonlight Sonata,' Paul supplied, wiping down the cooker, which he kept meticulously clean. Sophie stacked the dishwasher, making sure to put everything in the exact order he'd specified, since she'd apparently stacked it completely wrong last time. 'I find this one particularly calming. It's scientifically proven that calm classical music is an effective way to alleviate stress. Did you know that? Listening to soothing music has a relaxing effect on the body and mind. It mesmerises you.' He paused in his rigorous wiping. 'Captivates you, almost. Allows you to explore your emotions, delve deep inside and...'

Sophie watched him interestedly as he narrowed his eyes, glancing off somewhere.

He obviously sensed her watching him. 'And you don't really like it, do you?' He looked at her with a tolerant half-smile.

'I do,' Sophie refuted. 'I like most music, but...' She screwed up her nose. 'It's a bit maudlin, isn't it? This particular track, I mean.'

Paul sighed and shook his head, clearly despairing of her musical ignorance. 'So, what mood-inspiring music do you fancy then?

'Adele?' Sophie suggested hopefully.

He rolled his eyes. 'Adele it is,' he said, instructing Alexa accordingly.

'Brilliant.' Sophie grinned and turned back to her task. 'I've missed my music… without my phone.' Dropping a subtle hint, she sneaked another peek at him.

Paul's sigh was longer this time. 'Go on then,' he said, retrieving a credit card from his phone wallet. 'Go and order one online,' he said, offering it to her.

Sophie stared at it agog. 'Really?'

'Well, you obviously can't live without one.' Paul shrugged good-naturedly. 'But run it by me before you hit purchase,' he said, as Sophie gleefully grabbed the card.

'Will do.' Sophie smiled, delighted. 'Cheers, Paul.'

'No worries. Get yourself some shoes, while you're browsing. Can't have you running around in your socks forever, can we? It's not very hygienic.'

'Yes. Right.' Sophie furrowed her brow. She hadn't heard that one before. 'Small problem,' she said.

Paul arched an eye curiously.

'I don't have anything to browse on,' Sophie pointed out.

'Ah. Of course you don't.' Paul downed his cloth and went to the dining area, where his jacket was hanging on a chair. 'You can use my laptop,' he said, retrieving his study keys to go and fetch it.

'No dipping into files, though, Sophie,' he said, coming back with the laptop and setting it up on the dining table. 'I have confidential client information on here, remember?'

'I won't,' Sophie assured him, her eyes straying to the jacket pocket he'd dropped his keys back into. He'd kept the study locked since he'd found her in there. She supposed it was fair enough, since he had all that confidential stuff. She still wanted to know what was in those desk drawers he'd been so concerned about, though, and why it was her mother's photo he kept on his desk.

CHAPTER FIFTY-EIGHT

ALICIA

Alicia couldn't shake the feeling that something was wrong. Justin had called every day since Sophie went missing, but today she hadn't heard a thing from him. Her useless attempt to explain why she'd taken a decision to ruin his life had driven him to some darker place than he had already been in. She would never forget the emotion in his voice when he'd confirmed that Sophie had given him something worth living for.

Had given him, was the thought that had been plaguing her. Assisted by far too much wine, she'd drifted off to sleep with that thought in her head. Her nightmares had been as bad as her reality. She'd found herself in an *Alice in Wonderland*, haunted distortion of her house, where she heard her family – voices and laughter and tears emerging from rooms she couldn't reach, no matter how hard she ran. Stairs – first one flight, then two – stretched before her like elongated rubber.

She'd left Justin in an empty house as haunted to him as hers was in her dreams, with nothing but the hope he might find Sophie. He'd been working on the studio to keep that hope alive. He would be so desperately lonely, so broken inside. She had to talk to him. If only to hear him say he didn't want to talk to her, she had to hear his voice, know that he was all right physically, if not emotionally. Hesitating for a second, she selected his number, and her anxiety increased as his phone went straight to voicemail.

'Any news?' Jess asked worriedly, coming into the kitchen as Alicia keyed in a text.

'No answer,' Alicia said, fear that something had happened to him gnawing away at her insides. He might have simply decided to stop contacting her – he wasn't beholden to her now, after all – but the nagging voice telling her something was wrong just wouldn't go away.

'He's probably busy. Out searching, possibly?' Jessica suggested, looking as concerned as Alicia felt. 'He might be in a bad reception area. Have you tried the hospital?'

'I'm doing that now,' Alicia said, waiting for the hospital to pick up.

Finding out he wasn't there either, apprehension settled like ice in the pit of her tummy. He might not want to talk to her – might never want to ever again – but for him to remain uncontactable when there was even the slightest possibility she might be trying to get in touch with news of Sophie, that just didn't make sense.

'Give him another half hour,' Jessica said, looking worried now as she checked her own phone. She knew, too, Alicia thought, that Justin wouldn't cut all contact under these circumstances.

He would call. *Please let him call.* Keying in a text to him, Alicia tried to quash the insistent niggle that told her he wouldn't. An hour later, she was half out of her mind with worry and incapable of sitting still. She had no idea where he was. He'd been looking for Sophie in the most godforsaken places. He could be anywhere. Lying injured in some backstreet. Unable to get help. Unable to call for help.

He was adamant he would find Sophie – or die trying. He'd said it. Alicia knew he would go wherever his search took him, with no regard for his own safety.

She was about to call DI Taylor when her phone rang. Terror gripped her stomach as the detective's number flashed up.

'Alicia, it's Justin…' he said, and Alicia reeled as even more of her world fell apart.

CHAPTER FIFTY-NINE

ALICIA

Yanked from a fitful sleep, panic flooding every pore in her body, Alicia's eyes shot to the monitor, and her heart rate returned to somewhere near normal. Reassured by the steady *blip*, *blip* indicating his vital signs were stable, she looked to where her hand still lay on Justin's, her fingers curled softly around his. He hadn't moved. No movement at all, apart from the rapid flicker of his eyelids as his eyes chased his dreams.

Or nightmares.

The cardiothoracic surgeons had worked relentlessly, and by some miracle they'd managed to control the haemorrhaging caused by the knife wound. And it *had* been a miracle. Even with fast surgical intervention, his chances had been slim. He was weak, but, God willing, he would recover physically. Mentally and emotionally, though, Alicia knew those wounds might be unlikely to heal.

He still looked deathly pale against the stark white of the sheets. Alicia studied his profile, a strong profile, which so often gave nothing away of the man inside. A good, dependable man, brought to his knees, by her. She desperately wanted to lie next to him, hold him, as he'd held her after the emergency surgery she'd had to deliver their baby boy. He'd been so gentle, so caring, both immediately after the birth and every day thereafter, until little

Lucas had been stolen away. Until Paul Radley had walked back into her life and stolen Justin's happiness away.

Squeezing his hand gently, she leaned to brush his cheek with a kiss. 'I never stopped loving you, Justin,' she whispered. 'Never.'

Forcing her tears back, she prayed silently that God would find it within his mercy to bring his daughter back to him. Then almost shot out of her skin as Justin said, 'Tell her I'm sorry.'

'What?' Getting unsteadily to her feet, Alicia searched his face.

'Sophie, tell her, will you? I—' Justin coughed and then squeezed her hand hard.

Alicia wasted no time, jabbing buttons and calling for help, and when it came, even while they were checking monitors and tubes, Justin didn't let go of her hand.

Finally, his pain medication adjusted and as comfortable as he could be, he dozed. It was a fitful sleep. He would jolt painfully awake, perspiration beading his brow and confusion in his eyes. He spoke occasionally – incoherently, mostly. 'Where's Sophie?' he'd asked several times. He'd asked where Luke was, too, which broke Alicia's heart all over again, for Justin. The nurse had confirmed that the morphine was feeding his confusion, but still Alicia worried. Justin needed help. Whatever kind of counselling he needed, she would support him, if he would let her. Whatever he wanted, she wouldn't fight him. She might not deserve to survive, but he did.

Alicia checked again. He was still sleeping. Knowing it might be the last time she would spend a night by his side, she brushed his damp hair from his forehead, pressed her lips lightly against it, and then settled back down to watch him. She wouldn't go, even if he didn't want her there, until he was out of danger.

CHAPTER SIXTY

JUSTIN

Drifting in and out of sleep, Justin opened his eyes as he heard a tap on the door.

'Only me,' Jessica said, giving him a bright smile as she poked her head around it. 'Bit of a drastic way to get out of our date, isn't it, Justin?'

Easing himself up in the bed, Justin smiled.

'I thought I'd bring you a few things.' Jessica came on in, rattling a carrier bag and walking across to him. Or rather, clip-clopping across to him on heels that could definitely be described as vertiginous. She was a little overdressed, surely, for office or hospital visits. Noting the tight skirt and top, Justin made sure not to let his gaze linger.

'Cheers.' He smiled. 'You really shouldn't have bothered. I intend to be gone as soon as I can.'

'Not too soon?' Jessica looked at him, alarmed. 'I mean, I know you're a doctor, but you're not infallible. You should be resting, Justin, building up your strength. You're exhausted – emotionally traumatised, to say little of being severely physically injured.' Her expression was almost tearful as she looked him worriedly over.

'Honestly, I could just shake Alicia sometimes,' she went on, with a despairing sigh. 'She's upset, too, of course she is. Devastated, poor soul,' she added, her tone switching to sympathetic, which didn't ring quite true any more in Justin's mind. 'But I do wonder why she couldn't just have been honest with you from the outset.'

'It is what it is,' Justin said, watching her warily. 'She wasn't, for whatever reason. I suppose I'm just going to have to learn to deal with it.'

'A mess is what it is,' Jess said, delving into her bag and producing juice, fruit and tissues. 'You two splitting up, poor Sophie missing, little Lucas… Not that I'm saying what happened to Lucas was Alicia's fault. Just so you know, I'm here, Justin. If you need someone to talk to, any time, just call me.'

Justin nodded, glancing down at the hand she'd placed on his arm. 'Have we?' he asked, looking back at her. 'Split up?'

Jessica looked taken aback.

'Did Alicia say we'd split?' Justin pushed it.

'Well, not in so many words.' Jessica busied herself with her bag, producing biscuits and a book.

'What words?' Justin asked. 'What did she say exactly?'

'I haven't brought any grapes, you'll be pleased to know,' Jessica answered evasively.

Justin kept his attention on her. 'Jessica?'

'She didn't say *exactly*.' Jessica arranged the things she'd bought on top of the locker. Stuff he didn't need, because there was no way he was staying. He'd haemorrhaged badly, but there was no major damage to vital organs. He would live. What he wanted to do was establish whether he had a life worth living. To find his daughter and get to the root of why he'd been lied to.

'She mentioned the house.' Jessica's eyes flicked in his direction, after a pause, and then away again. 'Something about needing to find somewhere to live. I—'

'On her own?' Justin cut in.

'Yes. A studio apartment, I think she said. She saw some somewhere. And with everything that's happened, I was assuming you wouldn't be rushing to get back with her.'

'Where?' Justin said. 'The apartments, where was it she saw them?'

Jessica looked flustered. 'I don't know. I can't remember. The Moseley area somewhere, I think. I've had a lot on my mind, too, Justin. Luke was my nephew. Sophie's my niece. I'm just trying to make sure you're both all right. I'm not quite sure why I'm suddenly under interrogation.'

Justin kneaded his forehead. 'You're not. I'm sorry.' He offered her a small smile. 'I'm just a bit confused, that's all. Emotional, I guess.'

Jessica looked him over uncertainly. 'You're bound to be,' she said, her tone back to sympathetic, her voice full of concern as she reached to fluff up his pillows. He didn't need his pillows fluffing. He needed to know what the hell was going on.

'Thanks.' He forced a smile anyway. 'Can I ask you something else, Jess? If you don't mind, that is?'

'Of course you can,' she said, seating herself on the edge of his bed.

'She said she'd been drinking,' Justin started cautiously. He didn't want to go in heavily. He simply needed to know how far Jessica was willing to go.

Jessica drew in a breath. Was that expression judgemental? Shouldn't it be guarded, for her sister's sake? 'That's right,' she said. 'She's drinking quite a bit now, actually. Regularly, sadly. It's understandable, I suppose, under the circumstances, but it's a worry, as you can imagine.'

Alicia wasn't teetotal. They'd both drunk more than was healthy on the odd occasion, but Alicia had never drunk regularly.

'How much? How much had she drunk, Jess?' he asked, running a hand across his neck. He didn't need to work at looking like a troubled man. 'Was she drinking a lot back then?'

Jessica looked hesitant, then, 'Yes,' she said, 'unfortunately.'

'So she could have been paralytic then?'

Again, Jessica hesitated. 'Not too paralytic to make her way to his room.' Her expression was definitely disapproving as she glanced briefly away and back again.

'No, I suppose not.' Justin heaved out a sigh.

He looked away then, appearing to ponder. 'There's something else,' he said, looking back at her.

Smiling caringly, Jessica took hold of his hand. Justin couldn't quite believe it. 'Why didn't you tell her about the forensic search?'

Jessica looked confused.

'Was it because you hoped we wouldn't be able to talk with police officers poking around?' Justin asked her point-blank.

'No.' Jessica snatched her hand away from his. 'Why on earth would I do that?'

'The photographs I asked about,' Justin went on. 'Why did you tell me Alicia had them?'

Jessica paled, considerably. 'I didn't. I just assumed, because of what you said.'

Justin nodded slowly. 'Making a lot of assumptions, aren't you, Jess?' he said, studying her carefully. 'Tell me, how much bullshit have you been feeding me, precisely?'

Dropping her gaze fast, Jessica got to her feet, her cheeks flushing furiously as she collected up her bag.

'It never was a date, Jessica,' Justin said quietly, as she walked to the door. All of this without once making eye contact with him.

Watching her leave, Justin cursed his naive stupidity. He really must be completely blind not to have seen what was right under his nose, he thought angrily, heaving his legs over the bed and pulling the tube from his arm. He didn't know how many lies he was being told, but one thing he did know for certain was that Alicia wasn't a closet alcoholic, as implied by her sister. If her propensity was to hit the bottle in a crisis, wouldn't she have done that when Luke died? Would she have been capable of coherent, albeit emotional, conversation every day since?

He also knew that photographs didn't lie.

She'd said she wasn't well. The photos he had of her at that wedding told him there was a hell of a lot more to this than met the eye. Alicia was holding something back. And Justin intended to find out what. Why she would hold anything back now, he wasn't sure. But he intended to get to the truth, one way or another.

CHAPTER SIXTY-ONE

ALICIA

Rounding the corner of the corridor Justin was on, Alicia was surprised to see Jessica coming towards her. Shouldn't she be at work? Concentrating on her phone as she walked towards her, Jessica didn't appear to notice her.

'Jess?' Alicia said, eyeing her curiously. Typing out a text, she still hadn't seen her.

Jessica's head snapped up. 'Alicia!' She looked surprised. 'I didn't think you were coming until later.'

'I had a few things I wanted to get for Justin, and then I had my doctor's appointment, but, to be honest, I couldn't face it. You know, having to go over why I'm not sleeping well.'

'Ah.' Jessica nodded, and pushed her mobile into her bag.

'I take it you came to see Justin?' Alicia asked, when Jessica didn't add anything else.

'I thought I would pay him a visit,' Jessica said, glancing down at her shoes. They must be killing her, Alicia thought. They were a least six inches high, and definite toe-pinchers. Not the sort of shoes she'd want to wear to troop along hospital corridors. 'He was a bit tired though, so I didn't stay long. I left him a few bits and bobs.'

'Well, I'm sure he appreciated the visit, and the bits and bobs.' Alicia smiled. 'But shouldn't you be at work?'

'I had to deliver some papers to a client. I've wangled the rest of the day off,' Jessica said quickly.

'Oh right. Well, I'll see you back at yours then.' Leaning in to give her a hug, Alicia noticed the troubled look in her eyes. 'Jessica? Is everything all right?'

'Yes.' Jessica said, her gaze flicking down and back. 'It's probably nothing, but…'

'But?' Her antennae on red alert for the next bad thing to happen, Alicia urged her on.

'Justin seems a bit… confused,' Jessica said, her expression now a mixture of sympathetic and guarded. 'Mixed up,' she elaborated, as Alicia looked at her worriedly.

'Mixed up how?' she asked apprehensively, praying that he wasn't heading back to the pit of despair he'd been in once before.

'It's probably just the stress of everything catching up with him,' Jessica said. 'He seems to think I've said things which I haven't, that you've told him things. He'll be fine after a good rest. Don't worry, Ali.'

But Alicia was worried. 'What kind of things?' She felt her eyes filling up all over again.

'Little things,' Jessica said, seeming reluctant. 'The missing photographs, for instance. He seems convinced that I told him you had them, and I distinctly remember I didn't. I mean, why would I when you don't? Like I say, it's nothing major. I thought I should warn you though.' Jessica gave her arm a squeeze. 'He's just a bit muddled. He'll be fine.'

Alicia nodded bewilderedly.

'I'd better get back to work,' Jessica said, kissing her cheek. 'See you later, sweetheart.'

Watching her go, Alicia ferreted in her pocket for the loo roll she'd grabbed from the patients' toilet, in the absence of tissue, and wiped her eyes. Earlier, she'd decided she would try again to talk to him. Not here, obviously, while he was so ill. She wasn't sure whether she would be able to talk sensibly, feeling as confused as she was, consumed with guilt, her heart fit to burst in her chest. And she wasn't sure whether he would ever be able to listen, but she knew she had to try. She'd even considered writing to him, because then she wouldn't have to see his face, read the expression in his eyes.

That would have to wait now. He needed to get well. And if he needed her to keep her distance until he did, then she would do that. At least he had Jessica to visit him, who clearly cared for them both.

She was pondering what Jessica had meant by *things she'd told him* as she went into Justin's room. Finding his bed empty, she frowned, puzzled. He was up and about but wasn't supposed to be walking very far yet with his drip. Perhaps they'd taken him for some test or other? Walking across to his locker, Alicia deposited her bags, and her heart stopped dead. His drip was still there, the cannula he'd had in his hand pulled out and abandoned on the bed. Holding her breath, she checked his locker. His mobile was gone. His clothes…

Oh God, no. 'Justin!'

CHAPTER SIXTY-TWO

ALICIA

Alicia ran back to her car, ringing Justin as she did, only to get his voicemail again, which only increased the knot of fear growing inside her. Where on earth was he? Why had he left? He'd pulled his drip out, for God's sake, and not even discharged himself.

What was he thinking? His emotions were raw – all of the stages of grief and more. Alicia couldn't even imagine how he must be feeling. He'd been confused, Jessica had said. He'd already been bewildered and broken, stuffed full of pent-up anger. He'd snapped at her, but he hadn't once lost his temper, though he had every right to. But he had attacked Paul Radley. Icy fingers ran the length of her spine. Aggressively, DI Taylor had said. Where had he gone now, disorientated and in pain? What would he do? He wasn't capable of defending himself if there were a confrontation of some sort. Physically, he wouldn't be able to, but that might not stop him provoking that confrontation.

She had to find him. Please, God, before he did anything reckless. He wasn't *well*. Gulping back her mounting fear, banging the heel of her hand against the steering wheel and cursing the slow traffic, Alicia drove straight to the house, hoping she might find Justin there. Her heart plummeted another inch when she saw his car wasn't on the drive. After Justin was attacked, DI Taylor had organised the collection of the vehicle from where it had been parked. One of his officers had driven it here and delivered Justin the keys, so that could only mean Justin was driving it now. Was he even capable of driving? There were no signs of life when she knocked on the door, no signs of him through the windows. He wasn't here.

Justin, please, please answer your phone.

Driving straight to the house where he'd said he was renting a room – a single room, no bigger than a shoebox, with one tiny window and tobacco-stained walls, not fit for a dog – she found he hadn't been back there either, and her heart sank without trace. She had no idea where else to look. He obviously wouldn't be at work – the hospital he'd just escaped. Might he have gone back to trawling the streets, compelled to carry on searching?

Was he searching for Paul Radley? She didn't imagine he would cross the line for her sake, but for Sophie he would. For Sophie, in his disturbed state of mind, he might do anything.

Alicia drove next to Jess's, and sprinted to the house, almost falling through the door as she fumbled to open it. She was hoping and praying that Justin might have rung there, that there was some logical reason she hadn't been able to get hold of him, like his phone wasn't working, perhaps because he had dropped it. She was clutching at straws. Desperate.

'Jess!' she called, checking the answerphone and charging straight to the lounge, and then to the kitchen. 'Jess?'

'Up here,' Jessica answered from the top of the stairs. 'I've just been speaking to Justin.'

'You've been talking to…?' Noting the phone in her hand, Alicia shook her head, confused. 'Where is he? I've been trying to get hold of him. His phone kept going to voicemail.'

'I'm not sure.' Jessica came on down. 'He obviously needed some space to think.'

'I see.' Despite the fact that he'd clearly been avoiding her calls, her heart settled clunkily back into its moorings. Alicia nodded, looking worriedly at her sister as she met her in the hall. 'Did he call you?'

'Yes. He said he's been trying to get hold of you.'

Her phone had obviously gone to voicemail, too. Relieved, Alicia checked it, but found no message. Growing more confused, she scanned Jessica's face. 'Is he all right?'

Giving her a small nod, Jessica glanced at her warily. 'As he can be,' she said.

'Are you?' Alicia asked, looking her over with concern. She looked pale and tearful. 'Jess?'

Jessica took a breath. 'There's something I need to mention, Ali,' she said, seeming reluctant. 'He asked me to meet him, before he was injured. I'm sure it was just to talk, but under the circumstances…' She hesitated uncertainly. 'I told him I didn't think it was a good idea, when I saw him at the hospital. I thought you should know. I…'

Stopping, Jessica fixed her gaze on the floor, while Alicia inwardly reeled. Did Jess think…? No, surely Justin wouldn't…? Unless to get back at her? But he wouldn't do that. She knew him. He wasn't vindictive. He wouldn't do something out of spite. It wasn't in his nature to… her thoughts ground to a halt as it occurred to her that Jessica might possibly be embroidering the truth. She noted her sister's body language, the downcast eyes, the phone still in her hand. It was never far from her side. But why would she…

'I didn't want there to be any bad feeling between us, Ali.' Jessica looked at her imploringly. 'I didn't want to mention it, but…'

'It's okay, Jess. I'm glad you did. He probably did need to talk. He obviously has endless questions going around in his head.' Giving Jessica a brittle smile, Alicia pulled in a breath. The 'why would she', she realised, was becoming blindingly obvious.

'Exactly.' Jessica looked hugely relieved. 'I'm happy to lend a shoulder, of course I am. You know me, always willing to help in a crisis. But I didn't want to seem to be going behind your back.'

'No, of course you wouldn't.' Alicia smiled tightly again. 'Did you go back to work?' she enquired casually.

Jessica looked at her blankly.

'It's just that you said you'd gone to see Justin because you were taking the rest of the day off.'

'Yes,' Jessica said uncertainly.

'And then you said you had to get back to work,' Alicia reminded her.

Jessica's brow furrowed. 'Did I?'

'Perhaps it's you who's a bit mixed up, Jess?' Alicia suggested.

Jessica looked somewhat po-faced. 'I hardly think it's me who could be accused of that, Alicia. I only mentioned it because I thought you should be aware, but if you're going to start bandying accusations about…'

'Aware of what, Jess?' Alicia stopped her, as Jessica turned towards the kitchen. 'That my husband's right up there alongside the "bastards" you've had the misfortune to be involved with? That, even though he's injured, out of his mind with grief, he's engineering some plan to sleep with my sister to get back at me?'

'That was *not* what I said.' Jessica whirled back around. 'You're putting words in my mouth, Alicia, and that's not fair after all I've done for you. I really wonder why on earth I—'

'Why didn't you text me?' Alicia asked over her. 'When Justin "guessed" about Sophie, why didn't you alert me, Jess? Your phone is never more than two inches away from you, after all.'

Jessica looked nonplussed. 'I don't know,' she said indignantly. 'I don't remember. I was in a state of shock. Of panic. For you!'

'Right.' Alicia narrowed her eyes. 'Did you also forget to tell me you'd mentioned Sophie's sixteenth birthday to Paul Radley, therefore supplying him with the exact information I *didn't* want him to have – her date of birth?' she asked furiously.

'Oh, don't be bloody ridiculous,' Jessica snapped, turning away again.

'He wouldn't have known!' Alicia shouted behind her. 'He wouldn't have done the maths if you hadn't told him!'

Jessica turned back, two bright spots on her cheeks, her expression livid. 'But Justin would have! He'd already done the maths, Alicia. He *knew*. And, if you ask me, it was about bloody time he did!'

Alicia stared at her, her heart feeling as if it was fragmenting piece by painful piece. 'You wanted him to find out, didn't you?'

'Of course I didn't want him to find out.' Jessica sighed short-temperedly. 'But if you're asking whether I'm glad he knows, then yes, I am. You should have told him, Alicia. It wasn't fair to keep him under false pretences. You should have given him a chance at another relationship.'

Alicia laughed – a short, disbelieving laugh. 'With you.'

Jessica notched up her chin. 'If that's what he'd wanted, then yes. Why not?'

'Why not?' Alicia almost choked out the words. 'He's my husband!'

'And you don't appreciate him!' Jessica countered angrily. 'You had the perfect life, the perfect family, everything I ever wanted. You didn't deserve it, Alicia.'

She was jealous. Alicia was utterly stunned. So jealous she would have risked Sophie's happiness? Justin's?

'You were so busy fluttering your bloody eyelashes and blushing the first time you saw him, it never occurred to you I might be interested in him,' Jessica ranted on, obviously letting go of the frustration she'd bottled up inside for many, many years. 'That he might have been interested in me. Oh *no*. You just moved in like a cruise missile, grabbing him for yourself, always getting everything you want because you're so obviously needy. But you didn't want him, did you? You lied to him, deceived him, cheated…'

Realising she might have gone a step too far, she stopped suddenly.

Alicia clenched her teeth hard. 'Did you give him Sophie's mobile number?' she demanded, her fury now bubbling white-hot inside her. 'Paul Radley. Did you give him Sophie's number?'

Jessica held her gaze. 'She's his daughter,' she said, tilting her chin defiantly.

'*My* daughter!' Alicia's fury spilled over. '*My* husband!' She stepped forward to land a stinging slap on Jessica's face, who was even now unrepentant. 'You're sad,' she seethed. 'A very sad, bitter woman, who I was fool enough to listen to for far too long. I hope you'll be happy on your own, Jess.' Looking her over contemptuously, Alicia turned to fly up the stairs for her things.

'Where are you going?' Jessica shouted after her.

'To find my family!'

CHAPTER SIXTY-THREE

JUSTIN

Sitting with the heels of his hands pressed hard against his eyes, his chest heaving with a toxic mixture of raw anger and anguish that far outweighed his physical pain, Justin struggled to get a grip on his emotions. He needed to. Coping mechanisms weren't going to work. Nothing was going to work, but he needed to.

Picking up the photos from that long-ago wedding, several of which he'd now had enlarged, he studied them again. Her bridesmaid's dress was pastel blue; the colour suited her fair complexion and caramel-coloured hair. It was a sleeveless dress with thin shoulder straps. He recalled how she'd slathered herself in fake tan the night before – to hide her pale skin, she'd said. Her first lie, one of a succession of lies. How could he have been so blind? *How?* He was a doctor! He'd seen this type of bruising a thousand times. The concealer she'd also applied, some of which she'd got on the front of the dress – he vividly remembered her trying to sponge it off before she left the house – had clearly eventually worn off.

She'd worn a cardigan at the reception. Said she was cold. He'd been sweltering. But he'd also been preoccupied, too busy with his own problems to see the evidence that was right before his eyes. Bruises. Finger-shaped bruising on both of her arms. Livid, purple-black bruises – meaning they were only a few days old, inflicted, therefore, around the night she'd stayed with her friend. Got so drunk with her friend she'd been ill.

Had it just been drink, he wondered, his gut tightening, his jaw clenching. She'd been hungover the next day; that much she'd told him. She'd also been dizzy, her movements sluggish, her limbs heavy. She'd had an upset stomach. All the symptoms of a bug. They were also the after-effects of any number of sedative-hypnotic drugs: flunitrazepam, gamma-hydroxybutyrate, ketamine, Rohypnol. All available on the black market, the latter easily purchased in Europe for use as a sleeping pill – or to render someone helpless in order to carry out a sexual assault.

Swallowing back the bile in his throat, Justin pressed his knuckles against his temples and tried to think rationally. Was he going completely insane? Imagining this? Looking for explanations for the inexplicable that were in no way preferable? She'd seen Paul Radley more than once. She'd *said* she had.

Why?

And if he was right about this, why the hell would she have lied to him?

It made no sense. None of it. But going slowly out of his mind or not, one thing he wasn't imagining were those bruises.

Sucking in a breath, he glanced upwards and then pulled himself to his feet. Walking across to the drinks table, he considered his options, picked up the whisky, tested the weight of it, then – emitting a roar that came from his soul – hurled it against the far wall.

Sitting by and doing nothing simply wasn't an option.

CHAPTER SIXTY-FOUR

ALICIA

Alicia jumped as her phone rang.

Thank God! Alicia seized on it. 'Justin, where are you?' she said immediately, unable to keep the wretchedness from her voice. 'I've been so worried. I thought something might have happened to you. Are you all right?'

'Yes,' he said. 'Sorry, I didn't mean to disappear like that, or not to call you, I just…'

'Needed some space?' Alicia filled in sadly.

'Definitely.' Justin drew in a breath. 'I have to see you, Alicia. Can we talk?'

Alicia felt the familiar knot of tension tighten in her stomach. He didn't sound agitated. Drained, yes, but not angry. 'When?' she asked him.

'Now. I'm outside.'

Outside the house? Alicia went to the window, and sure enough, he was parked outside. Clearly, he didn't want to come into the house, which he would always normally do. Presumably because he wanted to avoid Jessica, which confirmed what her sister had said. Something had gone on between them, but not the something that at least one of them had hoped.

'I'll be one minute,' she said, nodding as he glanced up at the window.

Debating whether to take her things out with her, Alicia decided to leave them where they were. Appearing with her bags would only raise more questions, and she didn't want that. No doubt Justin wouldn't want to wonder about what she might be up to or where she might be going either. She actually didn't have a clue where she would go. A hotel, she supposed, at least for tonight.

'Alicia?' Jessica came out of the lounge as she reached the hall. 'Can we talk?'

Alicia shook her head, incredulous. Did she honestly think they could? Now? Could she not see the damage she'd done? They still didn't know what had happened to Sophie. It was something Alicia tried hard not to imagine. She'd thought they were close – as close as two sisters with completely different lifestyles could be. That they would be there for each other in a crisis. She'd been so wrong. Jessica had never been the sister she'd thought she was. Instead, she was a twisted person, driven by jealousy. She'd wanted children desperately. She'd wanted what Alicia had, and was obviously prepared to go to any lengths to get it. Alicia felt for her, even now, but she couldn't ever forgive her for manipulating her own situation – or, more hurtfully, Justin's – to her own ends.

'I have to talk to Justin,' she said, still not able to even look at her.

'He's not coming in then?' Jessica asked.

'No, Jessica. Are you surprised?' Letting herself out, Alicia steeled herself for the questions Justin was bound to have. She hoped this time she would be able to answer coherently, and that he would be able to listen. If there was one good thing that had come from her confrontation with Jessica, she supposed it was that she was determined now to tell Justin everything.

Breathing deeply as she approached his car, she pulled open the passenger door and slipped inside.

'Thanks,' Justin said, glancing in her direction. 'For coming out.'

'You shouldn't have left the hospital, Justin,' Alicia ventured, after an awkward second. 'Your wounds won't be healed yet.'

Justin grimaced. 'No, they won't, not for a good while, I imagine.'

His tone wasn't caustic or reproachful. If anything, it was subdued. 'There are some things I need to ask you.' He turned towards her, his eyes cautiously scanning hers. 'I was hoping you could answer me honestly. If you can't... well, then I suppose I'll have my answer.'

Nodding, Alicia closed her eyes. She would give him honest answers, however ludicrous they sounded. She would have her answer, too, then, to the question she'd asked herself over and over: *Would he have believed her?*

'You said you'd been drinking.' He tugged in a breath, closing his own eyes briefly, Alicia noticed, possibly because of the pain in his chest. 'Were you drunk?' he asked, looking back at her.

'Very,' Alicia said, as she remembered it.

Justin waited a beat, then, 'Not drugged?' he asked tightly.

The question hit Alicia like a thunderclap, instantly propelling her back there, to the hotel room where she'd woken up to the unfamiliar smell of Paul Radley – a cloying mixture of body odour, bitter lemons and alcohol – with only jagged memories of how she'd got there. She felt again the peculiar bruises on her body that she'd had to hide. The reason she'd lied and then compounded her lies.

'I... don't know. I...' she faltered. 'I honestly don't remember. I've tried. I've gone over it a million times trying to remember, but I don't. I recall being at the bar. People drifting off. After that, nothing apart from hazy images, until the next morning.'

'Jesus Christ!' Justin said, pushing the heels of his hands hard against the steering wheel and dropping his head back against the headrest.

A heavy minute ticked by. Alicia was sure she could hear her heart beating, the rustle of the leaves on the wind outside.

'Why didn't you report him, Alicia?' he asked throatily. He turned towards her when she didn't answer.

Her mouth dry, her throat parched, Alicia met his gaze. Here was the crucial question, the absurdity of the choice she'd felt she had to make. 'You asked if I was drugged?' she said, as calmly as she could.

Justin looked confused.

'Would it have made any difference if I wasn't? she asked him. 'If I was *only* drunk, would that have meant it shouldn't have happened? That I could have stopped it in some way?'

'No,' Justin said categorically. 'I'm just trying to establish the facts, Alicia. I'm not judging you.'

'Aren't you?' Alicia studied him. 'What would you have done, Justin? Knowing you might not be believed, what would you have done?'

Justin raked his hands through his hair. 'You went back, Alicia. You saw him *again*. That's the part I'm struggling with. Make me understand. For Christ's sake, I *need* to. Tell me.'

Alicia swallowed, seeing the look in Paul Radley's eyes as clear as day: dark, intent, calculating. He'd told her she'd been insatiable. Justin would never have to find out, he'd said, gliding his hand down her back as she'd groped desperately for her clothes, sending a shudder of utter repulsion right through her. Though she'd had no idea what had happened between the bar and the hotel room – in the hotel room – she'd known with absolute certainty that he'd meant Justin *would* find out. She'd questioned herself over and over since, guilt overriding her anger, doubt clouding her recollection. But she *had* known. Justin's world had been falling apart, and, if she didn't agree to his terms, Paul Radley would make sure it did. How in God's name was she ever going to explain that, she'd thought then. She'd been young, naive, stupid, ashamed. Terrified. Finally, she'd been pregnant. No way to tell, no way to make anyone believe she hadn't known how to say no.

Alicia glanced down and then back, making sure to hold Justin's eyes this time. 'He threatened to tell you,' she said. 'Obviously, it would have been his version of events. When he went abroad, I thought everything might be all right.' She felt a tear wet her cheek and didn't bother this time to wipe it away. 'I prayed it would be, every day and every night. I was wrong. I lied. And now I'm being punished. I only have the word sorry, Justin. There's no other way to tell you how I feel.'

Justin stared at her, a myriad of emotions in his eyes: incomprehension, shock and pure, unadulterated rage.

He didn't respond initially, dropping his gaze and pressing his thumb hard against his forehead instead. And then, 'You should go back in,' he said gutturally, twisting to start the engine. 'I have to go.'

'Go? Go where?' Fear gripped Alicia's stomach. 'Justin! *Where* do you have to go?' she asked frantically.

Justin breathed hard. 'To finish the job.'

'Justin, *no*.' Cold foreboding sweeping through her, Alicia clutched his arm, immediately reliving the sickening impact on that dark day, when their little boy had been taken from them. 'Please…' she begged him. 'Don't, Justin. You're not well. Please, just let him go. I want him out of my life. Out of our lives. If you do this, he won't ever be, don't you see?'

Searching his face, she waited, her heart palpitating manically as she watched him suck in a long breath. 'You should have reported him,' he said hoarsely. 'You should have told me, Alicia. You should have been able to. *Fuck!* He slammed his hand against the steering wheel.

Alicia caught hold of his hand as he moved it again to his forehead. 'I should have,' she said hesitantly. 'I know, now, that I could have.'

He looked at her, his eyes awash with tears. 'Jesus, Alicia.' He gulped hard, 'I am *so* sorry.' Moving his hand tentatively to her face, he grazed his thumb gently across her cheek. 'So sorry.'

'Don't be,' Alicia said, pressing her forehead to his. 'We don't have time for any more regrets. We have to find Sophie.'

Blowing out a ragged breath, Justin nodded. 'Can we talk more?' he asked her hesitantly. 'Just generally, I mean,' he added quickly, clearly noticing her uncertainty.

She wanted to talk to him, so badly wanted to reach out to him, for him to reach out to her and talk about all they were going through. Even to lie silently next to him, rest her head on his chest and listen to the reassuring thrum of his heart – that's when she'd always felt safest, able to shut out the world and all the bad things in it – would salve the raw pain inside her. To delve into this, though, to relive the memories she'd tried so hard to forget… She wasn't sure she would be able to do that.

'I don't need the detail, Ali,' he said. 'I'd like to think you could talk to me, but only if you wanted to.'

Smiling tremulously, Alicia nodded. She hadn't been wrong about this man. She hadn't been wrong to love him completely.

Justin reached to wipe another errant tear from her cheek. 'We'll find her,' he said softly. 'If you don't want to be at the house, I get that, but…' He paused. 'I miss you, Alicia. Come back to me.'

Alicia's heartbeat picked up in a different way as she saw the hopeful look in his eyes. Nodding again, she hesitated for the briefest second and then pressed her lips softly to his, possibly giving him a very snotty kiss.

'I have something urgent I need to attend at the hospital,' Justin said, easing away from her. 'I'll come straight back, if that's okay with you?'

Alicia hesitated, and then nodded. She didn't particularly want to go back inside, but she had her things to collect. 'I hope you're going to get yourself checked over while you're there?' She gave him an admonishing look.

Justin managed a smile. 'I will. I promise.'

Alicia nodded, relieved, and then glanced back to the house. She would have to tell him she wanted nothing to do with her sister, possibly ever again, but there was another conundrum: how to explain that without seeming to be accusing him of anything or embarrassing him.

'Alicia, about Jessica,' he said apprehensively, raising the subject for her. 'I realise this is a big ask, but do you think we could maybe not share information with her?' He glanced awkwardly away. 'I think we need to trust each other now. No one else.'

Alicia scanned his eyes, as he turned back to her. His expression was definitely awkward, but it also held a warning, communicating all Alicia needed to know. He was aware, as she now was, of the hurt Jessica had caused, and still could.

Holding his gaze, she nodded resolutely. They had an understanding. There were no words needed.

'I'll ring you,' Justin said. 'As soon as I've finished at the hospital. It shouldn't be too long. Will you be okay until then?'

Again, Alicia nodded. 'I need to get my things together,' she said. It would never be whole without her children, but it was possible her heart might have started functioning again.

'One more thing, Alicia.' Justin stopped her as she reached for her door. 'Radley – he's dangerous. He's possibly a danger to Sophie, should she contact him again. I understand why you felt you couldn't say anything before, but…' He hesitated, studying her carefully. 'I think Taylor needs to know everything now, for her sake.'

Seeing the genuine fear in his eyes, Alicia felt a shudder run through her. He was right. Paul wouldn't hurt Sophie, surely? But even the slightest threat, in whatever form… Swallowing, she closed her eyes and took a deep breath. 'I'll ring the station,' she said. 'I'll do it from my car, out of earshot of Jessica.'

Justin sighed, clearly relieved, and then leaned towards her. 'For what it's worth, I'm here for you, Ali,' he said, brushing her lips with his own. 'Just so you know.'

Alicia immediately did what she'd been aching to do and threw her arms around him. 'It's worth a lot,' she assured him tearfully. 'And just so *you* know, there was never a second I didn't love you. I always will.'

Justin squeezed her back. 'I'll call you,' he promised, pulling away to kiss her forehead softly. 'As soon as I can.'

Watching him go, Alicia realised that Jessica really was a bad judge of men. Justin would never have got involved with her. Perhaps another woman, in time, possibly, if they'd had no future together, but he wouldn't have jumped at the first available female, particularly if that female was Alicia's sister. He just wasn't made that way.

Turning to the house, she was going over in her mind what she would say to DI Taylor – it was going to be one of the most difficult calls she'd made in her life – when her phone received a text. It was from Paul Radley, as if he'd known he was under discussion. Reluctantly, she checked it, and then froze, her stomach lurching violently as she stared down at the photograph: Sophie, lying asleep on her stomach, one hand resting on her pillow, her passport lying beside her. A single rose on the duvet. *A significant gesture*, that's what he'd said when he'd given one to her. He'd quoted something. Something to do with a rose bush growing in the pool of blood spilled from Aphrodite's slain lover, Adonis. He'd said it symbolised immortal love, love that would never fade, even through time or death… meaning they would be together forever.

She read the text.

Meet me. 8.00 p.m. Central Plaza, Apartment 153b. We need to talk about the future. Come alone.

CHAPTER SIXTY-FIVE

SOPHIE

Bored with the TV, Sophie wandered towards the kitchen for a drink. She quite fancied a huge glass of fizzy Coke, but guessed she'd have to settle for one of the fruit juices Paul made in his blender. The lime and cucumber was okay, but the apple, mint and spinach was foul.

'Won't be long,' Paul said, sailing past.

Dressed in his gym clothes, Sophie noticed. He'd offered to get her a membership, but Sophie wasn't all that into gyms. She'd said she'd try it. Despite all this healthy eating, though, she'd been so exhausted lately, she wasn't sure she could be bothered to drag herself as far as the lift.

'Did my phone arrive yet?' she asked him, coming back with her juice and trying hard not to wince as she swallowed a mouthful.

'Afraid not.' Paul smiled regretfully. 'We'll see about chasing it later.'

He still didn't trust her to use his laptop or his phone in his absence. He turned down her requests nicely, pointing out the importance of client confidentiality and all that crap, but it rankled that he didn't trust her enough not to poke around in his files. Like he'd got more to hide than boring old financial reports.

'Why don't you have a browse through the new Florida brochures I bought,' he suggested. 'We'll be going in a few days.'

That was a little vague, Sophie thought. He'd said he hadn't confirmed the flights when she'd asked him, and, while she realised it would be him forking out for them, she still had to have some clothes if she was going on holiday. 'I might,' she said, yawning.

'Manners, Sophie,' Paul reminded her, with a tolerant smile.

'Sorry,' Sophie said, pressing a hand to her mouth as she yawned again, and then watching with interest as Paul checked his jacket pocket for his phone, bringing out his study keys as he did and then plopping them back in his jacket.

'Half an hour,' he said, heading for the front door. 'Don't forget to take your vitamins.'

'I already did,' Sophie assured him, yawning widely again.

Waiting until he'd gone, Sophie stopped yawning, nipped to the loo, flushed the vitamin tablets away – she was sure the bloody things were making her sleepy – and then flew over to his jacket to retrieve the keys. It was now or never. He'd kept that door locked religiously since the one time she'd been in there, even coming back an hour after he'd gone out once. He'd made some other excuse, but he'd come back to make sure he'd locked the study, Sophie was sure of it. Plus, she hadn't been able to get the photo on his desk out of her mind, and the fact that Justin had been cropped out of it. Then there was the envelope. Sophie had glimpsed more photos in there.

She'd bet those were of his family. She was hoping they were. He'd been okay to her – generous – but despite being under the same roof as him, she still didn't know that much about him. He didn't talk about his family, didn't have a single photo of them anywhere around the apartment, and to Sophie, who'd lived in a home where family photos were dotted about everywhere, that just seemed odd.

Two minutes later, she was in the study, fumbling to find the right key for the drawer in which she'd seen the envelope. *Bingo!* Finally, she unlocked it, hurriedly extracting the envelope and peering inside. She squinted and tipped the contents out. These weren't photos of his family. Furrowing her brow, Sophie splayed them out on top of the desk. They were *their* family photos. Photographs taken mostly by Justin, of her and her mum. She recognised some of the backgrounds. Their bloody back garden, for one. Their lounge at Christmas. The holiday chalet they'd had in France. The boat they'd hired to tour Ireland. There were some later ones, as well, that she'd taken herself, of Justin and her mum, and Justin had been crudely cropped out of every one of them. Chopped out, with scissors. He hadn't even cut the photos in straight lines.

Why had he done that? How had he got them? Surely her mum hadn't given them to him?

Her heart like a big bass drum in her chest, Sophie shuffled through a few more and then stopped, a knot of apprehension tightening her tummy as she noticed that there were also much more recent photographs. Photographs that Luke should have been in – a family portrait, in particular. Sophie remembered that one so clearly. Her mum had had it framed for the hall wall. Justin had a copy of it in his office. In the photo, Sophie was sitting next to her mum on the sofa, her arm around her shoulders. Luke had been in her mum's arms, but now he was gone. Cropped out. Like he didn't exist.

There were more photographs in another drawer, all exclusively of her mum. Not posed, these photos hadn't been taken by Justin or her. They'd been taken by Paul, Sophie realised. Photos from over the years: Alicia walking along the street; loading her shopping into the car; coming out of the office where she worked. There was one of her painting their house, for fuck's sake. Hadn't he been in Dubai, time slipping by while he worked himself to death trying to get over the loss of his family?

Liar!

Scraping the photos together and furiously shoving them back in their envelope, Sophie put it back, slammed the drawer shut and moved to the last drawer.

It was stuck. *Shit!* Checking the time on the desk clock, she glanced worriedly towards the door and then yanked at the drawer. It was definitely jammed, not locked. Crouching down, pressing one hand against the desk for leverage, she tugged harder, and then fell back on her haunches as it gave.

Scrambling back, Sophie peered into it, and her heart skittered to a stop inside her. It was fairly obvious what had caused it to jam. Swallowing back a sick taste in her throat, Sophie reached for it: Luke's pink elephant toy. One of its floppy ears had got caught between the desk and the drawer and been torn clean off. He'd stuffed it in there as if it didn't matter. As if it wasn't the most important thing Sophie had ever, or would ever, possess in her life.

He'd taken it. Taken it from her.

A huge lump in her throat, Sophie lifted it to her face and sniffed it. His scent was still there – barely. Her little baby brother. Choking back the tears that stung the backs of her eyes, she delved further into the drawer. Feeling something smooth and cold towards the back of it, something with a chain attached, she fished it out. It was a locket. A gold locket, decorated with a flower motif.

Her mum's?

Sophie stopped breathing. With trembling fingers, she prised it open. Luke's little face looked back at her. His perfect cupid lips were curved into a delighted, gummy smile. His beautiful blue eyes, wide with the innocence of childhood, were dancing with glee.

Oh God, Luke.

Her mum hadn't given him this. She hadn't given him any of this. He'd taken these, too. Feeling the room shift around her, Sophie tried to breathe slowly, like Justin had once taught her, when she'd had a major panic about her part in the school play. Calm – he'd always been that. Calm and measured. Suddenly, Sophie wanted very much to go home.

Having a final check in the drawer, she wasn't surprised, somehow, to find her old phone as well as the new one.

Breathe. Doing what Justin would, Sophie tried to focus. Sliding the phone into her back pocket, she fastened the locket shakily around her neck, making sure it dropped below her neckline. Then, resting pink Ephalump, as they'd christened him, on the desk, she used her foot to shove the stuck drawer back into place and then relocked the other drawers.

Checking everything looked as it should at first glance, her gaze snagged on something she hadn't previously noticed on the top of his in tray. Seeing the letter was from The DNA People, she snatched it up, quickly pulling the contents out.

It was a paternity test. The report included all sorts of indecipherable tables – Genetic System Table, Combined Paternity Index – and figures relating to 'case number', 'child, mother', 'alleged father'. Nausea almost choking her, Sophie hurriedly scanned it. She couldn't digest the information enough to understand it. It made no sense – until she reached the Paternity Test Conclusions, which clearly stated that 'Paul Radley is excluded as the biological father.'

Shaking, Sophie blinked at it, uncomprehending for a second, and then froze.

'Do you not understand basic instructions, Sophie?' Paul said, his face white with anger as he walked quietly through the study door and saw the letter in her hand.

CHAPTER SIXTY-SIX

JUSTIN

Justin had parked as close as he could to the apartment block he'd previously followed Radley to, and was now walking away from his car, his intention to have a quiet word with the piece of scum that walked around in the guise of a man. He thought of Alicia, his chest constricting as he pictured what she might have gone through, even without knowing the details. It still hurt that she had lied to him, but now he was pained because she'd felt she'd had to. That was on him, not her. He needed to put it right – or try to. To listen to her, if she wanted to talk. To be there, if she didn't. Assuming Radley didn't report him, that was. Justin had an idea he wouldn't, given the implications for himself. He wasn't quite sure how this would go yet, what he would do to him, though the temptation to give in to his anger was overwhelming – show the bastard what it was like to be raped with a very intrusive object and then castrate him and render him truly powerless.

Possibly not a good idea if he did want to be there for Alicia and find Sophie. But the threat might be sufficient. The knowledge that Justin could render him helpless any time he wanted to might give Radley an inkling of how he'd made Alicia feel. Had there been other women? Probably. It wouldn't be enough – not nearly enough – to quash the burning rage inside him, but Justin supposed it would have to do.

Hearing his phone ring, he checked the number. Not Alicia. Jessica. She'd already called once, leaving him a message: an attempt at an apology for misreading the signs. He'd rung her back and told her it wasn't a good idea to call him again, as reasonably as he could. And now here she was, doing just that. Sighing, Justin hesitated, and then thinking that it might actually have something to do with Alicia, he took the call.

'Justin, you need to do something. She's going to meet him,' Jessica said immediately.

'What?' His stomach turning over, Justin stopped in his tracks.

'She's going to meet him,' Jessica repeated frantically. 'He said she should go alone. I don't know what to do. I've tried to convince her to let me go with her, to call you, but she won't. Justin, he has her.'

Reeling on his feet, Justin told her to slow down. He couldn't keep up with her. Couldn't make sense of it. Couldn't breathe.

'Sophie!' Jessica cried. 'Paul Radley has her! He has her passport, too. Alicia thinks he must have taken it from the house when he was there. You have to do something, Justin.'

Sophie? Justin's heart careered to a stop in his chest – and then kicked back hard. 'Where?' he asked, his emotions colliding, his adrenaline pumping, his mind focussing.

Breathe, he commanded himself, sucking air deep into his lungs. Ignoring the pain that seared through his chest.

'At his apartment – Central Plaza, 153b. Eight o'clock. He sent Alicia a photo of Sophie. It could only have been taken by him.'

Justin's gut twisted violently. 'What kind of photo?'

'Nothing explicit,' Jessica said quickly, clearly understanding his meaning. 'She was sleeping. He'd placed her passport next to her. He's obviously trying to tell to Alicia that he'll take her away if she doesn't turn up. Oh God, Justin, I have no idea what to—'

'How do you know where he lives?' Justin demanded.

'I… don't. I saw it… on the text,' Jessica stuttered. 'The address, I—'

Right, and she'd just reeled it straight off. *Bullshit!* 'How long have you been in contact with him, Jessica?' he asked her, barely controlling his temper. 'How long have you been feeding information to the man who *raped* your sister?'

'I haven't!' Jessica denied vehemently. 'I would never do that. I—'

'You're full of shit, do you know that, Jessica?'

'He's an old friend,' Jessica said. 'I could hardly lie to him if he asked me something outright.'

Justin laughed, astounded that she was trying to justify what she'd done. 'No, you couldn't lie to save your life, could you, Jess?'

'Justin, this isn't about me.' Jessica tried a new tack. 'What do you want me to do? Should I call the police?'

'I think you've done enough, Jessica,' Justin pointed out contemptuously. 'Stay out of it. As in, stay away from my family, full stop.'

Attempting to regulate his breathing as he ended the call, Justin tried to think with the mind of an animal intent on its prey. Radley had dangled the bait: a photo of a lost daughter sent to her mother. *Bastard!* Justin clamped his jaw hard. Would he have Sophie with him, knowing there was even a chance Alicia might call the police? Possibly, but wasn't it more likely he would be holding her somewhere else? That he would want to get Alicia in that apartment alone?

That thought slicing through him like a knife, Justin made his decision. The police might do something; they might do nothing. Either way, they were unlikely to turn up here and arrest the bastard. They might ask Radley some questions, might even ask him to go to the station. Would he admit to having Sophie though? To his perverse fucking intentions, which Justin had no doubt he had? Would he tell them where she was?

Not likely. At least not immediately.

And that, as far as Justin was concerned, was the critical factor. Assuming the police would even take any action, did Sophie have time on her side?

Justin checked his watch, calculating how long it might take Alicia to get here. It was the tail end of rush hour. Luck on his side, it might take her a while. He was already in situ. He needed to move. He needed to move now. Get to the bastard before Alicia arrived.

CHAPTER SIXTY-SEVEN

PAUL RADLEY

Listening to Rachmaninoff's Piano Concerto No. 2, which he preferred to the more popular third, Paul popped an olive into his mouth, rolling it around on his tongue and washing it down with a sip of cabernet sauvignon. He hadn't enjoyed what he'd just had to do to Sophie – it wasn't what he'd planned for her – but she'd left him with no choice.

He had been a touch disappointed with young Sophie, he had to admit. Their relationship had started so promisingly. He'd hoped she'd love him as readily as her mother had, but that didn't look like it would ever happen. Paul could see that now. He traced a drip of wine from the side of his glass with his finger, sucked it off and then scowled as he noticed another drop bleeding onto his natural wood worktop. Tugging a leaf from the kitchen roll, he moistened it at the tap and rubbed at the wine, and then, immensely irritated when he realised he would possibly have to have the surface stripped and resealed, banged his wine down, separating stem from glass, which made the situation ten times worse.

Temper, Paul, he cautioned himself. She would be here soon. Focussing on the calming music, he reached into his pocket, retrieving the lock of caramel-coloured hair he carried there, the smell of which – a woman's scent, with undertones of vanilla and innocence – he found soothed him.

Pressing it close to his face, he inhaled the sweet fragrance of her, and then glanced over at his ringing phone. Alicia. He'd guessed it might be. Paul breathed a deep sigh of satisfaction – and rejected the call. *Good things come to those who wait, my sweetest.*

He would bide his time. Soon she would be desperate enough to see him.

He'd been furious with her at first, but his anger had abated a little. He realised why she'd resisted his efforts to stay in touch, of course. She'd needed a father for her child, and who better than Justin Cole, who'd clearly been emotionally dependent on her, but also earned enough money to be someone she could depend on financially.

Yes, Paul could understand it, to a degree. It was clear she didn't want to hurt her husband now either; he was possibly still mentally unstable. That was admirable. A good quality in a woman. She shouldn't have deceived him though. He was Sophie's natural father. That was no way to treat a man she'd shared such intimacy with, was it?

CHAPTER SIXTY-EIGHT

JUSTIN

Taking another dose of fentanyl to take the edge off the nagging pain in his chest, Justin surveyed the apartment block from the opposite side of the road. He had no idea how he was going to get past the security guard. Ringing buzzers at random wasn't going to do it. The block was a new build, largely uninhabited. *Fuck.* Dragging his hand over his neck, he debated whether to try to bribe the guy. No. Too risky. He had no idea where this was going to end, but he definitely didn't want the man remembering he'd been here.

He'd considered the underground car park and had gone down there to take a look. He'd noticed there were two four-by-fours parked amongst a few other cars. Justin had tried not to let his mind go back to the day his son had been taken away, but it had anyway. Instantly transported back there, he'd felt the impact all over again, like a low blow to his stomach, and heard the cacophony of noise: horns blaring; people shouting; petrol spilling; sirens plaintively wailing.

Alicia. Screaming.

Sophie, her voice high-pitched, hysterical.

Luke… silent.

Not the car park, Justin had decided, his jaw tightening, his heart rate escalating, his mind refocussing. He had no chance of getting in without the security code.

Deciding his only real option was to go through the front entrance, he googled several local pizza parlours. Calling each of them, he ordered, prayed and waited. He needed to be in and out of there before Alicia turned up. He didn't want her involved in any of what he was about to do. And he would do whatever was necessary to get his daughter back. Once he'd established where she was, his inclination wasn't to leave the bastard capable of walking away.

Grabbing his overcoat from the boot, Justin fed his arms into it, pulled the collar high and then blew out a sigh of relief as two pizza delivery guys arrived in close succession, followed two minutes later by a third. It was now or never. There was no other way. He had no elaborate plan – he just needed to get to the lift, hopefully without providing a facial image on the CCTV. Pulling in a breath, he offered up another prayer as he sailed through the doors, the security guard being somewhat distracted.

'I've told you, there's no one here by any of those names.' The guy splayed his arms in despair as he addressed the disgruntled deliverymen. 'You must have the wrong building.'

Shaking his head as one of the men insisted he hadn't, the guy sighed, picked up his phone, then cried, 'Oh, for…!' He banged the phone down again as another pizza bearer appeared.

'Radley, fifteenth floor.' Keeping his head down, Justin grabbed his chance, pointing his thumb towards the lift as he passed by behind them.

'Yeah, yeah.' The guy waved Justin on, now looking considerably frustrated, as he picked up his phone again.

CHAPTER SIXTY-NINE

PAUL RADLEY

Paul was sizzling the bacon in preparation for his speciality – creamy courgette and bacon pasta – when his phone pinged. Setting the pan aside, he picked it up and checked the incoming text. It was from Alicia, as he'd expected.

How could she resist? His mouth curving into a smile, Paul went back to his culinary task. Patience was definitely a virtue, he decided. And he'd been very patient. Almost seventeen long years he'd been patient, living and working in a climate that didn't suit him. Not that that was Alicia's fault. Having sex with undesirable women rather than be unfaithful to her – that, he considered, was Alicia's fault. The last one had been particularly undesirable, making impossible demands on his time, imagining they were in a relationship. God forbid; the woman was a complete slut, leaving her underwear and feminine things – personal things no man would want to be aware of – all over the place.

He was back permanently now though. The wait would be worth it. Alicia would realise it. Now he was here in the flesh, she would recall – as he had every time he'd set eyes on her when he'd visited the UK; as he did frustratingly every night – how fulfilling their lovemaking had been.

Soon she would be here, where she should be: by his side, sharing the life they were meant to be living together, preparing meals together, experiencing the joys of making love to the soft strains of Rachmaninoff or Wagner in the background. She would be a good wife to him, keeping his house clean and lovingly pressing his shirts while he worked to put food on their table. Paul paused to ponder where they might live. In the country, possibly? A little cottage in Wales, perhaps – somewhere remote and cosy.

'Pass the wine, darling. I've let it breathe.' He smiled tenderly at the image of her he frequently conjured up to keep him company in the kitchen. An image so tangible sometimes, he could see the tiny fleck in her mesmerising cornflower blue eyes: a small imperfection, which he'd graciously overlooked.

'To us,' he said, raising his glass in a toast and then taking a large glug of his wine, before turning to the preparation of the rest of his ingredients. He did hope she wasn't as faddish as young Sophie with her food. He knitted his brow as it occurred to him they hadn't had time to appreciate the delights of fine cuisine together.

Ah well, she'd just have to learn, wouldn't she? She'd soon realise how things worked. Nodding to himself, Paul chopped at the garlic with vigour. He really couldn't abide faddishness of any sort.

CHAPTER SEVENTY

JUSTIN

His mouth dry, sweat tickling his forehead, Justin willed the lift to arrive. Sighing with relief when it did, he stepped in and kept his head down until the doors slid closed. Hitting the button for the right level, he wondered what the hell he was going to do next. Radley was hardly likely to open the door if he knew it was him.

Steeling himself as the lift doors swished open, Justin scanned the corridor. Empty. So what now? Pose as a workman? The building was still being worked on. A power supply employee? None of the above, he decided. Without a high-visibility jacket, which he might have thought of if he'd had more time to prepare, he wasn't likely to pull that off. A buildings' inspector?

Would Radley have a security camera or just a basic intercom system? Justin had no idea. If it was the latter, then his plan might work. All he needed was to get Radley to open the door enough to ask for ID. That would be enough. It had to work. Justin hadn't known who his assailant was that night outside the pub. He'd assumed, when it had been established his wallet was intact, that it had been some kind of revenge attack by the aggressive bastard who'd been abusing his girlfriend. But the possibility that it was Radley had crossed his mind. Didn't he have every reason to seek revenge after his attack on him? Justin hadn't thought him capable of it then. Now, though, after learning the animal was a rapist, someone who used blackmail to wield his power over the woman he'd raped, a piece of scum who would lure or kidnap her daughter to coerce her further, he believed him to be capable of anything. The man obviously had money enough to hire people to do his dirty work for him, if he was too cowardly to carry it out himself.

If the attack had been something to do with Radley, then Justin would have the element of surprise. He should still be in the hospital. But he wasn't. He was here. Assuming Radley, who'd clearly been stalking Alicia, had continued to monitor her, thereby establishing they'd apparently split up, this was the last place he'd expect him to be. And if he didn't have that element of surprise and couldn't gain access through the open door, then he would just have to kick the fucking thing down.

Hitting the buzzer, Justin braced himself and waited.

CHAPTER SEVENTY-ONE

PAUL RADLEY

Alicia had arrived – a little bit late, but Paul would overlook that on the basis she'd had the good manners to text him and alert him to the fact that she would be. Clearly, their daughter had picked up her sloppy manners from her husband. Collecting up his homemade olive dressing, Paul placed it on the dining table alongside his Italian-inspired salad, and then, pleased with the table arrangement, went to greet his long-anticipated visitor.

'Darling,' he said, his warmest smile in place as he reached to open the door, 'I—'

'You *bastard*!' someone rasped furiously on the other side of it.

Sprawling backwards as the door was shoved violently into his face, Paul didn't stop to wonder what had just hit him. He rolled over, attempting to scramble away from the terrifying intruder advancing towards him.

Gulping hard, his bladder almost failing him, he pulled himself up onto all fours and then to his feet, almost losing his footing as he glanced frantically around for means of escape. He quickly realised his only exit was through the front door, but he stumbled away from there, where some madman, probably armed with a knife, was advancing towards him.

Paul felt sweat saturate his armpits as he imagined what despicable crime this thug might be intent on, and then physically sick as he caught up with him at the patio window.

'Take anything you want,' he spluttered, spittle wetting his cheek as the side of his face was rammed forcefully against the glass. 'Anything,' he gasped desperately. 'I won't try to stop you, just… *please* don't hurt me.'

The person behind him, clearly some lowlife, thieving thug of the worst kind, said nothing.

'I have money,' Paul tried. 'In my wallet. There's at least two hundred in cash. My credit cards are there, too. I'll give you the PIN—'

Fuck! He trailed painfully off as his face was forced harder against the glass. He was going to smash his cheekbone, deform him for life, the mad son of a bitch.

'What do you want?' he said weakly, when his attacker didn't answer. 'If it's electrical goods, I have phones and— *Aaargh!* Don't, you're hurting me!' he screamed, finding his arm pulled back and jerked high up behind his back. 'For God's sake, just tell me what you want!'

The man moved closer, his face right up next to his. 'My daughter,' he growled, close to his ear. 'Where is she, you fucker?'

Shit! 'I don't know!' Paul gurgled, as Justin Cole clutched a handful of his shirt, tightening it at his throat and yanking him back. 'I have no idea!'

Cole didn't answer. Hanging on to him so tight he almost choked him, he reached for the locking mechanism on the doors instead. 'You might want to have a rethink,' he suggested, pushing him bodily out onto the balcony.

Oh God, no. Realising he was facing his worst fear, Paul struggled to turn away from the fifteen-floor drop, at the bottom of which was nothing but bone-crushing concrete. But Cole was on him, pressing his arm hard across his shoulders, pushing him towards certain death.

'Where is she?' he repeated, his tone now menacingly quiet.

God, please help me. He couldn't tell him. How could he? The mad bastard *would* bloody well kill him. 'I don't know,' he whimpered, blinking hard as the ground loomed up towards him. 'I swear to God I don't.'

He heard Cole draw in a ragged breath. Paul had no idea how he was breathing at all. Gulping hard, he waited. He wouldn't do it. He wouldn't stand a chance of getting away with it. And then getting out of the building unnoticed, if he did. Would he?

After a second, Cole relaxed, just fractionally, the arm he had locked across his back, to Paul's huge relief. He hadn't thought he would. He was bluffing. And Paul had called his bluff.

'So now what are you going to do?' he asked him, his voice shaky, despite his attempt at bravado. 'Electrodes? Pull my fingernails—'

He stopped, emitting something between a squeak and a scream as Cole's arm snaked its way around his throat.

'*Shhh*,' he whispered, pressing a cold syringe to the side of his neck. 'You wouldn't want to attract any attention, would you, Radley? Because if you do, I may be forced to drop you after all, and that really would be very messy.'

Paul's eyes bulged as the man tightened his hold.

'Do you believe in karma, Radley?' he asked him, talking almost companionably, to Paul's disbelief. 'You should.' He squeezed still tighter. 'Because I'm going to hurt you. I'm going to do to you *exactly* what you did to my wife. I imagine you have one or two kitchen implements that might serve my purpose. Or something from the bathroom, maybe? It will hurt, but then pain turns you on, doesn't it, you sick, sad bastard.'

He let it hang, leaving Paul with a graphic image and his insides turning to liquid jelly.

'If I find you've hurt my daughter, in any way,' Cole growled, 'the pain is going to be so, *so* much worse. Last time, you fucker, where *is* she?'

'I don't know,' Paul cried. 'I swear—' He stopped, terror gripping him as Cole pressed the syringe closer. 'Don't,' he rasped, clamping his eyes shut.

Cole didn't answer, breathing slowly and heavily instead, like some lunatic psychopath.

He was insane, Paul realised, knowing with certainty that if he did tell him, the chances of the madman not doing him permanent damage were nil. 'What are you going to inject me with?' he croaked, perspiration popping out on his forehead.

'Just ketamine, Paul,' Cole said matter-of-factly. 'Nothing harmful. Just enough to render you incapable. You know, unable to speak, move or control your own body? *Powerless*, Paul. As in, unable to fight back. I take it you're getting my drift here?'

'Please, don't…' Paul's voice came out a hoarse whisper.

Cole, though, just tightened his grip.

CHAPTER SEVENTY-TWO

ALICIA

Waiting in the foyer for the security guard to ring up and announce her arrival, Alicia felt every hair on her body rise with repulsion. She was nauseated at even the thought of being near him, the look of calculated triumph she would see in his eyes, the cloying, too spicy, alcohol-soaked smell of him. A cold knot of fear gripped her stomach, twisting her insides so tight she couldn't breathe, as she imagined what he might have done to her daughter. That's what was forcing her to stand there on legs she thought might fail her. That's what was compelling her to go up to his apartment, to beg him, plead with him, do whatever she had to do to get him to let her go.

'He's still not answering,' the man said, having tried him for a second time.

'Did you see him go out?' Alicia asked, feeling more desperate by the second. Was he playing some sick, twisted control game, she wondered, her fear for Sophie intensifying as she realised that was very probably what he was doing: teaching her a lesson for being sloppily unpunctual. Like a child amusing himself by pulling legs from a spider one by one, until it had no ability to run, he'd played games with her from day one. How had he enticed Sophie? What sordid game might he have lured her into? Had she gone willingly?

The security guard frowned uncertainly. 'Come to think of it, no. Mind you, there was a right kerfuffle here earlier. Umpteen bloody pizza delivery men trying to deliver pizzas to non-existent residents.' He sighed despairingly. 'Hold on a sec. I'll see if his car's still in the car park.'

He turned to his monitors. 'Useless twits,' he muttered. 'Call themselves security systems experts. If the circuit breakers don't need replacing, there's a bloody power outage. Could have done a better job myself.' Finally, he banged one of the blank monitors, which flickered uncooperatively and then sparked into life, giving a visual of the car park. 'Yup.' The man squinted at it, apparently identifying Paul Radley's car. 'His car's definitely here, at least.'

Staring at the monitor behind him, Alicia's heart froze. Realisation hitting her with the full force of the impact that had occurred on the darkest day of her life, she gripped the reception desk hard. 'I didn't know he had a new car.' She forced the words out lightly.

The security guard glanced back at her. 'That's his usual car. He's been driving a rental while it's been in the workshop. Prefers his Discovery though, he said. Personally, I prefer the Range Rover Evoque. Production's slowing off a bit now though, apparently, to make way for the new model.' He twirled back towards her, obviously on a roll on the subject of cars. 'It's a shame. I reckon the Evoque's more reliable. Mine's never been in the workshop yet. Then again, you won't catch me driving like a madman. Treat your car with a bit of respect and she'll run as sweet as a nut, that's what I told him.'

'He does tend to hare around, doesn't he?' Alicia's smile was too bright, her voice tight. 'He's a bit of a stickler for punctuality.'

'Better to arrive safe than not to arrive at all, that's my motto.' The security guard sighed piously.

'A man after my own heart.' Alicia nodded in agreement and tried to keep breathing. 'He's probably in the shower,' she said, desperate now to get past him. 'He takes ages in the bathroom. Fastidiousness is in his nature, I'm afraid.'

'Tell me about it. He had a go at me for there being dust on the reception desk the other morning, like there wouldn't be, with builders all over the place. I mean, do I look like the cleaner? I wonder why I stick this job sometimes, honestly.'

'That sounds like Paul.' Alicia laughed. 'Sorry about that. I'm trying to train him out of it. Do you mind if I go on up?'

Narrowing his eyes, the man looked her over. 'Go on then,' he said, his face creasing into a smile as he nodded her towards the lift. 'Good luck with that training.'

'Thanks.' Alicia waved behind her as she walked away. Then she fixed her gaze forwards, hatred for Paul Radley coursing through every vein in her body as she headed determinedly for the fifteenth floor.

CHAPTER SEVENTY-THREE

JUSTIN

'Don't!' Radley pleaded, as Justin allowed the sharp point of the needle to pierce his flesh. 'Please. Stop. I'm begging you. You'll kill me.'

Not yet, you bastard. That would be way too merciful. 'When you've told me what you need to, Radley, then I'll consider it,' Justin said tightly. 'Possibly.'

'Oh, sweet fucking Jesus.' Radley squeezed his eyes shut. 'You really are mad.'

'As a hatter,' Justin assured him. 'The opiates I've been taking after someone attempted to have me knifed to death won't help my state of mind, of course. They tend to affect my concentration, I find. It's probably best not to struggle while I'm holding a syringe next to your jugular.'

'I don't know where she is!' Radley repeated the same bullshit he'd already spouted. 'How can I tell you something I don't know?'

'Wrong answer, you piece of shit. I'm running out of patience. And you're about to run out of time.'

'For God's sake!' Radley screamed, as Justin tensed his thumb against the plunger. 'Wait!'

Breathing in hard, Justin paused. He guessed from the gulp sliding tellingly down Radley's throat that he was considering his options, imagining his brains spilling out on the concrete below, and realising he hadn't fucking well got any options.

'There are some keys,' he blurted, 'in my jacket pocket, hanging on the dining chair.'

'Keys to where?' Justin tightened his hold around his throat.

Radley gagged hard. 'Her bedroom,' he rasped, his hands seeking to release Justin's hold on him. 'The door on the right, in the hall. That's where she is.'

She was in the apartment? Silent? *Subdued?* Justin could feel sweat tickling his eyelashes, prickling his spine. It took every ounce of his willpower not to plunge the syringe deep into the bastard's temple.

'I just wanted to talk to Alicia. I know she loves me. She had my *child*. She wanted to be with *me*.'

Justin's jaw clenched, a new image assaulting him: Alicia, with this *thing*, who had no respect whatsoever for women. Being touched by him. Raped by him.

'*My* child. *My* wife.' A small tic tugged at his cheek. His hand shaking badly, he pressed the syringe home.

Calmly, Justin counted, forcing himself to wait the one to five minutes it would take for onset of symptoms. Once, he would have been shocked by the realisation he was an inch away from killing someone. They were fifteen long floors up. His skull would smash like an eggshell. He'd imagined, in his darkest hours, when dreams of his wife in the arms of another man had come to haunt him, how lost love could drive someone to acts of despair or even madness. How cold-blooded murder might have its basis in love, or unrequited love. In being unloved, spurned or wronged.

This man, gagging on his Adam's apple, a man who'd begged for his life, had wronged him. He'd wronged his family. His children. He had to pay. Left to the law, he wouldn't. He *wouldn't*. There was no other way.

But what about Alicia? Sophie? Would they ever be able to live with the fact that he was a cold-blooded murderer?

Sucking in a breath, he allowed Radley to slide to the ground and then banged the terrace doors closed and raced for the keys.

Heading for the bedroom, he was in the hall when his gaze snagged on something he recognised. Stunned, Justin walked towards it and picked it up from where it sat on an occasional table against the wall: Luke's pink elephant soft toy. Two images immediately emblazoned themselves across his mind: Sophie sitting on her bed after they'd lost Luke, the toy clutched tight to her, her eyes those of a frightened child; and Luke chuckling delightedly, his little arms flailing, as his big sister bobbed the toy in front of him.

Bastard! Justin clenched his jaw hard.

His limbs heavy, his heartbeat sluggish, he located the locked bedroom. Faltering for a split second, his hand shaking, he pushed the key into the lock and pressed down the door handle.

Seeing the light was off, he opened the door slowly and stepped tentatively inside. 'Sophie?' he said, only half daring to hope she would answer. That she would be capable of answering.

His eyes adjusting to the light, he saw a movement – a shape stirring on the silhouette of the bed.

'Dad?' she said weakly.

And Justin's heart damn near exploded inside him. 'I'm here, Pumpkin,' he said, his voice cracking. 'Close your eyes, sweetheart. I'm going to turn on the light.'

Oh Christ, no. Justin felt the walls slam into him as he looked at his baby girl, her long sable hair hanging over the hands she had clamped to her face. She was trembling, shaking all over.

'He's here!' Sophie screamed suddenly, stopping him in his tracks. 'He's here!' She prised her eyes open and then squeezed them tight shut.

'No, Sophie, he's not!' His gut churning, Justin spoke forcefully but calmly. 'It's me. Just me, Pumpkin.'

'I can smell him! Garlic,' she cried, tears streaming down her cheeks. 'Garlic and lemons.'

'It's all right, Sophie. I've got you.' Justin moved fast. With one arm supporting her as he sat beside her, he eased her towards him. 'I've got you,' he said throatily, pulling her gently into his arms.

'I tried not to fall asleep. I tried really hard, but… the vitamins… they were floating. He didn't like it. The study,' she mumbled, her speech slurred, her eyes wide as she looked up at him. Unfocussed, Justin noted immediately, the pupils constricted.

'I've got you,' he said again, hot tears of frustration and anger wetting his own cheeks. 'Breathe for me, Pumpkin,' he urged her. 'Big breaths in, long breaths out. Can you do that for me?'

It was the item hanging around her neck that caused his gut to turn over: a yellow gold locket, enhanced with a white gold floral motif.

Justin breathed with his baby girl, tightened his hold around her. It was obvious. Blindingly obvious. He closed his eyes against the image that would be ingrained forever on his brain: *SORRY FOR YOUR LOSS*, scrawled in red lipstick on the mirror. He'd known it. Deep down in his gut, he'd known it.

'The study,' Sophie said again. 'The photos. We have to get them. You have to see.'

'Later, Sophie,' Justin tried to soothe her. He needed to get her to the hospital, flush out whatever drugs she'd ingested. 'We'll get them—'

'No! Now.' Sophie attempted to pull away from him. 'You need to see. We need to—'

'Whoa.' Justin stopped her as she tried to climb off the bed. 'Wait,' he said, standing carefully, easing her back down, making sure she stayed sitting. 'I'll get them. Promise me you won't move.'

Sophie nodded firmly. 'The door at the end of the hall,' she said. 'Desk drawer. Top and second.'

Justin moved fast, cursing as he reached the study door and tried a key that didn't fit. Finally finding the key that did, he thrust the door open and went to the desk. More *fucking* keys. Justin searched for the right one. His gut clenched as he glanced at the contents of the envelope he extracted from the top drawer, but he wasn't surprised. Radley's reality was skewed. He was a sick individual who hadn't been about to let the proof that Sophie wasn't his daughter change his plans. He wasn't surprised at the contents of the larger envelope he found there either – nauseous, but not surprised. Their family photographs. Stolen. Desecrated.

The photographs in the second did nothing to quell the rage burning like a fire inside him. Radley had watched her, stalked her. The torture he'd put Alicia through fuelling his twisted fantasy, he'd waited like a viper until they'd been weak, and then chosen his moment to strike.

Sophie was right: they needed these. It was all evidence should he be arrested, which Justin had no doubt he would be. Stuffing the photographs furiously into the envelope, he headed swiftly back to Sophie. She wasn't sitting on the bed. Strong-willed as ever, she was on her feet, weaving as she walked to the door.

Justin caught hold of her, easing her again towards him, holding her steady.

'You're my dad. You know you're my dad, right?' Sophie looked uncertainly at him.

'I do.' Justin nodded firmly. 'Just so you know though, I didn't need the piece of paper. Whatever the biology, I've loved you from birth, Sophie. And I always will. Nothing can change that.'

Relief flooding her features, Sophie leaned into him. 'Can we go home now?' she whispered into his shoulder.

'We can go home now, baby,' he promised hoarsely, holding her trembling body a second longer before passing her the envelope and then lifting his beautiful daughter into his arms.

CHAPTER SEVENTY-FOUR

JUSTIN

The blue lights sweeping the road outside told Justin the police had arrived. He didn't stop to ponder who had called them and why. His focus was all on Sophie – his aim to get her to his car and straight to the hospital. No one was going to stand in his way. No one!

Pulling her protectively closer in his arms, he shot a warning glance at an officer approaching him, who stopped uncertainly a yard off.

'Get an ambulance here, *now*!' someone yelled. *Taylor*. Justin kept going towards his car. Even as Taylor's car careered to a stop alongside him, he was determined to keep going.

'Justin!' Taylor called. 'Climb in.'

Justin didn't pause.

'For God's sake, man, climb in!' Taylor yelled. 'We'll get to the hospital a lot quicker with blue lights.'

Justin stopped. His breath short, his chest thudding, he watched Taylor spill out, yanking the back door open and gesturing him inside. Nodding shortly, Justin made up his mind, turning towards the car to ease Sophie carefully into it and then climb in beside her.

Taylor threw himself into the front passenger seat, slamming the door closed behind him. 'Go!' He turned to the driver and then twisted to face Justin. 'Is she all right?' he asked, glancing at

Sophie as Justin slid across, wrapping an arm around her as she burrowed again into his shoulder.

No, she's very much not all right. He looked down at her. 'She will be. We'll all be, hey, Pumpkin? Together.'

A slight nod told him Sophie was hearing him. She understood his meaning. He was her father. He would always be there for her.

Radley. His mind went to him, briefly. Should he just leave him? If the police presence here was anything to do with him, wouldn't they already be up there, rather than here? Justin shut it down. *Not now.* He needed to focus on his family. 'Alicia,' he said gruffly. 'I need to call her.'

Guessing he couldn't access his phone in his pocket, Taylor nodded, twisted back around and pulled out his own mobile. 'Number?' he asked him, keying it in as Justin reeled it off. 'Alicia?' he said a second later. 'I have Justin with me. He has Sophie.'

Turning back, he handed the phone to Justin.

'Sophie?' Alicia asked, incredulous, her voice choked, as if she was squeezing the word out through all the pain she'd been holding in.

'She's here,' Justin assured her. 'She's—'

Hearing the wretched sob that escaped her, he stopped and waited. 'She's all right, Alicia,' he said softly, after a second. 'She's right here.'

Sophie eased her head up as he spoke. 'Mum?' she asked, her beautiful chestnut eyes, dulled by drugs, seeming, at last, to focus.

Justin nodded. 'Hold on,' he said. 'Alicia, she wants to speak to you.'

Cradling Sophie, he held the phone gently to her ear.

'Mum?' Sophie said, and caught her breath. 'Mum? I'm sorry. I'm so sorry. I didn't get it. I still don't get all of it, but—'

'Hey, hey.' Justin squeezed her closer as she, too, broke off with a sob. 'No apologies, Pumpkin. They're not necessary. We'll get through this. I promise you we will.'

Pressing the phone back to his own ear, he spoke to Alicia. 'We're on our way to the hospital,' he said. 'Just to check Sophie over,' he added quickly. 'She's okay, I promise. I'll meet you there.'

'Okay,' Alicia managed emotionally. 'How?' she asked. 'How did you know where she was?'

Justin hesitated, his gaze flicking towards Taylor. 'Jessica gave me his address. I went there to talk to him,' he said, hoping it sounded feasible to Taylor. Whatever happened, he wanted to keep Alicia, and the fact that she was supposed to be seeing Radley, as far out of this as possible.

Taylor held his gaze for a long, hard minute, the look in his eyes dubious at best. 'Strange coincidence, that,' he said. 'We were just about to pay a visit to Mr Radley's apartment too. We had a 999 call from this geographical location. Cut short, unfortunately,' he went on, as Justin eyed him questioningly.

'Me,' Sophie said. 'That was me.'

'Ah.' Taylor nodded and smiled – for Sophie's benefit, Justin guessed. 'Well, that clears up the mystery. Don't worry, Sophie, we can have a chat later, when you're feeling better. We'll be having words with Mr Radley in the meantime. I have officers on their way there now.'

Shit! Justin squeezed his arm around Sophie a fraction tighter.

CHAPTER SEVENTY-FIVE

SOPHIE

Finally at home – her real home – Sophie sat on her bed, not quite able to believe she was here. Everything was exactly as it was when she'd left. Normal. The bedroom, which her mum and dad had decorated, knowing who she was, was *hers*. She was an individual, with a mind of her own. The only thing out of place was her notebook. She couldn't remember where she'd left that. In her drawer, she'd thought, but certainly not neatly placed on the dressing table. Her dad had done that. Not her mum. Her mum rarely touched her things. She'd once said she'd hate her to think she'd been snooping. Though she doubted her dad had been snooping. More likely it had been pulled out by that freak when he'd come in here, touching her things.

An involuntary shudder running through her, Sophie pulled her knees up to her chest, closed her eyes and rested her head. And then she snapped her eyes open as her mind conjured up an image of him, the look in his eyes changing from fondness to fury like the flick of a switch.

Sliding off the bed, she walked across to her mirror, her arms wrapped about herself as she examined her reflection. She couldn't believe how stupid she'd been. How utterly naive. How badly she'd misjudged people. She hadn't listened to her mum or her dad, just made assumptions and then charged off to nurse her own wounds. She'd listened to Paul Radley instead, been impressed by him, completely taken in by him. She wasn't sure she could ever trust herself again. She'd acted like a moody, selfish brat. And there she'd been yelling at her mum and dad because she'd wanted to be treated like an adult.

'Knock, knock,' her mum said behind her, tapping on the open door. 'Penny for them?' she asked, coming to place an arm around her shoulders.

'Just thinking.' Sophie shrugged.

Her mum eyed her warily. 'About?'

Sophie hesitated, and then decided that maybe getting through this together meant being truthful with each other whatever. 'That maybe I'm not as mature as I thought I was.'

Her mum moved around her. 'We go through life growing up, Sophie, trust me. Learning from our mistakes. And we all make them. My gran used to say something, I don't think I really got it until I'd suffered true loss, but when I was young, crying over something or other, she used to say, "Beautiful things make life worth living. Pain and sorrow turns to wisdom in time." I think she was right. If you're beating yourself up because you're imagining any of what happened is your fault, then don't. You have nothing to reproach yourself for.' She locked her eyes firmly on hers. 'You're fine just the way you are: individual, quirky, caring and beautiful. You make my life worth living. Okay?'

Sophie's mouth twitched into a smile. 'You forgot the super-intelligent and hugely talented bit.'

'And that.' Smiling back, her mum took hold of her shoulders. 'You're okay, Sophie. A normal, well-balanced teenager.'

'Apart from the odd moody moment,' Sophie pointed out.

'Um, well, there are those.' Her mum furrowed her brow and then laughed. 'They're normal, Sophie. Allowed. It's called being human. Trust me, you're an extremely loving and much loved person,' she said forcefully. 'I've loved you from the second I felt you growing inside me. I love everything that you are. And what you are is good, through and through. No one can take that away from you. The only thing people can rob you of, if you let them, is your confidence. Don't let him do that, Sophie.'

Sophie nodded, but dropped her gaze. She was trying, but she just didn't feel confident any more. Her mum had done it though. Somehow, she'd managed to find the strength to move on with her life, despite what had happened to her at the freak's hands. She hadn't been honest with Justin, something she clearly bitterly regretted, but she'd always been there for him. For her, too. Maybe her great-gran's saying was right. Her mum had learned from her mistakes. Sophie would do the same. She would certainly be wiser in future and value those people who really did love her.

'Did he mention your surprise?' her mum asked her.

Sophie looked back up at her curiously.

'Your dad, did he tell you about your surprise sixteenth birthday present?'

Sophie's smile widened. 'No,' she said, betting it was something really cool. Her dad always got her cool stuff: her Red or Dead boots; the puffer jacket he'd seen her drooling over in Miss Selfridge. Her heart dipped again, though, when she remembered the luxurious things Paul Radley had tried to tempt her with, which she'd actually thought were cool.

'Well?' she asked, as her mum eyed her teasingly.

'Sorry.' Her mum held up her hands. 'I can't say. Your dad will kill me if I tell you before he does.'

'Yeah, right.' Sophie rolled her eyes. 'I very much doubt that. Dad wouldn't hurt a fly. That's why he's a doctor.'

Her mum glanced down. 'No,' she said, smiling sadly now. 'No, he wouldn't.'

Noticing a tear plop down her cheek, Sophie looked at her, startled. 'Mum,' she said, pulling her into a hug, 'I thought we weren't supposed to be letting him win.'

'We're not.' Alicia squeezed her hard back. 'They're tears of relief, that's all. That you're here. *God*, I've missed you. Come on,' she said, easing away and running the back of her hand under her nose. 'Let's go and find your father. He can give you the guided tour.'

'Tour?' Sophie's mind boggled. 'What's he got me, Buckingham Palace?'

Following her mum to the door, Sophie quashed another bout of guilt as she realised how upset they both must have been on her sixteenth. They'd always pulled out all the stops on her birthday – having her friends over, buying a cake. Her mum had even made one once. It had taken her hours. She was rubbish in the kitchen, she'd always said, making no excuses for what she called her deficient domestic goddess gene. Sophie's thoughts swung again to Paul Radley. She'd had no friends while she'd been stuck in that apartment, not realising she was actually stuck in it. No phone. No contact with anyone. She doubted whether he would ever have let any of her friends in it, so OCD was he. Whatever happened to him, after what he'd done to her mum and dad, he deserved it, she decided.

'It's not quite Buckingham Palace,' Justin said, looking rueful as they met him on the landing. Obviously, he'd overheard. Sophie felt bad about that too. She hoped he wasn't thinking she rated material stuff over what really mattered. Because she didn't, and now she never would. She'd make sure to tell him that. 'A bit smaller,' he added, allowing them to pass.

'A shoebox?' *Preferably containing new Red or Dead boots.* Sophie glanced hopefully over her shoulder, noticing Justin's hand going to the small of her mum's back, which she'd managed to strain somehow.

'Any better?' he asked her.

'A bit.' Alicia replied. 'Still painful though.'

'Bend at the knee next time,' Justin advised, as they followed Sophie down the stairs. 'So, when did you do it exactly?'

'I'm not sure,' Alicia said vaguely, stopping at the basement door.

'What? You can't remember when you shifted the furniture?' Justin sounded dubious.

'Not exactly, no. Not to worry.' She waved away his concerns. 'I'm sure it will be fine once I've rested it.'

Noticing they were both loitering at the basement door now, Sophie back-stepped. 'A tiger?' she said, looking bemusedly at them. 'Must be, if you're keeping it chained up in the basement.'

'Try again.' Alicia smiled, swinging the door open.

'My very own vat of vintage wine?' Sophie peeked down after her as her mum led the way.

'In your dreams,' Alicia called back. 'Well, come on then. Your dad will be having a nervous breakdown wondering whether you like it.'

CHAPTER SEVENTY-SIX

ALICIA

'You have to be kidding me.' Standing in the middle of the studio, Sophie's eyes grew so wide, Alicia was sure they would pop right out of her head. 'You mean you did all this yourself?' She turned in disbelief to Justin. 'The man who puts his foot in paint trays?'

Justin ran a hand over his neck. 'Yes, thanks for that reminder, Sophie,' he said, smiling embarrassedly.

'He's been working on his DIY skills,' said Alicia. She stepped towards her husband, sliding a hand around his waist.

'Obviously.' Sophie glanced around, clearly awestruck, though Justin didn't seem entirely confident she was impressed.

'So, do you like it?' he asked her tentatively.

'Like it?' Sophie's eyes boggled wider. 'It's like, wow!'

'I take it that's a yes?'

'Yes!' Sophie said effusively, launching herself at Justin. 'It's totally cool. I *love* it,' she assured him, almost strangling him as she threw her arms around his neck, and then promptly took off, inspecting the various bits of equipment Justin had installed: microphones and stands, recording software, headphones… Alicia didn't have a clue what half of it was.

'You got me a Macbook Pro.' Sophie turned to him, her eyes filling up. 'And a digital audio workstation.' She trailed a hand over it. 'It must have cost a bomb.'

'I'm selling my body to pay for it.' Justin shrugged, definitely looking pleased.

God, she loved this man. He'd never given up hope, not once. Whatever the future held, Alicia knew with certainty she would have had no future without him. He'd never been selfish or controlling. In his lovemaking, in every aspect of his life, he was generous – a giver, not a taker. She would always be grateful for every precious day she had with him.

'Is it okay, the DAW?' he asked her.

'Perfect,' Sophie beamed. 'I can't wait to show Chloe.'

'What about the monitors? I was shopping in the dark a bit.'

'The man done good,' Sophie assured him. 'You even got an audio interface. It's phenomenal.'

'I'll go and get the cake. Don't worry, it's not homemade.' Alicia smiled, leaving them to the technical jargon.

CHAPTER SEVENTY-SEVEN

ALICIA

Candles blown out and wishes made – hers perhaps an impossible wish – they'd decided on a family afternoon as a treat for Sophie's postponed birthday. It was the first workday they'd all been home together that wasn't tinged with unbearable sadness, and being with each other seemed fitting. Clearing up in the kitchen, Alicia went to join Justin and Sophie in the lounge, but stopped short of the door, wanting to simply listen to father and daughter talking, as they used to.

'So what do you fancy?' Justin asked Sophie, picking up the TV remote. 'A film, *Homeland* or a rerun of *Game of Thrones*?'

'Not fussed,' Sophie said. 'You choose.'

'A film,' Justin decided, flicking to Netflix. 'Something cheerful, hopefully, that your mum will fancy too.'

'Okay?' Alicia heard him ask softly a second later, as he browsed.

'Better,' Sophie answered, her voice sounding so young, so vulnerable, it almost wrenched Alicia's heart from inside her.

Paul Radley had tried to steal her daughter's identity. She'd suffered at his hands, because of her own mother. Alicia had been trying to keep their family together, yet she'd almost torn them apart. She'd worried that Justin and Sophie might never be able to forgive her, but she'd underestimated them both. What Sophie needed to do now was what her mother had felt unable to: talk about what had happened, not allow it to fester inside her, asking herself 'what-ifs'. *What if I hadn't…? What if I'd done this differently? Or that?* From that came self-doubt. That was the negative emotion that ultimately destroyed people, stifled them and robbed them of all they could be. If anyone could help Sophie get past that, realise she wasn't responsible for other people's actions, it was Justin, who'd loved her unquestioningly. Who always would. Alicia had made a mistake all those years ago in not telling him, yet she'd made at least one good decision in her life, of that Alicia was sure. There was no father more loving than Justin. He would always be there for his daughter.

'Dad… I'm sorry,' Sophie said hesitantly, 'about taking off like that at the shopping centre. About being so angry with you. I think I was a bit screwed up. After Luke, I mean. And then, when I heard… what you said… and realised…'

'You and me both,' Justin assured her, as she trailed off. 'We all say stuff, Sophie – heat-of-the-moment stuff, when we're hurting or angry, which doesn't reflect what we really feel inside. I think the best thing we can do now is move forward don't you?' he asked her tentatively. 'Be there for each other?'

Sophie paused. 'Just so you know, though, I never stopped thinking about you as my dad, no matter what I tried to tell myself. Not in my heart.'

'Looks like you're stuck with me,' Justin joked. 'So… are you going to eat the rest of that cake, or am I going to have to help out?'

'Ditto. For your sins,' Sophie answered, her tone sounding less uncertain and more like herself. Alicia felt hope rise inside her that she wouldn't be too affected by the monster who'd tried to control her. 'And, no you can't have my cake,' she added. 'It's, like, chocolate.'

'More than I dare do to go near that then.' Justin chuckled.

'Do you still love Mum?' Sophie asked, just as Alicia was about to go in.

Alicia stepped back, fearing his next words might truly kill her.

'I never stopped loving her, Sophie,' Justin said, after a second that seemed to last an eternity. 'Why would I have?'

'Can you forgive her for what she did?' was Sophie's next question. 'For not telling you about me, I mean?'

Again, Justin hesitated. 'I wish she had told me,' he said eventually. 'I wish she'd felt able to.' He paused, drawing in a breath. 'I think she did what she did with the best intentions though. It's not easy to accept, if I'm honest – not easy to accept my own culpability in why she felt she couldn't – but yes, I think I can. Can you?'

'Uh-huh,' Sophie said thoughtfully, after a second. 'Her decision-making was a bit shit, but I do think she made the choices she did for the right reasons.'

Sophie would heal. In time she would be whole again. And if she faltered in the future, Justin would always be there to catch her. Alicia swallowed back a different kind of lump in her throat.

'I've brought you an extra slice,' she said, going on in. 'I think we deserve to indulge—' She stopped as Justin's phone rang, an uneasy feeling of trepidation washing over her.

Placing his cake on the coffee table, she sat down next to where Sophie was parked on her favourite spot on the sofa.

Glancing worriedly at her, Justin got to his feet, nodding towards the hall to indicate he would take the call there.

'You forgot a crumb.' Alicia smiled at Sophie, who was dabbing up the last of the cream from her plate with her finger.

Justin came back into the lounge a minute later, his face pale, Alicia noted – worryingly pale. 'DI Taylor.' He smiled, for Sophie's sake. 'He wants to have a chat.'

Alicia nodded slowly. 'When?' she asked him, trying to remain calm, though her stomach knotted inside her.

Justin kneaded his forehead. 'He's on his way.'

CHAPTER SEVENTY-EIGHT

ALICIA

Justin had been like a cat on hot bricks. He was trying to keep his emotions under control, for Sophie's sake, but he was pacing endlessly, breathing slowly, trying to stay calm. He was concerned, as he obviously would be, that DI Taylor's visit was to do with what had happened to Paul Radley.

'Are you warm enough, sweetheart?' Alicia asked Sophie, who'd gone quiet, also anticipating DI Taylor's visit with apprehension, for her own reasons. Alicia knew she would be struggling with her own confused emotions – guilt being one of them. She just hoped Sophie would be able to talk more about how she was feeling as time went on, that she would realise she – and Justin, in particular – understood.

Sitting in the middle of the sofa, her legs tucked under herself and a faraway look in her eyes, Alicia guessed Sophie was going over things now, the chain of events since the day her dear baby brother had died, as they all would for a long time to come. Alicia made a mental note to try to encourage her to put the bad memories behind her and cherish the good ones, the time she did have with Lucas, as Alicia and Justin would try to alongside her.

She would never truly be able to forgive herself for her naivety in imagining the whole mess would go away the day Paul Radley had. That he wouldn't come back to haunt her. She'd never dreamed it would be her daughter he would haunt. If she had… But it was too late for that now. She would die to undo it, but she couldn't. All she could do was be there for her daughter.

'Sophie? Are you all right, sweetheart?' She reached to squeeze her hand.

Sophie nodded again, and then looked worriedly towards Justin, who was gazing out of the window.

'It's probably just a routine call,' Alicia tried to reassure her. 'Don't fret too much about it, Sophie. You're not obliged to talk about anything unless you want to.'

Sophie smiled distractedly at her, and then turned her attention back to Justin. 'Dad? 'What's up?' she asked him, clearly feeling his anxiety too.

Alicia followed her gaze to where Justin was still standing at the window.

'Dad?'

'What?' Justin turned around, looking preoccupied. 'Oh, sorry, Pumpkin.' He dragged a hand over his neck, smiled tiredly and came towards her. 'I was miles away.'

'I gathered,' Sophie said, her forehead furrowed with worry. 'What's wrong?'

'Nothing,' Justin said, glancing quickly at Alicia. 'That is…' He took a breath and sat down next to Sophie. 'There is something I need to tell you before Taylor turns up. You too, Alicia.'

Noticing the nervous look in his eyes, Alicia swallowed hard, feeling hot and clammy suddenly, as she imagined what he might be about to say.

'Dad, what?' Sophie urged him, looking as wary as Alicia felt.

Justin took hold of Sophie's hand, twisting around to make sure he had full-on eye contact with her, which sent a fresh wave of apprehension down Alicia's spine. 'I need you to know that I've loved you from birth, Sophie,' he said firmly. 'And before that, when you were just a tiny heartbeat on the monitor.'

He looked again at Alicia, whose heart was now thudding frantically. His expression was deadly serious. It was bound to be, under the circumstances, but Alicia prayed he wasn't about to announce something that would rock Sophie's world further. Her world. They needed him, both of them, now more than ever, if they were going to get through this.

'There was never a second I didn't love you,' Justin went on. 'There will never be. No matter what the future may bring.'

Justin hesitated, glancing briefly at Alicia.

'Dad, what do you mean "no matter what the future may bring"? You're starting to scare me.'

Justin took a breath. 'I, er…' he started, and stopped. 'If I should have to go away for any reason…'

Now Sophie looked extremely nervous. 'Away, as in something work related?' she asked, doubt clouding her eyes.

'Possibly.' Justin's gaze flicked again towards Alicia and then back to Sophie

'Like fictitious conferences because you don't want to be here?' Sophie attempted to pull away from him.

'What?' Justin looked confused, then, 'No,' he said quickly. 'God, no. I'd rather be here than anywhere. I'm not even sure I'll need to go away yet. I just wanted you to know that my love for you never wavered, Sophie. It never will. I needed you to know that, that's all.'

He squeezed her hand, took another long breath and waited.

Sophie's gaze travelled between her parents. 'So you're not telling me you two are going to split up then?' she asked him suspiciously, the anxious look now in her eyes almost splitting Alicia's heart in two.

'No, Sophie, we are definitely not going to split up,' Justin said adamantly. 'I'm… not doing this very well, am I?' He eyed the ceiling, despairing of himself. 'I was simply trying to tell you that no matter where you are, how old you are, where I might be, that I'll always be there for you. And you will always be right here.'

Pressing a hand to his heart, he smiled encouragingly. 'Both of you,' he said, reaching for Alicia's hand.

Alicia looked at him, emotion climbing inside her. She knew what he was trying to say, and why he'd needed to say it now, before DI Taylor arrived: he thought he might not be around to afterwards. 'I love you,' she mouthed, squeezing his hand hard. *And I will, always, whatever the future may bring.*

Looking somewhat reassured, Justin nodded and turned back to Sophie. 'Sorry I scared you, Pumpkin,' he said. 'I'll try not to be so clumsy in the delivery of my next emotional speech. I'll write it on my cuff or—' He stopped as the doorbell rang, his gaze shooting fearfully towards Alicia.

Alicia didn't need to see the police car outside to know who it was. Was DI Taylor accompanied by uniformed officers, she wondered, steeling herself for whatever news he'd come to deliver.

'I'll get it,' Justin said, getting quickly to his feet. Alicia guessed from his steely expression that he was also readying himself for bad news.

CHAPTER SEVENTY-NINE

JUSTIN

'Justin.' Taylor's smile was inscrutable as Justin pulled the front door open. 'How are we?'

'Disorientated, tired,' Justin answered truthfully. 'Trying to pick up the pieces.'

Taylor nodded understandingly. 'It will be a case of taking it one day at a time, I suspect.

'Definitely.' Trying not to look obviously nervous, Justin scanned his face, searching for some indication of why he was here. The small talk, along with the fact that he appeared to be on his own, didn't point to an imminent arrest.

'Do you mind if I, er…' Taylor nodded past him to the hall.

'We were actually about to go out. A belated meal for Sophie's sixteenth,' Justin said, testing the waters, hoping the man might say it could wait. A forlorn hope, he guessed. Taylor obviously wasn't here on a social visit to enquire after their welfare. 'Sophie was looking forward to it. Can it wait?'

'It's important, Justin.' Taylor smiled again, but still his expression gave nothing away. 'It's probably better if I have a quick word now, if I may?'

His stomach tightening, Justin nodded and stepped back to allow him access. It had to be about Radley. Why else would he be here? The ketamine he'd injected into him would have been easily tested for. Justin had handwritten the prescription requesting some from the pharmacy. He'd been right outside his apartment block with his daughter, Taylor as his witness. There was no way to deny what he'd done.

'Ah, Sophie.' Taylor's mouth curved into a warm smile as Sophie came through from the lounge, heading for the stairs, 'I'm very pleased to see you looking brighter, young lady,' he said, extending his hand.

'I'm feeling brighter, thanks to Dad.' Sophie glanced at Justin, beaming him a smile that would sustain him. It would have to. Justin had thought he was ready for this, that he was mentally prepared. He wasn't. His daughter was safe, he reminded himself. She had a future with the person most important to her – her mother. That was what mattered here.

'I'm not so sure I'm pleased to see you though,' Sophie added, looking the detective guardedly over.

Taylor chuckled at that. 'Such is a policeman's lot. We grin and bear it for the greater good.' He sighed stoically.

To her credit, Sophie didn't quite roll her eyes at his obvious theatrics.

'Do you mind if I have a brief word with your parents in private, Sophie?' Taylor asked her. 'I gather you have a dinner engagement, so I won't keep them too long.'

Justin felt a little of his anxiety dissipate. If it really was only a quick word he wanted, then hopefully he hadn't come to read him his rights.

Looking relieved that it wasn't her he wanted to speak to, Sophie shrugged easily. 'No, it's cool. I was going up to ring Chloe anyway,' she said, giving Justin an impromptu hug and then turning for the stairs.

Justin watched her go, grateful that she seemed to be getting back to somewhere near normal, wanting to get in touch with her friends and pick up the threads of her life.

'I take it she's glad to be home,' Taylor observed, as Justin led the way to the lounge.

Where she would have been a long time ago, if you'd followed up my suspicions, Justin wanted to say. He decided it was probably better not to point that out.

'DI Taylor.' Alicia smiled brightly, turning from the window – though Justin could see that beneath the smile she was as nervous as he was. 'I was just about to boil the kettle. Would you like something? Tea? Coffee?'

'No, thank you,' DI Taylor declined, his expression serious. 'I won't take up too much of your time. I've actually come with some news regarding Paul Radley.'

And there it was. Justin could almost feel the cell door clanging shut behind him.

'What is it?' he asked, swapping worried glances with Alicia. He'd known this would come. He'd resigned himself to prison the second he'd started out on the path to extract information from Radley regarding Sophie's whereabouts. He'd wanted to scare the bastard as much as he'd terrorised his wife. Once he'd known for certain that his instincts were right, that Radley actually had her, nothing had mattered other than finding out where he was holding her. When he'd realised what Radley had done to her, on top of the torture he'd inflicted on Alicia, his instinct had been to kill him. He'd convinced himself that being locked up for life was a small price to pay.

Taylor looked him over, taking his time. Justin wished he'd bloody well get on with it. 'Paul Radley is dead,' he finally announced.

Dead? The news hit Justin like a sledgehammer.

But he hadn't…? He'd *stopped*. It had taken every ounce of his willpower to pull back from tipping the man over. Even knowing the bastard might never be brought to justice, he'd stopped, unable to condemn his daughter to living the rest of her life with a murderer for a father and causing Alicia's nightmare to go on forever.

And now… the evidence all pointed to him having killed him anyway. Justin felt sick to his soul.

'Or fortunately, depending on your viewpoint,' Taylor added blandly.

Justin stared at him, uncomprehending. *But…* 'How?' He choked the word out, his gaze shooting towards Alicia. Her face was hard, resigned, almost knowing. He noted the straight set of her shoulders, the defiant tilt to her chin. She looked indifferent – satisfied, almost. *Jesus.*

'Suicide,' Taylor supplied, as Justin attempted to focus and failed miserably. 'Not long after we left the vicinity, it seems, which puts you in the clear, Justin. A detective inspector's sworn statement is about as cast iron an alibi as you can get, I imagine.'

Justin felt his blood stop pumping. 'By what means?' he asked, swallowing hard as his mind raced through all sorts of scenarios.

'Plunged fifteen floors from his balcony. Made a bit of a mess on the concrete.' Taylor had just confirmed what Justin really did *not* want to hear. He'd left the door open. He hadn't bothered to close the front door when he'd charged in there. Knowing he was in no fit state to take the man on physically, his aim had been to get to Radley before he'd realised what was happening. Alicia had been due to arrive. The door had been open the whole time – and Radley had been on the balcony, incapable of doing anything other than realise what was happening to him. *Jesus Christ.*

Justin pinched the bridge of his nose hard. He couldn't speak. He felt as if he might actually vomit. But… she *couldn't* have. He tried to still his ludicrous imaginings. Panic gripping his chest like a vice, he wiped a thin film of sweat from his forehead and tried to think rationally, rather than follow the insane road his thoughts were going down.

'Do you have any suspects?' Alicia asked, seating herself on the sofa, her tone calm, her movements tense but composed.

Taylor shook his head. 'Not yet, no. The circumstances surrounding his death are not being viewed as suspicious. Looks like he took his own life.'

Alicia nodded.

Justin looked back to Taylor, wishing he could read what was going through the man's mind.

Taylor locked eyes with him, studying him hard for a long, petrifying moment. 'There's something else you should know,' he said, his gaze travelling to Alicia and back to Justin.

His thoughts all over the place, Justin tried to concentrate as he waited for him to go on.

Taylor spoke, eventually. 'You might recall we didn't have much to go on in regard to the road traffic accident, apart from the colour and model of the car?'

Struggling to keep up, Justin nodded. 'A black four-by-four, as driven by half the population of the country.'

'A Land Rover Discovery,' Taylor said guardedly, and waited.

'The same car Paul Radley drives,' Alicia added quietly, after a second, her gaze now on the fingers she was knotting and unknotting in her lap.

'Apparently, yes.' His expression grim, Taylor looked from her to Justin. 'We made some enquiries, concentrating on body shops in the area and the suspected damage to the vehicle. One of the shop owners was reluctant to impart details of such a repair. The owner of the vehicle paid cash, it seems. The job was never logged, for tax-avoidance purposes. Obviously, we can't say for certain whether Paul Radley was involved without further examination of the car, but…'

'So the car he's been driving was a rental?' Justin asked, attempting to get his head around what Taylor was implying.

'It would seem so,' Taylor confirmed.

Justin dropped heavily down to the seat behind him. He'd known it. Deep in his gut, he'd known Radley had been involved in the murder of his son. He hadn't figured out how or why, but when he'd seen those photographs, Luke and him cut crudely out of them all, he'd been sure. The only thing he hadn't been able to fathom was why Radley would have taken the risk that he might have killed the woman he was obsessed with, too, along with the child he'd truly believed was his. But now he realised that he wouldn't have cared. In Radley's mind, Alicia and Sophie belonged to him. If he couldn't have them, then no one could.

Alicia knew it too. She'd just said so. She'd known Radley owned a Discovery before Taylor had confirmed it. Yet, she *couldn't* have. Unless… it had been one of the vehicles in the underground car park. He'd looked right at it. What state of mind would Alicia have been in if she'd seen it there too?

'I'm afraid there's more,' Taylor said, as Justin dragged his hands through his hair and tried to stop their incessant shaking. He didn't dare look at Alicia.

'We've been waiting for a forensics report to come back in regard to footmarks retrieved from the garden of your house, which bear a significant identifier, allowing us to narrow a specific pair of trainers down to brand, possibly even batch number.'

'And?' Justin held his breath.

'We were a bit stuck at that stage,' Taylor continued. 'More often than not, it's impossible to identify the actual wearer unless we have them in custody, other than by information already held on the database or divine intervention.'

'Is this leading somewhere, DI Taylor?' Alicia asked, still sounding quite calm, where Justin felt as if his chest was about to explode.

'It seems the divine did intervene,' Taylor went on. 'We can't be one hundred percent sure at this stage, but it seems Paul Radley was the owner of a similar pair of trainers, thereby indicating that it might well have been him who broke into your home. We'd need other substantiating evidence, of course—'

Justin exchanged glances with Alicia. *Leave it*, was the clear message he read in her eyes. They had the substantiating evidence: the locket, the photographs. Did they really want to share that with Taylor, thereby supplying further motive for possibly being involved in his death?

'I'm afraid it does look likely though,' Taylor concluded, with a heavy sigh. I'm so sorry. This must all be very distressing for you both.'

'I see.' Kneading his temple, Justin forced himself to look back at Taylor. He needed to maintain eye contact. He needed the man to go.

'Did you recognise him, Justin? Or his car?' Taylor asked him curiously. 'Did you get a look at him after the accident?'

Realising the man was looking for motive, Justin shook his head. 'No,' he stated categorically, making damn sure to hold eye contact. 'Do you think I wouldn't have mentioned it, if I had?'

Taylor narrowed his eyes, scrutinising him carefully. 'No, I don't think for one minute you wouldn't have mentioned it – volubly,' he said, his expression… conspiratorial?

His emotions now way off-kilter, wondering whether he dare read into this what Taylor seemed to be communicating, Justin looked bewilderedly back to Alicia. Her expression unreadable, she glanced briefly back at him before turning her attention to Taylor. 'Were there any extenuating circumstances?' she asked him, causing Justin to do a double take.

Taylor's expression went back to grim. 'There wasn't a lot left of the body to examine, to be honest,' he said. 'I doubt the post-mortem will produce anything that suggests it wasn't suicide.'

'No security footage?' Alicia pushed, causing Justin's stomach to drop like a stone.

'Nothing,' Taylor confirmed. 'It seems several power outages had damaged the security feeds, which basically means we have nothing to go on.'

Looking back to Justin, he held his gaze for a long minute, nodded almost imperceptibly and then glanced down at his watch. 'Right, well, I've taken up enough of your valuable time. I'll leave you to go out for your meal. No doubt you have a lot to discuss. One or two fences that might need mending, possibly?'

'A few.' Nodding, Alicia stood to see him out.

'I'm sure they'll all be fixable,' Taylor said. 'It never ceases to amaze me how strong a family unit can be when everyone pulls together.'

Turning to Justin, he reached to shake his hand. 'Sorry we weren't much help to you in your painstaking search for Sophie, Justin,' he said, now wearing his apologetic smile. 'All's well that ends well, though, hey? I'll find my own way out,' he said, turning towards the door with a wave – leaving Justin inwardly reeling.

CHAPTER EIGHTY

JUSTIN

Too shocked to move, Justin stayed where he was as Alicia went to the kitchen. She was making tea. *Tea?* She'd just learned that the bastard who'd raped her, killed their son and taken their daughter had fallen fifteen floors to his death, his insides undoubtedly splattered all over the pavement, and her reaction was to go and put the kettle on?

Christ. Running his hands up over his face, Justin took several slow breaths and then stood to follow her.

Seating himself at the kitchen table, he clasped his hands in front of him and watched her retrieve two cups from the dishwasher, wincing as she straightened up. She'd strained her back, she'd said, moving furniture.

When? She hadn't had a bad back when she'd met him in the car. And she would hardly have gone back into the house and started shifting furniture with the sister she wasn't exactly on very good terms with after certain events. Plus, there was the matter of Radley's twisted text. Was she likely to have been moving furniture after reading that?

'This heavy weight you lifted…' he ventured, mentally calculating Radley's weight, which he reckoned to be at least that of Alicia, plus half again. 'Did Jessica help you with it?'

Alicia didn't answer immediately, appearing to ponder as she poured hot water into the teapot to warm it.

Turning to him, eventually, she looked at him, her gaze long and searching. 'Yes,' she said. 'I was adamant I could do it on my own, but Jessica insisted on helping.'

'Right.' Justin studied his hands – hands that had come so close to committing murder. He would have done, if not for his wife and daughter, whose lives Radley had almost succeeded in destroying.

'How do we tell Sophie?' Alicia asked, her voice worried now.

Justin took a second to digest this, and then looked back at her. She was holding her breath. Her beautiful, cornflower-blue eyes wide with fear, she was waiting for his reaction.

Tugging in a tight breath, Justin got to his feet. 'Together,' he said softly, walking across to her. He needed to hold her, to be there for her, to try to the best of his ability to keep his family safe.

A LETTER FROM SHERYL

Thank you so much for choosing to read *The Affair*. I have everything crossed, hoping you will enjoy it. If you would like to join a mailing list for alerts on my future novels, please sign up here. You can unsubscribe at any time, and your email address will never be shared.

www.bookouture.com/sheryl-browne

I have to say, this wasn't the easiest story to write. Sadly, I suffered a family loss as I set out on this particular journey, which threw me. I'm not sure I could have continued to write without the wonderful support and professionalism of Bookouture behind me. I will be eternally grateful for that.

In the writing of this book, I struggled with Alicia: firstly, to get in touch with her emotionally; and then, once I had, once I felt her every emotion, I struggled to live them alongside her. Without going into great detail, I would like to add another dedication here: to any mother who has had to grieve the loss of a child at any stage, from pregnancy and beyond. When the daily pace of life takes over, when you are perhaps striving to be the best parent you can to other children, a short life lived and lost is often grieved silently. That life though, grown inside you, is never forgotten. This isn't my story but, yes, some of it is based on experience. Alicia was a little bit scared to admit how emotionally broken she was at first. I think we have given her a voice. This, then, is a story of a woman who was lost, and a man who was lost alongside her, trying to come to terms with their grief when their relationship was under threat. I think, with every milestone in life, we look back and reflect, and we remember those we've lost personally and those who were there to help us over life's obstacles. For me, those are the people who believed in me, even when I didn't quite believe in myself.

To all of you, thank you.

If you have enjoyed the book, I would love it if you could share your thoughts and write a brief review. Reviews mean the world to an author and will help a book find its wings. I would also love to hear from you via Facebook or Twitter or my website. If you would like to keep up to date with my latest book news, please do sign up at the website link below.

Keep safe, everyone, and happy reading.
Sheryl x

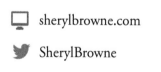 sherylbrowne.com

SherylBrowne

SherylBrowne.Author

ACKNOWLEDGEMENTS

Once again, I would like to offer a massive thank you to the team at Bookouture, without whom *The Affair* would never have happened! Special thanks to Helen Jenner and Peta Nightingale for their skill in making this book the best it could be – and for their tremendous patience and support through a family loss, which threw me completely off track. Special thanks also to Kim Nash and Noelle Holten for their unstinting support and amazing marketing skills. For your shoulder, too, Kim. When I needed it, it was there. That meant a lot. To all the other lovely, friendly and super-supportive authors at Bookouture, I love you! Thanks for the smiles!

I owe a huge debt of gratitude to all the fantastically hardworking bloggers and reviewers who have taken time to read and review my books and shout out endlessly for me. I so often say I couldn't do this without you. Trust me, I couldn't. Your passion, as always, leaves me in absolute awe. Thank you! Huge thanks, too, to Shell Baker, without whose support and encouragement my previous book might never have been submitted. You're all awesome!

Final thanks to every single reader out there for buying and reading my books. Authors write with you in mind. Knowing you have enjoyed reading our books and care enough to say so is the best incentive in the world for us to keep writing.